'Anot   njoyable story from an author who
excel   ving animals real character'   *Junior*

'The   ing tale of a very special kitten'
The Good Book Guide

'The   er of animal adventures'
Independent on Sunday

'Spa   ; humour and wonderful characters are
Dick   -Smith's trademarks'
Books for your Children

'Dick   g-Smith has brought magic into the lives
of mi   s of children'   *Parents Magazine*

Also available by Dick King-Smith,
award-winning author and creator of *Babe*:

From Corgi Pups, for beginner readers
Happy Mouseday

From Young Corgi/Doubleday Books
The Adventurous Snail
All Because of Jackson
Billy the Bird
E.S.P.
Funny Frank
The Guard Dog
Hairy Hezekiah
Horse Pie
Omnibombulator
Titus Rules OK

From Corgi Yearling Books
Mr Ape
A Mouse Called Wolf
Harriet's Hare

From Corgi Books, for older readers

The Crowstarver

Dick King-Smith

The
Catlady

Illustrated by John Eastwood

YOUNG CORGI

THE CATLADY
A YOUNG CORGI BOOK 978 0 552 55044 4

First published in Great Britain by Doubleday,
an imprint of Random House Children's Books

Doubleday edition published 2004
Young Corgi edition published 2005

7 9 10 8 6

Papers used by Random House Children's Books are natural,
recyclable products made from wood grown in sustainable forests.
The manufacturing processes conform to the environmental regulations
of the country of origin.

Set in Palatino by
Palimpsest Book Production Limited, Polmont, Stirlingshire

Young Corgi Books are published by Random House Children's Books,
61–63 Uxbridge Rd, London W5 5SA,
a division of The Random House Group Ltd,

Addresses for companies within The Random House Group Limited can be found at:
www.randomhouse.co.uk/offices.htm

THE RANDOM HOUSE GROUP Limited Reg. No. 954009
www.kidsatrandomhouse.co.uk

A CIP catalogue record for this book is available from the British Library.

The Random House Group Limited supports the Forest Stewardship
Council (FSC®), the leading international forest certification organisation.
Our books carrying the FSC label are printed on FSC® certified paper. FSC
is the only forest certification scheme endorsed by the leading environmental
organisations, including Greenpeace. Our paper procurement policy can be
found at www.randomhouse.co.uk/environment

MIX
Paper from
responsible sources
FSC® C013604

Printed and bound by CPI Group (UK) Ltd, Croydon, CR0 4YY

Chapter One

On the morning of January 22nd 1901, Muriel Ponsonby had, living in her house, sixteen cats (including kittens). By the evening of that day another litter of kittens had been born, bringing the total to a round twenty.

This event was, as usual, recorded in a large book titled BIRTHDAY BOOK (CATS ONLY).

Miss Ponsonby, it should be explained, was an elderly lady living alone in a large country house that had belonged to her parents. Because she had always looked after them, she had never married, and after their deaths she had allowed her liking for cats full rein. To be sure, she gave away some of the many kittens that appeared, but nevertheless Ponsonby Place – for this was the name of the family home – was always swarming with cats.

Miss Ponsonby kept herself to herself and did not mix much with the local villagers, save to go now and then to the local shop to buy provisions for herself and the cats. Most felt she was harmless, a rather sweet old lady, but there were some who said she was a witch. Partly because of this she was known to one and all as "The Catlady".

In fact she was not a witch but simply a somewhat strange old woman with odd habits.

For example, she talked constantly throughout the day, to herself a listener might have thought. But this was no sign of madness. She was, of course, talking to her cats, and they talked back. Colonel Sir Percival Ponsonby and his wife had always addressed their daughter by a shortened

3

version of her Christian name Muriel and all her cats used this. When spoken to, they would reply "Mu! Mu! Mu!".

Many would have found it odd to discover that she took all her meals with her cats. The long refectory table in the great dining-room was laid with a bowl for each adult cat and any kittens old enough to jump up on it, and the Catlady

would sit at the head with her own bowl before her. To be sure, she used a knife and fork and spoon, and afterwards wiped her lips with a napkin while the rest cleaned their faces with their paws. But on occasion, so as not to seem standoffish, she would fill a bowl with milk and lap from it.

At night-time she was kept very comfortable,

especially in the winter, for all those cats who wished – and many did – slept on her bed, providing her with a warm furry coverlet.

With her rather sharp features, green eyes, and grey hair tied back to show her somewhat pointed ears, Muriel Ponsonby looked much like a giant cat as she lay stretched beneath the purring throng.

Few people knew of her eating habits, for she had no servants, and only the doctor, called on a rare occasion when she was confined to bed, had ever seen the cat blanket. But no one at all knew the strangest thing about Miss Ponsonby, which was that she was a firm believer in reincarnation.

As a simple soldier, her father, who had served in the army in India, thought that the idea of reincarnation was a lot of nonsense, but he had talked about it to his daughter when she was a child. As she grew older Muriel came to believe, as Hindus do, that when a person dies, he or she is reborn in another body, and not necessarily a human one. She was sure that some of her feline companions had once been people she knew. Thus among her cats there was a Percival (her late father, she was certain, just the same whiskers), a Florence (her late mother), a Rupert and a Madeleine (cousins), a Walter and a Beatrice (uncle and aunt), as well as some newly departed friends. Ethel Simmons, Margaret Maitland and Edith Wilson (two tabbies and a black), all old schoolfriends of hers, had reappeared in feline form.

It was to these nine cats that Muriel Ponsonby chiefly spoke, and they replied by making typical cat noises like miaowing and purring. All were delighted to be living in comfort in Ponsonby Place, in the care of a human whom they had, in

their previous lives, known and loved.

Percival and Florence were of course particularly pleased at how well their only daughter had turned out.

"How fortunate we are, my dear," the Colonel said to his wife, "to be looked after by Muriel in our old age."

"Old age?" said Florence. "I think you tend to forget, Percival, that we have been reincarnated into new bodies and that ours are now comparatively young."

"You are right of course, Florence dear," Percival replied. "Why, we have our new lives ahead of us."

"And possibly other lives," said Florence.

"What do you mean?"

Florence rubbed her face against her husband's luxuriant whiskers. "We might have babies," she said.

Of course not all the kittens born in Ponsonby Place were reincarnations of human beings. Most were simply ordinary kittens born to ordinary cats, and were given names like Tibbles or Fluff. The Catlady could tell the difference merely by looking into their eyes once they were opened, and until this happened she did not attempt to name them.

So it was not for ten days that she examined the four kittens born on January 22nd 1901, the very day upon which Queen Victoria had died. Three of the kittens were tabbies, the fourth a ginger.

The Catlady picked up the tabbies first, looking to see what sex each was, and then peering into its newly-opened eyes.

"You're a tom," she said, three times, and, again three times, "Sorry, dear, you're only a cat."

But when she came to the fourth kitten, a small and dumpy one, expecting it to be another tom – for ginger kittens usually were – she found it to be a queen, as female cats are called. Then she

looked into its eyes, and caught her breath.

"Not just a queen," said the Catlady in a hoarse whisper, "but *the* Queen!"

Reverently she placed the ginger kitten back in its nest. "Oh, Your Majesty!" she said. "Reborn on the day you died! To think that you have come to grace my house!" and awkwardly, for she was not as young as she had been, she dropped a curtsy.

"Your humble servant, Ma'am," said the Catlady, and retired from the room, backwards.

Chapter Two

Hastily the Catlady made her way from the room in the East Wing where this latest litter of kittens had been born, to the principal bedroom of Ponsonby Place. It was a spacious chamber where her parents had slept in their lifetime – their previous lifetime, that is – and which they, in their reborn shapes, still naturally occupied. Once the Colonel had been a fiery old soldier and his wife a bit of a battleaxe, and now no

13

other cat ever dared cross this threshold.

The Catlady found them lying side by side in the middle of the great four-poster bed. Percival had been reincarnated as a white kitten that had grown into a very large and fat cat. His sweeping whiskers aped the military moustache of the human Percival. Florence was a tortoiseshell with

just the same small dark eyes that had once glinted behind Lady Ponsonby's pince-nez.

"Papa! Mama!" cried the Catlady excitedly (she could never bring herself to address them by their first names). At the sound of her voice they yawned and stretched themselves upon the fine silken bedspread with its pattern of damask roses, which was now much torn by sharp claws and dirtied by muddy feet.

"What do you think!" went on the Catlady. "Our dear departed Queen is come to stay! Edward VII may now be King of England but here at Ponsonby Place Victoria still reigns!"

"Mu," said Percival in a bored voice and Florence echoed "Mu", and they climbed off the four-poster and made their way down the curving staircase towards the dining-room, for it was time for tea.

How I wish Mama and Papa were still able to

speak the Queen's English – the King's English, I should say, mused the Catlady as, in the huge stone-flagged kitchen, she set about the task of filling a large number of bowls with a mixture of fish-heads and boiled rabbit and ox liver. For that matter, I wish that those others that have been reborn could speak too. How nice it would be to talk over old times with Uncle Walter and Aunt Beatrice, or chat about school-days with Ethel or one of the other girls.

Her thoughts were interrupted by a loud impatient miaowing from the waiting cats.

The Catlady sighed. "Coming, dears!" she called.

She sat at the head of the table, nibbling a biscuit. Later, when all had been cleared away and washed up, she would make herself a nice cup of tea, but at that moment she realized for the first time that she was not only lonely for human conversation but that she was tired.

The older I get, she thought, the more cats and so the more work I have, and it'll be worse soon. Both Cousin Madeleine and Edith Wilson are pregnant.

By the time she got to bed that night (after making her respects to the infant Queen Victoria) the Catlady had come to a decision. "There's only one thing for it, dears," she said to the patchwork quilt of different-coloured cats that covered her. "I shall have to get help."

Next day she composed an advertisement to be placed in the local newspaper, the *Dummerset Chronicle*. It was very short. It said:

Advertisements

HOME HELP WANTED.
Suit animal lover
Apply Ponsonby Place,
Dumpton Muddicorum.

For some days the Catlady waited, rather nervously, for replies. She had been a recluse for so many years now that she was not looking forward to the ordeal of interviewing a whole string of strange people.

She need not have worried. As soon as the locals of Dumpton Muddicorum read the Situations Vacant in the *Dummerset Chronicle* they said to each other, "Look at this then! It's the old Catlady, advertising for home help. What a job, eh? Great rambling place, crawling with cats, and stinking of them too no doubt, and as for her, well, if she ain't a witch she's as mad as a hatter! Anyone who applies for that needs their heads seeing to."

And no one did.

Muriel Ponsonby did not renew the advertisement. Perhaps it's just as well, she thought, I probably wouldn't have got on with the person.

I'll just have to manage somehow.

Nonetheless when shopping in the village, she did ask the shopkeepers if they knew of anyone suitable, but none of them did.

"Not at the moment, madam," said the butcher, tipping his straw hat to her, "but I'll be sure to let you know if I hear of anyone," and the others replied in the same vein. They winked at other customers when she had left their shops, and the customers smiled and shook their heads, watching her pedal rather shakily away on her tall black bicycle with the big wicker basket on the handle-bars.

Poor old dear, they thought. She needs some help, no doubt about that, but she'll be lucky to get anyone. Shame really, she's a nice old thing.

As for the village children, they sniggered behind their hands. "It's that old Catlady!" they whispered, and when she had gone by, they curled their fingers like claws and hissed and catcalled, pretending to scratch one another.

The weeks went by, and Cousin Madeleine and Edith Wilson both gave birth, one to four and one to six kittens. These were just ordinary kittens (for no one among the Catlady's family or friends had died), but with a total now of thirty animals in her house she found herself wishing very much that someone – anyone – had answered that advertisement.

By now the little tubby ginger female that was, its owner knew beyond doubt, the reincarnation of the late great Queen, was weaned. The Catlady found that, try as she would to treat all her animals alike, this one had already become special. She took to carrying her about, and had at long last decided what to call her.

After the first shock of finding who was within the little furry body, she had very gradually given up treating this kitten with such exaggerated respect. She stopped curtsying to it and backing out of the room. From first addressing it as "Your Majesty", she had then progressed to "Victoria", and later, so familiar did she now feel with this royal personage, to "Vicky".

The other cats, incidentally, on learning from the ginger kitten who she had been in her previous incarnation, treated her with much respect, Percival especially so, as in his former shape, his bravery in India had earned him the Victoria Cross.

One winter's day, when the snow lay deep around Ponsonby Place, there was a knocking on the great front door, and the Catlady went to see who it could be, Vicky perched upon her shoulder.

Muriel opened the door, expecting the postman, for no one else usually came all the way up the long drive to the house. But it wasn't the postman. Standing on the steps outside was a young girl, poorly clad and shivering with cold.

Though on the whole the Catlady preferred cats to people, she was of a kindly nature, and now she did not hesitate. "Come in! Come in!" she cried. "You'll catch your death, whoever you are. Come, follow me, I have a good fire in the drawing-room." As the girl followed her across the vast echoing hall, a host of cats watched curiously from doorway and stairway.

"Here, sit by the fire and warm yourself," said

the Catlady, "and I will go and make you a hot drink."

When she had done so and the girl had drunk and some colour had come back into her pinched face, the Catlady said, "Now, tell me, what can I do for you?"

As she said this, it occurred to her that perhaps the girl had come in answer to that old advertisement in the *Dummerset Chronicle*. I rather hope not, the Catlady said to herself. This is not the sort of person I had in mind. Not only is she badly dressed but her clothes are dirty, with bits of straw sticking to them.

The Catlady's face must have shown her distaste, for the girl stood up and said, "I won't trouble you any longer, madam. I'll be on my way now and thank you for your kindness."

She spoke with a Dummerset accent. A local girl, thought the Catlady. "Wait a moment," she said. "You knocked on my door so you must tell me what you wanted."

"I saw your lights," said the girl, "and what with the snow . . . and I was fair wore out . . .

and I hadn't eaten for quite a while . . . I just couldn't go any further."

"And you're not going any further now," said the Catlady decidedly. "Sit down again. I'll fetch you some food."

CHAPTER THREE

Muriel Ponsonby was not particularly interested in food. As long as her cats were well fed, she herself was content with very simple fare and seldom kept much in the house.

Now however she was not long in providing some good hot soup and some bread and cheese for the young stranger, and not until the girl had finished eating did she press her further.

"Now, tell me your name."

"If you please, madam," said the girl, "my name is Mary Nutt."

"But tell me, Mary," said the Catlady, "where are your parents?" Mary's not very old, she thought. Fourteen perhaps?

"Dead," Mary replied.

"Both?"

"Yes, madam. Mother died a month ago, and my father, he was killed in South Africa, fighting the Boers. He was a soldier, my dad was, a soldier of the Queen."

At this last word, Vicky jumped up onto the girl's lap, and Mary stroked her and added, "And the Queen's dead too now."

Yes and no, said the Catlady to herself.

To Mary she said, "I am very sorry for you. My father is . . . that is to say, was . . . a soldier."

And now he's a white cat, she thought.

"Thank you, madam," said Mary Nutt. "The fact is that since Mother died, I've had nowhere to live. These last weeks I've just been wandering about the countryside, sleeping in haystacks, as you can see, with no food to speak of, for I've no money. That was the first good meal I've had for many a day and I thank you for your kindness."

This telling of her troubles and the sight of Vicky snuggled down on the girl's lap would probably have been enough to make up the Catlady's mind anyway. But then something happened which absolutely decided her.

In through the drawing-room door marched the white cat Percival, straight up to the girl, and began to rub himself against her legs, purring like mad.

Mary Nutt put out a hand to stroke him. "Isn't

he handsome!" she said.

"You like cats, do you?" asked the Colonel's daughter.

"Oh yes!" replied the daughter of a trooper.

The Catlady looked at her, stroking with one

hand Colonel Sir Percival Ponsonby and with the other cuddling Victoria, Queen of the United Kingdom, Empress of India, and any doubts vanished. "I hope," she said, "that you will stay here with me, Mary, and help me to look after my family."

On that snowy day when Mary Nutt first set foot in Ponsonby Place, the house was as it had been for many years now. That is to say the floors were dirty, the ceilings cobwebby, the furniture dusty, the chair covers grubby, and the windows smeary.

The place was a paradise for cockroaches and woodlice and earwigs and beetles, and even, in the damper parts, for snails (though mice had the sense to keep well away).

On top of everything else the whole house stank of cat.

By springtime the change in Ponsonby Place was miraculous. The floors and the ceilings and the furniture were clean, the covers washed, the insects gone. If the Colonel and his Lady could have been reincarnated in human rather than feline form, the house would have looked to them just as it had been in their day. To be sure, there was still a smell of cat but, thanks to opening as many (clean) windows as possible when the weather allowed, it was much less strong now.

All this of course was due to the busy hands of Mary Nutt, who had turned out to be what the Catlady's mother would have called "a treasure".

At first from simple gratitude at being given a home and then because she quickly grew fond of the Catlady, Mary worked

from dawn to dusk in Ponsonby Place, dusting, scrubbing, washing and polishing, and indeed doing most of the cooking. Even more importantly from the Catlady's point of view, her new helper paid a lot of attention to all the cats, and, whenever she had a spare moment, it was spent grooming some happily-purring puss.

Percival and the rest spoke about her to each other with approval. "Good sort of girl, that, don't you think?" he said to Florence. "She's being a great help to Mu, what?" and his wife agreed, as did the uncle and aunt,

33

the cousins and the schoolfriends. Only Vicky made no comment.

The Colonel cleared his throat.

"I hope you approve of the young servant, Your Majesty?" he said respectfully.

Vicky looked up at the big white cat with her usual haughty expression. "We have only one criticism," she replied.

"What is that, pray, ma'am?"

"We do not have enough attention paid to us. We are after all the most important cat in the house, in the land indeed. The girl should feed us first."

"Certainly she should, ma'am," said Percival, and once Vicky had left the room, he had a word with all the other cats.

From then on, to Mary's puzzlement and Muriel's delight, when the food bowls were put upon the long refectory table, no cat touched a mouthful of its food until the tubby ginger cat Vicky had finished her meal and jumped down.

Just as it should be, thought the Catlady. Her Majesty must eat first. Perhaps one of these days I'll tell Mary about reincarnation. The poor girl has lost both father and mother, or at least she thinks she has. It would surely be a comfort if I could persuade her that each of them is no doubt enjoying another life in another form.

Chapter Four

As time passed the relationship between the Catlady and her young orphaned helper strengthened.

Miss Muriel (as Mary now addressed her employer) became a kind of replacement for the girl's late mother despite the huge gap in age.

Equally, for the childless Catlady, this hard-working, affectionate, cat-loving girl was a great blessing. Especially because once again the cat population of Ponsonby Place was increasing. Margaret Maitland and Edith Wilson had, between them, another half dozen kittens so that now the total was thirty-six.

Miss Muriel was pleased with the new arrivals, Mary could see, though she did not understand why the Catlady had picked up each new kitten, peered into its eyes, and then said in a disappointed voice "Oh dear, you're just a cat."

Just another cat, Mary thought, and more work for me. She knew, because she'd been told, that when the Colonel and Lady Ponsonby had been alive, they had employed a cook, a parlourmaid, and three housemaids, and of course there had not been an army of cats in the place. If only I could persuade Miss Muriel, Mary thought, to get rid of some of them. Every bit of furniture is covered in cat hairs, in wet weather every floor is dotted with muddy little pawprints, there are litter trays everywhere to be emptied and often the kittens don't use them. What can I do to get Miss Muriel to part with some of them?

As though in answer to this question, a cat walked into the room Mary was dusting. It was a tomcat, she could see from its big round face, and ebony in colour. A black male, thought Mary Nutt, and "Blackmail!" she said out loud.

Suppose I told Miss Muriel, she thought, that if a lot of the cats don't go, then I will? I wouldn't actually go, of course, I couldn't let her down like that when she's been so good to me, but it might just work. And we could shut up some of the rooms, so there'd be less cleaning to do. Let's just hope I can persuade her.

As things turned out, luck was to be on Mary's side. While she was plucking up the courage to tackle her employer, the Catlady was herself beginning to feel that perhaps there were rather too many cats in Ponsonby Place. It's not the

expense of feeding them, she said to herself, I don't mind that, and it's not the work involved, for now dear Mary prepares their food and washes their dishes and cleans out their litter trays. It's because of Vicky, I suppose, she's become so important to me (well, she would be, wouldn't she, she is . . . was . . . the Queen) that I don't pay as much attention to the others as I used to. Except for Papa and Mama, of course, and the relations and friends. But as for the rest of them, I suppose I could do without them. That cat blanket's getting too much of a thing. I'd sooner just have Her Majesty on the bed.

But then something happened that was to settle things for both Mary and Muriel. For some time the Catlady had been a trifle worried about her late mother (that is to say, about the tortoiseshell cat Florence within whose body Lady Ponsonby had been reincarnated) because she seemed to be getting a bit fat.

"Oh Mama," said the Catlady as she entered the master bedroom, carrying Vicky, "I shall have to feed you less. Just look at the tummy on you!"

Following her own advice, she looked more carefully and then gave a gasp of horror as the truth dawned upon her.

"Oh Mama!" she cried. "You are pregnant!"

Florence stretched languidly on the four-poster bed, and Percival purred proudly.

"And at your time of life!" said the Catlady.

Then she realized that though her mother if still alive would have been in her nineties, the cat she had become was young. What's more, when the coming kittens were born to Percival and Florence (to Mama and Papa, that is to say), they would be, strictly speaking, her own little brothers and sisters!

She hurried downstairs to the kitchens. "Mary! Mary!" she cried. "She is going to have kittens!"

"Who, Miss Muriel?"

In the nick of time the Catlady stopped herself from replying "My Mama".

"My Florence!" she said. "I had thought she was just putting on too much weight but now I see what it is!"

More kittens, thought Mary, as if there weren't enough cats about the place already. Maybe this is the moment to suggest cutting down the numbers.

"Wouldn't it be a good idea to get rid of a few of your cats, Miss Muriel?" she asked.

"Get rid of them?"

"Yes. Find good homes for them."

"But how?"

"I could put an advertisement in the local paper."

43

A few days later readers of the *Dummerset Chronicle* saw the following notice:

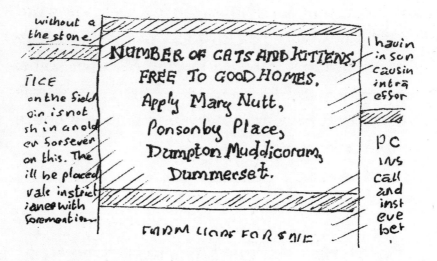

"You don't have to do anything, Miss Muriel," Mary said. "I give you my word I'll make sure they go to good homes."

In the next few weeks a lot of people came walking, cycling, or riding up the drive to

Ponsonby Place. Some owned a cat but fancied having another, some had lost their cat and wanted to replace it, some had never owned a cat before but were attracted by that one word FREE. Many were just curious and keen to take this chance to see the Catlady in her own home.

Such was the demand that soon Mary was having to turn people away. She pinned a notice on the front door that said:

"All those that have gone have got good homes, I'm sure, Miss Muriel," she said to the Catlady, who was sitting in an armchair in the drawing-room, with the Queen of the United Kingdom on her lap, reading a book called *The Care of Cats.*

"Well done, Mary dear," the Catlady said. "Though I shall miss them all very much."

Let's hope, she thought, that my Florence (Mama, that is) has a lot of kittens.

As though to compensate for the losses, Florence gave birth the very next day, on the fine silken bedspread of the four-poster in the bedroom of the Catlady's late parents.

"Oh Mama!" breathed Muriel Ponsonby as she bent over the two new-born kittens. One was a tortoiseshell like the mother, the other white like the father who sat nearby, purring with pride.

The Catlady had been an only child, but now she thought – I have a baby brother and a baby sister!

"Oh Papa," she said, "what shall we call them?" But of course Percival merely replied "Mu".

"I'll ask Mary," said the Catlady and she followed Vicky (who always liked to lead the way) down to the kitchens.

If only Mary knew, she thought as she told the good tidings, that these two new kittens are the children of my dear Mama and Papa, so that now I have the brother and the sister I never had as a child.

"Come up and see them," she said, and then as they stood looking down she said, "What shall we call them? Why don't you choose, Mary Nutt?"

Mary laughed.

"We could call them after some sort of nut!" she said.

"What a good idea," said the Catlady. "Let's see now, there's walnut and peanut . . ."

". . . and chestnut and beechnut and ground-nut . . ."

". . . and coconut and hazelnut," said the Catlady.

"Hazel," said Mary. "That would be a nice name for the little female, wouldn't it?"

"Oh yes!" said the Catlady. "But what about the little tom?"

"Coco, Miss Muriel," said Mary. "Short for coconut."

"I like it!" cried the Catlady.

My sister Hazel, she thought, and my brother

Coco. What fun! How lucky I am to believe in reincarnation. It would be nice for Mary to believe too. Just think – her father for instance, Arthur, I think he was called, suppose he's now a boy or a horse perhaps or a dog or maybe even something as small as a mouse. No, not a mouse, they don't live long enough, he'd have gone into yet another body by now, dead of old age or, worse, killed by a cat. Just think, if dear Papa had eaten Arthur Nutt!"

But it might help Mary, she said to herself, to know that I at least believe that her father is not dead and gone. His body might be buried on some

South African battlefield, but his personality, his spirit, his soul, call it what you like, has been reincarnated, has entered some other body. Maybe I should try to explain it to her.

"Mary dear, tell me, is it very painful for you to talk of your parents?"

"Painful?" replied Mary. "Yes, it will always be painful. But they've gone. I just have to accept that."

"Gone," said the Catlady. "Gone where?"

"To Heaven, I suppose. They were good people."

"Have you ever thought," asked the Catlady, "that they might have been reincarnated?"

"What does that mean?"

"That they might have been reborn, in some other shape or form?"

"Oh, I don't think I could believe in that," Mary said.

"I do," said the Catlady.

Mary Nutt looked at her employer, the elderly green-eyed Catlady, grey hair tied back as usual. She's aged quite a bit in the time I've lived here, she thought, rather bent, a bit unsteady on her feet, but her mind is still clear, I think. Or rather, I thought. But this reincarnation thing!

"Do you mean," Mary asked, "that you believe you were someone else in a previous life?"

"Someone. Or perhaps somebody. I wasn't necessarily human."

"You could have been an animal?"

"Yes, indeed. I may be one in the future, when my heart stops beating. I don't expect you to believe in the idea, Mary, but I thought it might be a comfort to you to know that I am sure your mother and father are still enjoying lives of some sort. As indeed my dear Mama and Papa are."

"Your mother and father?"

"At this moment they are in their old bedroom, resting upon their four-poster bed, while my brother and sister play on the floor."

"I don't understand," said Mary.

"Percival and Florence. My father and mother."

"Those were their names?"

"Those are their names. New forms they may have acquired, but I know without a shadow of a doubt who they were before they became cats. Just as I am absolutely certain about Vicky here. She was born at twenty past four on the afternoon of January 22nd 1901, the very instant that the last breath left her previous body."

"Whose body was that?" Mary asked.

"Vicky, as I most disrespectfully call her, is in fact Victoria, Queen of the United Kingdom and Empress of India," said the Catlady.

She picked up the stout ginger cat and began, with great deference, to stroke her. "So now you know, Mary," she said. "Vicky here is the late great Queen Victoria."

Did I tell myself her mind was clear, Mary thought. She's barmy.

CHAPTER FIVE

The shopkeepers in Dumpton Muddicorum had always thought Miss Ponsonby a bit mad. You'd have to be, they said, to keep as many cats (and spend as much money on their food) as the Catlady does.

Nonetheless they were still rather fond of her. She was always smiling, always polite. "She may be a bit strange," they said amongst themselves, "but she's a proper lady."

Of course they knew nothing of her belief in reincarnation, but had commented, first, on her kindness in giving away some of her cats ("Free," they said. "She never asked for a penny"), and, secondly, on the fact that the years seemed to be telling on her. Riding her bicycle was patently becoming a big effort.

"Good job she's got that nice young girl living with her, what's her name . . . Mary . . . Mary Nutt, that's it," they said. They were not surprised when Mary appeared in the village one day, riding the Catlady's tall black bicycle, to do the shopping. They each made regular enquiries of Mary as to how Miss Ponsonby was getting on.

One day Mary came back from the village to find the Catlady standing at the front door, leaning on the walking-stick that she now always used, and looking, Mary could see, very worried.

"What is it, Miss Muriel?" Mary asked before beginning to unload the shopping from the big wicker basket on the handle-bars. "What's the matter?"

"Oh Mary!" cried the Catlady. "It's my brother!"

"Your brother?"

"Yes, Coco. I can't find him anywhere. I've asked Mama and Papa and my sister Hazel where Coco has gone but of course they couldn't tell me. Could he have been stolen, d'you think, or run away? I've searched the house but I can't find him."

"He must be somewhere about," Mary said. "I'll just unload this shopping and then I'll make you a nice cup of tea. I'll find him, don't you worry."

In fact the white kitten Coco, adventurous as most boys are, had decided to do some exploring.

In the master bedroom of Ponsonby Place there was a large fireplace, once used to keep Sir Percival and Lady Ponsonby warm on winter nights. When Coco was alone in the room, he began to nose around it. Looking up, he saw the sky through the chimney stack. He also saw that there were little stone steps on the walls of the chimney, steps up which, long ago, children had been sent to sweep down the soot with bags full of goose-feathers. Coco began to climb. As he did so, the soot began to fall and he became covered in the stuff. It got in his eyes and his nose and his mouth, and he became very frightened. He did not know whether to go on up or to come back down or what to do. He sat on one of the steps, mewing pitifully for his mother.

He was there, of course, when the Catlady was searching for him, but her hearing was too poor to catch his muffled cries and her eyesight not sharp enough to notice the fallen soot in the fireplace.

But Mary, when she began to search, both heard the kitten and saw the sootfall. Cautiously she peered up the chimney and saw the crouching figure of the tiny adventurer.

"Oh Coco!" she called. "However are you going

to get out of there?" The answer was immediate.

Perhaps it was the sight of her face, perhaps the sound of her voice, perhaps he simply lost his footing, but the next minute Coco came tumbling down into the fireplace.

Mary, by now very sooty herself, carried him down to the kitchens where  the Catlady still sat over her cup of tea.

"Here he is!" she said.

"But Mary," the Catlady cried, peering through her spectacles, "my brother Coco is a white kitten, like Papa, and that one is coal-black."

"Coal-black's about right," Mary said, and she set about cleaning the unhappy Coco, while on the floor below the sink, his parents watched and waited.

"Whatever has the boy been doing?" Percival asked his wife.

"Went up the chimney by the look of it," replied Florence.

"Why?"

"I've no idea, Percival. Boys will be boys."

The Colonel looked smug. "Chip off the old

block," he said rather proudly. "I was always an adventurous lad."

But Coco was not the only adventurous one. A few days later it was Hazel who went missing. Coco had gone up. She went down.

Below the ground floor of Ponsonby Place were the cellars, though the door to them was nowadays seldom opened. The flight of steps that led down to the racks where Colonel Sir Percival Ponsonby had kept his wine (when he was a man) were very steep, and the Catlady hadn't been down there for years.

But recently Mary had taken to using the racks for storing things and on this particular day she had gone down to fetch some cloths and some shoe-polish. Unbeknownst to her, someone else slipped down too.

Mary came back up the steep steps and shut the cellar door. She got out Miss Ponsonby's bicycle and set off to do the shopping.

When she returned, she found, once again, the Catlady standing at the front door, leaning on her walking-stick. This time, however, she looked delighted, her old face wreathed in smiles.

"Oh Mary!" she cried. "It's my sister!"

"Your sister?"

"Yes, Hazel. I lost her. I couldn't find her anywhere. But someone else did find her!"

"Who?"

The Catlady pointed down at Vicky, who was sitting at her feet, looking extremely smug.

"Her Most Gracious Majesty found her," said the

Catlady. "How Hazel got there I do not know, but she was in the cellars. Somehow she'd been shut in there."

"Oh," said Mary.

"I was getting so worried," the Catlady said. "I looked everywhere, I listened everywhere, but as I think you know, these days neither my sight nor my hearing are what they used to be. I asked Papa and Mama but they didn't seem to understand. And then something extraordinary

happened, Mary. Vicky came up to me and put a paw on my stocking – something she has never done before – and then turned and walked away, stopping and looking back every so often. Clearly she wanted me to follow her, so I did. She led me to the cellar door and when I opened it, there was my poor sister sitting on the steps. How glad I was to see her, and so were Papa and Mama and Coco. And how grateful I am to Her Majesty!"

The Catlady bent down and, very respectfully, stroked Vicky's fat ginger back.

"Thank you, Ma'am, thank you so much," she said, and Vicky purred loudly.

Percival and Florence of course discussed this latest event in their own language.

"How in the world did the girl come to be shut in the cellars?" the Colonel asked his wife.

At that moment, Vicky came into the master bedroom. She was the only cat in the house to be allowed in that room, though normally she spent her days and nights on the Catlady's bed.

Percival and Florence, who had both been lying on the carpet, sprang up, and Percival stood rigidly to attention like the soldier he had once been.

He waited for Vicky to speak (it was customary among all the cats not to address the Queen first but to wait to be spoken to).

"Well, Colonel," Vicky said, "I trust that your daughter is none the worse for this latest incident?"

"She came to no harm, Your Majesty," Percival

replied, "but she might have been imprisoned for a long time had it not been for your skill in finding her, Ma'am. My wife and I are truly grateful."

"It was nothing," Vicky said. "We happened to be passing the cellar door and we heard the child mewing. 'Kittens should be seen and not heard' as the saying goes, but on this occasion it was fortunate that the child cried out."

"And that Your Majesty's hearing is so sharp," said Florence.

"All our five senses are in perfect working order," said Vicky imperiously and she waddled regally out of the room.

Chapter Six

Probably on account of the Catlady's strangely respectful treatment of Vicky, Mary Nutt began, despite herself, to think quite a lot about this strange idea of reincarnation.

In the Catlady's library she first consulted an encyclopaedia. "This belief", she read, "is fundamental to the Hindu and Buddhist concepts of the world."

So millions of people believe in it, she thought.

They can't all be barmy. Perhaps Miss Muriel isn't, either.

Reincarnation, she read, accounts for the differences in the character of individuals because of what each had once been. So was the fact that Vicky was short and tubby and bossy and that the other cats always let her eat first and seemed to be very respectful towards her – was that all because this ginger cat had once been Queen of England? Rubbish, one part of her said.

Millions believe in it, said another. Of course it would be a comfort to me to be able to believe that my mother and father are alive again, in some shape or form. If only I could, she thought.

I wonder what form Miss Muriel believes she will assume, when she dies? Which may not be all that long, she thought. She's aged a great deal in the years that I've been here.

For some time now the Catlady had not come

down for breakfast. She ate very little anyway, and Mary, seeing how frail she was becoming, persuaded her to have a tray with a cup of tea and some toast and marmalade brought up to her bedroom.

One morning Mary knocked as usual and took in the tray.

"Shall I pour for you both, Miss Muriel?" she asked.

"Please, Mary dear."

So she saw to the Catlady's tea and then, as usual, filled a saucer with milk and put it on the floor for Vicky.

"How are we today, Miss Muriel?" she asked.

"A little tired. I'm not getting any younger, I fear."

"You stay in bed," Mary said. "I can bring you some lunch up later."

You're really looking very old now, she

thought. But not unhappy. Maybe because of this belief of yours that when you die, you'll start again as someone or something else.

"I've been thinking quite a lot," she said, "about what you said to me some time ago. About being reborn, in another body."

"I shall be," said the Catlady firmly.

It still seems odd that she's so sure, Mary thought.

The Catlady did not get up at all that day, saying that she did not have the energy. It was the same all that week, a week that by chance contained two bereavements for Muriel Ponsonby. The cat that had once been her Uncle Walter died, and then her old schoolfriend Margaret Maitland.

"Both cats were very old though, weren't they?" Mary said in an effort to console her friend.

"As I am," said the Catlady.

"Anyway," said Mary, "it's nice for you to think they will both be reborn, isn't it?"

"As I shall be," said the Catlady.

What am I saying, Mary asked herself. I'm barmy too.

She could not make up her mind whether the

Catlady was just tired or whether she was ill. And if so, how ill? Should I call the doctor, she thought?

What decided her was a request that the Catlady made.

"Mary dear," she said. "Would you fetch Percival and Florence and Coco and Hazel? I should like to say goodbye to them."

When Mary had done so, she telephoned the doctor. He came and examined the old lady, and then he took Mary aside and said to her, "I'm afraid Miss Ponsonby is very ill. To be honest with you, my dear, I don't hold out much hope."

"She's dying, you mean?" Mary asked.

"I fear so."

Shall I tell him about Miss Muriel's beliefs, she thought? No, he'll think I'm mad as well as her. The next morning Mary Nutt woke early and dressed. As she went downstairs from her bedroom in what had been the servants' quarters and made her way to the kitchen, she noticed something odd. There was not a cat to be seen, anywhere.

She was about to put a kettle on to make tea when one cat walked in through the kitchen door.

It was Vicky, who stared up at Mary with her customary grumpy look and made a noise which meant, Mary had no doubt, "Follow me".

Up the stairs
went Vicky, Mary
at her heels, and
in through the
open door of
the Catlady's
bedroom.

Dick King-Smith

On the floor, in
a rough circle
around the bed,
were sitting all
the other cats
of   Ponsonby
Place: Percival and
Florence and their
children, Rupert
and Madeleine,
the newly
widowed Aunt
Beatrice,   Ethel
and Edith, and a
number of others.
All sat quite still,
gazing up at the
bed, on which the
Catlady lay stretched

and still. On her face was a gentle smile.

Mary picked up a hand. It was icy cold. "Oh Miss Muriel," she whispered. "Who or what are you now?"

Chapter Seven

The vicar was afraid that the funeral of the late Miss Muriel Ponsonby might be very poorly attended. Her mother and father were long dead, he knew (though he did not know that they, and other relatives, still lived, in different shape, in Ponsonby Place). The only mourner he expected to see was Mary Nutt.

What a pity, he thought, that the daughter of Colonel Sir Percival Ponsonby and

Lady Ponsonby, of Ponsonby Place, one of the finest old houses in Dummerset, should go to

her grave almost unmourned.

In fact, on the day when the Catlady was buried, the vicar's church was jam-packed.

All the villagers of Dumpton Muddicorum and all the tradesmen and a number of other people in the neighbourhood who owned cats that had once belonged to Muriel, all of these turned up to pay their respects. All the Catlady's oddities were forgotten and only her kindness and cheerfulness remembered.

"She was a funny one," they said, "but there was something ever so nice about her. Always so polite too."

"Yes and she was a kind lady, taking in Mary Nutt like she did."

Nor were humans the only mourners. At the back of the church, behind the rearmost pews, sat a silent line of cats.

*

When it was all over, Mary ate her tea in the kitchen while on the floor the various cats ate theirs (Vicky first, of course). What's to become of me, she thought. I can't stay here now that Miss Muriel's dead. The house will be sold, I suppose.

"I don't know," she said to the cats. "I just don't know."

But a week later, she did.

She was summoned to the offices of the

Catlady's solicitor in a nearby town, to be told some astonishing news.

"This, Miss Nutt," said the solicitor, "is a copy of the will of Miss Muriel Ponsonby. As you know, she had no remaining family, no one for whose benefit Ponsonby Place might be sold. She therefore decided that she would leave the house to the RSPC."

"RSPC?" asked Mary.

"The Royal Society for the Protection of Cats.

So that the charity might use Ponsonby Place as its national headquarters. More, the will states that, because of your loyal service to her and her deep affection for you, you should continue to live there, rent-free, for as long as you wish. I am delighted to tell you that Miss Ponsonby has left you a substantial sum of money, to cover your day-to-day expenses and to enable you to employ such help as a housekeeper and a gardener. You are a very fortunate young lady."

Fortunate indeed, thought Mary afterwards. But oh, how I shall miss her! And so will the cats.

Six months later the RSPC had not yet moved in to Ponsonby Place but Mary, with help, was keeping things in apple-pie order. The only change she made was to remove Vicky from the Catlady's bedroom, and Percival and Florence from the master-bedroom, and to shut both bedroom doors.

"You'll just have to find other rooms to sleep in," she said to them all, and fat ginger Vicky

gave her a look that said plainly "We are not amused".

Six months to the day from the death of the Catlady, Mary saw a strange cat come walking

up the drive towards the house, in a very confident way, as though it knew just what it was about.

It was a grey cat, about six months old, Mary guessed, with a sharp face and green eyes and rather pointed ears. A female, she was sure, by the look of it.

It walked straight up to her and began to rub itself against her legs, purring very loudly indeed. Then it walked straight in through the front door. Mary followed.

The stranger set off up the stairs and along the landing, to the now closed door of the bedroom of the Late Muriel Ponsonby. Standing on its hindlegs, it reached up with a forepaw

as though trying to turn the door-handle.

Mystified, Mary opened the door for it, and it ran into the room and leaped upon the bed. It lay there, ears pricked, its green eyes staring into hers with a look that told Mary Nutt exactly what had happened, something that, up to this moment, she had never quite been able to believe possible.

This strange green-eyed grey cat, this lady cat was . . . the Catlady!

"Oh Miss Muriel!" Mary breathed. "You're back!"

THE END

ABOUT THE AUTHOR

Dick King-Smith was a Gloucestershire farmer until the age of 45, when he gave up farming to become a primary school teacher. Now a bestselling full-time author, his work has received many awards including a Bronze Medal for the Smarties Prize of 1997 for *All Because of Jackson* and the Children's Book Award in 1995 for *Harriet's Hare*.

In 1992, he was also voted Children's Author of the Year. In 1995, his top-selling title *The Sheep-Pig* was developed into a box-office movie, *BABE*, introducing hundreds of thousands of youngsters to his work. In 2005 he was the first recipient of the Peter Pan award.

SILENT WITNESSES

Crime scene crowds are a strange lot. Since my death, I had learned just how strange they truly were. For one thing, I always spotted familiar faces among the crowd—the very same faces, in fact—at virtually every crime scene since my days tracking Maggie had begun. I called them The Watchers. There was a blank-faced black man with tattoo stripes on his cheeks, a pale, blonde lady wearing a light cotton dress and no shoes, two teenagers with greasy hair and even greasier skin, and a rigid dark-haired man with military posture. They were always here, scattered among the crowd, waiting, though I was not sure what they were waiting for. I'd see them when I first searched the faces of the crowd, but when I looked again—they'd always be gone.

If these were my colleagues in the afterlife, I was in sad shape indeed.

Praise For

DESOLATE ANGEL

"I do not want Kevin Fahey to rest in peace. I want him to hang around until he's solved every one of the cases he bungled when he was a live detective. Happily, there are enough of those to let me look forward to many more hours of reading pleasure."

—Margaret Maron, author of *Sand Sharks*

Berkley Prime Crime titles by Chaz McGee

DESOLATE ANGEL
ANGEL INTERRUPTED

ANGEL
INTERRUPTED

Chaz McGee

BERKLEY PRIME CRIME, NEW YORK

THE BERKLEY PUBLISHING GROUP
Published by the Penguin Group
Penguin Group (USA) Inc.
375 Hudson Street, New York, New York 10014, USA
Penguin Group (Canada), 90 Eglinton Avenue East, Suite 700, Toronto, Ontario M4P 2Y3, Canada
(a division of Pearson Penguin Canada Inc.)
Penguin Books Ltd., 80 Strand, London WC2R 0RL, England
Penguin Group Ireland, 25 St. Stephen's Green, Dublin 2, Ireland (a division of Penguin Books Ltd.)
Penguin Group (Australia), 250 Camberwell Road, Camberwell, Victoria 3124, Australia
(a division of Pearson Australia Group Pty. Ltd.)
Penguin Books India Pvt. Ltd., 11 Community Centre, Panchsheel Park, New Delhi—110 017, India
Penguin Group (NZ), 67 Apollo Drive, Rosedale, North Shore 0632, New Zealand
(a division of Pearson New Zealand Ltd.)
Penguin Books (South Africa) (Pty.) Ltd., 24 Sturdee Avenue, Rosebank, Johannesburg 2196,
South Africa

Penguin Books Ltd., Registered Offices: 80 Strand, London WC2R 0RL, England

ANGEL INTERRUPTED

A Berkley Prime Crime Book / published by arrangement with the author

PRINTING HISTORY
Berkley Prime Crime mass-market edition / September 2010

ISBN: 978-0-425-23314-6

BERKLEY® PRIME CRIME
Berkley Prime Crime Books are published by The Berkley Publishing Group,
a division of Penguin Group (USA) Inc.,
375 Hudson Street, New York, New York 10014.
BERKLEY® PRIME CRIME and the PRIME CRIME logo are trademarks of Penguin Group
(USA) Inc.

PRINTED IN THE UNITED STATES OF AMERICA

10   9   8   7   6   5   4   3   2   1

My death has given me hope. And though hope is all my solitary existence offers me, I find I am luckier than many of the living I pass each day. Not having hope is a terrible fate. Those who lack it are more dead than me.

Prologue

A man with no past and no hope for the future walks through a playground. It is spring. He is cataloging all the things he does not have in his life: family, happiness, love, innocence. If he ever had any of these things, he no longer remembers. His life has been one of fear and shame for as long as he can recall.

This knowledge fuels a rage in him so profound he is convinced that if he were to open his mouth wide enough, he could spew flames like a dragon, scorching the laughing children before him in a single, awe-inspiring fireball.

There are days when he longs for the power to annihilate the world, and this is one of them.

Who is he kidding? He cannot annihilate the world. He doesn't even have the power to leave. But he could annihilate a family. Perhaps that would satisfy the anger that burns inside him, searing his heart with each peal of laughter he hears.

Besides, if he says no, he will be left with no one. He

will be utterly alone in this world. He will have nowhere to go and no one to care for him.

He cannot bear the thought.

The playground air smells like green. The sounds of songbirds surround him. The sunshine is warm on his cheeks and the air tastes of rain. A small boy squeals with delight as he swings from one monkey bar to the next.

Yes, the man thinks. *The boy is perfect. He will be the one.*

Chapter 1

Love is squandered by the human race. I have seen people kill in the name of love. I have watched others torture themselves with it, bleeding every drop of joy from their hearts because they always hunger for more, no matter how much love they may have.

Love is different when you are dead.

It becomes less self-serving and less specific. It transcends the whims of the chemical for a simple desire to be near. My love for a stranger can be as profound as my love for the woman and children I left behind when I died. Love has become both more tangible and more important. Could it transform my fate? Love is, I tell myself, the answer.

I have come to know all these things and more in the months since my death. I try hard to remember these lessons, since I failed so miserably to learn any when I was alive. I was too busy drinking my way through my days and running from the love I was given. Death is my second chance to understand life. So far, I have learned that no one is as important or as alone as they think, that kindness is the reason why people survive—and that evil is as real as love when it comes to the human race.

I have learned these things while wandering the streets of my town, unseen and unmourned, contemplating the failures of my life and the mysteries of my death.

I could dwell on the mysteries of my death—god knows I still don't understand it—but on a fine spring morning I prefer instead to dwell on the mysteries of love. For example, why do we give physical love such importance when it is, truly, the most fleeting love of all? Love comes in as many forms as there are people walking the earth. Just this week I have loved, among others, three children playing school in the park, especially the small boy wearing glasses who took his pretend role as a student very seriously indeed; the waitress at the corner coffee shop who smiles at her solitary customers out of happiness, not because she feels sorry for them; the pimple-faced grocery boy who stopped to pet a stray dog outside his store and fed it hamburger when no one was looking; and, of course, my Maggie, my replacement on the squad.

All of my infatuations, with the exception of Maggie, tend to come and go. They are as different as each day is new. Today I was in love with an old woman. It amused me to no end. I would never have noticed her when I was alive. I would have looked right through her, walked right past her, relegated her to the ranks of all the other white-haired ladies that crowded the edges of my life. But now that I am dead, I find I cannot take my eyes from her. She is exquisite.

She doesn't look like you would expect. If she had looked the part, she would have been tall and elegant with slender hands and silver hair and a finely carved face of angular perfection. Instead, she is a plump dove of a woman, round faced and rosy cheeked, her eyes bright pools of blue among crinkles of pink skin. Her hair is cropped short, often tucked behind her ears, as if she does not want anything to get in the way when she looks life in the eye.

And that, I think, is where my love for her is born. I have never met anyone quite like her, not in life and not in death. She is content to be exactly where she is. She feels every moment of her day with a willingness that takes my breath away. Life glints off her in bright flecks; she is sunlight sparkling from a spinning pinwheel. She sprinkles diamonds in her wake as she moves through her house and sits in her garden. She is always alone, and yet she is always content.

I have searched the hidden corners of her life and seen the photos of younger times. I have followed her, unseen, through her tidy house, certain I would spot signs of regret. But though she lives alone—the man in the photographs has obviously passed over, and I see no evidence of children to comfort her in advancing age—I do not feel sadness in her, not even at those times when she slows to examine the images of her past life. Happiness flows from her like silver ribbons and entwines her memories. She pauses, she feels, she moves on. I envy her certainty.

This morning, she was sitting on a small metal bench in a corner of her garden. Her tranquility was so great that rabbits hopped along the garden path without fear and chewed clover at her feet. Birds bathed in their concrete bath inches from where she sat. A sparrow lit on the arm of the bench, inches from her, rustling itself back into order. The old lady saw it all with bright eyes, soaking in the life surrounding her.

I could not tear myself away from her. I had followed her for days now, absorbed in learning the secrets of her serenity. To be near her was to live life in infinitesimal glory. She was the opposite of what I had been.

A breeze blew past, ruffling her hair. She closed her

eyes to enjoy the sensation. I was so lost in watching her that I failed to notice I was not her only observer.

"Excuse me," a timid voice said.

The old woman opened her eyes.

A man stood on the edge of her garden, waiting permission to speak. He was a weighed-down man in both body and spirit. His flesh sagged with years of bad food, though he could not have been older than his early forties. He reeked of cigarettes. His face, though perhaps once almost delicate, had become doughy and lackluster. His spirit, too, was heavy. I could feel it clearly. All the things he had not said in his life—love left unspoken, anger swallowed, regrets not voiced, apologies that stuck in his throat—they all encumbered him. His body slumped under the weight of these unvoiced emotions and I knew he would grow old before his time.

"Please, come into my garden," my white-haired muse said calmly, unsurprised to see him at her gate. "I believe we are neighbors, are we not?"

"We are," the man said, shuffling into her tiny paradise with an awkward politeness. He stood near the birdbath and did not seem to notice the flash of wings or the frantic thumping as creatures fled from his presence.

He smelled of stale beer and fried food, an odor I had lived with perpetually while alive but had since come to think of as the stench of self-neglect and disappointment.

"I live six doors down," he explained. "With my mother. Or, I did live with my mother. She died last fall."

"I see." The woman's voice was kind. She recognized the loneliness in him and, though she did not feel it herself, she understood how it could cripple others. "I'm so sorry to hear that. I had not seen her for a long time. I wondered where she had gone."

"She was bedridden for several years before she passed," the man explained.

"And you?" the woman asked. "What are you doing with your life now that she's gone? Here, please—sit." She waved her hand at a metal chair by a flower bed blooming in a riot of blues and purples around a miniature pond. But the man chose only to stand behind it, his hands gripping the curve of its back.

"I work," he explained. "I'm a chef at the Italian restaurant on Sturgis Street. And I volunteer. Actually, that's why I'm here."

"I hope you aren't here about me." The old woman laughed. "I am quite fine. I have no need for meals, on wheels or otherwise."

He smiled with an effort that told me it was an expression he seldom wore. "No, not that." His fingers twitched as mine used to when I needed a cigarette. "I keep watch, you see, in the park. I watch over the children."

The lady waited, her face betraying nothing.

"I'm part of an organization," he added quickly, as if her silence meant she thought him peculiar or, worse, suspected him of being the evil he purported to prevent. "It's not a big deal. I just keep tabs on the people who come and go. Jot down license plate numbers sometimes. Keep an eye on the children. I mostly work nights, preparing food for the next day, so I like to walk in the mornings when they play."

"I see," the old lady said. "You are Holden Caulfield in *The Catcher in the Rye*."

A spark lit inside him. This time, the smile came easily. "That's my favorite book," he admitted. "How did you know?"

"Many years of teaching school, my young friend."

He nodded and wiped his hands across the tops of his pants, leaving streaks of flour on the denim. "I have a favor to ask. But you'll think it's strange."

"I'm too old to think anything's strange," she assured him.

"There's a man in the park. Sitting on a bench."

"Perhaps he is enjoying the weather?" She lifted her face to the sun. "It is the finest of spring days. I have been sitting here for an hour myself."

"I don't think so," the man said reluctantly, as if hating to spoil her pleasure. "I've seen him now for several days in a row, sitting on the same bench for hours, watching the children play. Sometimes he sleeps or pretends to read the newspaper, but he is secretly watching the children. I'm sure of it. Once you suspect, it's easy to tell."

A cloud of sadness passed over the old lady's face. She knew too much about the world to question the possibilities of what he implied.

"I wonder if you might go with me?" the man asked. "To the park? To take a look at him to see."

"To see what?" she asked.

"To see if you think he is a danger or if, maybe, well . . ." His voice trailed off.

She looked at him and waited, unhurried, willing to let him take his time.

He glanced about him as he searched for the right words. "I need you to tell me if you think he is a danger to the children or if he's just someone like me who lives alone and likes the company of the park. His life could be ruined if I made an accusation. But a child's life might be ruined if I don't."

"Well, then," the old lady said, rising to her feet as she made up her mind to trust him. "Let's just have a look, shall we?"

Chapter 2

I was a surly bastard when I was alive, rejecting small talk and daring others to encroach on my silence at their peril. I would park myself at a bar, ignoring everyone and everything around me. I feared the kindness of others, knowing that glimpsing anything less than abject misery would remind me of how I had given up on life and other people had not.

But in the months I've spent wandering my town since my death, I have come to understand that people need meaningless chatter. They use small talk to fill the spaces between themselves and others, as the old lady's neighbor was doing now. He prattled on in a nervous monologue about his job; his mother; his desire to do the right thing; and, most of all, his fear that he might accuse an innocent man, thus triggering an avalanche of injustice.

My god, but he never stopped talking. It was as annoying as a thousand sand flies buzzing inside my head. The chattering of monkeys would have been more soothing.

I do not trust people who talk too much.

As a detective, I pegged suspects as guilty the instant they offered unasked-for information. And I had been right, most of the time, at least before I descended into ineptitude. Guilt made people talk, as if they could regurgitate their shame in words.

None of the man's inane chattering seemed to ripple the surface of the old lady's calm. She was kinder than me. She understood the man's need for contact and, perhaps, his need to exorcise the thoughts he had about the man in the park.

The trouble was, I suspected there was no man in the park. *He* was the man with the thoughts that should be feared. And how would I protect her if I turned out to be right?

"It's an organized effort, actually," he was telling the old woman, who was busy admiring her neighbors' gardens as they walked past each. "It was started by a retired colonel. I was his first volunteer, actually. He's in a wheelchair because of a war injury, so he relies on other people, like me."

The old lady smiled at him. "It seems more worthy than watching television."

They turned a corner toward the park. I hurried to keep up, an unseen interloper on their privacy. "I've never had a problem until now," he told the old lady. "And I've been keeping an eye out for months. They make those sorts of fellows register. You can look up their names and addresses on the Internet and know right away if one lives near you. It's public information. We keep track of them all."

"Oh, dear," the old lady said, her calm finally ruffled. But I could not tell if she rejected the idea of such men living near her or the idea that they were tagged for life like animals in the wild.

"What's your name, dear?" she interrupted firmly

when her new friend had gone on too long about his idea for basil ice cream, a suggestion I am certain revolted the old lady as much as it did me. "I remember what your mother looked like quite clearly, but I cannot remember her name. I am a bit forgetful these days."

"It's Robert," he said. "For my father. He died when I was young. My mother named me Robert Michael Martin. She said three first names were better than one."

"And her name was Eleanor," the old lady remembered. "I recall it now."

"That's right," the man said. "I already know your name."

Oh, really? Then why had he said nothing until now?

"At least," he continued, "I know part of your name. You're Mrs. Bates."

"But you must call me Noni," she insisted.

Noni, Noni, Noni—*no, no, no.* Did your mother never tell you not to talk to strangers, not to invite them into your life?

"Isn't the park the other way?" Noni asked when he led her down a side street.

"Yes. But if we go this way, we'll be able to approach the bench from behind and you can study him without him even knowing, maybe get a better read that way."

And if you do that, you'll also be marching straight into a deserted bramble with a strange man, far from anyone who could hear you, with me as a powerless witness unable to sound the alarm. No! I wanted to shout. *For God's sake, have you been living in a bubble? You don't even know this man and you surely don't know what he is capable of, no one can know just by looking. Oh, the things I have seen, the moments that have turned people's lives from triumph to terror, the decisions that have brought on suffering—how small they can be, how the smallest of choices can end a life.*

"We shall go your way," my friend Noni declared. "There are some hydrangeas on this block I have been wanting to see up close."

Choices like that one.

A hundred thoughts ran through my head, accompanied by a hundred paralyzing images. I had seen so much violence in my life, before violence cut my life short. I had long ago learned that people had no shame when it came to inflicting pain on others. They'd murder a sweet little old lady as surely as they'd kill a soldier in his prime, all to fill some terrible void that yawned inside them. There are wounded people walking this earth, people whose souls have been poisoned and whose minds have been warped and whose selfishness has risen to such heights that they can take a human life as casually as stomping on an ant.

But what could I do about it but follow them? I had no power over the physical world, just a slight ability to influence wind and water and, sometimes, fire. Even then, my influence was meager. I could inspire a breeze, ripple the surface of a pond, maybe even create a spark or two, but none of that could stop a man. If he wanted to hurt my morning's muse, there would be nothing I could do except witness her suffering—and I was not at all sure this was something I could endure. Having wallowed in human misery while I was alive, I was not anxious to have it follow me in death.

They were approaching the undeveloped edge of the park, hidden from the playground and picnic area by acres of untamed overgrowth. Early in my career, I used to bust men in the shadows of the ramble ahead, hauling them in for lewd conduct and indecent exposure. This was code for some poor bastard groping another poor bastard in the dark, both seeking something raw and real to counteract the charade of their lives. Back then, I'd enjoyed arresting those men with the same enthusiasm my father had reserved for hunting deer. But I was ashamed of my actions now—and I'd have given anything to encounter another human tramping among the shadows. Anyone at all. I feared for my new friend, Noni. Could she not see what this man was up to? He was a loner who had lived with his mother his entire life. Did she need a Hitchcock movie playing right in front of her to realize the truth? You'd think someone named "Mrs. Bates" would know better.

"Look," Noni said suddenly. "Did you see that? Follow me." *And she's leading him even deeper into the brush. It is hard to be a guardian angel given what humans bring upon themselves.* She placed a finger over her lips, and the chubby man dutifully followed, tiptoeing closer as she bent forward and parted the branches of a bramble bush. "See?"

There, nestled under a protective layer of thorny branches and thick leaves, a mother rabbit had just returned to her nest of grass. Eight newborn kits crowded around her, seeking her warmth.

"They're very good mothers," the old lady whispered to her new friend.

Something profound rose in the man named Robert Michael Martin at her comment: sorrow, panic, need— emotions flared like a fire doused with gasoline before he pushed it all back into the past and concealed it with a rush of self-assurance.

Where did that come from?

I would have no time to wonder. The stillness of the spring morning was split by the sound of sirens, arriving from all directions. Their wails filled the air, terrifying the rabbits and flushing birds from the brush. Even I, so used to sirens when I was alive, felt a dark cloud pass through me.

"Oh, dear," the old lady said.

"We're too late," Robert Michael Martin said in despair. "He's taken someone."

"You don't know that," Noni said firmly. "It could be a fire."

It was not a fire. I reached the scene well before the pair hurrying across the park behind me. But it was a not a kidnapped child, either. Squad cars were converging on a cottage across the road that bordered the playground in the park. Already, there were three first responders at the curb and more arrived within the minute. Whatever had happened was bad—and the possibilities were made worse by the fact that the cottage did not look like a crime scene at all. It seemed more like a perfect home for happy endings. It was a white-clapboard, copper-roofed house only one story high, a modern fairy cottage among the larger homes surrounding it. The yard was well tended and in full spring bloom, though its glory would not survive the day. Already, heavy-booted patrolmen were trampling the grounds as they stretched crime scene tape from corner to corner, barricading the cottage inside a perimeter of officially sanctioned space that none could cross but the anointed.

And me, of course. No crime scene tape could stop me.

Unseen, I entered the house and found a tidy home with pink-painted walls and plump furniture heaped high with pillows. There were family photos displayed on shelves and fresh flowers in a vase set on a delicately carved table in the foyer.

Death waited a few feet beyond.

I felt it before I saw it: a flat, cold void, as if in taking life away, death had taken all the oxygen and light with it.

Death is always startling, even when you live in it. Sprawled across a pastel carpet lay the body of a small woman. In her stillness, she seemed as frail as a broken-boned bird. She had been dead for some time, perhaps as long as a day. No trace of life lingered around her.

She was lovely even in death. Her delicate face showed few wrinkles, and her dark hair flowed out behind her in thick, chocolate waves, luxurious in a way that seemed obscene in the face of death. Her skin was pale and she was dressed in the floral scrubs of a nurse. She had not voided, as so many others do in death, and I was glad for that small dignity.

Her mouth was slightly open, as if she were waiting for a kiss that would never come. Snow White without her prince. Her eyes stared up at the ceiling, as if looking through infinity and beyond. In her right hand she clutched a small, gray pistol. It was a delicate weapon that looked like a toy. But she was proof the gun was real. A bullet hole bloomed neatly in the center of her right temple, as precisely defined as if a surgeon had drilled a hole there. It seemed impossible that such a tiny opening had taken her life in an instant, but I had seen such deceptively neat wounds before. I knew they had the power to obliterate all.

As I grew accustomed to the heaviness of death, I sensed the undertones beneath it. Emotions filled me, giving me a glimpse of what her final moment had been like. I felt, strangely, a strong vein of deep love but, most of all, betrayal of the most terrible sort.

What had happened here?

Blood had seeped out in a halo around her head, staining the carpet beneath. A patrolman was kneeling by the body, examining it with the curiosity of someone confronting death for the first time. He touched her left arm, then lifted it by the wrist and checked for a pulse, even though she was clearly gone. He let the arm flop back down, out of place, and then moved to her right side. He touched one of her fingers, curled around the gun, checking it for rigor, pushing it away from its original position without realizing what he had done.

I had been careless like that once, I knew. But I still wanted to take the gun out of the dead woman's hand and shoot the guy right then and there for maximum stupidity.

"What the hell are you doing, Denny?" a voice cried out from across the room. Excellent—maybe I wouldn't have to shoot the dumb bastard after all. Maybe his partner would do it for me.

An outraged black woman in uniform stood at the edge of the carpet glaring down at the wide-eyed patrolman. "Get away from the body," she ordered him. "Go stand over there by the door and remember *exactly* what she looked like when you first got in this room, because Gunn is going to lay you out."

Gunn? My heart skipped a beat. Maggie was on her way.

"I didn't touch anything," the patrolman mumbled.

"I saw you touch her hand."

"I was checking to see if she was breathing," he said defensively.

"I ought to do the same for you. There's no blood getting to your brain. Get over there." The cop shuffled, ashamed, to a corner of the room. He mumbled something as he passed her, but his partner was in no mood to hear it. "Hell, no," she said to him. "You're going to tell them yourself. Look at the body, you dumbass. You might have just screwed up evidence we needed to tell us whether this was murder or suicide."

She was right. There was something odd about the curve of the dead woman's right arm and the way she held the gun. I'd seen many an unhappy human blown to the other side by a self-inflicted gunshot. They dropped like rocks in a pond, arms flopped out in instantaneous surrender to death. I'd never seen a suicide with an arm curved as gracefully as a ballet dancer's. Something was off.

I tried to read the emotions lingering in the room more closely, but the emotions of the living interfered. Already, crime scene specialists had started to flood into the house, including several I recognized. Peggy Calhoun, an older woman just a few years from retirement, had arrived, even though she usually stayed in the lab to supervise her less-experienced colleagues. Her cat's-eye glasses dangled from a chain looped around her neck and, as always, she had orange lipstick smeared on her teeth.

"What are you doing here?" the female cop asked her.

"Gonzales sent me," Peggy explained, naming the department's commander which, in our town's case, meant the de facto chief of police, since our chief had long since slid into a state of moldy senility after five decades of distinguished service. I knew Gonzales wouldn't wait much longer before he went for the top job.

"What's Gonzales got to do with the victim?" the cop asked.

"He knows her."

The cop stepped back, ceding the crime scene to Peggy's expertise. But Peggy looked around the small house instead. She saw the unlived-in bedrooms and the single place setting still on the kitchen table from breakfast. "She lived alone?" Peggy asked the cop.

"Looks that way. No sign of anyone else. All the clothes in the closet look like hers. A couple prescriptions in the bathroom are made out to her, nothing big. Mild antidepressants, I think, that's all. I checked her bureau drawers myself." The cop looked at Peggy meaningfully. "I thought another woman should do that, know what I mean?"

Peggy nodded, understanding.

"None of the usual, you know, toys or anything. No guy stuff left lying around, no signs of outsiders at all, except for the photos." She nodded toward a shelf where younger versions of the dead woman posed with relatives at graduations and birthday parties. "It's not going to be easy telling all those people she's gone. I'm hoping they live out of town so someone else has to do it."

Peggy's eyes filled with tears. I was surprised. She'd seen many a crime scene before. She bent over the body to disguise her lack of composure, and was examining the carpet for trace evidence when the female cop announced, "Doc and Gunn just arrived. Plus that slimy new partner of hers."

Maggie. Salvation had arrived.

Chapter 3

Maggie entered a crime scene the way she entered a church. She stopped on the threshold to gather herself, emptying her mind of all else so she could be a worthy receptacle for what she learned inside. She calmed her thoughts, steadied her heart, and opened herself up to absorbing gifts beyond the tangible. With reverence and humility, she then stepped inside, determined to do her best.

Her eyes went to every corner of the room, cataloging everything. Well, everything but me. Though I could follow her every move if I desired, Maggie could not see me. At best there were times, I thought, when she sensed my presence or I felt a connection binding us across our worlds. But mostly I was little more than an observer to her competence as a detective. She was all I had failed to be.

The young patrolman in the corner could not meet her eyes. Maggie noticed, and the smallest of frowns flickered across her face. "Has anything been touched or moved?" she asked, without judgment, knowing that keeping her anger under control was the best way to preserve the truth.

"I'll let Denny tell you for himself," the black cop said as she headed outside to help corral the onlookers who were already clogging the sidewalk and driveway.

Maggie stared at Denny, waiting. He blushed. "Just do your best to remember exactly what it was you might have touched or moved," she said quietly. I could feel the cop's world shrink to Maggie and nothing else. She had that effect on people, and it made her one hell of an interrogator. The beat cop's heart rate slowed, and he searched his memory carefully. He wanted to help and it did not hurt that Maggie, my Maggie, was as fine a specimen as the human race could offer. She was not beautiful, nor even pretty, by most people's standards. Her face was plain, her hair an ordinary brown. But she was in incredible physical shape, and she moved through the world like a panther might cut through the jungle—focused and utterly unafraid.

Denny was staring at her arms. She wore a sleeveless black blouse, and her muscles were perfect.

"Your name's Denny, right?" Maggie said more loudly. "Help me out here, Denny."

"I picked up her left arm," he finally said. "To check her pulse and make sure she was dead." When Maggie nodded, as if understanding, he continued. "I guess maybe it slipped out of my hand and I let it flop a little?" He looked like he might faint.

"Flop how?"

Denny leaned over the body, trying to remember. "It was straight by the body when I first picked it up, very straight, almost like someone had pulled it into place."

"Good," Maggie said. "What about the other arm, the one with the gun?"

"I touched her hand, a little. The finger was coiled around the trigger. I thought it might be dangerous."

"And that's it?" she asked.

Denny nodded.

"Thanks. We can take it from here."

Maggie knelt next to Peggy Calhoun, the crime lab head, and the two women began to whisper in low tones, conferring over what they had just heard. Denny, ignored, headed out the door—but found a less forgiving detective blocking the way: Maggie's new partner, Adrian Calvano.

"Way to fuck up a crime scene," Calvano told the terrified patrolman as he scurried past. "Hope you enjoy walking the beat."

"Give it a rest, Adrian," Maggie said automatically, her mind on the body before her. She sounded like she said that phrase a lot.

What a jerk Calvano was. How could Gonzales have made him Maggie's new partner? Adrian Calvano was an unctuous douche bag I'd hated when I was alive and now loathed well into the afterlife. He'd never missed an opportunity to tear someone else down, be it partner, perpetrator, or passerby. I hated him for so many reasons it was hard to keep track. Replacing me as Maggie's partner was just the latest one. For one thing, Calvano was in his midforties, but had stayed thin and still had all of his hair. He probably dyed it, since it was still jet black, but you couldn't quite be sure. He wore it brushed straight back like he thought he was some sort of Italian count. Women loved it. Women loved *him*. The rest of the word thought he was an asshole.

Maggie deserved so much better.

"Adrian?" Maggie asked. When Calvano, a world-class ass-kisser, responded right away, I realized she was the senior officer on the case. That made me feel better. I was sure

Calvano hated taking orders from a woman. "I need you to screen and interview all those people standing around outside," she said. "Talk to her neighbors. The usual. Peter's filming them, but I need you on it. Find me people who know the victim, who can tell me about her life."

Clearly, Maggie was unaware that Calvano's usual interview technique was to insult people, then alienate them completely, and, eventually, make them hate every cop they met from there on out. But there was nothing I could do to stop him as he headed out the door, leaving Maggie kneeling with Peggy Calhoun among a sea of forensic techs so intent on their own tasks that they paid no attention to the two women.

"It's really sad," Peggy said. "It looks like she was completely alone. There's not a trace of anyone in this house but her."

Maggie glanced at her friend. "That bother you?"

"A little," Peggy admitted. "I mean, look at her. She was so beautiful. How can a person like that end up alone?"

"Some people like being alone," Maggie said. "I live alone."

"I know," Peggy conceded. "And I've lived alone for thirty years. It's just that she seems so delicate, and this house is so filled with love. As if she had a lot of love to give. It's horrible for her to die alone this way. What made her so unhappy?"

"My guess is someone else," Maggie said. "She'd have been better off alone."

Maggie was on her hands and knees, her eyes level with a spot only a few inches from the floor. "You know what? I don't think this woman was alone when she died. Look at the position of the hand, the way it's wrapped around the gun and the fingers are curled around the trigger. You ever see that before?"

Peggy shook her head. "Not in a suicide."

"Exactly," Maggie said.

"Calvano is going to want to call it self-help. He always does."

"I can handle Calvano," Maggie said confidently. "This one is not being marked closed anytime soon. Not until we catch the guy."

Peggy gave a sound that was halfway between a sob and a sigh. Maggie looked at her sharply. "You okay, Calhoun?"

"I knew you would take her side," Peggy said, nodding toward the victim on the floor. "I knew you'd be the one to fight for her."

Maggie patted her on the back. "I'm going to need you on this one. Together, we'll find out who did this to her. He won't get away, I promise."

"Gonzales knows her," Peggy said. "She's a trauma nurse. He says she saved his son's life one night after he'd been hit in the temple at a baseball game. The doctors said not to worry, that it was just a minor concussion. But she saw something in the kid's eyes and wouldn't let it go until they finally did another scan. Turns out the kid had a serious internal cranial bleed. They caught it in time because of her."

Together the two women stared down at the dead nurse, searching for a reason why she might be lying there while others walked around alive.

"It's always the good ones, isn't it?" Maggie asked.

"Seems that way," Peggy agreed.

Chapter 4

Outside the cottage, Calvano was busy pissing people off. "Get back behind the tape before I take you in myself," he told one woman who had leaned so far over the crime scene tape in her efforts to see inside the front door that her breasts were spilling out of her shirt. The lady's husband sputtered at Calvano in outrage, but he'd already moved on to insulting someone else. His tall figure in its well-cut suit towered above the sea of neighbors who had come running from their homes and from the park across the street to see what the fuss was about.

Crime scene crowds are a strange lot. Since my death, I had learned just how strange they truly were. For one thing, I always spotted familiar faces among the crowd— the very same faces, in fact—at virtually every crime scene since my days tracking Maggie had begun. I called them The Watchers. There was a blank-faced black man with tattoo stripes on his cheeks, a pale, blonde lady wearing a light cotton dress and no shoes, two teenagers with greasy hair and even greasier skin, and a rigid dark-haired man with military posture. They were always there, scattered among the crowd, waiting, though I was not sure what they were waiting for. I'd see them when I first searched the faces of the crowd, but when I looked again—they'd always be gone. Today I was late, having lingered inside with Maggie, and I'd caught a glimpse only of the black man with the tribal tattoos on his cheeks. I tried to find him again, but he had disappeared.

If these were my colleagues in the afterlife, I was in sad shape indeed.

Calvano was scanning the crowd, just like me, examining faces, looking for anyone who seemed out of place. Most of the people were from the neighborhood. They came in all ages, all shapes, all sizes. Most looked curious and very little more, although a few seemed frightened. Only my old lady friend, Noni Bates, looked upset.

"You knew the woman who lived here?" Calvano asked abruptly, not bothering to conceal his use of the past tense.

"Yes," Noni said in a voice that lacked her usual preciseness. "I give her advice on her garden. She's a nurse in the emergency room at the hospital. What happened?"

"She killed herself. Stay here," Calvano told her. "We'll want to talk to you."

She blinked, taken aback by his abruptness. Her new friend, Robert Michael Martin, interceded. "Are you sure?" he asked Calvano. "Isn't it a little soon to make that call?"

Hoo-boy. Calvano was going to love this one. He looked at Martin with contempt. "Who are you?" he demanded.

"I'm her neighbor."

"Did you know her?"

"No."

"Then shut up and leave the scene to us."

"There was a man in the park," Martin said. "He was sitting on the bench right over there." He pointed straight across the street to where a row of benches lined two sides of the playground, forming a neat right angle that gave one row of benches a perfect view of the cottage's front door.

"That's what benches are for," Calvano said impatiently. "For sitting on."

"But he'd been there for days," Martin insisted.

"And you know that *how*?" Calvano asked brusquely.

"I've been watching him." Martin started to explain, but Noni put a warning hand on his arm. She knew people like Calvano on sight. Martin fell silent.

It was too late. Calvano was staring at Martin more closely, sizing up his sloppy clothes and intense gaze. "What's your name?" he asked abruptly.

"Robert Michael Martin," the chef said promptly.

"Well, Robert Michael Martin, I'm going to need your address, too." Calvano held a pad out to the man. "Print, please. We'll be in touch."

Martin wrote his address down, eager to help, not knowing he would likely pay dearly for speaking up.

The old lady knew better. She'd lived longer. She'd run into bullies like Calvano before. "Robert, you go home and wash up," she said firmly when he was done printing his address. "I have some things to tell this nice detective and then I'll stop by."

"But someone needs to—"

"I can do that," Noni interrupted firmly. "You go on and I'll stop by when I'm done." Even Robert Michael Martin got the hint. With a look at Calvano that was part scorn and part fear, Martin started marching resolutely down the block, trying to maintain his dignity. Calvano's only choice in stopping him was to tackle him and risk damaging his expensive suit, possibly for nothing, or let him go.

Naturally, Calvano let him go. He was an even worse detective than I had been. At least I'd had the excuse of being a drunk to explain my sloppiness.

Calvano took it out on Noni. "Lady, I don't appreciate you—"

"Did you want to talk to me or not?" Noni demanded. "I can give you ten minutes and then I intend to go to church and pray for this young woman's soul."

I was impressed. Her voice had gone from cooperative to steely in an instant. I bet she'd been one hell of a teacher in her day. Calvano actually flipped to a new page in his notebook, ready to take notes. What a grand old dame.

"What did you know about . . . ?" Calvano asked, his voice faltering. He flipped back a few pages and checked for the victim's name, one he had already managed to forget. " . . . about Fiona Harper?"

"Her name was Fiona *Harker*," Noni correctly him grimly. "She lived alone. She never married. She didn't have a boyfriend that I know of. And she would never have killed herself. You're quite mistaken on this point. Fiona was a practicing Catholic. She would not have killed herself."

Calvano looked bored. I wanted to brain him. Fiona Harker deserved better. Yes, I had been just as careless when I was alive. But I was different now. I was sensitive. Which was why I knew he needed a good beat-down. Watching Calvano reminded me of how sloppy I had been, and I didn't like looking in the mirror.

"What else can you tell me?" Calvano asked Noni.

"She was very private and a little shy. We only met because she stopped by my house to ask me about some perennials in my garden. People say she was an excellent nurse, and I know she was an excellent gardener."

"But no boyfriend?" Calvano asked skeptically.

"Not that I know of," Noni said. "Although I'm not the one to ask. We did not discuss our personal lives." She managed to make it sound like Calvano had been a pervert for asking, even though it was his job to know. I totally enjoyed his shamefaced reaction. Noni had his number.

"Are people in this neighborhood tight?" Calvano asked, trying to regain his authority. "Can you point out other people who might have known her?"

"I can't help you," Noni said. "I didn't know her well enough to say."

That was when the screaming began. We all heard it: uncontrolled, feral panic, so intense it made you want to flee first and ask questions later.

The crowd turned, searching the park, trying to put it all together. A woman in her late twenties stood on the edge of the playground, face flushed, her hands held over her mouth, her eyes searching the park as she screamed and screamed and screamed.

Noni was the first to realize what it meant: a playground, a panicked mother, the strange man in the park. She pointed to the woman and yelled at a stunned Calvano, "Go. A child is missing. *Go.*"

Chapter 5

The crowd of onlookers outside the cottage came as close to stampeding as I have ever seen people do. Calvano was helpless to stop the flood. They surged across the road in a pack, terrifying the already frightened children who had been left alone on the playground while their parents rubbernecked at the crime scene a few yards away.

While some in the crowd ran to the screaming woman, others found their children and scooped them up, holding them tight, circling the wagons of their hearts while they waited to hear who and how tragedy had struck. A few knew the screaming woman and guided her toward a bench, getting her to sit long enough to elicit the story: her son was missing. He was a four-year-old boy with curly brown hair, small for his age, wearing blue shorts and a T-shirt with dinosaurs on it. His name was Tyler.

She had only left him alone for a couple minutes. Drawn by the sirens and the gathering crowd, she had drifted toward the cottage, leaving her son on a swing. When she returned a few moments later, he was gone. No one had seen a thing. They had all been focused on the small, white house rimmed by crime scene tape. The mother had immediately started pushing through the crowd, expecting to find her son. The little boy loved policemen; he wanted to be one when he grew up. Surely he had wandered across the street, searching out his heroes?

He was nowhere to be found.

Unnoticed by the distracted crime scene crowd, the mother had searched the open lawn with a rising sense of panic before, in full-blown terror, she had begun to run blindly through the park, calling out her son's name, each step without an answer sending her further over the edge of reason. The scratches on her face and hands told of how frantic and alone she had been during her search. Not finding him anywhere and too overwhelmed to continue, she had returned to the playground. There, she'd overheard two women repeating a rumor: the dead nurse in the cottage across the street had been shot to death.

The mother was sure the killer had taken her son. No one could tell her otherwise.

She was a heavyset woman with curly red hair and freckles sprinkled up and down her arms and legs. Her face was splotchy, and she could not stop shaking as she sobbed out her fears. She carried an immense sorrow with her, as if her whole world had been lost. But it was not a new emotion; I could sense she had grown as used to it as a beetle to its shell. Her fear was fueled by past tragedy as much as by the present circumstances.

A small crowd had surrounded the sobbing woman, wanting to lend support. Other playground mothers, grim-faced, tried to calm her as their children, ashen-faced, tried to understand what was happening.

Calvano pushed away those trying to comfort her and

sat beside the mother, assuring her that he was a detective and that they would find her son.

It was as if the woman were deaf. She continued to sob uncontrollably, unable to assist at all.

After a few minutes of cajoling, Calvano started to lose patience. I could not say I blamed him. They were losing precious moments better spent looking for the boy. Others realized this as well. Spurred into action by Calvano's increasingly impatient voice, a woman who was holding on firmly to the hand of her daughter tapped Calvano on the shoulder and beckoned him to follow her. They stood away from the bench where they would not be overheard by the sobbing mother.

"She lost her husband in Iraq a year ago," the woman told Calvano. "She was hospitalized for a month when she found out. I don't think she'll be of much help at all. If you don't find Tyler, she'll have nothing left and she knows it. I think you better call her doctor."

Now it was Calvano's turn to panic. The mother's help was essential. If the cases were related, they needed to know. If not, if someone had just taken advantage of the distraction and snatched the boy, it could be the worst kind of case. Without the mother's help, they had nothing.

It was about to get even worse. Calvano left the sobbing woman with her friends and went to consult with Maggie just as dozens of well-meaning neighbors and strangers alike organized into search teams. They scattered across the park and began calling the young boy's name, pulling bushes apart, searching the branches of trees, trampling the ground with their feet. Within minutes, before Calvano or Maggie could stop them, any evidence had likely been destroyed by well-meaning strangers. They would have nothing to go on at all.

Which meant it was all up to me. If I hurried, I might be able to pick up a trace of where he had gone.

Maggie had reached the edge of the playground, angry at being called away from her crime scene. But when told of the boy's disappearance, she looked every bit as disbelieving as Calvano had. She began arguing with Calvano in a tight circle formed by patrolmen to keep civilians out. It looked oddly like a football huddle, and it did little to conceal the heated argument they were having. Calvano had about three theories, all of them confusing. Maggie had one: the two crimes were not related. Both she and Peggy Calhoun had estimated the nurse's time of death at least twenty-four hours before, and there was no reason to suspect the boy being taken was anything but a crime of opportunity.

Calvano was of the opinion that they should take the missing boy's mother over to view the nurse's body just in case it turned out that she knew the woman—proving there might be a connection between the two cases. The silence that met this suggestion did not faze him. "It's fast and efficient," he insisted.

"Let me get this straight," Maggie asked, trying to keep her voice neutral. "This poor woman loses her husband to war, and now her only connection to him, their son, is missing, and you want to ask her to go look at the dead body of a woman with a bullet through her head?" Maggie's voice broke with frustration. "I've called in Gonzales. Let's let him make the call about how to approach this."

"There's not going to be anything left in the park to go on," one of the beat cops said. "People are trampling any evidence there might have been."

"All we can do right now is try to talk to the mother and pray that someone she knows did this," Maggie said. "If it's a stranger abduction, we're done."

"It was that weirdo," Calvano told the others. "This fat guy with flour in his hair. I questioned him earlier. I got a weird vibe off him. And he lives around here. He'd know how to get out of the park fast."

Some of the gathered officers looked hopeful at this, but Maggie knew Calvano too well to believe his hunches were worth a damn. "We'll let Gonzales make the call," she repeated. "In the meantime, I need the door of the cottage under guard at all times, no one gets in or out, and, for God's sake, keep the search for the missing boy from spilling over into my crime scene. No one goes near that yard. The rest of you need to search the surrounding neighborhood." When Maggie gave orders, she had a way of sounding as if she were asking for your help personally, and that you and you alone could help her out. The uniforms began their organized search for the boy without hesitation.

Maggie sat by the sobbing mother, waiting patiently while the woman fought for control. She was hoping to get something from her before Gonzales arrived. I didn't think it would happen, and I could feel that Maggie didn't either. Still, she had to try.

Meanwhile, Calvano went running after some civilian searchers so he could blow off his frustration by screaming at them

And me? I went in search of the abductor.

Chapter 6

I could find no trace of the boy. Too many lives filled the park and too many emotions muddied the air. The taking of a child is a transgression that strikes a chord of visceral terror in everyone, whether they have children or not. It is a primal reaction beyond our control: no one likes to be reminded of how helpless we are to stop the worst from happening. Because of this, everywhere I turned, the way was blocked, either by well-meaning searchers or by the residual energy from their frenzied emotions.

A child that small, barely four years of age, would be so trusting. I could almost see him lifting his innocent face to the stranger's, listening intently to his story, wanting to be a good boy, and, believing the story to be true, slipping his tiny hand into the man's larger hand before marching away with him like the big boy he believed himself to be. The child would be unformed, his emotions fleeting and hard to trace—which meant I needed to concentrate on the abductor. He would leave an emotional trail like a snake slithering though grass. I had tracked evil before.

Where had the boy been taken to hide? With this many people searching and no trace of him to be found, I was pretty sure the child was no longer in the park. I would concentrate on the exits and picking up the predatory scent of his abductor. I circled the edges of the park, seeking an indication of darkness that might lead me to the boy.

There.

Along the back edge of the park, I discovered what had to be lingering traces of the kidnapper. It was near the side street where my dear old lady, Noni Bates, and her lonely middle-aged neighbor, Robert Michael Martin, had discovered the rabbit's nest. A vein of darkness lingered in the air, surrounded by more troubled emotions. Ambivalence, perhaps, and a hint of shame. Self-loathing. *Lots of self-loathing.* And something that felt very much like sadness.

This was either a conflicted kidnapper or someone who had never done this before.

Had he taken the boy out of opportunity? If Robert Michael Martin was telling the truth, he had seen the abductor watching the children all week. Had he been fighting his urges the entire time and then been unable to resist the perfect opportunity that unfolded before him, taking the child on a whim?

Or, an unwilling thought intruded, *perhaps Robert Michael Martin was the abductor after all*. He had left the nurse's cottage and surely followed this route on his way back home. He had been angry and felt overlooked. He had been in need of power. And he certainly seemed obsessed with children. Perhaps the temptation had been too much.

I wished for my new friend Noni that it was not so, but I hoped it *was* him, so that the boy might be found.

I see what others miss, as mortals often overlook the nuances of their world. Or perhaps the searchers were simply moving too fast. But there, green among the green, just along the outer edge of the park's back lawn, I discovered a plastic dinosaur, about three inches long, lying on its side in a patch of grass that concealed it from human eyes. It was a deeper green than the lawn, but it was the feeling of it that drew me to it. My intuition is akin to a sense of smell in that it affirms the existence of the invisible. But it is different in every other way. It's just that smell comes closest to what I experience. It fills me until there is no doubt as to what I know. When I knelt next to the plastic toy, I felt the joy of a cozy kitchen on a weekend morning. The smell of pancakes and a mother's lingering perfume permeated my mind. I tasted grape juice and heard the din of cartoon characters crashing into one another, felt the soft scratch of a favorite stuffed toy on my cheek and, to my deep joy, experienced the humanness of hunger.

Yes, the toy belonged to the boy. He had been taken out this way.

The volunteer searchers had left this end of the park. But a crime scene crew would probably come through in hopes of finding anything that might yield a clue. I owed it to them to make sure they found the toy.

I had broken the boundary between my old and new worlds once before, and the pain had debilitated me for days. I could not afford to tear the fabric between the two worlds now; I needed to keep searching for the boy. I would have to find a way to reveal the toy without attempting to move it.

In the end, the best I could do was to summon a light breeze to rustle the grass around the toy. With concentration, I was able to flatten the blades slightly around it. But it would still take good eyes to spot it.

That job done, I searched the sidewalk leading away from the park, losing the trail at a parking space halfway down the block. The abductor had driven away in a car.

I headed back to the crime scenes, knowing Gonzales would have arrived by now and wondering who would win the battle of strategy—Maggie or Calvano. The three of them were sitting in a town car parked near the nurse's cottage, the driver dismissed in the interest of discretion. He was standing outside the car, smoking a cigarette and bullshitting the female cop who had been guarding the crime scene earlier.

The town car belonged to Gonzales. It was a luxury sedan designed for bigwigs and politicians. Gonzales was both. He had risen rapidly though the ranks of the department and had been named commander a few years before. He was impossible to pin down and therefore impossible to contradict. Like all politicians, he had no core of his own. He was as close to being a shape-shifter as humans ever get, morphing his opinions and attitudes to mirror those he was with at the time, eluding all attempts at revealing who he really was. It served him well. He'd gone far being all things to all people while, essentially, being no one at all

This was unfortunate for Calvano. I have done a lot of watching since I died, my voyeurism extending behind closed doors. Gonzales had a soft spot for Maggie. He looked upon her as a daughter or, perhaps, a protégée. He knew her father, and I had eavesdropped on many a conversation between them. Maggie's father was the old guard, and it would be a few more years before Gonzales could ignore their wishes. Calvano was deluded if he thought that Gonzales would take his advice over Maggie's.

It didn't take Calvano long to find this out. "Absolutely not," Gonzales was saying to him. "Leave the mother alone. If you want to look for a connection, question her friends or other mothers in the park. Ask if any of them know Fiona." When Calvano looked blank, Gonzales shook his head. "That's the murder victim, Calvano. Her name is Fiona Harker. Just ask if anyone knows her and leave it at that for now. We'll find the connection, if there is one."

Calvano looked as if he had been just passed over for captain of the football team. Pouting is not an attractive trait in a grown man.

"Have you got anything else?" Gonzales asked him.

"Yes," Calvano said, refusing to meet Maggie's eyes. "There was one guy I talked to, a neighbor. There's something wrong with him. I can feel it. He tried to interject himself into the investigation. The boy was taken right after he left the first crime scene. It could be he came sniffing back around after killing the nurse to see what we knew, and when I blew him off and didn't play his game, maybe he got angry and took the boy?"

"Because nurse-murdering pedophiles are our number one problem in this state," Maggie offered, although sarcasm was not one of her preferred weapons. Calvano was starting to get to her. Partnering with him would be like babysitting a chimpanzee.

Gonzales tried not to smile. "Take a team and talk to him. Do you have his address?"

"Right here, Commander." Calvano held up his notebook.

"If he gave you the right address," Maggie pointed out.

Calvano looked momentarily alarmed, but recovered. "I know what he looks like," he said confidently. "We can smoke him out."

Oh my god, better that I had been a broken-down lush than a total dweeb like this guy.

"Fine," Gonzales said. "Pull six men from across town to visit your suspect. No lights, keep it low-key. They should be out of uniform. Ask for a voluntary search of the house. Get back to me if the owner refuses, and I'll arrange for a warrant."

Calvano left the car as supremely confident of his abilities as when he had first entered it. Nothing, not reality or the scorn of others, could put a dent in his ego. The sad thing was that it had carried him this far.

With Calvano gone, there was plenty of room for me. I made myself comfortable in the driver's seat and pretended to steer as I eavesdropped on Maggie and Gonzales. There were times when I badly missed my old life or, rather, badly missed the life I wish I had lived. This was one of them. I wanted to be one of the good guys. The best I could do was to eavesdrop while they talked.

Gonzales had relaxed the moment Calvano left the car and became as close to human as he can manage. "Don't say it," he said to Maggie.

"Don't say what?" she asked innocently, though she was trying not to smile. Maggie's plain face is transformed when she smiles, but she doesn't smile very often. She feels the world's pain a little too much than might be healthy for a woman her age, but it's the price she pays for being a better detective than I ever was.

"You're angry I put Calvano with you," Gonzales said.

"You couldn't have put him with one of the other mouth-breathers?"

Gonzales looked apologetic. "I can't afford another nonfunctioning team," he explained. "I'm still paying the price for Fahey and Bonaventura."

Ouch. That hurt. The reference to my old partner and

me stung. Were we never to be posthumously rehabili-
tated? They did it for politicians all the time.

Maggie started to say something—I let myself imagine she had been about to spring to my defense—but
Gonzales stopped her with an upturned palm. "For another reason, too," he said. "I can't take another lawsuit
in the department. You don't put up with his crap. If I let
him partner with any other woman, it would be a disaster. If I let him interact with witnesses or victims without
someone like you to keep him in line, it would be a disaster. That's why he's in your lap. I promise it won't be
forever."

"Sir, why have him at all?" she suggested. "I'm just
asking."

"Being a pigheaded bully is not incompatible with law
enforcement," Gonzales said. "You just have to know
how to use his special talents."

"And the fact that his uncle is a councilman has nothing to do with it?"

"Of course not," Gonzales assured her with his politi-
cian's grin, but at least he had the decency to know he
was full of it. His smile faded. "Maggie, I need you to
take the lead on Fiona Harker's murder. It means a lot to
me."

"I heard about her treating your son."

"She didn't just treat him, she saved his life," Gonzales said, his voice taking on an edge of genuine emotion
I had never heard in him before. "I owe her. The emergency room was crashing in around us. It was a Saturday
night and the ER was crowded with drunks bellowing
and people brawling and all the doctors were just pushing the cases through and that—" His voice broke and
he stopped to regain control. "That woman cared enough
about my son to take a second look at his scan when the
doctors had dismissed it and, because of her, they had

him in surgery within half an hour. It saved his life. She deserves some justice. It's all I can give her, but I owe it to her."

"I understand, sir," Maggie said. "I won't let it go."

"I know you won't. That's why I put you on it."

"Unfortunately, that means Calvano needs to be lead on the missing kid case," she said for him. "They might be related."

"Do you think they are?"

"Only in the sense that whoever took the boy used the first crime as a distraction and was able to get away unnoticed."

"You're sure?' Gonzales asked.

"The time frames are different. MO is different. No connection between victims."

"What about the mother?" he asked. "Could she have harmed her boy?"

Maggie looked so sad at the mention of the missing boy's mother. She wasn't just empathetic to people, she assumed their sorrow and carried it inside her for the duration of a case. "It's not her, sir. I talked to her briefly, but I had to have her taken to emergency psych. She's broken. Lost her husband a year ago. Her kid is all she has. She thinks it's her fault. It's not her."

"You're sure about that?" Gonzales was being very careful; he'd had enough public relations disasters thanks, in part, to me.

Maggie nodded. "She didn't have the time, she doesn't have the motive, and she didn't have the means. Witnesses saw her with her kid seconds before the crime scene distracted everyone, and there's no way she could have killed him and hidden the body far enough away to avoid detection. We'd have found something. He was taken, sir. I put three offices on a closer search of the park, though it's been trampled by volunteers. I doubt they'll find anything."

"We can't stop people from wanting to help."

"Not when there are six of us and sixty of them."

"We're going to have a lot more than six people on our side, and you don't have to worry about Calvano screwing it up. I made a decision, and then I made a call. The feds are coming in on the missing child case." Gonzales noticed Maggie's smile. "Yes, Gunn, Calvano will have to deal with them instead of you."

"When will they be here?"

"They're in Baltimore wrapping up another case, but they'll be here tonight."

"You know that Calvano's going to roust that poor neighbor before they get here," she predicted. "He'll want to get his licks in while he can."

"The guy might be involved," Gonzales warned her. "Calvano's been right before."

"From what I hear, Robert Michael Martin is just some poor guy who wants to be a hero," Maggie said. "He's not organized enough or motivated enough to have done what this abductor did. I think we're looking for a pro."

Gonzales sighed. "What kind of world has professional child abductors?"

"Our world?" Maggie suggested.

Gonzales regained his professional detachment. "I want you to ignore the media, ride herd on Calvano, and find out who did this to Fiona."

"What about the boy?" She sounded wistful. Like everyone, she wanted to help.

"You're going to work on that, too."

"How?"

"Use the Harker case as a cover but, when you can, I want you to pursue any local angles on the kid, all right? You and I know the feds are going to come in with a profile and they're going to broaden the search—but this is a small enough town that someone, somewhere, knows who it was. Or at least suspects who it was. He was taken from the heart of town. There's got to be a local connection. I want us to be the ones who find it."

"So you want me to solve the Harker case, and find out who took the boy, and keep Calvano in line all at the same time?"

"That's about it," Gonzales agreed.

"Do I at least get overtime?" Maggie asked, joking.

"I know you can do this," Gonzales told her solemnly. "You can do it and more, if you need to." For once, I agreed with Gonzales.

Chapter 7

If ever I am sent back to the world of the living, I want a friend like Noni Bates to be with me. She beat the cops to Robert Michael Martin's house, having correctly surmised that Calvano would set his sights on him. But it was more than that, I realized, when I found her on his front porch. A vein of anxiety ran through her, a fear he might turn out to be the most evil of beings her school-teacher's heart could imagine. I realized it took courage for her to be there at his house in pursuit of the truth. She was sturdy, but she was small, and she was no match for a man Martin's size.

I wanted to search his house before anyone else arrived and polluted it with their own agendas. I didn't think Martin was connected to the boy's disappearance, not after feeling the residual emotions the kidnapper had left behind. But I'd racked up a lifetime of being wrong. So I felt it was prudent to check, just in case.

I lingered in the front hallway, soaking in the loneliness of the dusty old house, while Noni rang the bell outside. Martin appeared promptly, shambling along like a bear awoken from hibernation. I get to see the things people do when they think no one is looking, and sometimes it's not pretty. Martin was sleepily scratching his belly and blinking as if surprised to find it was still daylight outside.

"Mrs. Bates?" he said when he opened the door—without checking to see who it was first, I might add. He was lucky he'd not been swept off his feet by a sea of cops and flattened against the hallway walls. "What are you doing here?"

"Get dressed," she said firmly. "And call a lawyer now. I am certain that detective is on his way to arrest you."

"I haven't done anything wrong." He sounded so dumbfounded, I almost felt sorry for the poor slob. He actually thought being innocent might protect him. That only told me he'd never run into cops like Calvano before.

"May I come in?" Noni asked. He stepped aside and she entered his front hall as if it were Buckingham Palace. If she noticed the musty air, the dust on the furniture, or the lingering smell of fried meat, she gave no sign that she found it in the least important.

But she did eye his attire. He'd ditched the flour-dusted jeans and was wearing a dingy T-shirt and boxer shorts. "Really, dear. I taught men like that detective when they were still boys and pushing other children around on the playground. He will be here soon. You get dressed and call a lawyer."

"I don't need a lawyer," Martin said again, affronted at the implication that he might.

"Then at least get dressed." The steel was back in her voice, and he blinked once, then obeyed, climbing the stairs to the upper chaos of his second floor. I followed.

It was as uncared for as the rest of the house. I moved

from room to room, picking up on the vague fear that had driven his mother's existence. It permeated every room, including the one where she had died: a hospital bed still dominated the interior and pill bottles still littered the bureau surface. Only the bed, stripped clean of its linens, had been touched since the body had been removed— what had he said? A year ago? The dude seriously needed to move on.

I felt sorry for the guy. He was just some schlep who'd never been loved enough as a kid because his mother had been too overwhelmed and afraid of sliding into poverty to spare the time. He didn't have friends because he didn't know how to make them.

I searched the rooms, all the while expecting to hear Calvano and his men entering below. There was no trace of a small boy anywhere, not in any of the two empty bedrooms or the chaotic one Robert Michael Martin clearly occupied and used, it appeared, for sitting in bed and eating pizza while he watched television. I even searched the attic. It was filled with the detritus of his mother's life. She had apparently saved everything she ever owned, just in case she might need it again. The basement was dark and dirt-floored in that way of old houses that have never been updated. The boy had never been there. No one had ever been there. Martin lived in isolation. The rooms were half dead, as devoid of energy as his life.

I returned to the first floor just as Calvano arrived. If he was surprised to have Noni Bates answer the door, he did not show it.

"We're here to search the house," Calvano said, and I realized, appalled, that he did not recognize her from earlier. "We would like permission to search, but we can get a warrant, if necessary."

"Wait here," Noni told him, and shut the door firmly in his face, locking the dead bolt. I enjoyed that immensely.

She called upstairs to Martin, who promptly appeared, attired in a short-sleeve checked shirt and chinos he had obviously not worn for several years. His belly spilled over the waistband like bread dough, but he did look far more respectable, like an actual taxpaying citizen, for example. For some of the cops waiting to search his house, that might make a difference.

"The police are here," she told him with her usual conciseness. "They want permission to search your house."

"Let them in," he said at once. "Of course they can search. I have nothing to hide."

Noni visibly relaxed. He had passed the test. She was back to believing him to be the innocent she hoped he was. "You be the one to let them in," she advised him.

Martin opened the door. When he saw the rows of officers waiting to invade his life, words failed him. He simply stepped aside and let them enter.

"This constitutes your official permission to search the house," Calvano said to him. "Please state so for the record."

"It does," Martin said in a weak voice. I caught a whiff of anxiety rising from him, a distress I could not pinpoint until I realized that this dark cave of a house was where he was safe from a world in which he felt off-kilter and, like all creatures, he did not like his lair disturbed. Noni sensed his anxiety and stood beside him, a hand on his shoulder as six men swept past them, fanning out to their assigned rooms.

"I expect you to put things back where they were," Noni called after them, but only her forgiving eyes could have missed the obvious—this particular house could look no worse after a search than it had looked going in. How could anyone tell the difference?

I had not been able to check out the entire first floor before Calvano arrived, so I was anxious to continue my own brand of searching. Martin and the old lady were still in the front hall, where both seemed unable to decide whether it was okay for them to sit down or if they should remain standing the entire time. Dredging up a flash of gallantry, Martin fetched a kitchen chair for Noni, who sat in it numbly. Some of her courage was a façade. Six cops could be intimidating.

As they tore Martin's house apart looking for signs of the missing boy or evidence of nasty habits, I checked out a kitchen that seemed oddly unused for someone who was a chef. The refrigerator held dozens of take-out cartons in varying stages of decay, coffee creamer, and two six-packs of Dr Pepper. Pizza boxes lined the counters, paper plates smeared with tomato and grease filled the sink, and a couple crusty frying pans that smelled of old hamburger sat, unwashed, on the stove.

The guy definitely needed to get a life, but I found myself thinking that maybe he ought to get himself a maid first.

There was nothing that stamped the house as his until I discovered an office at the back of the first-floor hallway. A plainclothes officer was methodically flipping through a shelf of videos and books along one wall. He was soon joined by a colleague who had completed the search of his assigned room. He went right to a large-screen computer that dominated the room. A few spiral-bound notebooks and a row of pens were lined up next to its keyboard, but otherwise the counter was uncluttered, which was pretty remarkable given the old soda and fast-food wrappers filling every other surface.

"This is it," the first cop predicted. "We've got him now."

"Bingo," the other said. He'd pulled up Martin's browser history on the computer. "I'm no expert, but name a kiddie porn site or chat room and I'm betting it's here. It's all the guy ever went to."

"Of course I went to those sites," a voice said from the doorway. Martin had followed the extra man to his office. It was the only room in the house he really cared about. "I volunteer for an organization that tracks child abusers and sex offenders. I go online and pretend to be a kid. That's how we know who to track online."

The men stared at him blankly.

"It's called KinderWatch," Martin said proudly. "We have members up and down the East Coast, even a few in the Midwest. The founder lives right here, about a mile away. Ask him. He'll tell you. I'm one of his best volunteers."

Had he been better able to read the mood in the room, Martin's sense of pride would have deflated in favor of fear. They'd seen the sites he had visited. Their judgment was swift and it was final.

"What's going on?" Calvano asked from the doorway. Noni stood behind him, craning her neck, trying to see into the room.

"Kiddie porn sites," one of the men said loudly. "I'm checking his hard drive next."

"Looks like I need you to come to the station," Calvano told Martin, a petty note of triumph in his voice.

"But I'm not one of them, I *watch* them. For you guys," Martin protested.

"You need to come with me," Calvano answered, pushing him toward the hall. That was Calvano for you. Why use persuasion when a little bullying would do?

"He's not answering any questions without a lawyer present," Noni announced, inserting her small frame between Martin and Calvano.

"Who are you?" Calvano asked rudely and, focusing on her for the first time, realized he had seen her earlier, but was unable to make the leap from the sweet, little old lady before him to any connection to a kidnapped boy. "What's it to you?"

"I was a friend of his mother's. I promised to look after him," she said firmly. Martin gave her a look of gratitude so raw I felt as if I had invaded his privacy just seeing it.

"I will not permit you to ask him questions without a lawyer present," Noni said. She turned to Robert Michael Martin. "You go with the detective but you sit there and you do not say a word until I bring a lawyer to you. Do you understand?"

Martin nodded mutely. Calvano still had a hand clamped on his shoulder, and the poor bastard was starting to get seriously scared.

"Furthermore," Noni added. "He withdraws permission for you to search his house. You'll have to get a warrant."

"It's way too late for that, lady," the man at the computer said. "Way too late."

Calvano pushed Martin forward and he began to shuffle toward the front door as awkwardly as if he were wearing leg irons. "Don't handcuff me," he said. "I don't want the neighbors to see."

Calvano was mean enough to laugh. "You need to lay off watching so much television. You're doing this voluntarily. No one's arresting you. Yet." He pushed him out the front door. A handful of neighbors had already gathered, drawn by the cars parked outside. Regardless of what happened to Martin now, neighbors were drawing their own conclusions. His name would be repeated all up and down the blocks of his neighborhood. God knows what people would say. By sundown, he'd have murdered the nurse and taken the boy and eaten him alive.

Noni lingered behind. As soon as Calvano's car drove away, she walked through the house, evaluating the men searching through Martin's belongings, trying to decide which one she wanted. She finally selected a young officer who'd been pulled from his beat because of the manpower shortage—Denny, the young cop who had disturbed the nurse's crime scene earlier in the day.

"You," Noni said, pointing at him. He was peering under Martin's bed and he froze, startled.

"Ma'am?" he asked weakly.

"Come here, young man. I want to have a word with you."

Chapter 8

Calvano was doing what he did best: rousting a suspect. I had been a bully, too, because bullying was a lazy man's best option. Slowed down by hangovers and a perpetual depression caused by constant drinking, I had barely been able to rise and shower each morning, and sometimes had not even managed that. I'd soon discovered that browbeating required no advance work, no investigating, no remembering what you'd done the day before. You just jumped in and started harassing a suspect and hoped it might take you somewhere. Sometimes you got lucky, maybe even enough times to convince them to let you keep your badge.

But I didn't want to watch Calvano work on Martin. I'd had enough of Calvano for one day. When a man is dying of thirst, he doesn't dream of muddy waters, he dreams of a pure mountain stream. I needed Maggie.

I knew I'd find her at the hospital, working on Fiona Harker's murder. Once Maggie started an investigation, she didn't stop until she had solved the case or someone like Gonzales pulled her from it and pointed her in another direction. That had rarely happened to her—Maggie almost always solved her cases, something my old partner and I had never been able to do.

The dead nurse had no personal life to speak of, so Maggie, I reasoned, would go to the place where she had spent most of her life: the hospital. There was only one in our small town, but it was large, well funded, and served the surrounding county. It was a sprawling, four-story building constructed five decades ago, when architects had designed one public building after another as huge, utilitarian boxes. It had kept up with the times, though. Inside its walls, county residents could be treated for everything from a splinter in a toe to terminal cancer.

I had not visited the hospital much since my death. For every three people surrounded by loved ones celebrating a successful procedure, there was someone in a bed nearby, alone in the dark, facing their own mortality. The trouble was that I could tell the difference. The dying had a glow about them that grew stronger as their bodies grew weaker, as if their life force was being leeched from their physical bodies and gathered for the transition. Many of them sensed this and met their deaths with so much courage and strength it made me ashamed I had squandered my life when I'd once had it. Others lay fearfully in bed, awaiting the worst. And a lucky few slept, blissfully unaware that they were never to wake.

They all died in the end.

It wasn't the death that bothered me, though. It was my knowing in advance. It was the fact that each of them so far, at least the ones I had witnessed, had moved on to someplace unknown, leaving me behind. That alone made the hospital an infinitely painful place for me.

But Maggie would be there, at least. I could endure anything for Maggie.

I found her in a staff lounge on the first floor near the emergency room, talking to a tall man with brown hair. He was unremarkable looking except, perhaps, for his eyes, which were copper. He was thin in that way of doctors who, annoyingly enough, look like they run sixteen miles a day and perform in triathlons every weekend. He was at least ten years older than Maggie, though his voice sounded older than that. I could feel his fatigue as surely as if it were mine. He had been working for many hours in the emergency room, I suspected. Wisps of other people's misfortune clung to him like cotton candy.

I didn't like the way he was looking at Maggie. He looked like a man who'd watched his ship go down, only to spot a dinghy filled with enough food and water to last him until help arrived.

"Did you know her?" Maggie was asking him.

I sat down behind the doctor and made faces at him. It was childish, and no one could see me, but it made me feel better. That was good enough for me.

"Of course," he told Maggie. "Fiona was, hands down, the best nurse we had. She never lost her cool, ever. I once saw her walk in behind a stretcher, cradling the bottom half of a leg like it was a baby, the whole time telling the guy on the stretcher that he was going to be okay. She didn't blink an eye. Nothing fazed her. She did what had to be done and she wanted to save lives. No matter how tired the rest of us got, we knew Fiona would have our backs. Everyone is devastated about her death and I am, frankly, concerned about our quality of care without her."

Well, that was quite the eulogy—I wondered just how well the good doctor had known Fiona Harker.

"You sound as if you two were close," Maggie said.

Personally, I'd have gone for a bigger bite—but Maggie had her ways. Though I didn't like the way she was staring into his copper eyes. At all.

"I only knew her professionally. I've been going through some difficult personal times," he explained. "I haven't had time for anything but work and straightening out my personal life. I haven't had time for friends for years, in fact."

You hear that, Maggie? *The man is a mess.*

"That seems a bit sad," Maggie said quietly.

What kind of line of questioning was that?

The doctor shrugged. "I'm good at what I do. Sometimes, that has to be enough."

Maggie blinked. He had struck a chord.

I did not trust the good doctor.

"Did she have a boyfriend, someone she was involved with?" Maggie asked.

The doctor shrugged again. "She might have. She was a lovely woman, not just on the outside, but inside as well. Kind. Caring. Infinitely patient, and when you're talking about the emergency room and people anxious about their loved ones, well, her patience kept things from getting ugly on a weekly basis. But I never heard any talk about her personal life. You'd have to ask the other nurses that."

"Was anyone here at the hospital particularly close to her?" Maggie persisted.

"I'm afraid you'll have to ask the other nurses that as well." The doctor rose to his feet. "I would like to answer any other questions you have, but we've got a head trauma on the way in. Perhaps you would like to get a cup of coffee later?"

What the hell? He was hitting on her. What had happened to being "good at what you do" and that being enough?

Maggie's smile was professional. "I'm afraid I can't."

"Right," he said, ducking his head and looking defeated just long enough for her to feel sorry for him. "I should have known better than to ask."

"Maybe if circumstances were different," Maggie offered, which was going a little too far, in my opinion. He was a grown man. He could take rejection.

The doctor smiled at that and, this time, Maggie's answering smile was way too close to her prime smile for my comfort. *What the hell is it about doctors anyway?*

"Well, time to go save lives," he said reluctantly, still holding her gaze.

Oh, yeah, well, there is that. The whole saving lives thing and all.

"It was nice to meet you, Dr. Fletcher," Maggie answered, holding out her hand.

"Call me Christian." He held on to her hand just a beat too long. She didn't seem to mind. "You can find most of the staff in the nurses' lounge sooner or later," he offered, stalling. "It's at the end of the hall."

"Thank you."

Maggie's *thank you* was enough to cause the doctor to bump into the door frame on the way out, but it was scant punishment for his audacity in daring to take my Maggie from me.

Dr. Christian Fletcher? What a jerk. Fletcher the Lecher, more likely.

I took a good look at what I was feeling, and I had to admit it: jealousy was alive and well in the dead.

Chapter 9

You'd think nurses would like cops. But not this one.
She looked like Nikita Khrushchev wearing a black wig—
and she was not letting Maggie talk to any of "her nurses."

"I'm sorry," she said. "I am sure the staff would like
to talk to you and we are certainly all devastated about
Fiona. But we are understaffed tonight and it's simply not
possible until the shift is over and a new shift arrives."

"How long?" Maggie finally muttered after the third
time she was told this. She was not used to having to give
up. It unleashed something unpredictable in her that fascinated me.

"Three hours. But you might be able to catch some of
the new shift if you get here a little before that. Some of
them knew Fiona."

"What about you?" Maggie asked, peering at the
woman. Her forearms were as big as hams and she was
guarding the nurse's station like a mother bear protects
her cubs.

"What about me?" the woman shot back. She had mean eyes, like she was looking for a puppy to kick. I'd hate to see those eyes coming at me if I was dying. Or being born, for that matter.

"Did you know Fiona Harker?"

"No," she said abruptly. "Not at all." She turned her back on Maggie and began stacking patient files. Maggie knew it was a waste of time to argue with her and left.

I followed her out of the hospital and amused myself playing hopscotch on the colored lines that had been painted on the floor to help people find their way through the maze of white hallways. I don't know if anyone actually thought the twisting lines of green, red, blue, and yellow were helpful—they confused the hell out of me—but it sure was fun to jump from one color to the other, chanting old childhood songs.

"Step on a crack, break your mother's back," a high voice said.

Where did that come from?

I stopped abruptly and noticed a little girl of around nine wearing a hospital gown. She was standing in the doorway of a vending machine nook, a pack of potato chips in one hand. Her feet were bare and she had no hair. Not a strand. Her head was shaped like a giant Brussels sprout.

"Those aren't good for you," I said, nodding at the chips.

She shrugged. "Neither is chemo, but I'm doing it anyway." And with that, she followed me in hopping from color to color down the hall for a few moments, then disappeared through two swinging doors, labeled PEDIATRIC ONCOLOGY.

The girl had been real.

It's things like this that mess with your head when you're dead.

Maggie was taking the long way out of the hospital, as if she was lost. Perhaps she should have followed the colored lines. *Unless . . .* I noted with a flash of jealousy that she was heading out through the emergency room exit doors, looking around as she did so. But the fantastic Dr. Fletcher was nowhere to be found. Most of the staff was clustered by a double-wide entrance door, ushering in stretchers of people covered in blood. A car accident, I suspected. Their agony engulfed me, and I fled the building, thinking, *It's not death that people ought to fear, it's life. Life hurts way more than death.*

I can get across town in minutes if I need to, but I like to ride shotgun with Maggie and pretend that we're partners. It's difficult to do that if Calvano is along for the ride, of course. There's no way in hell I'm sitting on *his* lap, but today we had her car to ourselves. Maggie doesn't play music when she drives. She hums. Not very well, either, but I like to think everyone is allowed a few imperfections.

Maggie hums because she is thinking. Her tuneless melodies form the soundtrack to her mind and she was burning synapses that day as she sorted through the case she had been given. She had an amazing ability to compartmentalize her thoughts. I knew she had put the issue of the missing boy aside while she concentrated on the dead nurse. She cared about the boy—everyone did: there were AMBER Alerts and volunteer search teams and media blanketing our town—but Maggie had been given the nurse's banner to carry into battle, and that was where her allegiance lay.

I tried to read her thoughts. There was a connection building between Maggie and the nurse. I did not know if I had simply gotten better at reading Maggie's emotions and this was a connection she forged with all victims, or if she felt an unexpected kinship with the nurse because they had their solitary lives in common. Whatever the cause, Maggie went through sadness, regret, fear, and a little bit of fury. I found that flicker of anger interesting. Fury at someone unknown who had killed the nurse—or fury at someone in her own life who had loved her and left her? But who could ever do such a thing? Who would leave someone like Maggie?

We reached the station at the same time as my old lady friend, Noni Bates. She was not alone. A well-dressed man in his early forties was gallantly helping her from a late model Lexus. He held a briefcase and wore expensive shoes. Dollars to doughnuts he was a lawyer, maybe even a good one. He was definitely a well-paid one. I had expected Noni to bring a fussy, old, retired lawyer to Robert Michael Martin's rescue, perhaps one with bushy, white eyebrows and hair sprouting from his ears. But, of course, she had been a teacher and probably had a network of professionals from here to Shanghai she'd once taught and could forever call on.

It would take the two of them a while to get past the front desk sergeant, Freddy, who was in a bad mood because his wife was cheating on him with his brother. I knew this because one of the perks of being dead is that you know everyone's secrets.

"But they may be questioning him right now," Noni was telling Freddy.

"Not if he asked for a lawyer, they aren't," Freddy said politely, recognizing the steel in her voice and not wanting to antagonize her.

"He's much too . . ." Noni paused. "He probably did not *insist* on one."

Freddy shrugged. "I can't help you there, ma'am. There's no crime in being stupid."

And stupid Robert Michael Martin was. Despite Noni's warning, he had agreed to be questioned by Adrian Calvano without counsel present, believing his innocence would protect him.

I could have joined the interrogation and amused myself by making faces behind Calvano's back, but I felt high-powered energy emanating from the observation room next door, and when Maggie headed for it, I drifted in behind her.

Gonzales shivered. "There's a draft in here. Can you shut the door? I've got to get the air conditioning fixed." *Not a draft, my friend, just little old me.*

"Anything shake loose?" Maggie asked.

Gonzales shook his head. "It's the usual disaster." He seemed to remember that a couple of department lawyers were standing behind him and amended his remarks. "I don't think there is anything to shake out of him."

We all peered through the one-way glass. Robert Michael Martin sat, perplexed, in a straight-back chair across from Calvano—who was hammering on the table between them with his fist. It seemed a little early in the performance to be pounding on tabletops, but that was Adrian Calvano for you: no finesse.

"So, you are admitting that you actually go by the park every single morning to watch the children?" Calvano shouted at him.

Martin looked like he was going to cry. I felt his fear, but something else, too. I concentrated on it until I had it: the more Calvano screamed, the more Martin seemed comfortable with it. Not only was he accustomed to being yelled at and ridiculed, he expected it. I felt even sadder for him. His mother must have been a real joy.

"I told you," Martin said, his voice cracking. "I volunteer for KinderWatch. Ask Colonel Vitek. He'll tell you. He's the founder of the group. I'm his best volunteer."

"You've said that," Calvano said with disgust. "Several times." He sat back in his chair and crossed his arms. "You like watching the little kids every day?"

"Come on," Maggie said to Gonzales. "This is unproductive and beneath us. And there's a lawyer downstairs coming up to represent Martin any minute. Let me talk to him and see what I can get before he shuts down. Maybe he saw something in the park that would help." I felt a spark from her as she made one of the connections only Maggie can make. Her voice grew more excited. "Sir, let me ask him who was in the park *yesterday*. He may have seen whoever killed Fiona Harker."

Gonzales turned to her, interested, but a knock interrupted their exchange. I was sure it was Martin's lawyer, there to call off the dogs, but it was Peggy Calhoun from the lab. She held up a small, clear evidence bag holding a plastic dinosaur. "We got something from the park. Not much, but something."

Gonzales and Maggie eyed the small green toy. "Are we sure it's the boy's?"

Peggy shrugged. "The officers that brought it in say some other kids at the playground identified it as belonging to Tyler Matthews. Its name is Rocky."

"The dinosaur's name is Rocky?" Gonzales asked dubiously.

"That's what the other kids say he called it," Peggy explained.

"Can you get anything off Rocky?" Gonzales said drily.

"Maybe a print. And if we're lucky, not the kid's." Peggy didn't sound too sure.

"See what you can do," Gonzales told her absently. Calvano's voice had risen to a roar and we were all distracted by his histrionics.

Peggy looked appalled at the scene unfolding behind

the one-way mirror. "Sir," she said firmly, staring at Calvano.

"What is it?" he asked, annoyed that she hadn't left.

"There's a rookie patrolman outside who wants to speak to you. I really think you'd better talk to him."

"Go talk to him," Gonzales ordered Maggie, not paying much attention. He was watching Calvano as one might watch a lab specimen, studying his behavior and trying to figure out the cause, cataloging Calvano's triggers so that he might use that behavior for his own purposes one day. To my real dying day, and that could be a long time coming, I would never quite get Gonzales.

Maggie left to speak to the rookie patrolman and I, naturally, followed. It was Denny, the cop who had disturbed the crime scene a few hours before. He turned purple when he saw Maggie coming at him.

"Ma'am, I would just like to say again how sorry I am that—"

"What is it?" Maggie interrupted. She didn't like groveling, but she didn't like incompetence, either, so he was not getting off the hook entirely.

The poor kid was so nervous that he almost stuttered. Maggie took pity on him. "Take a deep breath," she told him. "Now order your thoughts like you're writing an essay. Get you facts in order. One, two, three . . . ready?"

He nodded.

"Now tell me," Maggie said calmly.

"I talked to an old lady who is a neighbor of the man being questioned. She was there when we searched his house. A friend of his mother's, I believe she said."

"Very good," Maggie told him. "Keep going."

"She says Martin came to get her this morning, very excited about a man in the park who was watching the children. He was quite concerned the man might do something."

"And this was before we found the nurse or the kid was taken?"

"Yes, definitely before." Denny looked at Maggie. "That's important, right? It means he didn't just make it up after he was a suspect."

"Yes," Maggie said. "It's important. Was the neighbor telling you the truth?"

"The old lady?" Denny looked startled. "Ma'am, I don't think she's capable of not telling the truth."

Maggie smiled. "I've known a few people like that myself."

"There was one other thing. The old lady knew the nurse. She says Calvano interviewed her about it."

"Yes?" Maggie asked, trying to pull it out of him.

"She says the nurse would never have killed herself, that she was a Catholic."

"We know she didn't kill herself," Maggie assured him. "Thank you. I'll let the commander know."

Denny scurried away and Peggy, who had been watching Maggie from a spot against the wall, spoke. "What is it? You look troubled."

"Just one Catholic girl looking after another," Maggie said. "That could have been me, you know. Seriously."

"Except you're the best shot in the department," Peggy offered. "It wouldn't have been you lying on that carpet."

Maggie looked at her friend. "Peggy, when I was in the house, I felt . . ." She hesitated.

"What?" Peggy asked. "Go with it."

"I felt this sense of betrayal," Maggie said. "It sounds silly, I know."

Yes, I exulted. She had picked up on it, too. Or maybe she had picked up on me. Maybe I had helped.

"It's not silly," Peggy said firmly. "I felt it, too."

"Like someone she loved had betrayed her?"

•

"Exactly," Peggy said.

"Like someone who loved her had killed her," Maggie said sadly.

"Ah, Maggie." Peggy was her senior by three decades. "When you get as old as I am, you will know one thing for sure: people kill the people they love all the time."

"You're right," Maggie acknowledged. "And, god knows, I know that."

Peggy was staring at her oddly.

"What?" Maggie said. "Spit it out."

"Hypnosis," Peggy said firmly.

"Hypnosis?"

"If that poor schmuck in there actually saw something, I'd put him under and get it out of him quickly, before Calvano buries everything under a mountain of fear."

"You really think that will work?"

"We used it a lot during the eighties when there was a spate of carjackings around here. We got better descriptions and a few license plates. It helped with a murder in '97 and a couple of rapes the same year. A few other times, too."

"Why not recently?" Maggie asked.

"Gonzales thinks of it as hocus-pocus, and evidence gathered through hypnosis is not necessarily admissible in court. But the woman we worked with still lives in town. She's good. She has a private therapy practice and is a certified forensic hypnosis specialist. Plus, she helped me quit smoking." Peggy smiled and there it was again: her signature smear of orange lipstick on her teeth. I had come to love that smear.

Maggie shrugged. "I can give it a try."

"I'd do it before the feds get here if I was you," Peggy suggested. "You won't have a say in it after that."

"How did this place ever run without you?" Maggie asked.

"It's never had to," Peggy admitted with a laugh.

Maggie stared at the green dinosaur in Peggy's hands. "Do you really think you'll get something off it?"

"I have to," Peggy said simply. "Calvano's getting nowhere."

And with that, she left Maggie to clean up Calvano's mess, disappearing down the hall toward her lab, where evidence was orderly and answers were logical and whole new worlds awaited her beneath the lens of her beloved microscope.

Maggie reached Gonzales at the exact same time that Martin's lawyer finally made it to the interrogation room. She reentered the observation area just in time to see the lawyer say to Calvano, "This interrogation is over."

Gonzales sighed.

"He wasn't getting anywhere anyway, sir," Maggie offered in consolation.

Gonzales looked at her intently. "Give me good news."

"I think this guy is legit," Maggie said, nodding toward Martin. The poor slob had started to sweat like a seal in a sauna, but he also looked completely dumbfounded at his good fortune: he had a lawyer, a real one, who had rescued him just as he realized he had truly screwed the pooch by not listening to Noni's advice. There was conferring, cards were passed, hands shook. Calvano was pouting, as usual.

"He was sounding the alarm about some guy in the park before any of this took place," Maggie told Gonzales. "He might have seen something important. Not just about the missing kid, but maybe the nurse, too."

Gonzales looked interested. "What are you suggesting?"

Maggie took a deep breath. "Hypnosis."

His smile disappeared.

"Sir, the department has used it before, and there's a very good, certified specialist here in town. Her testimony

has been accepted in court before. I'm not looking for
that, though. We just need something, anything, from this
Martin guy to narrow it down. Maybe with some help he
can give us a good description—or, just as important, a
more *objective* description—of the man he saw. It might
tell us whether the man in the park was a real threat. Or
maybe Martin saw a car, or a license plate that leads us
somewhere. I'd take anything. I don't have a clue, literally, and neither does Calvano."

"I'm not a believer, Gunn," was all Gonzales said. He
turned his back on her and stared wistfully through the
observation glass. Martin was being hoisted upright by
his lawyer, who was angry at Calvano and giving him a
lecture about Fifth Amendment rights for any cameras
that might be rolling.

Gonzales was distracted, or he would never have
thought he'd get away with saying no to Maggie. It was
like waving a red flag at a bull.

"I'll make you a deal," she said sweetly, which told me
she was up to something, even if Gonzales missed it.

He turned to look at her. She held his gaze.

Gonzales gave up first. "Let's hear the deal."

"I'll swap you a polygraph for hypnosis."

"Pardon?" Gonzales looked amused.

"I know you like your polygraphs," Maggie explained.
"If I can convince that poor schlep in there to take one, and
if he passes, will you consent to one hypnosis session? I'm
offering you one quasi-scientific method for another."

"All right, Gunn," Gonzales said. He always called her
"Gunn" in front of others. "You're on. But good luck con-
vincing the suit his client should take a polygraph."

"No worries, sir," Maggie said confidently. "I can do
that."

And she did. She started by humiliating Calvano the
moment she entered the interrogation room. Only slightly,

mind you, and not nearly enough for me, but enough for Robert Michael Martin and his lawyer to feel a little vindicated.

"I'm taking over," she announced to Calvano, turning her back on him dismissively. I was close enough to catch the wink she gave her partner. Calvano saw it, too, but he was such a dumbass, it took him a few seconds to process it. Once he did, he mumbled, "Fine," and stalked from the room.

"Sorry about that," Maggie said to Martin, throwing him her hundred-watt smile. "Everyone gets on edge when a little kid goes missing."

"Well, of course," Martin stammered. "It's the worst possible thing that could happen." He stared at Maggie, worried about where she was going with the whole thing. He did not look as worried as his lawyer, though. Maggie read the mood in the room and changed directions.

"Here's the deal," Maggie said, ignoring the lawyer and talking directly to Martin. "I believe you, and I need your help."

"You need my help?" Martin asked eagerly.

"Yes. I'm working the case of the murdered nurse and my partner . . ."—she dropped her voice to make it clear she thought her partner was an idiot, which probably wasn't hard—"well, he's in change of the missing boy case."

The lawyer looked scandalized at the thought of Calvano being in charge of anything. I guess word about Calvano had gotten out in the legal community.

"Until," Maggie added.

"Until what?" the lawyer demanded.

"Until later tonight went the feds arrive and take over and all hell breaks loose."

Martin looked alarmed. So did his lawyer. "As in the FBI?" Martin asked.

"At the very least. They'll be taking over the missing boy case. It'll be out of our hands at that point."

"What are you suggesting?" the lawyer asked.

"He takes a polygraph," Maggie said quickly, "for screening purposes only. Nothing will be used in court, you have my word."

"Screening for what?" the lawyer asked. Martin looked mystified.

"If he passes the poly, I want to bring in a hypnotist."

"Cool!" Martin said before his lawyer could react.

"Not cool," the lawyer said firmly.

"Listen to me," Maggie said earnestly, once again addressing herself directly to Martin. She knew his type. He wanted to be a hero. He wanted to help. He wanted his quiet, uneventful life to have meaning. She looked deep into his eyes, and I felt him falter. "I really need your help," Maggie said softly. "It's something only you can do."

The lawyer made a sound that seemed a lot like a snort, but she ignored him. "You were in the park yesterday and this morning," she said. "Do you know what that means?"

"It means your idiot partner considers my client the number-one suspect in the boy's disappearance," the lawyer said drily.

"It means that you are in a position not only to help with the missing boy's case —"

"It's *Tyler*," Martin interrupted.

"I beg your pardon?"

"The little boy's name is Tyler. Tyler Matthews."

Maggie blinked. "I'm sorry. You're absolutely right. My apologies." She smiled at him, and Martin melted some more. "You can help me find whoever took Tyler, but that's not all. You may have seen who killed Fiona Harker and not even realize it."

"The nurse?" Martin said eagerly.

Maggie nodded. "You are in a unique position, my friend. You could help us with two cases, not just one."

Martin stared back at her, trying to engage his brain. I don't think women looked at him like that very often.

"The only thing is," Maggie prodded him, "you need to do this before the feds take over. They won't want any part of this. They have their own ways. If you want to help us, you need to do it now. They're not going to care what you saw and they are most definitely not going to let you help. I'll be lucky if I get to help."

The lawyer looked from Maggie to his client, and he knew when he was beat. "I need a word with my client," he said firmly. Maggie left the room.

Gonzales was already outside in the hallway, shaking his head.

"What, sir?" she asked defensively.

"He's going to agree," Gonzales predicted.

"I know," Maggie said matter-of-factly. "Is there a problem?"

"Not if you keep those big, brown eyes to yourself." With that, he walked away.

"Okay," the lawyer announced, popping his head into the hall. "He'll do it. But I'm to be present at all times."

"Deal," Maggie said.

"But my client gets to go home first and put on clean clothes and take a deep breath," the lawyer added. "You can send someone with him if you need to."

"Deal," Maggie said quickly. "I'll set it up for early evening."

"Keep your partner away from him in the meantime," the lawyer added.

"No problem," Maggie agreed with a smile.

Chapter 10

Maggie had a few hours free until she had to return to the station, so she headed back to the hospital in hopes of questioning some nurses before they started their shifts. I decided to make my own way over in hopes of picking up something useful on the missing boy along the way. I detoured down side streets, into neighborhoods, hoping to pick up a trace of Tyler Matthews. My search uncovered nothing. But I'd had to try. After a while I gave up and drifted over to the hospital to see if Maggie had done any better gleaning information about Fiona Harker.

I found Maggie in a staff lounge, talking to two tearful women who had clearly known Fiona Harker. They were dressed in fresh scrubs and waiting for their shift to begin. One was from Trinidad, I guessed, given her accent and the fact that half the nurses in our town had been recruited from there. "Fiona was one of the good ones," she was saying in a musical lilt. "She never crossed nobody, ever." The other nurse was a pale, little bit of a thing with curly brown hair. But she must have had strength in there somewhere if she was a nurse. I'd never met a weak one.

I loved nurses. They were the one good thing about the hospital. Even though you ran across the occasional gorgon like the one who had turned Maggie away earlier, most of them led lives connected to dozens of other lives and reveled in their connections. There was such beauty in their willingness to be a part of other lives. I had seen people in great pain have that pain eased when a nurse walked into the room; put a hand on their brow; and, without even realizing it, took some of the pain onto themselves. Their ability to accept the humanness of others put the rest of us to shame.

Of course, those bonds could hurt when they were severed. The two nurses dabbed at their eyes with tissues as they answered Maggie's questions. Taken together, their comments allowed a portrait of the dead nurse to emerge:

No, Fiona had not been involved with anyone. They would have known if she had. It was impossible to keep your personal life private at the hospital.

No, they had never even heard of her being involved with anyone in the past, which was odd when you stopped to think about it, given how lovely she was. But then Fiona had always been a very private person, and she did not gossip. She did ask people questions about their lives and she was a wonderful listener. It was only after she'd left that you realized she hadn't offered any information about herself.

Yes, she had family, they thought, somewhere on the West Coast. They did not know why Fiona lived so far away from them. She'd grown up in San Francisco. Or was it Sacramento? Neither could remember. They only knew this detail because once, when an earthquake in

California had been reported on the news, Fiona had excused herself to phone her family to make sure they were safe.

All the doctors loved Fiona. If you were a good nurse, they never had to ask twice for an instrument or for a test to be run or a patient to be checked on. With Fiona, you never had to ask at all. The instrument was there, waiting for you to take it. She had written down the tests you wanted before the words were out of your mouth. She gave everyone special treatment, so you always knew your patients were in good hands.

It was enough to make some nurses resent her, sure, but not enough to kill her. Nurses don't kill, they insisted to Maggie. Nurses healed.

A third nurse joined them just before the current shift ended. She put her feet up and waited to hear more about Fiona's death. She was a big woman with an upturned nose and a jolly smile. Her breasts were enormous but, I imagined, comforting when you were sick and in need of motherly care.

"I liked her," the new woman declared in a booming voice. The other nurses seemed awed by her volume. They glanced at Maggie with a look that clearly said, *Don't get her started.*

"Was that unusual?" Maggie asked with a straight face. "You liking someone?"

"Hell, yeah," the nurse boomed. "I can't stand a soul. Just ask those two."

The other two nurses nodded rapidly, eyes wide.

I decided I liked the new nurse, big mouth and all. She was only testing Maggie's mettle.

"What did you like about Fiona?" Maggie asked.

The big nurse did not hesitate. As she took off her shoes and massaged her feet, she counted off what she had liked about Fiona Harker. "Fiona minded her own business. Fiona knew her job. Fiona liked her patients. Fiona had a sense of humor."

The other two nurses looked startled at this.

"Yes, she did," the big nurse insisted, seeing their expressions. "A great sense of humor. She just saved it for patients. They're the ones who need it. And she was kind. When my mother died, she came to the funeral."

"Your mother died?" the thin nurse asked faintly.

"Three years ago," the big nurse shouted back, then laughed at their expressions. "It's all right. I didn't tell anyone. But Fiona found out and she was there. It meant a lot to me, more than I thought it would. I don't know why, but it did. Just seeing her made me feel like everything was going to be all right. That life would go on and I could make it through and that better things were ahead. Fiona calmed you. She let the bullshit roll right off her. And believe me, we get a lot of it around this place. Especially from the hallowed doctors." She looked up at her fellow nurses with a solemn expression. "Let us all now kneel and pray."

Maggie looked up, puzzled, but the big nurse was laughing again. "That's what Fiona used to say when the doctors would sweep through and leave us with a shit pile of work to do. Because that's what the doctors acted like they expected us to do. Kneel and pray to them and hail them for gracing us with their presence. They all act like that. Fiona hated that about them."

"Fiona Harker was having an affair with a doctor."

Everyone in the room looked surprised at this declaration. The voice had come out of nowhere. We all looked around and there, standing against a row of pink lockers along one side of the room, stood an older nurse, maybe midfifties, who was taking off her ID badge and storing it in her locker.

"Get out of here!" the big nurse boomed, not believing a word of it.

"She was." The older nurse was tall and thin with gray hair cut short and not a dab of makeup on her rather pretty face. She had strong, almost masculine hands. Now, I'd want *her* beside me if I were dying, I decided. She had not pronounced judgment on Fiona, and I don't think she was in the habit of pronouncing judgment on anyone, ever. Her demeanor was matter-of-fact and her energy shone like silver steel. I could tell she seldom questioned life. She accepted the world as a series of irrefutable facts and then set about to do what she could with them. She would have made an awesome doctor.

Maggie stood up, as impressed with the newcomer as I was, and introduced herself. She took the nurse's name and invited her to sit.

"I'd just as soon stand, thanks," the nurse explained. "My back hurts from lifting two-hundred-pound patients."

Before Maggie could ask her to tell them more about Fiona Harker, the big nurse blurted out the questions on everyone's mind. "Give us the dirt already. What doctor? For how long? How did you know?"

"I don't know which doctor. Is that important?" The older nurse crossed her arms and looked the other nurses over as if they were failing to measure up to her high standards, and could they all not try just a little bit harder?

"Hell, yeah, it's important," the big nurse said. "She was probably killed by him."

The older nurse looked at Maggie. "I thought Fiona killed herself."

Maggie shook her head. "We don't think so."

The older nurse looked a little relieved, as if her world had been disturbed but could now resume its regular orbit. "I wondered about that. I didn't think she was the type. And I've met a lot of people who tried to kill themselves in my time."

"What do you know about her personal life?" Maggie prodded. "It's very important. Not many people seem to know anything about her."

"I don't know all that much either," the older nurse admitted. "I think she'd been having an affair for about a year. At least that was when she changed, a year ago."

"Changed how?" Maggie asked.

"Went from being very self-contained to reaching out more to patients and others. She was always an excellent nurse, but she held herself back before then. Kept it very, very professional. People in here are scared. They need more than that. Fiona began giving more of herself about a year ago. Smiling, telling the young patients stories from her own childhood."

"Why the change?" Maggie asked.

"She was happy. Happier than she had ever been in the twelve years we worked together."

"What makes you think it was an affair?" Maggie asked.

"Yeah," the big nurse said. She was a human echo. "What makes you think it was an affair?" The look Maggie gave her was quick, but it was enough to cause the big nurse to sit back in her chair and drag her fingers over her mouth in the universal "zipped up" gesture. The younger nurses exchanged a glance—Maggie had impressed them.

"I knew it was an affair because Fiona was secretive about it," the older nurse explained. "I was her shift supervisor for almost a year, so I noticed the difference. Sometimes she'd take phone calls on her cell while on duty, which she'd never done before, or excuse herself to make calls outside the hospital. Which everyone is supposed to do, of course, but no one ever really does, unless they want privacy. She'd ask for time off at the last minute, which I tried to give her, because she rarely took time off otherwise."

"Who was she involved with?" Maggie asked.

"I have no idea. It wasn't any of my business, and I didn't want to make it my business. What people do to each other as consenting adults is their business."

"Was there a pattern to her time off?" Maggie asked. She was hoping to match it to the still-unknown doctor's schedule once he was identified.

The nurse shrugged. "Not that I could tell. When she was working for me, the only pattern I could see was that the other person was calling all the shots. I know how it goes. I've seen it before. She rarely asked for time off in advance, it was always at the last minute. Which meant one thing to me: when he asked her to take time off, she did. Which is why I figured it was a doctor. Probably a married one."

"Fletcher!" the big nurse almost shouted.

Maggie looked alarmed, the two young nurses were scandalized. And me? I felt a stab of satisfaction at the news that maybe the good doctor was not so good after all.

"Christian Fletcher?" Maggie asked. "The emergency room head?"

"I bet it was him," the big nurse decided. "His marriage broke up. No one really knows why. He was married, and now he's not and, besides, the guy's a catch!"

This pronouncement caused the small, curly-haired brunette to turn a deep scarlet. "Dr. Fletcher is very nice," she protested. "He would not cheat on his wife. He flies to Honduras and Afghanistan each year to help people who need medical care, and he does it for free."

"He is a good man," her friend agreed.

"He's not a good man if he killed Fiona," the big nurse pointed out.

"I don't know who she was having the affair with," the older nurse said loudly, sending the big nurse a definite glare. "I have no idea if it was Dr. Fletcher or the man in the moon. And I should think the last thing the detective needs to hear is gossip."

Maggie looked like she'd take anything, including gossip, but the older nurse was already on her way out the door. "Call me if you need more from me, but honestly, I've told you everything I know."

"That's right," the big nurse called after her. "Drop a bomb and then leave so the rest of us have to clean it up."

"Do you really think it was Dr. Fletcher?" the youngest nurse asked breathlessly. Her own dreams for Dr. Fletcher had just taken a nosedive.

"No," her friend said scornfully. "Why you listen to her?" She cocked her head at the big nurse and shook a finger at her. "Stop messing with people's heads."

"Oh, come on," the big nurse protested as she pulled vigorously on her toes. "Who in this place is worth having an affair with besides him?" She went through a litany of doctors and why they were unworthy. The reasons ranged from halitosis to wearing a toupee to several cases of extreme narcissism, and there was also one wife-beater and a small circle of closet cases. When she was done, I had to agree: the pickings were slim at County General.

"What can you tell me about the breakup of Dr. Fletcher's marriage?" Maggie finally interrupted—and part of me wondered whether she had asked out of professional or personal curiosity.

"No one really knows, but it broke his heart when it happened," the young nurse said, looking at the others. "He did everything he could to hold it together, but . . ."

"Oh, I'll say it for you," the big nurse volunteered. "His wife is a grade-A bitch, intent on becoming the most famous and beloved doctor this hospital has ever produced. She wants it all. Fame. A foundation named after her. More money than the rest of us will see in a lifetime. And she wants a husband just as driven as she is, though not one who overshadows her, of course. But Dr. Fletcher likes working in the emergency room. He feels he can make a difference there, and he does. That's not good enough for her. She should've married a cardiologist or a brain surgeon when she had the chance. She could have, too, believe me. She's one of those tall, thin blondes you just have to hate on principle." The woman laughed merrily at this and the others even smiled their agreement.

"Dr. Fletcher's wife works at this hospital?" Maggie asked.

"In pediatric oncology," the small brunette nurse told her. "She's the head of it."

"She is a very good doctor," her friend added. "But an unpleasant woman. She's always very friendly to big donors to the hospital, but she treats us like dirt. And she can be cold to her patients and very patronizing to their parents, like they don't know what's best for their own children."

"One of those," the big nurse said.

"One of those," the brunette agreed.

"If you ask me, Dr. Fletcher left his wife because no one in his right mind could live with her," the big nurse added. "That's my take on the situation."

"Why are you so certain Fiona was having an affair with a doctor?" Maggie asked. "It could have been with someone outside the hospital."

"Who else could we get involved with?" the little brunette asked Maggie. "It's not like we have lives."

"True that," her friend agreed with a nod.

Maggie was ready to ask more questions, but a new

shift was starting, and her cell phone was ringing. She stared at the number calling and flipped it open. "Something happen?" Her frown was immediate. "He *what*?" I could feel her frustration grow as she listened. "I'll be right there," she told the caller, and snapped the phone shut angrily. My Maggie was pissed off.

The nurses eyed her, hoping for an explanation. They did not get one.

"Thank you," Maggie told them. "I'll be back."

"We'll be here," the big nurse said with a sigh as she massaged the heels of her feet. Just for fun, I sent a puff of air straight at the arches of her size elevens. She jumped and then giggled, an oddly disconcerting sound coming from such a large woman. The other two nurses looked at her blankly.

"Don't ask," she boomed.

They didn't.

Chapter 11

"What the hell, sir?" Maggie asked Gonzales.

That cracked me up: What the hell, *sir*. It was pure Maggie.

"Don't look at me, Gunn. The guy just showed up. Wanted to help us find Tyler Matthews. Let Calvano do his job. He might stumble across something."

I winced and wondered if people had ever said that about me. Probably. Stumbling was what I'd done best.

The guy who had showed up to help was in a wheelchair and compensated with ramrod posture, as if he wanted to prove he was in control. Calvano was sitting with him in the interrogation room. They were sharing coffee and cigarettes like a couple of old ladies in Boca Raton. The guy was somewhere in that gray area between fifty and sixty years of age. He had reddish brown hair swept back on top and cut short on the sides, and his face was pockmarked from long-ago acne.

"Who is this guy anyway?" Maggie asked. She and

Gonzales were huddled together in the observation room close to the one-way glass, whispering so the others in the room could not hear. But I had a prime spot to overhear all.

"Colonel William Vitek, US Marines. Retired."

"He get the injury in battle?" she asked.

"Car accident," an old-school beat cop named Morty said from behind them. He had stopped by to see what the excitement was all about. "His wife and son died in the accident. He's only been in town about six months. Inherited a house he's looking to sell. Big war hero. At least that's what people in the neighborhood say."

That's how Morty's sentences often ended. He had walked his beat for decades and knew his neighborhood like a younger cop never would.

Maggie flashed Morty a smile. He was her father's oldest friend. Morty called her "Rosie" and had since she was a little girl. He was also the only one on this planet who could get away with calling her that.

He'd been allowed to join them in observing the session because Morty was a lot more than just an old beat cop. Between him and Peggy Calhoun, they pretty much remembered every case from the past thirty years. They were the department's memory, and Gonzales knew how valuable that was. He pretty much let Morty stick his nose in wherever he liked, provided it was on his own time. Morty was tall with bright white hair and the kind of rounded potbelly that comes with age.

"What are you doing here?" Maggie asked her old friend.

"Just thought I'd see Calvano work his magic," Morty said cheerfully, letting a hint of brogue creep into his voice, even though he was about as Irish as Mohammad Albaca, who ran the coffee concession in the lobby.

Maggie looked at him skeptically.

"I worked on a case sixteen years ago," Morty confessed. "A missing boy. Bobby D'Amato. He was taken from a rest area north of town. I responded to the initial call. They were only about ten miles from home, but the kid had to take a pee and the mother made the father stop to let him. They were still arguing about it when the kid ran inside to the bathroom by himself. He never came back out, not that they could see."

"I remember that," Gonzales said. "Never found the boy, right?"

Morty shook his head. "We figured the perp grabbed him, hit the highway, and was gone. The mother still lives in town. The father moved away for a better job and fresh start. But we never found the kid's body. Nothing."

"And you think the two abductions are connected?" Gonzales asked.

Morty shook his head again. "No, but I thought maybe . . ." He shrugged.

"You thought this guy might know something that would help with the old case? Or give you a fresh idea about what might have happened?" Maggie guessed. Her voice was kind. Like Morty, she never let go of an old case. They haunted her until solved.

"Especially this guy." Morty nodded toward the man in the wheelchair. "Colonel Vitek is some big-deal defender of kids. Tracks all the online predators. Works for law enforcement departments up and down the coast."

"Not ours," Gonzales said firmly.

"*Works* for them?" Maggie asked, one eye on the interrogation room where Calvano and Vitek were trading stories about how stupid criminals are. Ironic, I thought, as I was sure somewhere criminals were sitting around and trading stories about how stupid Calvano was.

"Unofficial arrangements," Morty explained. "With departments too small to have their own Internet divisions. What he does is manage a group of volunteers who pretend to be underage kids. They visit the right chat rooms, they wait to be approached, they make it plain they're underage, and, eventually, someone always asks to meet in person. The volunteers agree and suggest an actual location, usually the town they're pretending to be from, and that's when Vitek notifies local law enforcement. The local cops wait for the pervert when he shows up, video games and candy in hand, and they've got their man."

"You sound like you admire this guy," Maggie said. She stared at Colonel Vitek, and I could tell she was thinking, *I'm not going to canonize him yet.*

Morty had no problem with Vitek's methods. "If he gets even one creep off the streets, I'm all for it," he admitted.

Maggie disguised her distaste. Anything that even approached entrapment was just lazy police work, in her opinion, even if it was for a good cause. "Is he any good at what he does?" she asked, staring at Vitek though the one-way glass.

"People say he is," Morty said. "I wouldn't know. But maybe he knows something that might help with the Bobby D'Amato case. You never know."

I felt a flash of love and regret toward Morty. He was old, he was fighting off time and disease, but he had promised the parents of that missing boy that he'd never give up and, sixteen years later, he was still keeping his word. I wished I'd been half the cop he was, and I was ashamed that I had made fun of him when I was alive for never wanting to be anything but a beat cop.

Gonzales tapped impatiently on the window, signaling for Calvano to knock off the bullshitting and continue the interview. The feds were arriving that night, and he wanted something to show them.

Colonel Vitek heard the tap and nodded toward his unknown watchers. He knew he was being filmed—hence
the ramrod posture, I decided. He enjoyed being the center of attention.

I wasn't sure I liked him. For one thing, he had fleshy
lips that he curled around his cigarette like he was suck-
ing on a pacifier. For another, his energy was muddy
and hard to read. I tried to enter the part of his thoughts
that stored memory. This was where I usually had the
most success in reading people. Memories could tell a
lot about someone—what they chose to hold on to, what
they had tried to let go, who they cared about, and what
they feared.

The colonel had very unpleasant memories.

Not battles, like I had expected, or headlights bearing
down on him before a crash, but memories of a different
kind of war.

Most unpleasant indeed. No wonder he had devoted
his life to catching child abusers. He was waging a personal war of revenge.

"Okay," Calvano was saying to the colonel in a buddy-
to-buddy tone. "Let's get back to it." Calvano smiled like
he was Vitek's best friend. Like a lot of guys who never
got near a barracks, Calvano thought military men were
the epitome of manhood. I was pretty sure I was about to
witness a display of thorough ass-kissing—quite a con-
trast from the way he'd acted toward that poor slob Robert Michael Martin earlier in the day.

"You say your group has chapters all over the eastern
US?" Calvano asked.

"That's right," the colonel explained. "We started out
in New Jersey and we've spread from there. As you can
see"—he patted the armrest of his wheelchair—"I'm limited in what I can do. But I manage volunteers from my
home easily enough, and most of what we do is online. I

was based in Philly, but I have some personal business
here to take care of. It was easy enough to move headquarters here for a few months."

"So you just cut your volunteers loose and let them do
their thing?" Calvano asked. God, he was an idiot.

"No, sir." The colonel shook his head vigorously.
"They undergo extensive training. We don't want to be
accused of entrapment." I could tell his unctuous smile
had pissed off Maggie as much as it pissed off me. She
did not like the colonel.

Interesting. I didn't like him, either. But Maggie? Maggie *really* didn't like him. Maybe because the colonel was
a man who had to be in charge, and men like that are
rarely big fans of strong women. She'd put up with more
than a few Colonel Viteks in her battle to become a detective. I could understand her distaste. He was a reminder
that the number of men in the world waiting to put her in
her place was pretty much endless.

"What kind of training?" Calvano asked, with the ea-
gerness of a groupie.

"After training, they do practice sessions," the colonel explained. "While we conduct a background check to
make sure we don't invite a fox into the henhouse."

"And Robert Michael Martin passed the background
test?"

The colonel's smile faltered slightly. "Martin passed
our standard background check, yes."

"Meaning?"

"Meaning if he had an official record, it didn't show
up. The guy is clean." The colonel paused. "So far as I
know, that is. So far as official records show."

Maggie winced. He had just damned Martin with faint
praise.

"Did you ever notice anything unusual about Martin?"
Calvano asked. Subtle, buddy. How about a flashing neon

sign above your head that says, "Accuse him! Accuse him!" just in case the colonel missed the message?

"He is very zealous," the colonel admitted. He leaned toward Calvano and lowered his voice. "I get a lot of damaged people as volunteers. And I understand why. They come to me for a chance to fight back at what happened to them or someone they loved. They need to get some power out of the dynamic. I don't ask people why they want to volunteer. I don't have to. Robert is one of those. He has a personal stake in stopping child abuse."

"So the guy is a little off?" Calvano asked.

Even Gonzales flinched at that one.

"Maybe a little," the colonel conceded. "He volunteers all the time, and I prefer that my volunteers lead more balanced lives. If he isn't online, he's checking out the parks, keeping an eye on the homes of registered offenders. He's very thorough."

"He ever bring anyone in?" Calvano asked.

"Not yet," the colonel admitted. "Sometimes . . ." He shrugged.

"What?" Calvano asked. "Give me some background here."

But the colonel just smiled like he had said enough. "I have had a lot of very, very dedicated volunteers," was all he offered Calvano. "And there have been a few bad apples in the mix. People whose motives aren't so pure. I can never see them coming until we're in the middle, though."

"What do you mean?" Calvano said.

"I'm always keeping an eye out for the shady ones. And there's always this moment where I start to get a feeling about someone and this voice inside of me says, *Something's off.* I've learned to listen to that voice. When someone gets on my radar like that, I have special software I use to track them online without their knowing and read the transcripts of any chats they engage in. And I've caught a few, a very few, about to go over to the dark side."

"And Martin is one of them?" Calvano asked, excited.

But the colonel shook his head. "I wouldn't say that. But . . ." He shrugged. "My radar started to go off about him. He just seemed a little too excited about the possibility of something actually happening. Know what I mean?"

Calvano nodded. "He told you about the man he supposedly saw in the park?"

The colonel nodded. "He left a few messages. Yesterday. Again this morning."

"But you didn't talk to him?"

"I have over fifty volunteers to oversee. I can't talk to everyone right away. Not unless it's a real emergency."

"And you figured he was just blowing smoke?"

"I figured he was a troubled young man," the colonel said.

Maggie had heard enough. She turned to Gonzales and preempted any attempt at straying from their plan. "All the more reason to give Martin a polygraph," she said. "He'll be back here in an hour."

"Relax, Gunn," Gonzales said. "We're sticking with our deal." He turned his back to Calvano and the colonel. "I think I've seen enough."

Gonzales was restless, a little peeved, but I could not tell what the cause was. Was it just the tawdriness of the situation, the scummy nature of a world where even fifty volunteers had a hard time keeping the wolves from the lambs? Or, like Maggie, did he not like the slightly holier-than-thou attitude the colonel emitted? It was hard to tell.

There was a knock at the door of the observation room and Freddy, the desk sergeant, stuck his head inside. His face was grave.

"What's up, Freddy?" Maggie asked.

"There's a lady downstairs I think you better see . . ." His voice faltered. "She heard about the boy who went missing this morning."

"Who the hell is it?" Gonzales asked. The last thing he needed was another complication.

"It's Rosemary D'Amato, the mother of the boy who was abducted north of town sixteen years ago," Morty explained. "She comes in every time there's a child ab- duction or, really, any case that she thinks might tell her what happened to her son. She shows up here two, three times a year and has for the last sixteen years."

Gonzales looked a little stunned at this.

"I'll go talk to her," Maggie volunteered.

"I'll go with you," Morty offered. "I've talked to her before."

"Go," Gonzales agreed, looking at his watch. "Sixteen years of waiting for us to do our jobs? God, just go to her."

I had a feeling the feds couldn't get here fast enough for Gonzales. He wanted to be rid of this case.

Chapter 12

Rosemary D'Amato looked exactly like a million other middle-aged mothers who drive their kids to soccer practice and try unsuccessfully to find a little time to take care of themselves. She was overweight with short, dark hair, no makeup, and an indifferent outfit that did nothing to flatter her figure. The only difference was that her son had disappeared off the face of the earth one ordinary morning, and her self-neglect was caused by apathy. She was sitting in a plastic chair in the waiting area of the lobby, eyes fixed firmly on her lap, as if fighting off the memories the station house held.

It made me sad to see her sitting there alone without someone to support her. I was pretty sure her husband had moved to another town because he was unable to hold on to the immense sorrow his wife clung to. I'd seen that happen before. And I could feel it around her. It was a sense of overwhelming loss very like what I had felt in the park earlier when little Tyler Matthews had been taken—

only this woman's sorrow was tempered by resignation. Yet she could not give it up. Rosemary D'Amato had held on to her terrible sadness for sixteen years. I didn't know where she had found the energy to keep living under such a burden. I had seen people crippled by losses like that for life and, even as I'd failed to do anything about it when I'd been a detective, I had known that grieving loved ones were the final victims of whatever terrible crime I'd failed to solve.

Maggie was kind to Rosemary D'Amato. Morty was respectful and grave. Mrs. D'Amato recognized him and a wave of gratitude welled in her. She clung to Morty like a lifeboat. "I heard another little boy was taken," she told him. "Have they found him?"

Morty led her to a table in the coffee bar. "They have not found him yet," he said kindly. "This is Detective Gunn. She can tell you more. Let me go get you some tea."

Mrs. D'Amato looked at Maggie apologetically; she was not a woman who wanted to trouble anyone. My heart ached for her. What must it be like to have to beg people for scraps of information year after year—and get only apologetic smiles in return—because you could not bear to give up the only thing you had left of your son: the hope that you might see him again?

"Mrs. D'Amato," Maggie said quietly as she sat with the woman at a small table by a window through which sunshine flooded almost obscenely. Such beauty to illuminate such sorrow. "I don't have anything to tell you, really. We believe this little boy was taken by someone who took advantage of the distraction caused by another crime nearby. We have no idea whether this is a repeat offender or someone who just took advantage of the situation. I am afraid it is very unlikely it's the same man who took your son. Your son's abductor was probably a transient."

"I know," Mrs. D'Amato said. "But I owe it to him to ask." Her hands were clenched into tight fists and she could not lift her eyes from them; it was as if those fists were her anchors and without them she might float away.

"I understand." Maggie took Rosemary D'Amato's hands and unfolded them gently, then held them in her own. I had never really seen this side of Maggie before. She often only showed her determined side to the public, as if she knew the families of the victims needed the strength of her anger to get them through the unthinkable. But with Mrs. D'Amato, she was infinitely kind.

"I have lost people who were my whole world," Maggie said to the downcast woman. "I understand how hard it is to let go. And I would never ask you to break your promise to your son."

Mrs. D'Amato looked up, searching Maggie's face.

"I know you promised to protect him," Maggie said. "And I know you will never stop trying to find him so you can keep your word. I give you my own personal word that if I get even an inkling that these two cases are connected in any way, I will let you know. But you must promise me in return that you will call me anytime you need to. I'm going to read over your son's file, and if I see anything that's been missed, I promise to follow up."

Mrs. D'Amato began to cry. Morty arrived with a cup of hot tea for her. He had remembered she took two sugars with her tea, and when he set the packets next to her cup, Mrs. D'Amato cried even more. I understood then that the hardest thing in the world was to depend on the kindness of strangers when that was all you had.

"That poor woman whose son was taken this morning?" Mrs. D'Amato said through her tears. "She doesn't know what it's going to be like. What each day will bring."

As if on cue, the doors to the parking lot slid open and

the missing boy's mother entered, supported by a friend
on each side. She had aged fifteen years in six hours. Her
face was splotchy from crying, her hands shook, and her
eyes had the glazed look of the sedated. I didn't think
she was fit to be at the station, but my guess was Gonzales wanted a first go at her before the feds took over.
Either that or she was here of her own accord, desperate
for news of her son.

Rosemary D'Amato stared at Callie Matthews as she
shuffled across the lobby, supported by her friends. She
had to look away. "I can't bear to," she whispered. "That
poor, poor woman."

Anxiousness radiated off Maggie, and I knew why.
She wanted to help Rosemary D'Amato, but she wanted
to head off Callie Matthews even more, especially since
the only thing that protected her from Calvano's ineptitude was a short elevator ride.

"Go," Morty told her, reading her face.

"Yes, please go," Mrs. D'Amato echoed. "I know you
can help that woman more. I'll be okay. I just had to come
by and check. I know it doesn't do any good, but I have
to."

Maggie gave her a business card. "Call me personally, anytime. And make sure Morty knows how to get in
touch with you. Will you do that?"

Mrs. D'Amato nodded and wrapped her hands around
her tea, finding a new anchor.

"I'll see she gets home," Morty promised.

As Maggie hurried after the trio of women struggling toward the elevator, Morty pried off the top of Mrs.
D'Amato's tea for her and poured both sugars into it.
"You'll feel better after a cup of tea," he said. "I know I
always do."

"Are you sure you're not an Irish cop?" Rosemary
D'Amato asked him through her tears and, just like that,

they were laughing. It was amazing to me how a spark of laughter could heal the human heart.

"I'm sure," Morty told her. "My mother was even more sure."

They smiled at each other. Their banter was a ritual for both of them. "How are you?" Morty asked. "Still at the construction company?"

She nodded. "They couldn't find a crane without me to tell them where it is."

"And your husband?"

She smiled ruefully. "Still in Scranton. His job is going quite well."

Morty waited for the rest.

"He wants me to join him, but I still can't bring myself to move," she finally said. "I just can't. What if Bobby were to come home one day and I wasn't there?"

"I'm sure your husband understands."

Mrs. D'Amato wiped her eyes. "That's enough for one day," she decided. "I know you must get tired of me."

"Never," Morty said firmly. "I don't expect you to give up until I give up—and that's just not going to happen."

She smiled at him. "You're a good man."

Morty colored. "Don't forget your tea. Take it with you. I'll walk you to your car."

"I walked." She laughed at Morty's expression. "You think you're the only one who can walk a beat? It's for my health. The doctor says I need more exercise."

"Don't we all?" Morty joked. But I could tell he was pleased that Mrs. D'Amato was starting to take an interest in her own well-being again, however small. "In fact, I will walk you home." He took her arm, making small talk as they headed for the door.

That was when I saw the little boy for the first time. He was so small and frail that he nearly disappeared in a sunbeam that cascaded across the lobby and fell like a spotlight on a corner of the waiting area. Mrs. D'Amato and Morty walked right past him without a glance, but the little boy hopped up from his chair and followed them out the door. Curious, I followed the boy.

He was about four years old, dressed in a black and green striped shirt and wearing khaki shorts. He had brown hair buzzed short, and his ears stuck out from his head. The back of his tennis shoes lit up, a style first made popular years ago.

Who was he?

The little boy walked within inches of a tattooed biker screaming obscenities as he fought off three officers, and then the boy passed between a weary patrolman and an overweight drunk being herded through the front door. No one gave the little boy a single glance.

I didn't think anyone could see him but me.

We made an odd parade, marching down the sidewalk in a raggle-taggle formation through the bright spring afternoon: Morty and Mrs. D'Amato, who had started slowly but picked up steam as the sunshine lifted her spirits; the boy with his spindly knees resolutely following them, his little body shimmering in the afternoon light; and yours truly, bringing up the rear.

We passed by the park where Tyler Matthews had been taken. Uniformed officers belatedly guarded its borders, and a few crime scene technicians still searched along its edges. We passed the cottage where the nurse had been killed. The officer guarding the door waved at Morty. We reached the thoroughfare that led to a small business district and passed right by the Italian restaurant where Robert Michael Martin worked as a chef. The smells of tomato sauce and garlic were truly heavenly but, alas, while my sense of smell has returned and I can enjoy the anticipation, there's no satisfaction for me these days.

Morty and Mrs. D'Amato paused at a corner for a traf-

fic light. The little boy had no such qualms. He stepped
right out into the traffic and was across the street before
I could follow. Oblivious drivers zoomed past me, and
some drove right through me as I hurried to keep pace.

The little boy knew where he was going and was in the
lead now, with Morty and Mrs. D'Amato a quarter block
behind. We kept marching in our odd parade of the dead
and the living through the neighborhood on the other side
of the business district. The little boy turned down a side
street about three blocks farther on.

By the time I reached the corner, he was sitting in the
branches of a tree overlooking a small brick bungalow,
the kind with walls that bulge slightly, as if the house
was holding its breath. The yard was neatly kept with tidy
flower beds blooming on each side of the front stoop. The
house looked familiar to me.

The little boy was already nestled in the crook of the
tree and had his spindly legs and jaunty sneakers propped
up on the trunk above his body. I got the feeling that, just
like me, he had his favorite watching spots.

Morty and Mrs. D'Amato had reached the corner.
They turned down the block and Morty gallantly took
her arm again as they approached her walkway. He even
tipped his hat as she stopped on her front stoop to wave
good-bye. Norman Rockwell could not have imagined a
more perfect scene of your friendly neighborhood officer
in action. Except for the dead kid in the tree and the dead
cop lurking in the yard, of course.

I thought the little boy would surely follow Mrs.
D'Amato inside. She unlocked her door and stepped into
her solitary fortress. I wondered what the house would
feel like after sixteen years of sorrow had eroded its comforting air, but before I could follow her inside, I felt the
oddest of sensations.

Someone was holding my hand.

I looked down and the little boy was standing beside me, gazing upward expectantly, his hand occupying the same space as mine. It was not a tangible feeling. It was not quite that solid. It was more as if I held a heavy fog in my hand. It tickled a little, and I wanted to laugh, but the boy's solemn expression invited no merriment. I have occupied the same space as the living before, and it is not pleasant. It tears at my insides, whatever those insides may be made of. But this mingling of the dead was not bad at all; it tingled as if the lowest level of electric current were pulsing through me and had found an exit point where our two hands crossed.

In fact, it filled my heart with life. I wondered if he really was like me, or different in some way.

The boy's steady gaze told me that he wanted something. I did not know what. When he stepped forward, I followed, and we walked hand in hand past the busy blocks of the living, across streets, retracing our steps and heading back in the exact same direction we had come from. When we reached the park, he turned and led me across the lawn toward the playground area. Unseen by any of the living, we drifted past the crime scene tape that had been stretched across the spot where Tyler Matthews had last been seen, then past the sandbox and monkey bars. But as we approached the swings, the little boy took his hand away. I felt the loss of his energy acutely.

He hopped on a swing and stared up at me, expectantly.

The kid was dreaming if he thought I could push him. It ripped me apart to tear the veil between my world and the physical. But that was not what the little boy wanted. What he wanted was to pretend.

So pretend we did, like a father and son lingering in the park on a fading spring afternoon. As the birds sang behind us and traffic hummed a few blocks away, as the sun descended lower in the sky and the clouds above turned from bright white to a faint pink, I stood behind the swing and moved my arms while the little boy caused the swing to move, first slowly and then faster, picking up speed until it swung back and forth as vigorously as any living four-year-old might like. He unnecessarily wrapped his hands around the metal chains on each side, as I am certain he had no corporeal presence. But he wanted to be a little boy again, and he needed me to be his father. I pretended to push him higher and higher, smiling when he glanced at me over his shoulder. The sun spiraled behind the boy, setting his whole silhouette awash in fire; he was a burning bush soaring through the skies.

His laughter rang through the afternoon, high and pure, unheard, I was certain, by anyone but me. What joy it gave the little boy to swing on a fine spring afternoon, with someone there to watch over him.

I thought then of all the days I had missed with my own boys, of all the afternoons I could have been home with them but sat, instead, in some lousy dive bar, drinking in bitterness and inhaling the boozy stench of everyone else's disappointments as a way to mask my own. How many hours had I squandered that I could have spent listening to the high, pure joy of my sons and seeing them fiercely alive on a sunny day?

I felt a flash of regret so acute, my mind reeled with longing. *I had had so much and experienced so little.* But the pealing laughter of the little boy on the swing rescued me from my memories and brought me back to where I was. I couldn't undo the past and I could do very little to affect the future. But the present? At least I was here, enjoying the end of a sunshine-soaked afternoon. I looked around, making the most of it, and noticed the uniformed officer on guard in the doorway of the cottage where the nurse had died. He was staring across the street at us, a puzzled look on his face. I realized what he was seeing: a deserted playground, a windless afternoon—yet there it was, an empty swing distinctly soaring first one way and then the other, without a trace of anyone in sight.

I began to laugh at what he must be thinking, and my laughter mingled with that of the boy's. We made a fine pair, he and I, and for just a moment I felt the exultation of feeling that I belonged.

Chapter 13

I left my young friend hanging by the tips of his toes from the monkey bars, out-tricking even the most agile of living children. He did not see me go, nor did he care. He was done with me. He, too, lived in a solitary world and I was but a visitor to it.

The air smelled of twilight. Another day had passed. Lives had been shattered, fortunes made, and love found, all on one ordinary day. I don't know how people can ever find life boring. It's one big soap opera that never ends. And I knew exactly where the next episode would take place. I headed to department headquarters, where Robert Michael Martin was being polygraphed and hypnotized. It was my first chance to experience the human mind as it was probed by other humans, and I did not want to miss it.

I was not the only one. Martin had been seated in the largest interrogation room, one adjoined by a spacious observation room concealed behind an entire wall of one-

way glass. In all my years on the force, I had never rated
the use of this room. But despite its size, I felt eerily as if
I were part of a crowd witnessing an execution. It did not
help that Martin was connected to various wires leading
to a polygraph machine.

Because he was undergoing the test voluntarily, his
lawyer had negotiated the right to sit beside him; he was
the only other person allowed in the room besides the
dark-haired polygraph specialist with intense energy, who
was asking Martin control questions about his name, age,
and address. Innocuous as these questions were, Martin
had already started to sweat. The white dress shirt he had
so carefully donned was soaked, and perspiration covered
his doughy face. When the operator asked him to confirm
his occupation, I thought the poor bastard was going to
pass out. This was not a man used to being around other
people, I decided. His worry over what others thought of
him created a level of anxiousness that was sending his
baselines through the roof.

Noni Bates looked concerned. She had been allowed
to observe and had worn a straw hat for the occasion. She
had also, I noticed, sat directly in front of Calvano and
completely blocked his view, forcing him to move to a
seat in the corner. The chairs in the observation room had
been set up in front of the one-way mirror as if we were
watching a special preview of a new movie. I thought
popcorn would have enhanced the mood, but everyone
looked way too businesslike for that. Maggie was staring
intently though the glass, while Gonzales sat, immobile
and taut, as Martin was led through a series of innocuous
questions and, finally, queries about the man in the park.

"That dude sweats like a pig," Calvano observed.

"What astute powers of observation you have," Noni
Bates said sweetly. "You must be a detective."

Sarcasm, from that lovely old lady? Oh, I liked that.

So did Maggie, who clamped her lips shut tightly and avoided Calvano's eyes. Gonzales had not even heard.

Calvano stared at Noni and once again failed to recognize her. In this case, it worked in her favor. He had made a few comments to Gonzales about "people going over his head" but had not yet figured out it was Noni who had sent the patrolmen to let Gonzales know what Martin had originally tried to tell Calvano about the man in the park. Calvano seemed under the impression that Noni was Martin's mother and, I suppose, in a way he was right. She was there to watch over him, and we all need that at times like this, no matter our age.

Despite his anxiousness, in the end, Martin passed the polygraph handily, as the operator explained to Gonzales after the session was over.

I did not need this news to know Martin had passed. I had discovered that no mere polygraph machine could hold a candle to me. I had followed the changes in Martin's heart rate and blood pressure through every question, and then had gone a step beyond, absorbing the flood of memories each question triggered in Martin's mind. I knew with certainty now that he was who he said he was, and that he might be of real help if he could only remember more.

A rare feeling overtook me when I realized Martin could help, one I had seldom experienced when I was alive: the hunt was on, there was hope, we were on the trail and moving forward—and I was in the lead.

Gonzales took the news of Martin's test results calmly, listening politely while the polygraph operator explained what he had already figured out for himself. "He shows a high level of concern over the missing boy," the operator said. "But he knows nothing about where the boy is or who took him, in my opinion. The man he says he saw in the park is absolutely real, at least to the subject, and I see no signs of deception on the subject's part. There was some reaction when I asked him control questions about his name, address, residency, and living situation, but I attribute that to the recent death of his mother, who apparently shared his living arrangements. Otherwise, this is a truthful subject. However, he is compliant and very eager to please. I would be wary of disinformation caused primarily by his overwhelming desire to be of help."

"I want a drug test," Calvano said loudly.

We all stared at him.

"It's easy to beat the test," Calvano explained defensively. "I want the guy tested to see if he took anything to help him beat the test."

Before anyone else could speak—and they all looked like they wanted to— Gonzales nipped that thought in the bud. "We're the ones who suggested a polygraph and put it forth as an acceptable screen. We're not changing our minds now."

"I would have detected the signs of drug use," the operator said coldly. "It's part of what I am trained to do."

Calvano looked like he was about to say something else, but a look from Gonzales inspired him to sit back and shut up instead. Few people got that look from Gonzales. Those who did remembered it.

"Thank you," Gonzales told the polygraph operator. "We can stop here. This was background only."

The man nodded and returned to the interrogation room to collect his equipment. His job was over, and he was happy to turn the more complicated task of sorting out which truths mattered to others. Martin had been waiting anxiously, as if he had just endured a particularly grueling job interview and now wanted to know if he had gotten the job. But the polygraph operator evaded his questions and left so quickly that it was all his lawyer could do to inquire after him, "What were the results?"

When the operator answered by leaving the room, the lawyer stared at the wall of one-way glass and announced, "My client will not agree to the hypnosis session until we are informed of the results of the polygraph test."

"He always was a smart boy," Noni told the room before anyone else could react. "Wanted to be a lawyer all the way back in sixth grade. I knew he would go far."

Gonzales looked at his watch. Time was ticking away. The feds would be taking over in an hour and a half. "Handle it," he told Maggie while Calvano stifled his outrage at being overlooked.

Maggie left the room to confer with Martin's lawyer.

"She's quite a competent detective, isn't she?" Noni asked after she had left, winning a weak smile from Gonzales and a lingering glare from Calvano.

When Maggie told Martin he had passed the polygraph, the poor bastard turned into a different man. He visibly relaxed, let out a long sigh, and unbuttoned the top two buttons of his shirt.

"Look at that. He's hiding something," Calvano announced in the adjoining room. "See how relieved he is that he got away with it?"

This did not sit well with Noni. She lit into Calvano. "Young man, you remind me of a bully I taught back in 1978. He was a smart young man who could have gone far, but he was so busy trying to cut others down that he missed the attempts at friendship that came his way. My guess is that his insecurity ensured he would be a bully his entire life. Last I heard, he was a tow truck operator, despite the fact that he had an IQ of one hundred and forty. I suggest if you intend to remain a detective that you learn to listen more to what others are saying and point fingers a little bit less."

She turned back around, having said her piece, and left a stunned Calvano to stare at the back of her head. I could feel him beginning to wonder who the hell she was and if they had met before. But then his self-preservation kicked in and he glanced at Gonzales, seeking his reaction. Gonzales was too smart for that. The moment the tirade began he had pulled out a cell phone and feigned a call. I knew he was faking it but admired his restraint. A cornered dog is a dangerous one—he would let Calvano save face and delude himself that no one had overheard the upbraiding.

He would not, however, let Calvano embarrass the department in front of the FBI. Maggie had accepted a piece of paper from Martin's lawyer after confirming his client had passed the polygraph, and she was looking it over intently. Gonzales knew what it was.

"Calvano," he barked. "Gunn's got the list of the license plate numbers Martin took down over the past couple days. These are cars that were parked near the playground. I want you to run them. Look for patterns, check out the owners, you know the drill—who doesn't belong near a park on a weekday? I want the list narrowed down by the time the feds get here. We need something solid to show them."

"Yes, sir," Calvano said smartly, as if he had just been handed a vital undercover assignment instead of grunt work that any clerk could do. Noni made him nervous and, like all bullies, he was anxious to leave the battlefield when others started fighting back.

Chapter 14

Calvano made the most of taking the list of license plate numbers from Maggie, emphasizing that Gonzales had asked him to handle it personally. She couldn't have cared less. The specialist trained in the forensic application of hypnosis had arrived to conduct her session with Martin, and that was what Maggie was most interested in—not just because she wanted to find the little boy, but because she hoped Martin might have seen something that would help solve Fiona Harker's murder.

The specialist was also a certified therapist, a fortunate skill considering Martin's mental state. She did not look at all like what I had expected. She was in her forties, small and blonde, with the lithe body and turned-out feet of a dancer. She also had kind eyes, a reassuring smile, and such a sweet voice that Martin was relaxed enough to start the session within moments. Although she had a PhD, she insisted Martin call her Miranda and asked if she might call him Robert. The poor guy was so unused to female attention, I suspect he would have consented to anything she asked, but then again, I would have, too.

When the therapist began to make small talk in preparation for relaxing Martin and putting him under, Maggie returned to the observation room. She nodded politely to Noni, who was still there as a condition of Robert Michael Martin's cooperation, then sat beside Gonzales. "You sure you want to stay for this?" she asked him.

"I wouldn't miss it," he said grimly. We both knew he was more likely ducking the press, but he was the commander, and who was I to second-guess his judgment?

While the specialist made small talk with Martin, I amused myself by fantasizing about combining polygraph and hypnosis techniques into one awesome witness-screening process, conducted exclusively by me. I would guide people through all they had seen surrounding a crime—but buzz them to a halt whenever they tried to embellish the truth. Oh, to be alive again.

Robert Michael Martin was ready.

"Robert, I want you to hold both hands out, as if you were playing the piano," the therapist told Martin. *Okay, Miranda,* I thought, *you can't see me, but today you're going to do a doubleheader and I will be glad to play along.*

With a goofy grin half caused by the fact that he was already a bit besotted with her, Martin complied, and I copied him, holding both palms open toward the floor.

"Good." Miranda smiled. "Now move each finger in turn as if you were pressing down on piano keys, one by one. Go all the way through both hands and reverse directions, again pressing each finger down in turn." She demonstrated the rapid finger movement technique and Martin and I imitated her, making it look like we were running up and down imaginary scales on a piano keyboard.

"Keep moving your fingers like that while I take you

back three days to Monday morning. Just keep doing that and listen to my voice."

I had no idea why she was asking Martin to do it, but the effect was quite literally mesmerizing. As Martin continued to move his fingers and listened to her sooth- ing voice take him back in time, I could feel his mind move further and further away from the present. Barriers between the conscious and unconscious areas of his brain began to fade as Miranda's hushed voice led us into the twilight of his thoughts. Part of him knew he was still in the interrogation room, but his consciousness was else- where, brought back to the days just passed.

"I want you to imagine a clock turning backward, backward, still backward," Miranda intoned. "Taking you back beyond breakfast this morning and the night before and another day and another night's sleep and yet another day and night to Monday morning."

I was right there with Martin. These were not my memories, but, as his mind opened, I entered and took a step closer to being one with him.

"You are standing at the front door to a very big house," Miranda told him. "I want you to go inside, where you will see a long hallway lined with many doors." She waited, and I saw the hallway come alive in his mind. "What do you see?" she asked Martin.

"Red carpet on the floors. Wallpaper. It looks like a hotel my mom and I once stayed in when we visited Denver."

"Very good," Miranda said. "Now behind each door, you will find a day. I want you to go to the door for this past Monday. It will be the second door on the right side of the hallway. Do you remember what happened leading up to Monday morning?"

Martin nodded. "Someone left the door to the walk-in open and my tiramisu was ruined. I had to make a new pan because Mr. and Mrs. Wheeler order it every Monday and they are very disappointed when we run out."

"Okay," Miranda said. "Let's keep that memory behind the door for Sunday. I want you to walk to the next door, the one for Monday. Open that door and go inside."

I could feel Martin reaching a hand out in his mind; it was a sensation as physical as if it were really happening. I saw the flash of a brass doorknob, a heavy oak door pushing open, and then, there it was: the sidewalk outside the restaurant where he worked, as he emerged from the solitude of his night shift into the early morning.

"Tell me where you are now," Miranda said.

I could have explained that we were standing outside the Italian restaurant, a night's worth of cooking and baking behind and a sunny day stretching out before us. It was a little cool, not like the fine day that would dawn later in the week. This was a still-crisp, slightly wintry day that teased of spring, just enough to ensure that Robert Michael Martin would want to take the long way home. As he walked, I walked beside him, inhaling the odors of baking bread followed by the starch and steam smells of the corner Laundromat.

Miranda talked Martin farther down the sidewalk, asking him questions about how he felt, what he smelled, if there was a wind, why he had decided to walk toward the park. Martin gave his answers dutifully and honestly, that much I could tell, as he had somehow gone back to that day in his mind completely, as if there were two Robert Michael Martins: the one sitting in a chair in the interrogation room and the one who had left work three days before and decided to check on the children in the park.

"It's really nice," Martin said to no one in particular. "I think maybe spring is not far away. I want to see what the park looks like."

Somewhere in that last block between restaurant and park, I ceased walking beside Martin and became a part of him, as if our beings had merged. I now saw the world through his eyes. There was no pain, no disharmony—he had invited me inside when he opened his mind through hypnotism. I felt as he felt leaving work: heavy, weary, my lungs choked with flour dust. I breathed deeply of the fresh air and was grateful for it.

We grew nearer to the playground and began to pass cars parked along the street that led to it. Martin slowed to note the license plate of each, jotting the numbers down in a small notebook he kept in his pocket. I memorized each one as he wrote, filing it away for future reference. Then he turned into the park and followed the brick path to the sandbox area, rimmed by benches. We sat and he tilted his head back to feel the sun; I could feel the warmth spreading through me as he did so. Children laughed and shrieked in the background while mothers chatted about their lives nearby.

Martin stiffened. He'd felt something, so I felt it, too. Someone was staring at us. He opened his eyes and scanned the playground area, noting the regulars: two stout Dutch nannies on a bench, chatting away in their language while their wards played nearby. An old man feeding pigeons from the crumbs of toast he had saved from his breakfast. A sanitation worker resting his feet before he headed back for a second shift. An old lady sitting alone, hands folded in her lap, watching the children and wondering how it was that her own had grown up so quickly and disappeared. And then, at the very end of one long row of benches, a man reading a newspaper—or pretending to. He held it at eye level, and every now and then would raise his head slightly and peer at the children playing, his eyes lingering on each as if he were hungry and intended to choose the plumpest to take home and eat. He wore sunglasses and a baseball hat pulled low over his face. All you could really see of him were his ears sticking out below the hat. He was the one who had been staring at Martin. I was sure of it.

I felt such danger—and longing—coming from the man that I lost my place for the briefest of moments. Martin and I parted, and I had to will my way back to him. I could not afford to lose the connection. I needed to see and feel everything he was feeling, yet find a way to tap into my own abilities at the same time.

"What does this man look like?" Miranda asked Martin.

"He is about my height but very thin," Martin answered, confirming what I was seeing in his mind's eye. "He looks awkward, like he doesn't quite know what to do with his arms and legs. His hands are long and elegant, like a girl's."

"What else?" the hypnotist prodded gently. "Look at his face. Tell me what you see."

"I can't," Martin explained, his voice distant. "The newspaper is in the way, and he's wearing a baseball hat and sunglasses. That's creepy. But his hair is brown and cut a little crazy. You can see wisps of it sticking out below the hat. He's wearing jeans that are too short for him. And sandals, even though the day is cool."

"Sandals?" Miranda asked. "Can you describe them?"

"The thick, ugly kind that are good for your feet," Martin said. "With socks. He wears white socks with them. I would never in a million years do that."

I could have told her even more. The newspaper did not disguise the fact that the man was, indeed, only pretending to read while he watched the children. I could feel him cataloging them in turn: *a girl, a girl, a boy, then another girl. Yellow-haired, red-haired, that one's too dark. Too old. I need a boy, a brown-haired boy, maybe four or five. Skinny, with big eyes. There must be one here somewhere.*

"Is this the man you told the police about?" Miranda asked.

"Yes," Martin said. "But maybe his kid is playing somewhere nearby, or maybe he's just lonely and likes the sound of the children at play. I think he lives alone in a big house with no one to talk to. Maybe that was what it was like even when he was a child. I think maybe he needs the company of sitting here in the park."

Whoa, buddy, I thought to myself as feelings of loneliness and despair overwhelmed Robert Michael Martin, leaking from him as if a dam had just burst and years of isolation had come pouring forth.

The therapist felt him veer from what she needed him to do. "Let's leave the park on Monday morning now," she suggested gently. "Let's go back into the hallway and close the door on Monday. Are you there? Good. Take a step down to the next door. Let's open it and take you to Tuesday morning. Work is over. You are leaving the restaurant again. Tell me what you see."

Martin complied, and she led him through Tuesday morning. It was very much like the day before, except that Martin was in the mood to admire cars and stopped to examine a red Lamborghini parked on a side street near the park. When he finally got to the park, the man was not there, at least not that Martin saw, nor did he see Tyler Matthews. Miranda quickly led him forward twenty-four more hours to Wednesday, the next door down in her hallway of memories.

This time, when Martin stepped through the door, the morning was cloudy and the day smelled of rain. Rain and urine. Martin sounded indignant when he spoke. "A bum slept inside the back stoop again," he complained. "I don't know why the cops can't keep him away. He stinks the whole place up."

And you, buddy, don't smell too good yourself after a

night sweating in the kitchen, I thought as we once again left the restaurant and walked down the sidewalk. I was still wholly in his mind, seeing the world exactly as he saw it.

"It's very overcast," he told Miranda. "I think it might rain. That would be good. I'm too tired to water the flowers, but if they die it'll be because I'm lazy and I promised my mother I'd take care of them. She would like this day. She loved rainy days."

Sadness welled in him, and I felt sorry for the man. His mother had been all he had.

"Where are you now?" the therapist asked. "Are you taking the same route to the park as yesterday?"

"No," he confessed. "I want to go home. I'm really very tired and kind of hungry." He hesitated and I felt an inner voice rise inside him, as if someone were chiding him. "I better not, though," he said out loud. "I heard on the news last night that a man took a little girl out in California, right from her front yard. But her friend across the street got a partial license plate number. They caught the guy and now she's a hero. I better take down some license plate numbers before I go home. The colonel says I am very thorough, the best volunteer he has. He says he depends on me and I must keep bringing him information and I must be his eyes, as he cannot get around the way I can." I saw it all as he took the notebook from his pocket and began jotting down numbers, just as he had the day before.

"What do they look like?" the hypnotist asked him. "Can you tell me the color and make of the cars as well? You did a good job of that yesterday."

As he recited a litany of minivans and sedans, along with their colors and approximate years and makes, I knew Maggie was taking notes, ready to test the accuracy of Martin's memory against whatever information the Department of Motor Vehicles would provide. Not only would it give her an idea of how valuable the hypnotism session had been, if the DMV records helped identify a car whose make and model did not match the official data, it might indicate stolen plates—and lead her to the abductor.

As Martin spoke, I realized for the first time that I could see far more than just what he was describing for Miranda. I was there every bit as much as he was. He was describing the cars to the hypnotist, but I was actually seeing the cars, along with the park or yard behind each car, the housewife walking her dog on the sidewalk, the mailman pushing his cart full of mail past them all. The details Martin was leaving out were visible to me, and I looked hungrily around, seeking clues only I could be privy to. I checked out the cottage across the street, where the nurse had lived, and saw a woman dressed in a rain-coat leaving the house and getting into a car and driving away. I realized with a start that it had been Fiona Harker, that she was still alive, but that within hours death would visit her and, a day after that, she would be found murdered on the floor.

"That's about it," Martin declared, talking to himself as he relived stowing his notebook and pen back in a pocket. "Let's see what the kids are up to today. There's this one kid in the sandbox who bullies the little ones. I'm going to keep an eye on him. I don't like the way he pushes other kids around. I may have to say something to his nanny."

"Do you know the children by name?" Miranda asked, to remind him she was there. I knew she was hoping to find information on Tyler Matthews, including whether he had followed any patterns that might help the police.

"I have names for them," Martin explained. "I make them up. And sometimes if they get called enough by their mothers I even know their real names."

"What about Tyler Matthews?" Miranda asked. "You know him by name, right?"

"Oh, sure," Martin said promptly. "His mom is a worrywart. My mom was like that. I couldn't go five feet away without her calling me back. His mother is even worse. It makes it hard for him. He wants to run, he wants to join the other children, he wants to cut loose and be himself for a while."

Is Martin talking about himself or Tyler Matthews?

"Is Tyler there now?" the therapist asked.

"No," Martin said. "Because of the weather, there aren't a lot of kids here today. Just a small crowd that—" He stopped abruptly, and I could feel him hesitate as a flicker of fear licked upward. It was a physical fear.

"What is it, Robert?" Miranda asked. "Tell me what you see."

"The man from Monday is back," Martin whispered. "The man who was pretending to read the newspaper. He's hiding behind the paper again. But I can see him all right. I can see his sandals and socks. I can feel him, too. I don't like him."

I could feel Martin's dislike. It flooded through him like water rising. It was dislike, suspicion, and a hefty dose of fear, too, as if somehow he, Martin, were in personal danger from the man.

"What is the man doing?" Miranda asked sharply.

"He's sitting next to the old man who feeds the pigeons, but he hasn't even bothered to say hello. You're supposed to say hello when you sit next to old people on park benches. That's why old people sit there. To talk to other people. He's hiding behind his newspaper, watching the children again . . ." His breath began to come in heavy gusts. "He's waiting for the right one. He's—" Martin stopped abruptly. His mind went blank.

"What is it?" Miranda asked.

"I don't want to go any further into his head," Martin said.

"You can tell what he's thinking?" she asked, a note of worry creeping into her otherwise relentlessly calm voice. Something about Martin's comment concerned her.

"No, but I can feel what he's thinking, and what he wants, and I don't like it. I don't want to go any closer."

"Okay," Miranda agreed crisply. "Let's take a look elsewhere. I want you to look up and tell me what you see. Look across the street."

"A really cute little cottage," Martin said, relaxing a little. "It has a great garden. Maybe the owner could tell me what I need to do to keep my mother's flowers alive. And the hedges are trimmed so neatly. I wish I lived there. It's like something out of a fairy tale. It's funny how I never noticed it before."

"Is anyone home?" Miranda asked, approaching the territory Maggie asked her to cover.

Martin was silent and I could see the scene through his eyes: an empty cottage, an empty curb in front, a sense of abandonment about the place.

"No," Martin said firmly. "The lights are off and it's quite shut up. I don't think the owner is there very often. The cottage looks lonely."

"Okay. Let's go back to the playground. Can you tell me anything else about the playground or the man on the bench?" Miranda said.

"It's going to rain. That means the man behind the newspaper will be leaving soon. The children will be safe for today. But I'm going to tell the colonel about him. I do not think that man can be trusted." Something welled up in Martin. When he spoke again, he sounded much younger than he was. "I have a bad feeling about him. I think he's a bad man. He likes hurting people."

"Are you tired?" Miranda said gently, understanding

something about him that the rest of us did not. I tried to search his memories so I could understand, but I failed—the park was all he allowed me to share. "Do you need a rest?" Miranda asked.

"No," Martin said firmly, his voice growing in strength. "I want to go further. I'm ready to go through the next door." As he spoke, I got that same odd sense of being in two places at one time: in the brightly lit interrogation room in front of witnesses, but also back in time, on a bench in a park with the wind picking up and the smell of rain even stronger in the air.

"Okay," Miranda agreed. "Shall we leave this room and continue on to the next door in the hallway, the one for this morning?"

"Yes," Martin said clearly, and I could feel the resolve building in him. He was determined to help.

"Let's go to just before you left work this morning," Miranda suggested in her most soothing voice. "You are a grown man. You are a strong man. You have worked a full night and are just finishing up."

Martin nodded, agreeing with her. "I baked all night long because we got an order in from a new deli for whole wheat loaves and Mrs. Rotanni says if she can make some money selling my bread to other places, she'll give me a nice raise."

"You must be feeling very proud of yourself," Miranda suggested, as if she knew he would need extra strength for what he was about to go through.

"Yes," Martin said. "But I'm not feeling so good this morning. I need coffee before I go to the park. I want a grande latte with a shot of hazelnut syrup. It costs three times what it ought to, but I'm not feeling too good. I think a latte will help."

"You're not feeling well?" the therapist asked, still concerned about something only she could pick up on.

I felt something in Martin cringe as he confessed, "I asked that new waitress out last night, the pretty one with the long black hair, and she just laughed at me. I saw one of the cooks laughing at me, too, and the busboy. She could have just said, 'No, thanks.' She didn't have to laugh in my face."

"No, she didn't," Miranda agreed gently. "Aren't you glad it is a new day?"

"Yes," said Martin, talking to himself. "She's a thief anyway. I saw her take money from the till when she thought no one was looking. I may even tell Mrs. Rotanni about it. If she does it again, I will." He paused and Miranda began to lead him through the morning. I could feel his thoughts shift as she led him down the block to a new coffee chain store, where he bought a large latte and a chocolate chip scone. For a fleeting second, I could almost taste that scone, and it filled me with lost delight. He wolfed it down and then described taking his time walking to the park, enjoying the weather and the knowledge that, at long last, spring had arrived without equivocation. His routine was much like the other three days, until he got nearer to the park.

"I better take down the license plate numbers again," he muttered to himself. "I promised the colonel last night that I would. He is anxious to know if the brown-haired man is there again today. I can tell he is interested in what I think. He must really trust my judgment." Martin sounded proud of himself, as if marveling that anyone would care about his opinion. "Damnit," he said, sounding frustrated. "I should have thought ahead. I'll have to balance my notebook with my latte or put it down on the sidewalk each time I write down a license plate number. I'm really tired. And I don't see any new cars, these all look pretty familiar. I'll write the numbers down later. I just want to rest for a while and soak up the sun and finish my latte first." He leaned his head back as if he were sitting on the park bench and closed his eyes.

"Where are you now?" Miranda asked, reminding him that others were listening. "Can you describe what you are seeing?"

Martin smiled. "The playground is packed today. It's such a nice day and every kid in town is here." He laughed. "Some little kid not more than two years old just threw sand in the bully's face and told him to go away. Way to go, little buddy!" He was silent for a moment. "Poor Tyler. His mother is always calling him. He wants to play with the little girl with red hair, but his mother won't let him go in the sandbox. She says it's too dirty." Martin's face was suddenly very sad. "She makes him different from the other boys. Doesn't she know what that is going to do to him?"

"Where is Tyler now?" Miranda asked sharply, trying to keep him from turning inward into his own memories.

"He is waiting his turn at the monkey bars. He's a cute little fellow, all elbows and knees, and his hair is brown and curly. I bet he hates his hair and thinks it looks like a girl's, but I think he looks like an angel."

Suddenly he gasped, and I could feel the darkness spread in him. I could feel the tension in the room grow at the same time; his lawyer, Miranda, the people on the other side of the one-way glass—they all know an important moment had come.

"He's back," Martin whispered. "He's back, and this time he's tried to change the way he looks. That's not good. That's not good at all. Why would he need to do that?"

"Change the way he looks how?" Miranda prompted.

"He's wearing a white windbreaker and black slacks and a different kind of hat pulled low over his face. It's one of those English caps that are flat on top. He's pretend-

ing to sleep, but I can tell he's watching the children, like
he's counting them off. He's . . ." Martin's voice trailed
off and I could feel the fear growing in him, filling him,
the kind of panic that raises its head and then grows and
grows. "He has something in his pocket. It sticks out a
little. It's a rag. Oh, no, it's the tip of a rag and . . ." Martin
paused, struggling to understand.

"What is it?" Miranda said sharply. "Tell me the first
thing that comes to your mind."

"It's a leash," Martin said firmly. "He has a leash, but
he doesn't have a dog. He's going to take someone. I know
he is." Martin's voice rose and became more urgent. "I've
got to tell someone before he does. I've got to let the police know." He hesitated. "They won't believe me. He
hasn't done anything. Who is going to believe me?" He
paused again, thinking out loud. "Could the colonel do
something? Maybe the police would listen to him. But he
says we have to have proof first, that feeling as if something is bad isn't enough. And what if I *am* wrong? What
if it's just some guy who has nowhere else to go? I have
nowhere else to go, either. Someone could easily say the
same thing about me." He was talking faster now, trying
to find his way to a solution. I could feel the panic in him
give way as he stared at the man in his memory. I had
a view of the stranger as well. And even though Martin
did not say it, I noted that the man had a sharp chin and
gangly arms and legs, ears that protruded and sunglasses
that he once again slid down over his eyes to conceal his
features. Between the sunglasses and the cap masking his
face, it was difficult to tell his age. I tried to get a read on
his thoughts, but it was hard leaving Martin's presence. It
was not the same as if I were experiencing the scene in
real time. I could read a little off the man, maybe a little
bit more than Martin, but not as much as I could have if
I were really there.

I picked up on enough to think that Martin was right. The man was hunting. He was scanning the crowd of children for prey. His fingers drummed nervously on the bench as he abruptly crossed one leg over the other, leaning forward to conceal his lap. His head moved slightly to the left and then to the right—he was following Tyler Matthews as the little boy swung across the monkey bars.

Tyler's mother called out to her son and the man slumped back, disappointed, as the boy ran across the grass toward his mother.

"I wish my mother were still alive," Martin said suddenly. "She would know what to do." He sounded breathless, the panic returning. "I don't know who will believe me, I just don't . . ." He began to describe his neighbors in turn, searching for an ally. "Mr. Novak thinks I'm a bum; he'll call the police on me. The Johnsons are never home. There's that new lady, but she doesn't know me from Adam, and she probably won't even answer the door. Oh." He stopped abruptly and sat upright. I felt relief flowing through him. "There is that nice lady who lives on the corner, the one with hydrangeas and the water garden. Mom always said she was very kind, very smart. She used to tell me to run to her when I was little if ever something bad happened and she wasn't around. She said if anyone knew what to do, that lady would know. What was her name?" He frowned, not remembering, but I knew: her name was Noni Bates.

"I'm going to go ask her what to do," he decided, talking to himself. "I think her name is Mrs. Bates."

He led us through walking to Noni's house. He described the scene in Noni's garden and her kindness, how her voice calmed him and made him feel as if he was not imagining things. He talked of how he decided it would be better to enter the park from the back so she could observe the man without him knowing.

"I take her the back way," he told the therapist, Miranda. "Even though it is longer. She does not mind. She wants to get to know me. She is asking me questions. I like her. I think she will be my friend."

And yet I'd been right behind the two of them, convinced Martin was about to strangle her and leave her for dead. So much for my intuition.

I concentrated on being one with Martin as he spoke, anxious to know if he had felt my presence on any level. As I merged more fully with him, I could feel the sun on my skin, smell the fragrance of flowers as we walked past. I could hear Noni's gentle voice as she asked about his mother and Martin's droning monotone as she let him prattle on about sauces and bread and basil-flavored ice cream. And then we were there, at the rear entrance to the park, just before the bushes where Noni had spotted the rabbits.

And I saw it.

A blue station wagon was parked exactly in the spot where my search earlier in the day had led me after I discovered the plastic dinosaur in the grass. I had followed Tyler Matthews's essence to the space where the car was parked, only to find bare asphalt. But this was earlier, hours earlier, before the boy had been taken, and I could see quite clearly through Martin's eyes that the abductor had driven a blue Toyota Matrix station wagon, license plate number RPK6992.

I was back in business.

I wanted to leave that very moment and find the car, but I was afraid to sever my connection with Martin abruptly. I had begun to wonder about my role in Martin's ability to delve so deeply. How much did my being there have to do with the clarity of his memories? I forced myself to stay while Miranda led him through the rest of the morning, to the arrival of the police cars at the cottage across the

street, to Calvano's mistreatment of him and the shame
he felt at being suspected, to his horror when he heard he
had been right and a child had been taken.

By the time he was done and Miranda had brought
him back to the present, Martin was exhausted. But Calvano and Maggie now had a lot more to go on—and so
did I. I had a car. Cars could be found.

"You were very brave," Miranda told Martin at the end
of the session. "They may find the little boy because of
you."

Martin swelled with pride and something shifted in
him, as if, in undergoing the experience, he had become
someone new.

"Here." Miranda slid her business card across the table
toward him. "I want you to take my card. I'm a therapist,
too, you know." Her voice was kind. She was quite good
at being kind. "If you ever want to talk, just about things,
I want you to call me. Something like this can be trau-
matic. I have a sliding fee scale, so you'll be able to afford
it. Or maybe you'd like to go get a coffee one day? I'd love
to talk with you again."

"Talk about things?" Martin asked. "What kind of
things?"

"Oh," she said casually, "what you want out of life.
How you feel about your life. We can maybe even talk
about the past, if you want."

Their eyes met and something private passed between
them.

It was time for me to go.

Chapter 15

I knew whoever had taken the boy was still in town. The AMBER Alert had gone out within minutes, cameras had been activated at all intersections, they had traffic stops set up at the major exit points, and the face of Tyler Matthews was plastered on every website and television screen in town. The police didn't have a vehicle description the way I did, but they knew to look for a four-year-old boy, and soon they'd have at least a half-assed description of the abductor out to the field, thanks to Robert Michael Martin.

It would be tough for anyone to move around with the kid. And what the abductor wanted from him could be done anywhere that offered privacy. To me, that meant that it was likely that whoever had the boy was hiding right here in my town. I knew what car he drove, and I would find him.

I left the station house just as the FBI agents arrived to take over the case: four men in suits. I passed them in the lobby and they felt like a single person, their individuality sublimated to such a degree that I could not differentiate the essence of each. What happened when their working days were done? Did they go back to being unique, or simply half exist? Still, the department needed them, and I was glad they were there.

I had to be systematic about my search. Nearly one hundred thousand people live in my town, sprawled across a seven-square-mile area that ranges in density from packed housing projects to meandering subdivisions parceled out in multi-acre lots. It would take me days to search each street, alleyway, driveway, and garage, even moving as fast as I was able. And I could not afford to overlook a single home.

I began by searching the neighborhoods to the west of headquarters, a grimy area where people lived paycheck to paycheck, if they were lucky enough to have one, and where both disappointment and resentment rained down on me from the apartment windows above. I had answered plenty of calls in this neighborhood when alive and had rousted more prostitutes than a cruise ship could hold. But I had never really looked at the women before, thinking them all the same. As I searched up and down the urban blocks, night fell and the women began to appear on the corners, and I saw beyond the heavy makeup and ridiculous outfits for the first time. I saw weary, frightened, and defeated human beings, marking time, waiting for it all to be over, looking for a way to forget they were here.

I saw no sign of the blue station wagon, though, and felt no trace of the boy. I left the industrial lights behind and kept searching.

I began to encounter neighborhoods like the one I'd once taken for granted, tidy and comforting in the gathering dusk. Lights winked on behind curtains, televisions blared, children shrieked with laughter as they chased each other across lawns and dreamed of the coming summer. Smells wafted through the air, tantalizing reminders of people gathering to break bread together. Children were being bathed and loved and read to; couples were falling into bed after lingering glances; the weary were putting their feet up and enjoying the silence. All of the rituals I had run from while alive now surrounded me, mocked me, reminding me of what I had given up.

I shook off the regret and kept going.

On and on, down every street, exploring every garage, nook, or alley that might conceal a car. I searched and willed myself to pick up on every nuance of fear or evil or innocence I could possibly detect. By morning I was exhausted. I was filled with the details of thousands of lives, and burdened by hundreds of dreams plus far too many secrets for one man, in any incarnation, to bear by himself. I had not understood that sampling so many lives would prove so draining. I had not found the boy, nor found the car, and I needed to rest.

I ended up on a familiar block east of the town center just as the morning rush trickled into the hush of a weekday morning in a residential neighborhood. Tidy brick bungalows and small clapboard houses lined each side of the street, their yards barely big enough to require mowing.

Of course. This was the street where Rosemary D'Amato, the mother of the boy who had been taken sixteen years ago, lived, unable to move for fear her son might return one day and find no one at home. This was where I had discovered my little otherworldly friend, sitting in the crook of a tree.

I was lonely. Perhaps he was there.

As I moved up the sidewalk, I passed a young mother pushing her newborn in a stroller and looking anxiously over her shoulder. No one would feel safe until Tyler Matthews was found. The morning held a familiar air—the

fear and the street intertwined—until, through a memory
fogged by bourbon and infidelity and one endless hang-
over, I recalled my role in the D'Amato abduction case
more clearly. *How could I possibly have forgotten the taking of a small boy? Could I really have been so callous?*
My old partner Danny and I had been one of the teams
assigned to the case, I remembered, but it had been taken
from us before the day was over. I guess word had gotten
out by then that you didn't give Fahey and Bonaventura
a priority case, not if you wanted the department to solve
it or look good in the media. After a day of flounder-
ing through fruitless interviews with other patrons of the
rest stop where the boy had been taken, I remembered
clearly that we had been walking up this very sidewalk
to question the parents further when a department sedan
had pulled up to the curb and a pair of younger detectives
had jumped out to let us know that we had orders to stand
down, that they were taking over. I remember looking at
Danny and shrugging with appalling apathy before we
wandered off to find a bar where we could drink away the
bruising of our egos. No one at the department had even
noticed we were gone when we returned to the squad
room, hours later, reeking of whiskey and cigarettes.

I cringed, remembering who I had been.

I had not followed the D'Amato case much after that. It
was a reminder of what a loser I had been, so I had willed
myself to forget it. All I really knew was that the boy
had never been found, nor had his body ever been found,
and that I may have spent a happy hour pushing him on a
swing in the park yesterday.

I was now hoping to find him in the tree.

Alas, with the exception of a mother robin that was
guarding her nest and gave no notice of me, the tree was
empty. I sat at its base and looked up at the house beside
it, wondering how Bobby D'Amato's mother had ever

found the strength to go on living after her son had simply evaporated from her life. How had she survived what Callie Matthews was going through now? As I was thinking of this, the door opened and Mrs. D'Amato stepped out onto her front porch, carrying a bouquet of white roses and baby's breath as if she were a bride in search of a groom. Curious, I hitched a ride when she hopped into her car. Why not? I needed a break and, wherever she was headed, I'd keep my eye out for a blue Toyota station wagon, license plate number RPK6992.

I made myself comfortable in the back, where a child's booster seat was still strapped into place by a shoulder harness, cracker crumbs embedded in its seams, having waited sixteen years for its occupant to return.

Rosemary D'Amato pressed a button on the CD player, startling me with the blare of Beatles music. When I glanced at the booster seat again, there he was: my little friend, happily ensconced in his harness straps, bobbing his head along to "Maxwell's Silver Hammer," a grin on his face as he and his mom headed out for a ride. He gave no notice that he even saw me. Certainly, he did not care that I was there, too.

He was a fickle little bastard. I would not have minded another session in the park, but he had no use for me today. He was content to sit and watch the town rush by.

I think he knew where we were going. He had taken this trip before. Me? It was not until Mrs. D'Amato pulled through the iron gate of the cemetery that I understood. She was there to visit her son's grave, not knowing he had tagged along for the ride.

I remembered then how parenthood had been a terrifying mixture of joy, hope, and fear. Rosemary D'Amato was the embodiment of the inherent conflicts between them. She had consented to a grave for her missing child—but she had never given up hope that he might one day return. Had the grave been a compromise forged between her and her husband? Was it acknowledgment that he was right in urging her to accept the unthinkable? Or did she simply need a temple to his memory, a place where she could go and talk to him without the world telling her she had to move on?

The sun was climbing in the morning sky. The trees that lined the lanes of the cemetery were in full bloom, and their white blossoms floated on the breeze like a spring snow shower. It was an exquisite day to visit the dead; it was even an exquisite day to be among the dead. But as we pulled up to the section that bordered the far fence of the cemetery, my little otherworldly friend grew agitated. His eyes narrowed and I could feel him grow wary. Sorrow and something else, perhaps even anger, rose in him. He stared out the car window as if seeing something I did not see. Did he feel betrayed that his mother had moved on, even if she was just going through the motions?

I followed Rosemary D'Amato from the car, ready for a walk through what I like to call the Library of Souls. I loved the cemetery. I loved the neat categorization of the dead, the finality of the names and dates carved on the granite, and the intricate relationships marked by their designations: mother, father, beloved daughter, son, generation after generation flowering before moving on, family made eternal because life will always find a way.

I felt a flash of unexpectedly strong emotions from an unseen source: panic, remorse, longing, sorrow. *Where did that come from?* Was I picking up on the lingering emotions of the dead who lay beneath me, or was there someone hidden in the hardwood trees clustered to the right of the cemetery section before us? Mrs. D'Amato did not appear to notice anything but the lawn in front of her. She picked her way across the grass, carefully stepping around granite markers as she walked toward her son's grave. I felt a shadow cross my heart even as I saw a shadow kiss the outer edges of the lawn.

A man hid in the trees.

He was deep in the darkness of the grove's overhanging canopy and concealed from outside eyes—but he was there. I stood very still. After a moment of probing, I could feel his heart beating even from a distance. It was a rapid but steady beat, one fueled by an odd mixture of regret and yearning and fear.

The little boy—he might know what it was all about. But when I looked around, my otherworldly friend was gone. He had not stayed to meet the man in the trees.

As Mrs. D'Amato knelt in front of her son's grave and laid the white roses before his headstone, I saw the man in the grove start to dart through the trees, away from her, the panic in him rising. I followed. He kept to the shadows, winding his way through the perimeter of undeveloped growth that rimmed the cemetery. He reached a section divided by the end of the asphalt drive and dashed across it, then took to the open ground, running across the graves in his haste to escape. I picked up speed, flowing past the names and years of those who had gone before me. I could sense anger in the man now, and resentment. Something had been taken from him. He reached a small stone house where the caretaker stored his tools. He ducked behind it. I heard a car door slam—he had parked his car behind the structure where no one could see it. I picked up speed, hoping to catch him. But he was already in the car and on his way out by the time I reached the road in front of the stone house. I could do nothing but stand there as the car swept through me, filling me with the tornado of conflicting emotions that coiled inside the man. He was there and then he was gone.

I could do nothing but stare after the car winding its way toward the cemetery entrance: it was a blue Toyota Matrix station wagon, license plate number RPK6992.

Chapter 16

When I was alive, I had loved car chases. They were an excuse to unleash my recklessness. My old partner, Danny, would brace himself against the dashboard, whooping in drunken glee as I floored the car, sped through red lights, passed other cars inches before oncoming traffic hit us, rocketed around curves at insane speeds, and transformed my ever-present death wish into a series of terrifying yet exhilarating experiences.

It's different when you're on foot.

I reached the front gate of the cemetery just in time to see the blue station wagon pull through it and turn right, driving swiftly down a neighborhood street toward a nearby boulevard. I had a chance of keeping up if he kept to the side streets. He reached the intersection and, mercifully, a red light stalled him while I made up ground. The light changed when I was still a quarter block away, but the man did not turn onto the boulevard. He zoomed across the intersection and entered a neighborhood on the far side of it, one of the ubiquitous newer developments with wide, flat yards that had mushroomed all over town starting a few decades ago. I followed and saw the car turn left down a winding road that led me back deep into streets that all looked alike with names that all sounded alike and with homes that featured identical plans distinguished only by minor façade variations like the front stoop design or window placement. If I'd been human, I'd never have been able to find my way out again. But the driver knew where he was going. He made a quick right onto a paved road that took him nearly to the edge of a central lake. Although once our town's reservoir, it had been converted into a boating and fishing paradise that doubled the value of the homes surrounding it. The blue Toyota followed the road around the lake's shoreline for a half mile, then turned left and disappeared. If he'd turned onto a road with a lot of turns leading off it, I was in trouble.

The road had only a few turns. The first right turn was a cul-de-sac with five houses arranged around it in a horseshoe pattern. Each yard was landscaped with such a profusion of bushes, trees, and flowers that you could barely see the houses beyond.

The Toyota was parked in the driveway of a small cedar-shingled house nestled in an explosion of greenery at the top of the cul-de-sac. The curtains were closed, the lights were off, and a rotating security camera scanned the area near the front door in increments. Home-monitoring-service signs dotted the yard, but they meant nothing to me. Death has its perks. Invisibility is one of them.

The man I had seen running from the cemetery, the same one Martin had seen in the park the morning Tyler Matthews was abducted, was standing on the front stoop, unlocking dead bolt after dead bolt, a bulging plastic bag from Wal-Mart looped over one arm. When he stepped inside, I followed.

Little Tyler Matthews was sitting with his back to a large television set, ignoring the cartoons that raced and blasted behind him in favor of a set of plastic barnyard animals that he had carefully arranged in a tidy tableau of barn, fence, cows, pigs, chickens, and ducks. Plastic horses had been lined up on the carpet nearby so that they appeared to be grazing. The boy looked unharmed and, indeed, untouched. He was wearing the same T-shirt and shorts he'd had on when he'd been taken. On the couch, I saw a pillow and rumpled blanket and guessed that he had fallen asleep there the night before.

I felt no one else in the house. The boy seemed unperturbed at having been left alone and greeted the return of the man who had taken him with an innocent, trusting look. He also seemed completely unaware that the living room where he sat was rigged with four different cameras so that his every move was captured in detail. I did not know if the cameras were broadcasting live over the Internet or were in place for a future day. I did not want to think about it either.

"What did you bring me?" the boy asked in a high, piping voice. He was holding a pig in each hand, snout to snout, as if they had been having an imaginary conversation.

The man dropped to one knee, and his voice was friendly. "I brought you some mac and cheese—the kind you said you liked, with the little wagon wheels—and some chocolate milk and a bag of doughnuts as a treat." He spoke very carefully to the boy, as if he wanted to show his innocence the respect it deserved.

"My mommy doesn't let me eat doughnuts," the boy explained matter-of-factly. "They aren't very good for you."

"I think one or two would be okay," the man assured him. "We don't have to tell your mommy."

"Is she coming to get me soon?" The boy sounded hopeful.

"I'm not sure," the man said. He folded his gangly arms and legs in on himself and sat in front of the boy, then pulled some new toys from his shopping bag. "In the meantime, I thought you might like some soldiers. I liked soldiers when I was your age." He freed a set of a dozen plastic toy soldiers from their see-through prison and arranged them on the carpet for the boy. Unlike the crudely molded army men of my own childhood, these were carefully designed fighting men of the modern era, immaculately painted with bright daubs of yellow and red and blue for accents. Many of them carried the weapons of their specialty: bazookas, missiles, rifles, radios. They were irresistible to any young boy.

The boy smiled at the soldiers and that smile took my breath away. He was exquisitely beautiful, with large, dark eyes rimmed with thick, black eyelashes. His curly brown hair fell into his face in cherubic loops. His skin was a perfect, creamy pink and his tiny mouth pursed in concentration as he examined his new army. "My daddy was a solider," he said, excited, as he gazed up at the man.

"You mean he is a soldier?" the man asked.

"No," the little boy said, again matter-of-factly. "A bad man killed him and now he got dead." He knocked over one of the plastic soldiers with another one and then dragged the toy to a place by the barn. "Me and Mommy buried him and some real soldiers shot off their guns. It was very loud. Mommy said not to cry, so I didn't. She said I was very brave afterward and gave me an extrabig piece of cake."

The man was startled at this information. I felt a flicker of shame in him, which told me that he had not known the boy personally and that he'd had no idea the boy's father had been killed in Iraq last year.

"Are you hungry?" he asked the boy, who nodded solemnly. "Would you like some mac and cheese now?" Tyler nodded again.

As the man rose from the carpet, a voice came out of nowhere, echoing through the room, deep and disembodied. "Do not feed the boy too much. I prefer them thin." It was an order, uttered by a man who expected to be obeyed. Short and to the point, leaving no room for argument.

The boy looked up, unconcerned at this intrusion, and returned to his toys. The man who had taken him did not react so casually. I felt the agitation in him rise and give way to a tumble of emotions triggered by the voice. Where first I had felt nothing in him but sympathy toward the little boy, I now felt anger in the man, accompanied by a desire to hurt, a need to exert power, and something much darker, something very much like lust. Whoever the disembodied voice belonged to, he had complete power over the man who had taken Tyler Matthews.

The man walked toward the kitchen and spoke into a camera affixed to the edge of the door, speaking low so the boy would not notice. "He has to eat."

"I do not want you to spoil him." The deep voice had a dark quality hidden beneath it, as if the real danger lay in all the things he was not saying out loud.

"How can I possibly spoil him in a few days?" the man who had taken Tyler argued. The fear in him rose, though, as if he knew he was daring to push his boundaries.

"You misunderstand me," the voice said, then repeated more precisely: "I do not want you to *spoil* him."

The man in the house froze. "I would never do that," he said in a flat voice.

The laughter that answered him was so rife with evil it turned my heart to ice. It started out low, then grew in volume, as if it were alive and had fattened itself on cynicism and carnal desire and was now filled with a satisfied certainty that no man could resist taking the fruit from the tree. "We shall see," the voice said as the laughter tapered off. "We shall see."

There was a moment of silence as the man in the apartment looked at the floor, stifling the hatred and fear and, yes, desire that flickered in him. He looked up, startled, as the voice boomed suddenly from the webcam's speakers: "Turn him!"

"What?" The man still held the groceries in his hands.

"Turn the boy around so I can see him better."

The man in the house put the chocolate milk and frozen dinners down on the counter without a word and returned to the living room. "Hey, little buddy," he said in his most soothing voice. "Why don't we rearrange the farm and soldiers so you can watch TV at the same time?"

Before the boy could react, the man moved the toys and then gently turned the boy so his face was visible to a camera mounted on the far wall. The man gauged the distance between the boy and the camera, then carefully inched him back a bit. Satisfied, he stepped out of camera range and returned to the kitchen.

He was met with soft laughter from the unseen man on the way, laughter that told me the man was utterly confident in his ability to control what happened to Tyler Matthews next.

I knew it was only a matter of time. I had to find a way to get help.

Chapter 17

My town was in turmoil. That much was evident
everywhere I went. It had been invaded by the media
and infused with a hysteria you could feel on the streets.
Not even the missing boy's mother, Callie Matthews—
already a widow and now facing every parent's worst
nightmare—was spared the ugliness of speculation. And
this from people who knew her, not strangers.

I knew all this because I searched for Maggie at the
dead nurse's cottage first, then stopped by the park looking for my little otherworldly friend in hopes he was up
for another playground session. I needed some respite
from the evil I'd sensed in the cedar-shingled house near
the lake. Instead, I found a group of mothers, heads bent
together as their children played nearby for television
crews with nothing better to film than cheesy re-creations
of Tyler's last moments before he was taken.

"She's unstable, is my point," one of the mothers was

whispering to the others. "She's taking a lot of pills. Who knows what that can do to a person?"

"Tyler is her life," another disagreed. "She's not going to hurt him."

"She couldn't fake what she's going through," another agreed. "She's devastated."

"They're all devastated when people are watching," yet another mother insisted. "She could easily have lost it if he disobeyed her. You've seen how she gets. Was Tyler even here yesterday? I don't remember seeing him. Neither does Chelsea, and she is a very observant child."

"Oh, for God's sake, he was here," a stocky woman said with disgust. She walked away from the other mothers, ignoring the cameras, called her child to her, and left the park, probably wondering, as I did, what it was about tragedy that made people salivate and become so anxious to believe that even the best among us were capable of evil. I sympathized with her frustration, but I watched her go with sadness—her obvious rebuff of the group could cause a permanent rift. Crimes like this had a way of sending out fractures like earthquakes lead to fissures, carving divides that separate people and spread out in unpredictable directions, driving a wedge of destruction between friends and loved ones.

I left the park behind and went in search of Maggie. She was not at the station house, which was besieged by media vans. My guess was that Callie Matthews was inside being interviewed by the feds and that Gonzales would emerge as soon as the cameras were set up and the frenzy of reporters had reached the size of a large wolf pack. He'd appear, get his next five minutes of fame, then disappear back inside to cover the department's ass and plot his next move toward fame and fortune.

I kept going.

Maggie is a predictable creature, and she leads a soli-

tary life. I know her routine like my own, in part because
the patterns of her life fascinate me. She lives alone in a
condo and is friendly to her neighbors, but never stops to
chat with any of them; she works out at a gym four times
a week whenever she can, depending on her caseload; she
shops at a small market owned by a Korean couple who
save the best fruit and produce for her behind the counter;
she seldom buys anything that comes in a package, as she
is careful about what she eats, and her body shows it: she
is not a thin woman, but she is in superb condition and the
epitome of health and strength. It is one of the reasons I
remain so enamored of her after other infatuations have
come and gone. Everything about her celebrates life. She
is impossible for someone like me to resist. I am a moth
to her flame.

I checked her condo, then the market, the gym, and
a coffee shop she sometimes frequents for skinny lattes
sweetened with a shot of sugar-free vanilla syrup. When
none of those spots panned out, I knew she had to be at
her father's. She always ended up there at one time or
another during a difficult case, as well she should. Her
father, Colin, had spent ten years on the streets as a beat
cop and thirty more as a detective, rejecting all promo-
tions and attempts to pull him onto the department ladder
in favor of working the front line. He'd been allowed to
stay on well past standard retirement age and had only
left when, eventually, the ill health of his wife forced him
to. Maggie's mother had died a few years ago and, though
I had been too drunk and self-centered to notice it then,
I felt the sting of her loss in both daughter and husband.
Maggie and her father carried their sorrow around like
internal wounds that time did not seem to heal. Perhaps
she had been the glue that bound them.

I had not worked much with Colin Gunn when he was
on the force. Looking back, I realized it was because I had

not passed his worthiness test. Like dozens of burnouts before me, I had been placed in a category he avoided, because he was too busy getting the job done—including the jobs I was failing to do. He didn't waste his energy on losers like me. I can't say he was wrong.

Maggie was a lot like her father. She kept her head down, she never gave up, and she didn't waste much energy on the inevitable segment of the force that failed to pull its own weight, a group that included her partner, Calvano.

It was too bad Calvano was such a lousy partner. Maggie was not a talkative person by nature. She preferred to listen and to watch others talk; it told her much more about them than their words alone ever could. The exception was when she was working a difficult case. She liked to talk her way through the data, seeking a path among the collected evidence. If she'd had a decent partner, he would have been the perfect choice to listen, but since Gonzales always saddled her with losers in hopes of bringing them up closer to Maggie's level, she had started to turn to her father for advice.

I found them sitting on the front porch of Colin's house, his wheelchair pulled up next to Maggie's rocking chair. To my surprise, Peggy Calhoun was with them, a brown bag lunch open on her lap. She, too, had probably sought refuge from the media madness and left her lab for the quieter quarters of Colin Gunn's world.

"It's crazy," Maggie was telling her father as I settled into my favorite spot, a seat on the front step where I could lean back against a pillar and pretend to be a part of their family. Maggie never sensed I was there, but Colin? Sometimes, when he and I had the exact same thought at the exact same time, he'd look over to where I was sitting as if he could actually see me. It was an unconscious gesture on his part, but a thrill would zing through me nonetheless as I sensed a possibility coalescing in his mind before it was just as swiftly dismissed—Colin Gunn was not the type of man to believe in ghosts. He would not even allow himself to entertain the possibility.

I guess the joke was on him.

Maggie was frustrated in that charming way she gets when others are blocking her path. "You would not even believe what the quartet from Quantico are like," she told her father.

"I can believe it, Maggie May," he interrupted. "Trust me, I can believe it."

"Gonzales has told me to steer clear of them, but to keep poking around into the boy's disappearance, using the nurse's death as a cover."

"That's Gonzales for you. He wants to have his cake and eat it, too. Always has. He's a smart one. Smarter than me, god knows." Her father smiled proudly. "He likes you, Maggie. As he should. Keep it that way. He's going to end up owning this town. He's a good man to have on your side and a terrible man to have as an enemy."

"I can try," Maggie protested. "But I don't see how anyone can do their job when we're tripping over television cameras every time we turn around. And you should see the mother. They've had to dope her even more than usual just to face all those lights and shouted questions. It's insane. It's cruel. She's like an animal on display in a zoo. How is anyone going to find the boy with all of that in the way?"

Wow, she really was frustrated. This was not like my Maggie.

"I know," her father said sympathetically. "But that's the way it works these days, and all you can do is try to turn it to your advantage. Think of it this way: the whole state knows what little Tyler Matthews looks like now, as does most of the country, I'd imagine. That's a good thing."

Maggie's face clouded over. She hated to say what she was about to add to their conversation. "But you know he's unlikely to be alive, Dad. You know how long it's been. He probably didn't survive the first twenty-four hours."

"There's always hope, Maggie. There's always hope. What is this? We're Irish and we Irish have nothing, if not hope. What leads do you have?"

"Robert Michael Martin was able to give us a little to go on in terms of a description," Maggie explained. "Now Calvano is going through a list of license plate numbers while the rest of the special team is wading through an unbelievably long list of names that some former-military, overbearing, self-styled hero who runs some operation called KinderWatch has given them. Supposedly, it's a log of anyone seeking underage contact online in a five-state radius or some such nonsense. Everyone calls the guy 'the colonel' and he sits in his wheelchair like he's sitting on a throne, issuing orders like we're his grunts." She thumped the side of her father's wheelchair. "Trust me, you could run circles around him."

Colin Gunn looked at his daughter. "Are you saying we cripples need to learn to sit quietly and behave ourselves?"

"It's not that, Dad," she said, looking ashamed. This was a new look for her. It was adorable. "It's that he sits there, casting aspersions on everyone but the mayor, suggesting so-and-so might be doing this or that, and though he hasn't the proof, he's pretty sure they're dirty, and then, after pointing the finger at six dozen people . . . he just sits there, while everyone else runs off and does all the work. It's annoying. And it's counterproductive. But the feds are taking him and his list very seriously."

"I guess you're over your love of men in uniform?" her father asked, but a glance from Peggy warned him to say no more. I wondered what that look had been all about. Maggie's past was a mystery to me.

"He acts like everyone is under his command. You'd hate him, too."

"I'm surprised I haven't met him," Colin said. "There's only one wheelchair accessible VA van for the ride to Trenton. What's his name again?"

"Colonel William Vitek, retired, US Marines Corps."

"I'll be sure to keep an eye out for him, and hate him on sight when I do meet him. Of course, hating authority is a bit sticky when you have to depend on the Veterans Administration for your health care."

"Oh, you would hate him if you met him," Maggie said stubbornly. "Trust me."

"Rosemary D'Amato came into the station house again," Peggy told Colin, deciding it was time to change the subject. I was intrigued by the familiarity of her tone toward Maggie's father—had she been visiting the old man without Maggie around? I watched them for a few minutes until I was sure. *She had.* Why, that little vixen.

I enjoyed watching the way Colin Gunn looked at Peggy. To some, she was just a woman of a certain age with improbably red hair, cat's-eye glasses looped around her neck on a chain, and that ill-advised orange lipstick that always, inevitably, ended up on her teeth. But she was also a remarkably dedicated woman, who knew the mysteries of the earth's most minute worlds like no one else I had ever met. Her weapon was her microscope and she found justice for many families on that tiny battlefield. She was a scientist, but she was a wizard, too, one whose empathy for those who were grieving knew no boundaries. It had taken death to make me appreciate Peggy Calhoun, but appreciate her I did.

So did Colin Gunn, I thought to myself as I watched the way he looked at her and responded. One man's old lady was another man's younger woman, I reminded my-self. I think I liked knowing that about the world.

"That was a sad case," Colin remembered. "Little Bobby D'Amato. Your old partner, Bonaventura, caught part of it," he said to Maggie. "He and Fahey."

Maggie looked up at my name and my heart soared.

"Which was a disaster," Colin went on. *Ouch.* "I went to the chief when I heard and he pulled it and gave it to another team, but by then it was too late. We'd lost the first day and had to play catch-up from then on out."

Double ouch.

"Their son being taken split the D'Amatos up," Colin said sadly. "They stayed married, but in name only. That's always the way it goes. A child gets taken and you sit back and wait, knowing the marriage will never be the same, not when it's a reminder of what they've lost."

"She still lives in the same house," Peggy told him. "Still comes into the department to see if they have found anything new."

"That was a long time ago," Colin conceded. "But it's worse when you don't find a body. People can live the rest of their lives without being able to put it behind them."

"I don't want that to happen with Tyler Matthews," Maggie said. "God knows, I don't. But I'm not seeing what I can do."

"Maggie," her father said firmly. "Your job is to leave the boy to the others." He raised his eyebrows at her when she started to protest, and that alone caused her to remain silent. "There are plenty of people working that little boy's case, doing more than you could ever do for him. If anything breaks, Peggy here can tell you." He looked up and Peggy nodded. "Your duty is to that dead nurse. Where is she in all this?"

"Forgotten," Maggie said promptly. "Who cares about

a dead thirtysomething woman with no husband and no children? It makes for a lousy sound bite."

I think it is safe to say that everyone else on that porch, including me, heard the things that Maggie did not say in that sentence: she was a lot like Fiona Harker.

"It is frightening," Peggy agreed. "I could not get over the loneliness of her house. But, Maggie, she isn't you."

And this *isn't you*, I wanted to say. It was not like my Maggie to be sitting around, whining, when she could be relentlessly pursuing a lead.

Colin picked up on my thoughts. "Have you got any leads?" he asked his daughter. "Surely you've been interviewing her coworkers?"

Maggie shrugged. "I have gossip and innuendo."

You have Christian Fletcher, I wanted to shout. *He's a big, fat lead if ever I saw one.*

"Doesn't every lead start with gossip and innuendo?" her father asked gently.

"The nurses think she was having an affair with a married doctor."

"There you have it," her father said, spreading his arms. "A place to start."

"Except she likes the guy," Peggy said abruptly. They all let the comment lie there for a moment. I wanted to jump up and wave my arms and start shouting at Maggie: *No, leave that guy alone.*

"She likes what guy?" Colin Gunn finally asked.

"The doctor all the nurses think the dead nurse was having the affair with," Peggy said flatly. "When you told me about it, I could tell from your tone of voice that you liked him, Maggie."

"Traitor," Maggie muttered.

Peggy felt no need to apologize. She wanted the old Maggie back as much as I did.

"You cannot let your personal feelings interfere," her father told her. "Take yourself off the case."

"I can't," Maggie explained. "There's no one left to take it. They're all too busy running around in circles looking for the boy."

"Then get off your ass and go to the hospital," Colin suggested. "I don't care who you like or who you don't like. What is that nurse's name again? The victim?"

"Fiona," Maggie said. "Fiona Harker."

"Who?" Colin asked.

"Fiona Harker."

"Say her name one more time," her father ordered.

"Fiona Harker," Maggie said more loudly.

"Good. Now don't you forget she has a name. And don't you forget that this Fiona Harker is depending on you. You are all she has. Without you, she has no hope of justice. Without you, her killer gets to walk this earth free. And he will do it again. You and I both know that when someone gets away with murder, it eats at him and it invites him to try to get away with it again. It becomes as addictive as any drug. Getting away with murder is impossible to resist. You have to stop him, Maggie. You can't afford to have personal feelings, not about who might have done this."

"I know," she said, sitting up straighter. "I don't know what's the matter with me."

Peggy smiled ruefully. She knew. She knew all too well: Maggie was lonely. All those days of working long hours deep into the night, breakfasts alone in a silent house, nights spent with plenty of room on either side of her in bed, no one to share her triumphs and problems with . . . it was all taking a toll. I'd never understand why some people, like my new friend, Noni Bates, could embrace their solitude and not feel loneliness, while others, like Robert Michael Martin, felt it eating away at their sense of self, pulling them out to sea like an undertow.

My Maggie had become one of the lonely ones.

"Do your job," her father told her. His voice was kind. "First, do your job."

Maggie stood and kissed her father on the cheek. "I love you, Pop. And thanks. I needed that. I'm heading over to the hospital now."

"That's my girl," he called after her as Maggie skipped down the steps, inches from me. I wanted to touch her, but she slipped past as gracefully as a breeze.

"What did I teach you?" Colin Gunn yelled after his daughter.

Maggie turned, hands on her hips. "Fiona Harker," she said distinctly.

"That's right," her father said. His voice was full of pride. I realized that Colin missed the hunt and that Maggie was his surrogate. "Bring it home for Fiona."

As Maggie drove away, determined to regain her stride, Peggy affectionately ruffled Colin's thick hair. "She needs someone in her life," Peggy told him.

"But you don't," Colin said with a grin. "Not anymore." They kissed and then he smiled at her, his eyes twinkling with the light of a much younger man.

Chapter 18

I knew where Tyler Matthews was, but I was alone in my knowledge. I had no choice but to keep following Maggie—she was my best hope of getting through. I told myself that the child was safe for now, that the man he was with had good inside him—I had felt it—and that Tyler's innocence would be enough to keep that good alive for at least a little longer. But I had to find a way of letting Maggie know where he was. I did not think the kidnapper could hold out forever, not with the other man egging him on. The unseen man's voice had been more than evil; it had celebrated evil. I knew he must be hiding behind a cloak of respectability if he had sent another to do his dirty work in the park. What was his endgame? Whatever it was, it could not be good for the boy. I had to let Maggie know.

I try to control my baser human emotions. I really do. I know they won't be the ones to get me into heaven, if such a place exists. But I admit to feeling relief when

Maggie bypassed the emergency room, where the sainted Dr. Christian Fletcher worked, and headed for pediatric oncology, where Fletcher's wife served as chief. It was a good move on Maggie's part. If you want to get the dirt on someone, ask a soon-to-be-ex-spouse.

Word had gotten out among the nurses about Maggie's last visit. I saw the curious looks as she passed by and the troubled frowns as they remembered that one of their own had been lost. Maggie noticed none of this. Her concentration was focused solely on the task ahead. I felt relief at this, too. Her mind was back on the case.

The pediatric oncology ward was in one of the newer wings in the hospital. It was painted in cheery primary colors and the walls were lined with scenes from fairy tales. I don't think the patients noticed, though, at least not the ones I could see. Most were pale and wan, bald from chemotherapy and radiation treatments, and far too drained to do much more than lie in bed, eyes closed, as they tried to escape the pain. Their heads looked so small against their pillows. It did not seem fair that they should be here, suffering such intense physical pain before their lives had barely begun, when others who were much older, who had abused their bodies with drugs and alcohol and bad food for decades, thrived without consequence.

A tall doctor with long blonde hair pulled back in an elegant ponytail passed Maggie. She was trailed by a group of expensively dressed women who left a cloud of perfume in their wake. It had to be the other Dr. Fletcher, courting donors and donors' wives. She was extolling the virtues of the new ward with the ease of a tour guide, unaware that some of her guests were fighting back tears at the sight of so many young patients. This Dr. Fletcher did not give Maggie a single glance; she swept past her with the dismissive air of one who is used to being the most important person in the room.

Maggie reached the nurse's station and showed her badge to the plump black woman behind the counter. "Was that Dr. Fletcher?" she asked.

"She's Dr. Holman, now," the nurse explained, her eyes lingering on Maggie's credentials. "She's gone back to her maiden name."

"What's her full name?" Maggie asked, using her warm-up tone, the one that lets people know she represents authority and she's just getting started with the questions.

"Serena Holman," the nurse answered quickly.

"You keep her schedule?" Maggie asked.

The woman looked surprised. "Me? No. Dr. Holman keeps her own schedule."

"We're not competent enough, don't you know?" a nurse with short black hair broke in. She had one of those long, expressive mouths that signals her interior motives—but only when she wanted it to. She was smiling in a bitter, practiced way that made me think she had to defer to Dr. Holman far too often for her taste.

"Dr. Holman is tough on the nurses?" Maggie asked. She was doing that chameleon thing she does so well, where she can fit in with anyone at their level, becoming one of the boys just as easily as one of the girls, putting rich people at ease just as effortlessly as the poor.

"That's one way of putting it," the second nurse said. She snapped a file shut and handed it to the first nurse. "No change at all," she told her. "And I'm going to let you be the one to tell Dr. Holman that."

The first nurse looked terrified, and I wondered just how hard Dr. Holman was on the nurses.

"How long has she been separated from her husband?" Maggie asked them.

They stared at each other, trying to decide how much

to say. The second nurse looked up at Maggie. "You're the detective looking into Fiona's murder, right?"

"Right," Maggie confirmed.

That was good enough for her. "Dr. Holman went back to her maiden name about a month ago. I heard they're still living together, though. Neither one of them wants to be the first to move out of their house because of legal reasons."

"It's a *really* nice house," the first nurse interjected. "Waterfront."

"You hear why they decided to separate?" Maggie asked. Both women shook their heads and cast anxious glances down the hall, where Serena Holman was still leading her wealthy parade through the ward.

"Did you ever see Fiona Harker with Dr. Holman's husband?" Maggie asked abruptly, hoping to shock one of them into an answer.

The first nurse looked at the second one and her lips clamped down in a tight line, as if she was trying to hold words back. Boy, you could tell a lot from people's body language. I'd have been a better detective if I'd paid attention to that while alive.

"It's important," Maggie said quietly.

With another glance toward Serena Holman, the second nurse told Maggie that, yes, she'd seen Fiona Harker having coffee with Christian Fletcher a week or so before her death, upstairs in the hospital cafeteria. A lot of people had seen them.

"What did they look like?" Maggie asked. "How were they sitting?"

The second nurse looked perplexed at first, but paused, remembering. "They were at a table for four and sitting across from each other," she recalled. "He looked tired."

"He *always* looks tired," the first nurse interrupted. "He works like a dog."

"Fiona looked like, I don't know, something," the second nurse added.

"Something?" Maggie asked.

"Anxious. Maybe a little angry. That could be too strong of a word. I'd say Fiona looked anxious for sure."

"Thanks," Maggie said. "I appreciate it." She glanced down the hall. "Where can I wait for Dr. Holman?" she asked. "Give me a place where she can't possibly overlook me or make an easy escape."

They liked that, both of them.

"In there," the first nurse suggested, pointing toward a large door painted yellow next to the nurse's station. "She'll be going in there next to check on some of the kids. The ones who feel well enough to get out of bed go in there to play and socialize."

"Thanks," Maggie told them as she headed toward the room to wait. I followed, but not before noticing that the second nurse had picked up the telephone the moment Maggie's back was turned.

The room was a paradise for kids, but I wasn't sure the half dozen or so patients playing in it were in a position to appreciate the bright yellow walls, the smooth white floor dotted with colorful rugs, plush reading chairs beside shelves of books, or even the large-screen TV that dominated one wall and had dozens of family-friendly DVDs stored below it. Most of the kids had opted for quieter pursuits and were sitting at tables putting together jigsaw puzzles, coloring, or reading elaborate books about pirates and ancient Egypt. Two were even working on homework, I guessed, as they had math books open before them and were concentrating on equations they had scrawled on notebook paper. I hoped they would have the chance to ace their next math tests. The energy in the room was barely perceptible; it seemed impossible that six human beings, even this young, could survive on so little energy.

I wondered suddenly how many patients got to leave this ward to go home again.

Maggie took a seat on the couch, where she had a good view of the door. The moment Serena Holman entered, I figured she'd move and block the exit to gain a psychological advantage.

I sat at one of the empty tables on the other side of the room and watched the children, tracing the pain that flowed from them to the places in their tiny bodies where their cancers lived, pulsing darkly. I wished there was something I could do for them.

"Is that your little boy?"

A girl about eight years old stood in front of me. She was wearing a pink hospital gown and had fuzzy slippers on her feet. Her huge eyes were rimmed with dark shadows. I had seen her before. She had hopped with me on the colorful route lines painted on the hospital hall floors. She looked even more tired than she had yesterday as she stared at me patiently, waiting for my answer.

My little boy? Why had she asked if I had a little boy? I looked over and there he was: my little otherworldly friend, sitting at the table with me, hands folded precisely as if he were waiting for his teacher to begin a lesson.

"Not exactly," I told her. "You can hear me?"

"Of course I can hear you," she said, rolling her eyes at me. "I'm not deaf. I've just got acute lymphocytic leukemia. I saw you before. Remember?"

I smiled. "I remember." I was not as thrown as I might have been that she could see me. I had been seen by a child once before, albeit one as sick as she clearly was. My guess was that children, so open to possibilities adults have long since blocked, were closer to my world in general—and that those who were close to death sometimes had the power to see through to my side.

The girl was carrying a pad of drawing paper and a

box of new crayons. "Want me to draw him a picture?" she offered, and sat down before I could reply.

My little companion smiled at the young girl agreeably, as if to say, "Sure."

Looking at his face closely for the first time, I noticed a strange blankness in his eyes. He seemed a bit off to me; he was not quite like me.

No one else in the room noticed our exchange. To them, I suppose, it seemed as if the little girl were simply talking to herself. Maggie was flipping back over her notes, making notations in the margins. The other kids had just enough energy to support what they were doing. Playing with anyone else—or even noticing anyone else—seemed beyond them.

The little girl was drawing a picture of what I thought was a horse, or maybe it was a cow. The four-legged beast taking shape among enthusiastic blades of green grass on her art pad could have been anything from an Appaloosa to a zebra. My little otherworldly friend liked it, though. He beamed at her in encouragement.

"You're pretty good at that," I told the little girl.

"I know," she said confidently. Her arm was dotted with bruises where blood had been drawn and intravenous tubes inserted. "I'm going to be an artist when I grow up."

I hoped she was right.

"Here." She slid the completed drawing across the table to my friend. He smiled down at it. She looked up at me. "Your turn. What do you want me to draw you?"

Oh my god. *Of course.*

"Draw a lake," I said at once, with a glance toward Maggie. She had stopped reading her notes and was eyeing the sick children with a combination of sadness and frustration that there was nothing she could do to help.

"Like this?" the little girl asked, drawing a big, blue oval in the center of the page.

"Like that," I agreed, thinking hard. What shape had the reservoir been? "Only this end is longer and curves," I explained. "Like a dog's leg. It sticks down. Yes. Like that."

As she furiously colored in waves within the shape of the lake, I tried to place the house where I had discovered the little boy in context. If only I had paid more attention to the neighborhood when I was alive. I would not be able to attempt a real map of it, there were too many winding streets, and it would quickly become a confusing series of random lines. I'd have to keep it simple.

"What next?" the little girl asked agreeably, once the lake was finished.

"Put a boulevard there," I said, pointing to the bottom of the page.

"What's a boulevard?" she asked. "I've never drawn one before."

"A big road," I explained. "This one has six lanes. Three in each direction, with bushes in between the two directions."

She meticulously completed the boulevard, her concentration intense.

"Can you draw a road around the edge of the lake, too?" I asked. "Just a regular two-lane road?"

"Sure," she said confidently. "That's easy."

When she was done with the road, I had her draw a shorter road coming off the shoreline drive and then a cul-de-sac to the right off it. She finished the scene with a depiction of a house at the top of the cul-de-sac, then filled it in with small, brown squares to represent cedar shingles. It was surrounded by scribbly bushes and colorful flowers. Two plainer houses were arranged on each side of it.

"Now draw a little boy," I told her. "He lives in the house."

"Him?" she asked, staring at my little friend, who

seemed fascinated by the way she held her crayons and
drew colors across the white page.

"Like him," I agreed. "Only with curly hair."

She created a stick-legged little boy with a huge head
of brown curls and obediently colored his pants blue at
my suggestion. The T-shirt with dinosaurs printed on it
was beyond her, but she enthusiastically decorated the
upper half of the boy with a few blobs that had heads on
them and pronounced them dinosaurs. It didn't look a bit
like Tyler Matthews, but it was good enough to represent
him.

"Not bad at all," she said when she was done. "It might
be my best ever."

If only she knew, I thought. "Can you do me one more
favor? Can you give the drawing to the lady over there?"
I pointed to Maggie.

"Sure," she said, with the aplomb of one who has con-
quered far worse fears than approaching a stranger. "Is
she your wife?"

"No." I smiled. "But I wish she was."

"Should I tell her it's from you?"

"No, just tell her the little boy she is looking for lives
in that house and that it's by the lake where we used to get
our drinking water."

The little girl looked puzzled by this, but hopped from
her chair and marched across the room, drawing in hand,
willing to approach Maggie.

Unfortunately, Serena Holman chose that moment to
enter the room in search of her patients. She spotted the
girl and beckoned her over. "You were supposed to be
in radiation ten minutes ago," she admonished the child.
"We had a deal."

A nurse had followed Dr. Holman into the room. She
looked terrified but risked a comment. "I just thought it
would do her good to—"

"Thank you," Dr. Holman said abruptly. "When I want an opinion from you, I'll be sure to ask you for it."

She turned her back on the nurse and reached for the little girl, but the child twisted away and darted over to where Maggie was standing and thrust the drawing at her.

"I drew this for you," she said. "A little boy who's lost lives in the house and drinks water from the lake."

"How nice," Maggie said uncertainly as she stared at the drawing. She placed the drawing on top of her briefcase, her attention already elsewhere. I had lost my chance.

Serena Holman was examining Maggie suspiciously, having noticed her for the first time. Maggie took the hint. "Maggie Gunn," she said, showing her badge. "I'd like to ask you a few questions."

"I'm assuming this is about Fiona Harker?" the doctor asked with distaste. Emotions roiled in her—Fiona had definitely pushed some of her buttons, but I could not separate them out. This was one tightly coiled lady.

"Yes. It is." Maggie looked over at the children, wondering if they could overhear.

"Take her to radiation," Dr. Holman said, dismissing the little girl and nurse with a wave of her hand. "We can talk over here." Her voice was cold. Gone was the warm and caring doctor of the donor tour. It appeared the lady had two faces and the nurses, who seemed to loathe her, saw only one of them.

She led Maggie to the same table where I had been sitting. My little friend was gone. The doctor did not sit, but stood by the table, glancing impatiently at her watch.

"I just need a few moments," Maggie assured her. "Did you know Fiona Harker?"

"In passing," Holman said. "Our paths seldom crossed. She worked in the emergency room with my husband. Ex-husband," she corrected herself.

"Were they friends?" Maggie asked.

"What's that supposed to mean?"

"Were they friends?" Maggie repeated, more sharply. Uh-oh. Her personal feelings were creeping back in. She did not like Serena Holman.

"I suppose." The doctor glanced at her watch again. "If you consider coworkers friends. My husband—*ex-husband*—has no friends. He has his work and people he knows from work. Otherwise, I'd hardly call him a social animal."

Translation: *He hated going to all those hospital charity benefits that I dragged him to and, worse, failed to appreciate my utter divineness when I wore my designer ball gowns and showed off my boney shoulder blades. Others worshipped me, why not him? And by the way, I am really pissed that I married this brilliant med student only to find out he'd rather work in an emergency room than become chief of staff at Johns Hopkins.*

Oh, yes, I had run into Serena Holman's type before. And I now understood why Christian Fletcher chose to work all the time. Still, he was the one who had married her. If he had not been smart enough to see beyond her expensive good looks to her self-centeredness, then he had gotten exactly what he deserved.

Maggie was blatantly sizing the doctor up. Holman was returning the favor.

"Oh, don't tell me you've fallen for his noble-doctor act, too," Serena Holman finally said, breaking the silence.

"I beg your pardon?" Maggie sounded extremely professional. She was going to ice this lady's wings but good.

"Everyone always falls for Christian's saving-lives act," she said. "Every nurse in this hospital is after him now. The rest of us do good work, too, you know."

Maggie went for the jugular. "I've heard Fiona Harker was having an affair with a married doctor. You hear anything about that?"

Something inside the ice princess definitely flickered. I wondered just how much she knew about having affairs with married doctors. Something told me the answer was plenty. This was a woman who went for power. Her list of bed partners likely started and ended with the hospital's board of directors.

"My husband doesn't have enough blood in him to have an affair, if that's what you are insinuating," she told Maggie stiffly. "He wouldn't have dared."

"You'd be surprised what people do when they're unhappy," Maggie countered.

"I'm the one who asked for the divorce," Holman snapped back.

"Why?"

"Why is that any of your business? It has nothing to do with that dead nurse, and I fail to see how it is any of your concern."

Maggie snapped her notebook shut and handed Holman her business card. "I can't give you any more of my time today," she told the startled doctor, stealing her line right out from underneath her. "But I will be calling you in to the station at a future date to answer more questions."

Dr. Holman stared at her, too surprised to speak. Maggie retrieved her briefcase, noticed the little girl's drawing on it, grabbed it, and left the room. A spark of hope flared in me: Maggie still had the drawing.

I breezed right past Serena Holman, too. She was glowering after Maggie—this was one woman who was used to being the alpha female and did not like being outflanked.

I caught several nurses peeking out of patients' rooms

and enjoying the show as I raced past them and caught up with Maggie at the elevator. Just as the doors were about to close, a small redhead in a nurse's uniform stepped inside and stood silently beside Maggie. She held a brown paper grocery bag.

Maggie's ire was still up over Serena Holman, so it took her a moment to realize the red-haired nurse was glancing at her. When she realized the woman wanted to say something, Maggie pressed the stop button midfloor. The elevator jerked to a halt. Maggie was in no mood to mess around. "Yes?" she asked the nurse.

"I was a friend of Fiona Harker's," the woman said, her voice quavering. "I heard you were looking into her death."

Maggie's demeanor changed in an instant. "I'm very sorry about your loss," she told the nurse.

"Fiona was a really good person," the red-haired nurse said. "She deserved better than to die that way."

"Yes, she did," Maggie agreed firmly.

"She *was* having an affair," the nurse told her. "Some of the other girls said you were asking around."

Maggie hid her surprise. "Who was the affair with?"

"I don't know," the nurse said. "She wouldn't tell me. But it was serious. Fiona changed her schedule on Mondays and Wednesdays so they could spend mornings together. I was the one who swapped with her."

Maggie and I instantly thought the exact same thing: Fiona Harker had probably been killed on a Wednesday morning.

"You have no idea who it was?"

The nurse shook her head. "I didn't want to pry. Fiona was so private about her personal life. You just didn't ask her those kinds of things, not after you got to know her. You learned it was useless. She never talked about herself. I know he was married, but that's all I know. She said there were complications that would take some time to work out, but she was certain they were meant to be together."

"People tell me she was a good person, and a smart one," Maggie said. "But she was having an affair with a married doctor? That's not smart."

"It wasn't like that," the nurse insisted. "I think they were really, truly in love. The fact that Fiona was doing it told me that. It was very unlike her. And I'd never known Fiona to even go out with anyone before this. I know it makes her look bad, but you mustn't think ill of her. It must really have been love. True love."

Maggie looked as if she wasn't sure she believed in true love. I felt an unexpected sadness for her. She was too young to have given up on love.

"These are her things," the nurse told Maggie as she handed her the paper bag. "We shared a locker. I don't know if there's anything in it that might help, but I put everything in there, just in case." The nurse pressed the start button again and the car began to descend.

Maggie peered inside the bag. "I need your name," she told the nurse. "I have to establish a chain of evidence so that—"

The elevator stopped at the next floor and the nurse stepped out. "I'll find you," she promised. "Really, I will. But I have to be in surgery right now."

She scurried off before Maggie could protest. I know my Maggie and I could tell what she was thinking: she had gone off the rails, just a little, and lost her faith, but the moment she became determined to get back on track, the universe had rewarded her with a whole bag of leads. Maggie's faith in herself had been restored.

I was so absorbed watching the thoughts play over her face that I did not realize where we were going. When the elevator doors opened again, I saw we had ended up in the emergency room—she had not been able to resist another look at the good Dr. Fletcher. But she was not going to get close to Christian Fletcher that day. The sliding doors to the outside flew open and what seemed like stretcher after stretcher pushed through, bringing in a parade of maimed and bloody beings strapped to gurneys. Emergency medical technicians rushed in behind the victims, shouting their statuses at the staff. Fletcher was there in seconds, running from stretcher to stretcher, sorting out the patients who needed treatment first, assessing the situation with a calm competence that had a crystallizing effect on the entire treatment team. From what I could tell, a car accident had taken place involving two families. So far, no one had died, and Fletcher was determined that it stay that way.

Maggie watched as he directed five of the victims to treatment rooms, spoke urgently with a nurse over the head of a sixth, and quickly assigned staff to individual patients. Already his hands were moving over a final victim, the smallest one, evaluating her injuries with a gentle touch as a paramedic reported on her condition. Though he held it at bay so it would not interfere with his judgment, I could feel a remarkable combination of empathy and determination at his core. It was almost as if he could channel the victims' pain and felt personal outrage that a living creature should suffer so. He lived to stop their pain and reverse the damage at any cost. Yet his ego did not seem to be involved at all. He did it for them, not for himself. I could find no trace of arrogance in his heart, only outrage that the world allowed such anguish.

His soon-to-be-ex-wife had spoken derisively of Christian Fletcher saving lives, but seeing him actually do it told a different tale.

It was a profoundly humbling experience for me. He was ten times the man I had never been.

Chapter 19

Maggie returned to department headquarters, the paper bag of evidence cradled in her arms as she fought through the phalanx of reporters camped outside the front door, there to witness the pathetic parade of suspects being hauled inside one by one to face questioning by the task force in connection with the abduction of Tyler Matthews. Registered sex offenders and online predators flagged by KinderWatch were being brought in for questioning, and it was not a pretty sight. Heads down, eyes averted, they darted into the building like human cockroaches fleeing the light of the cameras. They came in all shapes and sizes and from different economic levels. It seemed the only thing they shared was a willingness to give up their dignity as humans and the respect of others in order to indulge their compulsions.

I did not feel sorry for them. I had seen too many lives destroyed by the selfishness of men like these; I had arrested too many of their victims after they had grown up and taken their anger out on the world with guns and knives. If I could find a hallway to hell, I'd happily herd the whole lot into the eternal flames.

I guess my newfound compassion had its limits.

Maggie had retreated deep into the Fiona Harker case and did not notice the terrified creature that rode the elevator up with her, flanked by two detectives. He was a desperately ashamed man with rumpled clothes and unkempt hair who loosely fit the description of the man Robert Michael Martin had seen in the park, but his frightened expression and the sense of despair that emanated from him made it plain that, despite whatever urges fought to be satisfied inside him, he was not their man. He did not have the nerve.

The trio got out on the second floor. Dozens of detectives, plainclothesmen, and administrative staff hurried through the halls. Inside the conference room, I could see an immense table stacked high with case files and surrounded by federal agents barking orders or talking into their cell phones. This was the hub of the Tyler Matthews investigation and, from the looks of things, few had been spared duty on the task force.

Maggie had never been more alone.

I rode with her up to the fourth floor, rifling through her memories, searching for a way to let her know that Tyler Matthews was only miles away. I could find no way in.

The squad room was deserted. Every available man and woman had been pulled into the madness two floors below. I felt a twinge of sympathy for anyone burglarized or assaulted over the next few days; justice for them would be delayed as long as Tyler remained missing. The fact that their suffering would not wait meant nothing in the face of reality.

I think Maggie was grateful for the silence. She could

work without interruption. She retrieved a diet soda from the break room before clearing her desk of all items. I watched this ritual with delight. Her desk had been my desk and, while once it had been a place of surrender where I waited out hangovers and pushed papers around in lieu of actually working, it was now a battleground where Maggie waged war against those who dared violate the rules that distinguished her world from chaos.

She had two large envelopes waiting for her in her mail slot and she placed these on one side of her desk, along with the slender case file on Fiona Harker. She put the grocery bag directly in the center of her desk, then sat down and stared at it. She was putting off opening it, afraid to risk disappointment if it held little of value. She glanced though the case file once again, fixing the timeline and death scene firmly in her mind, before opening the two envelopes marked to her attention. One was a ballistics report; the other held details on the autopsy. She spread both out across her desk and studied them intently. I perched on the edge of the desk, studying her.

Maggie's face was plain at first glance, slightly broad with a wide nose and thin mouth that seldom curled in a smile. Her eyes were large and dark, hard to read to those who had nothing but the surface to go on. But it was a mistake to think that Maggie was plain. Those who looked closer, like me, quickly discovered that her face was a mercurial wonder, her expressions constantly flowing from one nuanced expression to another as she processed the world around her. Maggie did not take a single moment for granted. Not one.

She read and reread both reports carefully, making a notation to search purchase records for the gun that had killed Fiona Harker. The autopsy confirmed that the nurse's death had occurred on a Wednesday morning and that she had been in excellent health before her death.

There was no surprise pregnancy, no evidence of sexual assault. The medical examiner had found the carefully nurtured, perfectly healthy body of a thirty-three-year-old woman, cause of death a single gunshot wound to the head. Without that wound, Fiona Harker would probably have lived to be a very, very old woman. Which meant that someone had stolen years from her. I knew Maggie was thinking the same thing as she read through the report—and I could feel the anger in her rising at the fact that someone out there actually thought they had gotten away with it.

When Maggie was done rereading the reports, she picked up the phone and let the medical examiner's office know it was okay to release Fiona Harker's body to her family in California. It would take a long and lonely cross-country ride to be welcomed by grieving family and friends, but it was all essentially for show, as I knew that any trace of Fiona Harker had long since moved on. Her family was mourning an empty vessel. I wondered if her friends would hold a memorial service here in town. Had she even had enough friends to warrant holding one? Fiona Harker had been a solitary woman, as alone in life as she was now alone in death. But she'd had coworkers, and they clearly felt her loss keenly. They needed a resolution, an explanation for her death. I hoped her belongings would tell Maggie more.

Before she opened the bag that had been given to her by Fiona's locker mate, Maggie inserted the ballistics and medical examiner's reports into the case file. As an afterthought, she folded the drawing the little girl had given her in the hospital and inserted it into the file folder as well. It had been my only hope, but was now likely to be buried in other paperwork. At least it had not gone into the trash. She made a few notes about her interviews with Serena Holman and the nurses in the file, then took a deep breath, moved the paperwork to a side drawer, and opened the grocery bag.

One by one, she placed the items that represented Fiona Harker's personal life onto her desktop, starting with a single tube of clear lip gloss and a pair of plain gold-hoop earrings. There was no other evidence of makeup or jewelry. Next came a framed photo of Fiona that was at least fifteen years old, showing her with an older couple who had to be her parents and another young woman who looked remarkably like Fiona. A mother, a father, and a sister to miss her. Their lives would never be the same, I knew; there would always be a hole in the place once occupied by Fiona and her love for them. Maggie then lifted spare clothes out of the bag, nothing more provocative than a plain gray T-shirt and a pair of jeans, extra socks, underwear, and black flip-flops. Fiona had not been an athlete, it seems: there were no workout clothes or tennis shoes. And then, finally, a peek into the kind of person Fiona Harker had been—a collection of books, mostly paperbacks, at the bottom of the bag. Maggie lifted the books out one by one and placed them on her desk: the poetry of Walt Whitman; another book of poems, this time by Gary Snyder; a biography of Helen Keller; a short story collection by Doris Lessing; and a hardback book entitled *Hostage to the Devil* by Malachi Martin. *Whoa.* Just seeing Maggie hold it made me want to destroy the book in a cleansing fire. Fiona Harker had not exactly gone in for light reading. She had lived an intense and brooding life, if her taste in books told Maggie anything.

That was it for evidence. There were no scribbled notes written in the margins of the books, no clues that might lead Maggie to her killer. Just more evidence of a solitary life by a very private woman who had spent her days battling death and, apparently, her nights trying to understand why. How had she ended up this way, with so few people and so little light in her life? I would never know, nor would the world ever know. The mystery of Fiona Harker's heart had died with her.

Maggie did something odd with her disappointment. She spread her arms out over Fiona Harker's belongings and put her head down on the desk, like a teenager sleeping through study hall. She closed her eyes and weariness swept through her. Maggie was tired, bone tired, but I could not pinpoint why. It had to do with Fiona Harker, I knew, and the sadness that permeated her life, but I did not want to accept the obvious explanation: that Maggie was tired from holding back the realization that her own life, too, lacked both human comfort and human contact. That she, too, was lonely.

I watched Maggie sleep. She fell deeper and deeper away from the waking world. Soon, I was able to follow her dreams as the living might follow a movie. She dreamed of a summer lake surrounded by longleaf pines, of a cedar cabin and a picnic table in the front yard. People sat around it, reading the books Maggie had found among Fiona Harker's possessions. Noni Bates, the old lady from the neighborhood, was engrossed in the Doris Lessing; a young boy I did not recognize was plowing through Walt Whitman; and, with amusement, I saw Gonzales moving a finger over the lines in Gary Snyder's book of poetry, silently mouthing the words as he read. At the far end of the table, an elderly Catholic priest sat reading the book about exorcisms, glancing up every now and then to stare disapprovingly at a dark-haired woman who lay motionless in the middle of the picnic table, as if she were dead or, perhaps, only sleeping. I could not find Maggie in her dream, though I saw it through her eyes— and heard it through her ears. In her dream, the buzz of a distant motor grew louder. A man in a powerboat was speeding toward Maggie from across the lake, plumes of water arcing in his wake. He arrived in a spray of cold water and offered Maggie a ride. His face looked familiar to me somehow. Who was he? Her father as a younger man, or was he a past lover?

I would learn no more from Maggie's dreams. Her partner, Adrian Calvano, pulled us both abruptly back to reality. He was shaking her shoulder and calling her name.

"Yo, Gunn," he said. "Wake up. What the hell? I've never even seen you close your eyes before."

"Get off me," Maggie said, swatting him away automatically. She was momentarily confused, unsure of where she was. "What time is it?" she asked.

"Time for you to wake up before the new shift gets here and you look like a complete loser."

She yawned and drank deeply from her soda. I touched the can. It was warm. How long had I been wandering through Maggie's dreams with her?

"You feeling okay?" Calvano asked with concern in his voice. He felt different somehow, I thought, less cocky and more, well, *real*.

"I'm fine," Maggie said. "I'm just tired of hitting dead ends. I've got nothing. What about you?"

Calvano sat in the chair next to her desk and stretched out his long legs. He stared at his ankles. He was probably thinking, *Man, those are sharp shoes*. Meanwhile, I was thinking, *What kind of an asshole wears argyle socks?*

"I need your help," Calvano said.

"Now who's acting weird?" She tossed her empty can into the trash.

"I mean it." He sounded downright human. What had happened to the Adrian Calvano I loathed so well?

"What is it?" Maggie asked.

"I've been shut out," he told her. "They're not letting me get near the investigation. That license plate bullshit was just bullshit. It got us nowhere. Now they're going through all the poor bastards on that KinderWatch list of pervs, pulling in anyone remotely local on the list, especially if they resemble that dude Martin claims he saw in the park. Even I know it's not getting us anywhere."

"I doubt there's much else they can do," Maggie said sympathetically. "I wish I could help, but I'm the only one around here who gives a crap about Fiona Harker's death. Well, me and Gonzales."

"Gonzales hates me," Calvano declared suddenly, his voice sounding younger. God help me, I felt a flash of sympathy toward the cocky bastard. I realized that maybe he wasn't kissing ass to get ahead; maybe he'd been trying to simply get attention from Gonzales. I wondered what Calvano's father had been like. I knew what it was like to have a father who was too busy to give a crap about you.

"Gonzales doesn't hate you," Maggie said, sorting the evidence from Fiona Harker's locker in preparation for sending it to the lab for processing. "He's just covering his ass. You know how he is. If we get nowhere—and chances are good at this point that we are never going to find Tyler Matthews—then he wants to make sure the feds take the rap for it, not him or the department."

"I could help," Calvano said stubbornly. "I'm not an idiot."

Maggie looked startled. "I never said you were."

"I look like an idiot, of course," he conceded. "I did go off the deep end a little about Martin, but, you know, I just wanted to find Tyler Matthews, and that Martin guy seems way too involved with a bunch of little kids he doesn't even know. There has to be something I can do. I know this town. I'm a local. I can do things the feds can't do."

Maggie recognized something in his voice and sympathized. She'd been shut out a lot when she first joined the force, by people like me. Or, rather, like I'd been. "How can I help?" she asked.

"What would *you* do?" he said. "Just tell me what you'd do. You're the best detective we have on the force."

Maggie looked at him, flabbergasted. "What?"

"Oh, come on," he said, annoyed. "You know you are. That's why you're Gonzales's favorite."

"I thought it was because we were sleeping together," she said sarcastically.

Calvano waved a hand. "That's bullshit. And I tell people so when they say that, which isn't very often around me. They learn. You're his pet because you're better than the rest of us slobs. Yeah, you don't have a life. But you're smarter. And you got a knack. So, tell me: what would you do?"

Maggie sat back, considering it. "You said they're looking at a list of suspects from the sex offenders' registry and from the KinderWatch list?" she asked.

Calvano nodded. "There's a lot of overlap."

"Are they cross-checking to see who on those lists inserted themselves into the investigation?"

Calvano nodded again. "That's the first thing the feds told us to do."

"No one came up?" Maggie asked.

"Not yet," Calvano said.

"But are they checking the volunteers?" she asked.

"What do you mean?"

"Well, you're checking the list of people KinderWatch is tracking, right? But is anyone looking into the volunteers for KinderWatch, beyond Robert Michael Martin?"

Calvano sat up straighter. "I don't think so."

"How better to insert yourself into any investigation that might take place?" she explained. "You were right to suspect Martin, it's just you focused on him and him alone too quickly. If I were one of those creeps, I'd want to know how close I was to being caught. What better way than to be a part of the group that's trying to catch you? I mean, think about it. That colonel guy says he does a routine background check. But I bet you anything he doesn't take the basic first step and verify that his volunteers are who they say they are. All you would need is someone's name, someone you know who has a clean record, and maybe a driver's license number, and you're probably taken at your word when you volunteer."

"Yeah," Calvano said eagerly. I felt it again: that need to please, just like poor Robert Michael Martin. He leaned forward. "How do I follow up on that, though, without getting shut out again?"

"Christ, Adrian. Do I have to tell you everything?" She was joking, though. I could tell she was thrilled that Calvano had come to her and treated her like one of the guys.

"Just tell me what you would do," he said. "You know I get . . ." He hesitated.

"Get what?" she asked.

"Too wrapped up in it to think like you. Too pissed off at the guy I think did it." Translation: even Adrian Calvano knew his ego got in the way.

"I'd go back to Martin," Maggie said. "Ask him about the other KinderWatch volunteers. He'd know who was a little off better than the colonel would. They'd act differently around the colonel, he's the boss. If you want to know what they are really like, ask one of their peers. Ask Martin."

"That dude is not going to talk to me," Calvano said. "He hates me."

Well, yeah, I thought. *Who doesn't hate you?* But then I felt mean—a least Calvano was trying. I hadn't tried for years by the time I died.

"Of course he hates you," Maggie said. "You zeroed in on him and no one else. The guy wants to be a hero. The guy probably wants to be a cop. You treated him like shit. I wouldn't want to help you either."

"Come with me to talk to him," Calvano asked. He was practically begging. I was starting to enjoy the show.

"I'm working on a case here," Maggie reminded him.

"You said yourself that you had nothing. Just come with me. It'll take half an hour."

She rolled her eyes, but the chance to be included was too tempting for her. "Only if his lawyer is there, Adrian. They'll crucify us if he's not."

"Whatever. Just come with me and, you know, set a friendly tone. Bat your eyelashes at him or something."

Okay, so Calvano wasn't going to be totally redeemed in a day. Neither was I, apparently, so that was something else we had in common.

"Let me get this stuff to the lab first." Maggie accepted Calvano's help in placing the items from Fiona Harker's locker into plastic evidence bags. I was amused at the timid way Calvano assisted her, like a little boy trying to please his mother. But I was touched, too. A man humbled is a man who can learn from his mistakes. I knew that from personal experience.

"Call Martin's lawyer now," she reminded him. "Let's talk to him at home, far from this mess. Make sure you explain why we're heading over, that we just want his help and that he is in no way a suspect. That's the only way Martin is going to override his lawyer's advice not to talk. If he thinks we can't move forward without him, he'll help."

"We can't move forward without him," Calvano admitted.

"Just let him know that."

Calvano nodded agreeably. Had Maggie finally found

a partner who wasn't a total disaster? Gonzales had been smart to put them together.

Maggie packed the items back into the grocery bag, this time every object neatly bagged and labeled, then headed out into the hallway. Of course, I followed. If you had the choice between listening to Calvano bumble through a phone call or watching Maggie walk through the halls, you'd have followed her, too.

She had her head down, thinking of the interview with Martin to come, and when she rounded the corner in the deserted hallway, she nearly crashed into Christian Fletcher. She jumped back, startled, and stared at him. His doctor's coat and hands were covered in blood.

How the hell had he gotten past the desk sergeant and the media looking like that?

"I lost three of them," Fletcher said, sounding shell-shocked. I noticed a waterproof jacket folded over one arm. He had come straight from the hospital, throwing it on over his bloody clothes, desperate to get to Maggie. That's how his bloody clothes had escaped attention from others.

"What?" Maggie asked, her hand inching toward her gun.

"I lost three of the crash victims," he said hollowly. Gone was the confident saver of lives. Christian Fletcher looked, and felt, like a crash victim himself. "I saw you over by the elevator when they first came in. Two families. Three kids. One of the fathers is dead now, a mother, too, and one of the kids. God took one of each."

"I'm not sure how much God had to do with it," Maggie said slowly.

Fletcher looked down at himself, as if noticing the blood for the first time. He quickly unfolded his jacket and put it back on. "I'm so sorry. I came right from the hospital." He looked up at Maggie with such naked need that even my envious heart ached for him. "I had nowhere else to go. I didn't have anyone else to talk to."

I could feel the confusion in Maggie. She was horrified: by the blood, by the deaths he had reported, by the raw need he was projecting on her. But she was filled with compassion, too, and she understood his need.

"Tell me what happened," she suggested gently.

"One of the drivers swerved to avoid a cat that ran into the road," he said. "He lost control and crossed the center line and hit another car head-on. He died and the mother in the other car died and one of the children, too. She was only three years old."

"I'm so sorry," Maggie said. "I'm so, so sorry. I know you did everything you could. I saw you."

"They made me leave," he said abruptly, slumping against the wall.

"What do you mean?"

"I'd been on for almost forty-eight hours straight, so they made me leave. Admin double checks all deaths. They acted like it was my fault those people died. That maybe I missed something when I treated them."

"No," Maggie said firmly. "I watched you working. You were amazing. I saw the other staff members there. They were looking to you. If you hadn't been there, no one would have been saved. I've never seen anything like it." A flame of jealousy licked at my heart. "They'll tell whoever signs off on the deaths that you weren't to blame. Surely you lose people in the emergency room all the time?"

"Yeah," he said quietly. "We do. Just usually not so many at one time and I'm so tired and I can't get Fiona off my mind."

Maggie looked around, whether for backup or to see if they were being overheard I could not tell. I knew she did not want to bring Fletcher back into the squad room.

When he saw Calvano, he'd shut right down. Calvano had that effect on other men.

"What do you mean about Fiona?" Maggie asked him quietly. He was sitting on the floor by then, his legs stretched out in front of him. She knelt by his side, her hand still resting on her gun, just in case, and spoke very gently to him. "What do you mean, you can't stop thinking about Fiona?" she asked him.

"I had coffee with her a week ago," he said in a distant voice. "The ER was slow and she asked if I wanted to take a break and I was hungry so we went upstairs. She was asking me all these questions about marriage and love and what it had been like to lose it all." He looked up at Maggie. "I guess word had gotten out about me and my wife, and she wanted to know if I was okay, if she could help in any way." He saw the look on Maggie's face. "She wasn't coming on to me," he said in a rush. "She made that very clear. She just wanted to be my friend." He ran a hand through his hair and seemed close to tears. "She got me talking, she was the first one I felt comfortable talking to about it, and I told her all about my marriage ending, how Serena had just announced it was over and I'd had no say." He was quiet. "I'm not sure I ever had a say in anything. It hurt. I told Fiona that. I told her how much it hurt and she looked so sad for me. She was a good person." He looked up at Maggie, eyes bright with tears. "She was a good person and she didn't deserve to die that way and I can't stop thinking about it."

"Why didn't you tell me about this earlier?" Maggie asked, fighting hard to keep her voice neutral.

He looked miserable. "I didn't want to talk about my wife or my marriage to *you*. I wasn't trying to hide anything. I just didn't want to have to talk about it to you." There was that naked need in his face again. I wondered if all of his strength went into fighting for his patients, leaving nothing left over to protect himself. "I'm sorry," he said. "I just didn't know who else to talk to about it or where to go. That little girl was only three and now she's dead. She can't have weighed more than thirty pounds. I could lift her as easily as a doll."

"What's going on?" Calvano's belligerent voice killed the mood instantly. But I was relieved he was there. Fletcher seemed so close to the edge.

Calvano towered over them both, looking pretty damn competent in his tailored suit and Italian shoes. I had to admit it—Gonzales was right. Calvano had his uses.

"It's okay," Maggie said. "I've got it. He's a background witness in the Harker case. He worked with her at the hospital."

Calvano was not mollified. "Is that blood on his hands?" he asked, staring down at Fletcher. The doctor had ducked his head, hiding his face from Calvano, and placed his hands over the top of his head, as if to protect himself.

"He's a doctor in the emergency room," Maggie explained, getting annoyed at Calvano, which was not a good sign. Fletcher had showed up like a crazy person, covered with blood, and she liked the guy even more for it?

"They don't have sinks in the emergency room?" Calvano asked, his voice still challenging.

"Give it a rest, Adrian," Maggie ordered him. "I'll be with you in a moment."

"Actually, I think I'll wait with you," Calvano decided. He sank down against the wall and slid to a seating position beside the doctor. "How's it going, dude?" he asked.

Fletcher looked over at Calvano and then abruptly stood. "I've got to go get some sleep," he told Maggie.

"Don't forget to shower," Calvano called from the floor.

"I'm sorry I bothered you," Fletcher told Maggie. "I shouldn't have come."

"I'm glad you came," Maggie said. "I need to know more about your coffee with Fiona Harker. What she might have said about her life."

"I'm off for the next twenty-four hours," he said miserably. He was a man lost without his work. "Let me catch up on my sleep and I'll call you in the morning."

I just bet he would.

He stuck his bloodstained hands in his pockets and walked down the hallway, shoulders hunched, looking miserable.

"You're an asshole," Maggie told Calvano as she hoisted him to his feet.

"Yeah, but I'm *your* asshole," he pointed out cheerfully. He gallantly took the grocery bag from her. "Carry your books to school?"

She rolled her eyes.

"Watch out for that guy," Calvano warned her. "He's got the hots for you."

"That poor man doesn't have the hots for anyone," Maggie said. "He's clinically depressed."

"He may be depressed," Calvano conceded. "But he still has the hots for you. Now, what do you say we both get some sleep and meet in the morning? Martin says he'll see us then."

That Calvano was starting to grow on me.

Chapter 20

Robert Michael Martin was waiting for Calvano and Maggie on his front porch early the next morning, looking anxious and eager to please. His hair was still damp from the shower and he wore a clean shirt with his baggy jeans. His slick lawyer was nowhere in sight, but Noni Bates sat on the porch swing near him, an enigmatic smile on her face. I caught a whiff of fatigue from her and realized that she might be older than I thought. For the first time, I acknowledged that perhaps the simplicity of her life had not only made her serene nature possible, it might have been all she could manage with what little energy she had. Trying to keep Robert Michael Martin out of trouble was taking its toll on my elderly Aphrodite.

"Where's your lawyer?" Maggie asked before she'd even reached the top step.

"He couldn't be here," Martin explained. "He's out of town for the weekend. He sent Mrs. Bates instead."

"He needs to be here," Maggie said firmly. Calvano

looked a bit panicked at that, like maybe he was going to pee in his tailored pants.

"It's okay," Noni said calmly. "I am perfectly capable of looking out for him. I will insist you keep to your word and ask him only about other volunteers."

"Deal," Calvano interrupted, unwilling to risk losing the interview.

Maggie looked annoyed, but walked through the front door when Martin opened it after suggesting they go into the living room. I saw why he was so anxious to install his guests there. He was playing at being the host. The room was cleaner than it had been a few days ago, so either the cops searching it had done Martin a favor, or he was getting used to the idea of actually having people in his house and had decided to clear out the pizza cartons and empty beer bottles. There was even a vase of flowers on the coffee table, a touch I suspected had been suggested by Noni.

"Would anyone like lemonade?" Noni asked. "I've made some fresh, and Robert has prepared Italian wedding cookies."

"Sweet," Calvano declared as he folded himself into the overstuffed couch. I hoped he didn't expect to be welcomed with such open arms by all the people he interviewed using Maggie's nonthreatening technique.

"That would be lovely," Maggie said. She sat in an armchair across from Martin and put him at ease with small talk about the restaurant where he worked. It had been a neighborhood institution for decades and, in fact, Maggie's parents had had their first date there. By the time Noni arrived with refreshments, they were all the best of friends, even Calvano, who managed to remain on Martin's good side by saying absolutely nothing. But Noni moved more slowly than she usually did when she brought in the lemonade and cookies, and I found myself annoyed at Martin for just sitting there—he was a grown man and he should not be letting that lovely old lady wait on him hand and foot. He needed to stand up, dust himself off, quit being such a mamma's boy, and be a man. He was going to wear her out if he kept it up.

Calvano cleared his throat like he was the chairman of the board about to call the meeting to order. I realized he was lost without his tried-and-true bullying approach, so I cut him some slack. "As Detective Gunn has mentioned, we are here to talk to you about the other volunteers for KinderWatch," Calvano explained. "One reason we came down so hard on you is because the type of person who commits crimes like abducting a child frequently insinuates himself into the investigation as a way to keep tabs on how close law enforcement is to catching him. We feel the same may be true about KinderWatch and whoever took Tyler Matthews."

Calvano unconsciously parroted Maggie's very words to him as he launched into a deeper explanation of the type of person they were looking for. Noni probably knew Calvano was a horse's ass, but Martin ate it up. He liked being treated as if he were a peer, never mind that the guy had wanted to throw him in prison for life just a couple of days ago. He listened eagerly, his eyes leaving Calvano's face only long enough to admire his stupid Italian loafers and gun. I knew he'd spill his guts about the other volunteers. Maggie could bat her eyelashes all she wanted, but what Martin was really interested in was playing cops and robbers.

"So you're looking for someone who was just pretending to be concerned about stopping online predators?" Martin asked eagerly when Calvano was done.

"It's a little more specific than that," Maggie said. "And you must be careful not to let your personal feelings about other volunteers color your judgment." I felt this comment was a zinger meant for Calvano. So did Noni, who hid her smile.

"What do you mean?" Martin asked, anxious to get it right.

Maggie searched for a way to explain, but knew Martin's limited social skills would make it difficult. "Let's say, hypothetically speaking, that there are some volunteers who are aloof, standoffish. Snobby. Who act like they are too good to talk to you." Martin's face finally signaled understanding, though that description probably applied to just about everyone at KinderWatch. Martin was a natural scapegoat, and he'd probably spent a lifetime being ignored or taunted by others. "Naturally, you would not like them," Maggie explained. "No one would. But that doesn't mean they're the kind of person we're looking for. We are looking for a very specific type of individual."

"Perhaps if you told him exactly what you were looking for?" said Noni, knowing Martin's imagination was a few seconds from exploding in wild accusations aimed at most of the other KinderWatch volunteers. It is a rare man who can resist retaliation.

"All right," Maggie agreed. "I'll start. Adrian, you know more than me about the profile. You add what you need to."

Right. Maggie would remember more from her standard training on child abusers undergone a decade ago than Calvano probably retained from earlier that day.

"This person would be a loner," Maggie explained. "He would likely give lots of their time to KinderWatch and volunteer to go the extra mile, maybe taking care of the mainframe or overall computer files in some way. He would not want to simply pose as a child online. He'd want to play a larger role, so he could see what other volunteers had picked up on."

Noni, sensing that Martin was realizing this description fit him to a T, intervened again. "You can see why Detective Calvano and the colonel might have suspected you," she said cheerfully. "But that's actually good, because it means you are in an excellent position to know who else might have done the same things you did." Maggie nodded gratefully.

Martin thought hard, both self-conscious and proud that so many people were waiting on him to speak. We waited in silence, and I was beginning to think it was useless, that the pressure was too much for him, when Martin finally spoke. "Most of the hardcore volunteers are women," he said. "They can get pretty intense. You're looking for men, right?"

"Yes," Maggie said firmly. "This was a man."

"There's the colonel," Martin said hopefully. "I heard that he all but accused me. Maybe I ought to return the favor." The rare note of belligerence in his voice told me he felt betrayed by the man who ran KinderWatch. I wondered if he would ever return as a volunteer, knowing what the colonel had said about him.

"He's in a wheelchair, dude," Calvano pointed out. "But, yeah, he did point the finger pretty hard at you. That's why I came at you so hard."

It was bullshit. He'd come at Martin hard because he was lazy and unimaginative, but it was as close as Calvano was going to come to an apology. Martin was angry enough at the colonel to accept Calvano's excuse with a nod.

"This person would have his own car," Maggie prompted him. "He'd be alone every time you saw him. Probably a little timid, especially around the female volunteers. He'd ask you questions, though, he'd likely approach you, wanting to know what you were up to, what you'd discovered online, if you had any new screen names of predators to track, if you'd discovered any new sites."

Martin only looked more confused.

"Why don't you just give them the names of all the other male volunteers who are local?" Noni suggested. She turned to Maggie. "What if they're married?" she asked.

Maggie shrugged. "The guy might be married, but he'd need a private place to take the boy. But I think Mrs. Bates is right. Maybe you should just give us all the names you know of for the local male volunteers, starting with the ones who are not married. I'm not asking you to accuse anyone, just use your gut feelings and tell us who among that group you think best fits the profile we gave you."

"Okay," Martin agreed, relieved he was not being asked to accuse someone and put them through what he had been subjected to. "There are three guys it could be, and about four more it *might* be, but they're all married."

As he provided the names, Calvano wrote them down in his notebook, occasionally referring to the information he'd gleaned from the license plate check but not finding a hit. His cockiness was returning, I realized, now that he had some leads. His kind of leads, too—all he had to do was intimidate the men Martin had named.

"What are you going to do to them?" Martin asked warily. "They're good people. Look what they volunteer their time for."

"We're not going to hassle them," Maggie said firmly, with a warning glance at Calvano. "We're going to start by finding out where they were on Thursday morning when the boy was taken. Most of them were probably at work, and that will rule out a lot. Don't worry, we'll be careful. No one will know their names came from you."

"It isn't that," Martin explained. "I'll probably never see them again. I'm not going back. Not after what the colonel said about me." He glanced at Noni Bates. "Not after what the colonel *thought* about me."

"I knew it wasn't you, dear," Noni said firmly. "I did not doubt you for an instant."

"After all I did for him," Martin added, his ire growing. "I was his best volunteer."

"Don't be too hard on him," Maggie advised. "You work in that field long enough and you start to develop a very dark view of human nature. It can change you. He just wanted to help find the boy."

"I never want to be that way," Martin declared, and I was unclear whether he meant like the colonel or like the predators the colonel tracked.

"You won't be that way," Noni said simply. "You aren't and you won't."

"Well, I think that will do for us," Maggie said, rising. She smiled at Martin. "You know, this area has a very active neighborhood watch organization. We train civilians for it. They get uniforms and ride around in cars, keeping an eye on things for us. They call in any problems they see. It's a lot like what you've been doing, only on wheels. I think you'd be good at it."

"Really?" Martin's face lit up. "I'll look into it."

Calvano followed Maggie out the door, but did not wait until they were far from the house to make his opinion known. "Alfredo is going to kill you for sending that guy to him for neighborhood watch. He's going to be one of those gung ho, fake-cop, live-for-the-job kind of guys who wear their uniforms all day, every day and scare the other volunteers away."

"We all have our uses, Adrian," Maggie told him with a smile. "We all have our uses."

Chapter 21

The hard work of being a detective—all the phone calls, the interviews, chasing down scraps of information in hopes of catching a break—had never been for me. Clearly. My partner and I had performed so dismally that our ineptitude became part of the department's permanent lingo: whenever a case remained unsolved, others on the force had taken to calling it "in FBL" as "in Fahey and Bonaventura Limbo."

The Tyler Matthews case was definitely in FBL, but Maggie and Calvano were going to put in their fair share of work to get it out of limbo. Calvano was following up on the list of volunteers Martin had given him; Maggie was going to lend a hand once she started the trace on the gun used to shoot Fiona Harker.

That was the kind of grunt work I'd avoided while alive. I avoided it now as well.

Using the names Robert Michael Martin had given them, Maggie helped Calvano pull together a list of addresses where the KinderWatch volunteers lived, or at least the ones that Martin felt might match the profile of Tyler's abductors. I memorized the list and headed over to the house where I knew Tyler Matthews was being held in hopes of finding a match. It would mean help was on its way to the boy, sooner or later.

None of the addresses provided by KinderWatch volunteers matched that of the small cedar-shingled house nestled among the grasses and flowers that thrived in its landscaped yard. I had no clue what the name of the man inside might be, but chances were good the house had not been rented under his real name. And that, if he had volunteered for KinderWatch, he hadn't signed up under the same name, either.

There would be no one coming for Tyler Matthews anytime soon.

By then it was Saturday afternoon and Tyler Matthews was facing another night without his mother. It was the best I could hope for. I had watched over him during the night before, noting that the man who held him had slept in a separate bedroom down the hall from Tyler. But anything could have happened to the boy since. He was being prepared for something terrible, I knew. I entered the house, fearful of what I would find. But it felt calm inside. The living room was empty, the cameras still there but clearly turned off. They were probably controlled remotely. The man who was staying in the house with Tyler had no say in the matter.

I checked the kitchen. No sign of the boy.

I got a bad feeling about that. I could feel the boy near—his innocence was unmistakable—and I could both smell his abductor's sweat and pick up on his internal conflict over protecting the child or destroying him by taking all that made him innocent. I searched a den, small bathroom, and one of the back bedrooms before finding the man and Tyler in a corner of the second bedroom, far from camera range.

That gave me a bad feeling, too.

But the little boy looked safe. He was wearing new clothes and sitting on a pillow placed on the floor, drinking chocolate milk while eating tiny powdered doughnuts from a bag. The man who had taken him was reading to him from a Batman comic while lying on his back on the floor, a pillow beneath his head. Had I not known the situation, I would have guessed that they were father and son.

"You can have another one," he told Tyler when he saw the small boy hesitating to pull another doughnut from the bag.

Tyler took a doughnut and nibbled it. "When is Mommy coming for me?" he asked.

The man put the comic book down. "I'm not sure," he said. "Your mommy is sick and in the hospital. You have to stay here for now."

Lying bastard. Tyler frowned at the news that his mother was sick and I felt anxiousness tug at his little heart. Even at his age, he knew his mother was fragile. How could this man have used that against him?

A cell phone rang and the man reached for it quickly, fear rising in him. I could hear the man on the other end. It was the same authoritative voice that had spoken from the other side of the camera feed. "Where are you?" he demanded.

"We're in a back bedroom," the first man said.

"Leave the boy alone until it is time," the unseen man ordered him.

The man looked up at Tyler, who had started to flip the pages of the comic book while he pretended to know how to read.

"Did you hear me?" the second man asked.

"Yes," the man in the house said abruptly. "I hear you."
He was filled with so many different emotions that it was
impossible to separate them out: rage, anger, fear, guilt,
lust, shame, hunger—and evil, too, I thought, but I could
not be sure if it was coming from the man or something
the man himself had sensed.

"Get back in camera range now," the unseen man ordered. "You're getting sloppy about this."

"I have followed your orders precisely," the first man
argued, his voice growing in pitch. The emotions in him
roiled and I felt his shame and guilt grow.

"You've been sloppy. Haven't you been reading the
papers? They're getting closer. I'm moving the timetable
up."

"I'm not ready," the first man insisted, panic in his
voice.

The second man laughed. It was an ugly sound that
filled me with darkness. It was so ripe and evil and filled
with certainty that the first man would fall. "You'll be
more than ready when the time comes. Then it will be all
I can do to control your appetite."

"I'm not like you," the first man insisted.

"Aren't you?" the second man challenged. "Now get
back into camera range and take the boy's shirt off."

The first man started to argue, but changed his mind.
He hung up his phone and coaxed the boy back into the
living room. He did not remove the boy's shirt. "I've got
to go out for a moment," he told Tyler. "I'll be right back.
I'll bring you a treat."

"Can you bring me my mommy?" the boy asked
hopefully.

"Not yet," the first man lied. "But soon. When she's
feeling better. How about some French fries. Do you like
French fries?"

"I like the toys that come with them."

"Okay, I'll bring you some. In the meantime, here are your other toys." The man arranged the plastic soldiers he had bought earlier in front of the boy and left. His cell phone was ringing again before he was even out the door. "What are you going to do?" he said into the phone. "Come over and make me?" The front door shut behind him and I was alone with the boy.

Or maybe I wasn't.

Tyler Matthews picked up a toy solider and held it out, like an offering, speaking to someone I could not see.

"I share," he said proudly. "I learned how in preschool. I will give you a soldier."

He smiled at whatever answer he alone had heard. He arranged the soldier on the rug and added a few more plastic men. "That's you, Pawpaw," he said, pointing to a toy soldier dressed in a paratrooper outfit. "See his gun?"

The boy touched a tiny gun painted on the plastic soldier's hip. "Let's play army." He cocked his head, listening intently. "No," he told his invisible friend. "I'm not scared. I'm a big boy. But I think Mommy will be mad about the doughnuts. Do you want one? I can get one for you." Whatever he heard in reply, he settled back into place on the rug, then stretched out on his stomach and, with the deep intensity of small children, became lost in his imaginary world, unaware that the cameras above him were recording his every move and that the man who would soon return was not his friend.

A few minutes later, the man who had abducted Tyler Matthews returned to the apartment, carrying a Happy Meal and a newspaper. He left the food with the boy and took a seat at the far end of the kitchen table, where the cameras could not see him. He lit a cigarette and began to read the newspaper intently. The front page was splashed with the news about Tyler's abduction. He pulled on a cigarette as he scanned through the articles on the front page. Both excitement and dread danced in him as he read of Tyler's abduction, the adrenaline overcoming any fear he had at being caught. Then I felt something in him catch, a curiosity and some sort of recognition. He let his cigarette drop and reread the article he'd been scanning, frowning as he did so. Images flickered across his mind as he searched to find meaning in something he remembered. Confusion followed, then a revelation, and, right on its heels, guilt again and a sense of obligation. He stood up abruptly from the table and joined Tyler in the living room, coaxing the boy to eat. I lingered behind, curious to see what he had been reading.

It was not an article about the abduction of Tyler Matthews. The article that had triggered his internal turmoil had been a story about the murder of Fiona Harker, relegated to a spot on the second page, juxtaposed ironically above a story detailing the success of a recent fundraiser for the hospital.

What in the world could Fiona Harker have to do with him? I wondered. *What was the connection?*

The man's cell phone rang again. This time he sounded angry rather than obedient when he answered it. "What do you want?" he demanded.

"Have you been smoking in the house?" the man on the other end asked.

"No," the first man said.

"You're lying. The smoke is spoiling the clarity of the shot. It's a filthy habit."

"You should know about filthy habits," the first man snapped. He was staring at Tyler Matthews, who was trying to feed French fries to his plastic soldiers.

The other man took a long time to think before he spoke again. "I forbid you to smoke," he said flatly. "It is forbidden."

"You smoke," the first man said. "Why is it you want me to pick up some of your filthy habits, but not all of them?"

"You will do as I say," the second man ordered, his voice growing in volume. It had an instant effect on the first man—I could feel overwhelming fear, shame, and revulsion fill him. It was a conditioned response. "You will do as I say or suffer accordingly. Need I remind you why I am this way? It's your fault and your fault alone."

Guilt flared in the first man, a crushing, overwhelming guilt.

"Did you hear me?" the second man barked.

"Yes," the first man said, his voice reduced to a whisper. "I heard you."

"Now, take off the boy's shirt and leave the room. I want to watch him alone for a while. I will call you when I am ready."

The first man gently removed Tyler's tiny T-shirt and folded it neatly into a square, as precisely as a soldier might fold his uniform, before leaving the room.

If there had been anything I could have done to protect the boy, I would have stayed. But I thought I knew who the man on the other end of the phone was. I prayed that the core of goodness languishing deep inside the man who was with Tyler would hold, at least for a while, and I left to find out if I was right.

Chapter 22

There are luxuries the living alone enjoy that I can no longer take for granted—picking up a phone, tapping at a computer keyboard, turning the pages of a police report. I have but two weapons left open to me when it comes to uncovering information: what I can see and what I can feel. I would need both to learn if what I suspected was true.

Robert Michael Martin was a lonely man sitting in a lonely room. He was perched on the edge of a chair in his newly clean living room, as if he was hoping for more company at any moment. The house seemed bigger than ever, the rooms even more empty. Not even Noni Bates was there to help him pass his suddenly empty hours. He was no longer welcome at KinderWatch, and his time in the sun helping Calvano and Maggie had passed. Now everyone else was frantically pursuing leads or resting at home with their loved ones, while he sat alone in a living room that had been cleaned for people who would no longer be coming. Without work to fill his hours, he had nothing.

I hated what I was about to do.

I sat across from Martin and concentrated on following the thread of loneliness that emanated from him. I followed it into his memories, memories that felt as lonely as his present. I caught glimpses of a solitary little boy, terrified of others, hiding behind his mother, peering out at the world, certain it would hurt him. I saw a pudgy boy sitting at a desk in a corner of a classroom, unnoticed by either teacher or classmates. I saw a grown man climbing the steps to a second-floor bedroom again and again, bearing food, offering flowers, administering medications, patiently adjusting pillows, doing what little he could to ease the suffering of the dying woman who lay there. I felt his certainty that, when she died, the only person in the world who loved him would be gone. Then I saw a grieving man at a graveside service, attended by few others, and then again, walking alone along the sidewalks of our town, nearly as unseen by others as I was, seeking out the noisy life of a playground to fill the empty hours of his days.

I hated the cruelty of what I was about to do even more.

Gently, I probed Martin's mind and found the fresh wound that was born of his memories of Calvano's treatment of him and Colonel Vitek's accusations. They had merged into a single, painful reminder that he was a man born to lose, a man who had stepped forward to help, only to be accused of the worst crimes imaginable. I concentrated hard on the feelings of betrayal their accusations had triggered and how they had torn at Martin's fragile ego. I felt his shock that this had happened to him give way to a sense of deep injustice, followed by outrage, recurring sadness, anger, and—finally—there it was: resentment. I fanned that resentment. I made him think of all the hours he had put into protecting children, of how he had trusted the colonel for guidance and how very hard he had worked for the colonel's approval. I made him remember all the times the colonel had asked favors of him, the hours he had given without pay to the cause, the children he had no doubt saved with his selfless vigilance. Like a singer with only one note to offer, I planted a thought in his mind over and over: *I trusted him, I trusted him, I trusted him. And he betrayed me.*

Then, like a man starting a fire with a tiny mound of tinder, I fanned his outrage ever so carefully by triggering the memories of Maggie and Calvano in his living room earlier that day. "We are looking for a man who would insinuate himself into the investigation," Calvano had said. "He would want to be of help, so he could keep an eye on what the police have found." Once Martin had that thought firmly in his head, I brought him back to his resentment toward the colonel and, finally, I intertwined those thoughts in his mind.

He got it.

Martin sat straight up and gasped. His face grew red with fury. His heart burned with outrage that he had been accused by a man he was now certain was guilty. *How dare the colonel have said such things about him? How dare the colonel have tried to ruin his reputation when his own hands were surely dirty?* But then Martin's conviction faltered. . . . *The colonel was in a wheelchair. How could he have managed to . . . ?* I felt Martin's resolve wobble and stepped up the cruelty of the thoughts I was planting in his mind. *He accused me of hurting children. . . . He accused me of unspeakable acts. He as much as said that he was certain I had taken the boy. . . . The things he implied I wanted to do with a child . . .*

That did the trick. Martin rose abruptly and raced to

his computer room, where he stuffed his pockets with those tiny computer thumb drives I had never bothered to master when I was alive. I wondered why he needed them and, for one brief moment of fear, grew afraid he would only lead me back to the station house. But no, he turned away from the direction of headquarters as he left home and strode angrily along the sidewalks of his neighborhood, leading me in the opposite direction.

I knew he was taking me to the colonel.

But then another thought rose in my own mind, one I should have considered from the start. What would happen when Martin tried to confront a man who was clearly more experienced than he was at harming others, a man who might even have a gun? What if I could not stop Martin from forcing a confrontation? The desire to hurt is easy to bring forth in the human mind; there are so many things human beings feel angry about it. But restraint? Impossible once you have set the wheels of fury in motion.

What had I done in my desire to find out where the colonel lived? Surely, pitting one man against another would not gain me redemption. What had I done?

Martin stopped in front of a small ranch house isolated from its neighbors by a large, flat lawn designed to discourage company. The front of the home was nearly obscured by an unbroken line of shrubs. The entrance door was on the left side of the house and it opened onto a low, wooden platform connected to a wide, concrete driveway by a ramp built to accommodate the colonel's wheelchair. The driveway ended at the rear of the house, where a garage and adjoining cedar fence blocked the backyard from view.

The driveway was empty. The colonel was not home. My relief was profound. I would remember this lesson and be more careful in the future. I had no business using people that way.

Martin had been there many times before as a volunteer, and he knew the house's weaknesses. He looked around to see if he was being watched, then quickly walked around to the far side of the house. He was completely concealed from the eyes of neighbors by the fence and shrubbery. A window had been left cracked open toward the middle of the house. Martin braced himself against the trunk of a tree, pried the window open farther, and wriggled through it with difficulty, finally dropping down into a bathroom. He waited until he was sure he was alone, lowered the window to its original position, and stepped out into the hallway of the colonel's house.

There was no evidence of a woman's touch anywhere, nor was there any attempt at decoration beyond the utilitarian. The floors were linoleum and the furniture crafted in a blocky, crate design. A large-screen TV and new couch dominated the living room. The dining alcove was barely big enough to hold a plain pine table. Chairs lined the table along three sides, while the fourth was kept clear for the colonel's wheelchair. The kitchen was big but outdated, with appliances and fixtures that were decades old. Cereal bowls and coffee cups had been washed and left to dry in the drainer next to the sink—did KinderWatch volunteers gather here for breaks, or did the colonel live with someone?

Martin knew where he was going. He headed down the hallway and passed two bedrooms. One was wheelchair accessible for the colonel; the other was as spotlessly clean and unadorned as a monk's cell. Toward the end of the hallway, Martin entered another bedroom that had clearly been converted into the headquarters of KinderWatch. My guess was that some of its volun-

teers worked from their homes, but others worked here,
at times, with the colonel watching over them. Counters
had been built along two of the walls and were lined with
computer monitors at intervals, their dimmed screens il-
luminating a room darkened by drawn blinds and heavy
curtains. The room was cooler than the rest of the house,
and the steady hum of electronics filled the air.

Martin knew where to find the main computer and,
within seconds, I realized why he was there. I had un-
derestimated Robert Michael Martin. Yes, he had been
bullied and disappointed his whole life. But he had yet
to embrace this fate as permanent: he was, in no way, a
willing victim. Martin wasn't just angry at the colonel for
accusing him of the worst crimes he could imagine, he
was determined to get even.

Martin peeked out a window, barely lifting the curtain
and blind to do so, verified that he was still alone, and set
to work. However awkward he was in the real world, however ill-equipped to deal with women or to live a normal
life among others, he was at home on a computer. Rapidly
typing in commands, he pulled up lists of files, sorted
them by date, culled the ones he apparently thought of
little use, and began copying the others onto the miniature hard drives he had brought with him. I didn't know
enough about computers to understand what he was copying, but soon he was working on three computers at once,
copying files simultaneously from all three to speed up
the time required to capture what seemed to be an endless
list of files. As the status bar of each file slowly filled, the
minutes ticked past. Martin no longer seemed nervous or
angry or awkward or uncertain. He had a plan. When the
thumb drives grew full, he took disks from a drawer in
a supply closet as casually as if he did it every day and
began to copy still more files to those.

It was fascinating to feel the strength growing in Martin as he moved around his electronic world. I knew there had been a time when the imaginary world of his computer had been the only one to welcome him and, somewhere along the way, Martin had become master of that world, and he felt like himself within it.

Almost an hour had passed when we both heard the slam of a car door. Without panic, Martin quickly aborted the copying of the remaining files and tapped out commands on the keyboards to return them to their screensavers. He grabbed his thumb drives, stuffed his pockets with disks, and slipped out the door to the hallway before either one of us heard the click of the colonel's key in the entrance door lock.

Martin knew his way around the house. As the colonel entered at one end, Martin quietly eased out a back door at the far end of the hall. It was not yet adapted to accommodate the colonel's wheelchair. It was narrow and opened onto a small back deck that held a grouping of plastic chairs clustered around a large gas grill. This was where the volunteers probably gathered to hang out, talk among themselves, and escape the colonel's overbearing manner. Cigarette butts littered the deck, and plastic cups half full of rain lined the railings. I don't know why, but it made me feel better to think that Martin had had some sort of a social life after all, even if it was along the edges of the occasional volunteer get together.

Martin was fast when he put his mind to it. The backyard was completely encircled by the tall cedar fence, its corners anchored by trees with overhanging branches ripe with the buds of spring. A swimming pool had been carved down the middle of the backyard in a perfect oblong. It gleamed a pristine light blue, as if it had been newly cleaned and was just waiting for the season to cooperate. Tables and chairs had been arranged around the edges of the pool. The KinderWatch volunteers probably kept the pool and backyard clean in return for being allowed to throw parties there.

Great bait for attracting volunteers and building a respectable façade.

Ignoring everything but his need to get away, Martin slipped out a back gate. I watched him gain speed as he drew away from the house. Soon he was practically running, the impact of what he had just done fueling his adrenaline. I was certain he was headed home to review the files in hopes he would find something to incriminate the colonel so that he could return the favor of hurling ugly accusations.

I returned to the colonel's house, my own goal satisfied. I knew where the colonel lived now. I just needed to figure out what to do with that knowledge.

The colonel had returned home angry. It radiated from him in dark pulses as palpable as sound waves from an explosion. He threw his keys onto the kitchen table and immediately wheeled back to his computer room. Switching on the lights, he took his place at the largest monitor, pushed a few buttons, and adjusted the lens of a web camera. He pressed a few more keys, bringing up an image of the house along the lake where Tyler Matthews was being held. But the monitor displayed nothing but an empty living room, and my heart soared with hope—had the second man left with Tyler?

The colonel leaned forward and spoke distinctly into a microphone attached to his computer's base. "Come here now," he ordered in a voice now familiar to me.

He stared at the monitor, waiting. When nothing happened, he pulled out his cell phone and made a call. Soon, the man who had taken Tyler Matthews came into view on the webcam, stumbling sleepily into the living room. "What is it?" he mumbled sullenly into his own cell phone. "I was taking a nap."

"Alone, I trust?"

"Yes, alone. What do you want?" The first man was angry.

"Put the phone down," the colonel ordered. "Look into the camera."

The man instantly complied. I realized he was used to performing for the colonel on cue. "What's wrong?" the man asked, a note of fear creeping into his voice.

"I have just spent a very unpleasant hour at the police station being interrogated about KinderWatch volunteers."

The other man flinched.

"You were careless," the colonel accused him. "Your name is at the top of the list."

"They won't be able to find me," the man said plaintively, and there it was again: he had dropped back into a much younger persona, almost as if he were two different people. He whined in his desperate desire to please the colonel. "This house is rented under a different name. They'll find no evidence of me."

"We're moving the schedule up," the colonel told him. "It's only a matter of time before they subpoena my records and files. I will not lose this opportunity. I have over a hundred customers willing to pay three thousand dollars each to watch."

"The boy is asleep right now," the other man protested.

"Then wake him." The colonel laughed. "It goes down tonight," he said firmly. "It's just a matter of time before they find you. Wake the boy, bathe him, and prepare yourself. I will notify the clients." The colonel laughed again. It was ugly. "When this night is over, you will be on your knees, only this time you will be thanking me."

The man on the other side of the camera looked stricken, but he seemed helpless to argue. "Tonight?" he asked weakly.

"Yes. Your whole life changes tonight." The colonel paused. I could feel the evil in the room grow thick, fed by a lust that had reared its head deep in the colonel's soul. His corruption of the man who was completely under his control excited him to a depth he had once thought lost to him.

This was what the colonel had been seeking.

He laughed again, more softly, then said, almost as an afterthought: "Tonight, I will make you into a man—and when it is all over, you will dispose of the boy."

Chapter 23

I could think of only one hope for Tyler Matthews: that the man who had taken him might somehow find the strength to go against the colonel's orders. I had sensed a fragment of goodness deep inside him, buried by years of abuse and pain and hatred. But some good was still there, and it had led him to care for the boy, if not tenderly, at least adequately, over the past few days. That same spark might lead to his, and the boy's, salvation.

How do you save a soul? I did not even know how to save my own.

I headed to the house where the boy was being held, moving through a town that was going about its usual business without any inkling that a young boy's fate hung in balance. People hurried, cars honked, drivers shouted, buses whooshed, trucks rumbled and roared—all the noisiness of a Saturday night suddenly seemed infinitely dear. I wished so badly that this cacophony of ordinary life was the soundtrack to my own existence, but I had moved well beyond that now. I was treading murky waters with no shoreline in sight.

Tyler Matthews was playing listlessly in a back bedroom, once again offering his soldiers to an unseen playmate, oblivious to the horrors that awaited him. The man who had taken him stood shirtless in the living room, dressed only in jeans that sagged beneath his boney hips. He was weeping from the sting of the words being uttered over the camera system's speakers.

"I took you in. No one else would have you," the colonel was telling him, not in a thunderous, commanding voice, but in a quiet voice ripe with malignant confidence—and, oh, it was so much worse, that sibilant whispering that gnawed away at the edges of the young man's soul with a power as corrosive and relentless as acid. The colonel knew he would win in the end; he was simply playing with his prey. "I took you in when no one, not even your own parents, would have you."

"What do you want me to do?" the man in the house whispered, his cheeks wet with tears. He had twisted his arms around his torso, as if he might explode if he let go.

"You know what to do," the colonel said scathingly. "It's been done to you often enough." The colonel's malevolent laughter filled the silence that followed. "Trust me, my friend, once you begin, you will not need to ask me what to do."

"Why?" the man pleaded. "Why are you making me do this?"

"Why?" The colonel sounded matter-of-fact. "Because I cannot do it myself."

He was lying. He wasn't doing it because he was confined to a wheelchair. Like all evil men, he was harming others because it fed a rapacious hole that burned within him, a nucleus of malice that fed on hatred of all that was good in the world, and a companion need to destroy anyone and anything that was happy. He did it because he could. Because he was strong and he had found someone weak. He did it for the power, and it was this power that fanned his lust.

"It wasn't my fault," the first man whispered.

"You were the one driving." I knew it had been years since the accident that had left the colonel in a wheelchair, yet his tone was confident he would prevail in this most familiar of arguments between them. "Do you want people to know what you are?" the colonel continued. "Do you really want people to know who you are, what I've done with you all these years?"

The man did not answer. He did not need to. His lowered head, the way his body shrank inward on itself, the twisting of his torso were all proof to the colonel that his words had found their mark. The man would do his bidding.

"Do not fight me anymore," the colonel advised in a deceptively kind voice. "You are about to discover your destiny. How many men can say they have achieved that?"

The first man could not bring himself to reply. His shame was palpable in the silence.

"Daddy?"

A child's voice cut through the silence with the purity of a handbell resonating in the hush of a church.

"Daddy?"

There it was again—Tyler Matthews calling out from the back bedroom, whether to the man twisted in agony a few feet away or to his own imagination, I could not say.

But the man in the house heard him through his pain. I could feel the good in him flicker as his heart responded to the artlessness of that single word.

"Where did you go?" the little boy's voice called out.

"I'm right here." The man turned his back on the camera and walked slowly toward the hall.

"Don't you dare move until I say you can," the colonel thundered after him, but the man did not turn around.

Tyler was lying on his stomach, holding a tiny plastic chicken and pretending it was pecking at grain on the floor. He looked up, his brown eyes wide. "I want my daddy," he said.

The man sat slowly beside Tyler and patted his back ever so gently. Once, I knew, someone had done that for him. But how long ago? Would the memory be enough to save them both?

"Your daddy isn't here," the man said. "Remember? He was in the war."

"He says you can be my new daddy," the little boy said confidently. "That you'll look after me." Tyler touched the man's cheeks with a chubby hand. "My other daddy had rough skin. He let me hold his razor once."

The man held his breath and something in him swelled and broke. It was sorrow, but it was sorrow that stemmed from the loss of love—and it was that love I needed to reach. I searched through his memories as he spoke to the little boy, promising Tyler that he would return him to his mother one day soon. I cannot bear to dwell on the memories I found within the man. They were of things no one should experience, of events dark and ugly and all too real in those places where evil souls walk the earth. But they were a part of him, and I had to go through them to find the good that lay underneath. At first, I could only detect the memory of smells. Of perfume as faint as gardenia bushes in a yard, of soap and aftershave and a kitchen warm with the heat from an oven. Then I could hear faint voices in his mind, a tune, though I could not discern which song it was. It was there, underneath that memory: the man had once been loved.

"I need to go to the potty," Tyler told the man.

"Okay," the man agreed. "I'll help you. You remember where it is, right?"

The little boy nodded and took his hand. The man led him out into the hall. I followed, trying to hold on to the thread of that one distant memory. I felt love surrounding that moment, and a total lack of fear, with no thoughts of the past or the future, just the warmth of a present that was utterly and unequivocally safe.

"I need help with my pants," Tyler told the man, struggling with the top button on his cotton shorts.

The man helped Tyler with the tiny fastener on his shorts, revealing underwear printed with colorful cars.

"I need some piracy," the little boy said proudly, repeating a lesson his mother had taught him.

"Piracy?" the man asked, confused.

The little boy nodded solemnly, holding his shorts up over his knees with two chubby fists, unwilling to give an inch.

"*Privacy?*" the man asked, understanding.

The boy nodded again.

"Of course," the man agreed. "Tell me when you are done."

He turned his back on the boy and I knew the moment had come. I let his memory of love and safety wash through me. It filled me and I gave it life. I held it within me, almost vibrating with the love and care the man had once, himself, been given, even if so very long ago.

"Get back here!" the colonel's voice boomed from the living room. "Get back in here at once."

Don't do it, my friend, I willed him. I did not know if it was presumptuous of me to interfere in this way, if my shaping human events was an affront to whatever power decided such things. But I was willing to risk everything I had, to risk my very soul if that was what it took, so that this man might turn from the evil the colonel embodied. I began to pray, though I did not know who or what I was praying to. I had often been angry over the last few months at being kept on this worldly plane. I had experienced bitterness and resentment, wondering why I was doomed to wander and others were granted the right to move on. But all that seemed petty now. All that mattered was that the man who stood in front of me do the right thing, a man who had once been as small and innocent as Tyler Matthews, a man who had surely been loved by someone, for however briefly, before his life had gone terribly wrong and he had joined forces with the colonel. I left my bitterness behind me. I thought nothing of myself. I lifted my heart to whatever power guided me through my lonely world, and I asked for help in turning the man. I prayed that he might break free from the terrible hold the colonel exerted over him. I prayed for his salvation.

"I'm done," Tyler announced proudly. "No drops, see?" The boy pointed to the toilet seat. "I'm the best at potty in all preschool. Of the boys. Girls are good at potty."

The man knelt before Tyler like a suitor proposing marriage, helping him untangle his shorts. "You're a big boy," he said in a kind voice.

Yes, remember those who once said that to you.

"Will you button them for me?" Tyler asked, wiggling as he tugged the shorts up over his legs.

As the man fumbled with the fastener on the waistband, Tyler wobbled and put his hand on top of the man's head to steady himself. It was a simple touch, whether made out of trust or a desire to stay balanced, I do not know. But I do know that this single touch, from that tiny, trusting child, turned the man away from evil.

He stood up abruptly and tucked Tyler's shirt back into his shorts. "There," he said. "Good as new." Something vulnerable in him shifted and grew, holding back the anger that usually commanded the man. He had made a choice.

"We're going to play a game," the man told Tyler. "Do you think you can remember the rules?"

The little boy nodded, anxious to make the man happy.

"I want you to stay here in this house alone for just a little while," the man told him. "I'm going to lock the door, and I don't want you to open it for anyone but me. Okay?"

The little boy hesitated. He did not want to be left alone.

"I just have to go out for a while, but I'll be back soon, okay? And when I come back, I'll take you to your mommy, as long as you wait for me."

The little boy's smile took my breath away. "We're going home to my mommy?" he asked.

"Yes," the man said. "I just have to do one thing first. Okay?"

Little boys are creatures of few words. Tyler had no words to express his feelings that he would soon see his mother. Instead, he wrapped his arms around the man's legs and held on tight, butting his head against the man's thighs in his joy.

The man laughed and pried him free. "I guess you're cool with the plan?"

Tyler nodded.

As the man left the bedroom, I could hear the song in his memory growing louder: his voice, a mother's voice, a father's voice, too, all joined together in one pitch-perfect sound.

It wasn't much to carry a man through an entire lifetime of pain, but it had been enough to save his soul.

Chapter 24

I sat next to the man who had taken Tyler Matthews as he drove away from the house, wondering what life had done to him to make him two separate people. He had left all feelings of goodwill within him behind in the house with Tyler. A rage now filled him, one that fed on its own momentum, rising like a tide that pushed him forward toward some unknown destination. I could not influence the emotion, because I did not understand the forces that fueled it. It was as if something profound inside the man fed it, perhaps memories of long-endured torments, but something external fed it as well. There was a source of fury coming from outside the man, egging him on.

With that recognition, I realized that I was not alone as a passenger in the car. The otherworldly little boy who had once let me pretend to push him on a swing on a fine spring afternoon was sitting in a corner of the backseat, where he had a direct view of the driver. Gone was any shred of innocence in the apparition. His childishness had been replaced by something terrifying and thunderous, far beyond either my control or my understanding. The boy barely moved and did not make a sound, yet the power he emanated was immense and ripe with vengeance.

I wondered if the man driving the car could see him. There was a connection between the two, that much was certain. The boy was staring at the man with his curiously blank eyes, eyes that lacked knowledge of life in some strange, vacant way, yet nonetheless burned with an intensity that led directly to the man and was filling him with immeasurable fury. I could feel it, and I feared for my own soul just being near that power. This was not a benign being, this small apparition of a child who had wanted to pretend he could swing, stretching his legs upward to the sky. He was not like me. He was something new to my world—and I did not think I liked him.

What I thought about him was immaterial to the otherworldly little boy. He gave me not a glance, not a single sign of recognition. All he cared about was the man driving the car. His control of the man's emotions was relentless and it was overwhelming.

The man began to drive faster and faster, running red lights when no one else was around, taking corners too quickly and clipping the curbs, his mind tumbling with a chaos of bitter memories and cascading pains that consumed him. The faster he drove, the more the little boy in the backseat seemed to enjoy it. His eyes had begun to glitter. He terrified me.

The man grew so agitated that he missed a turn and screeched to a halt, backing up a busy road despite the near certainty someone would come up fast behind him. He swung in an arc and sped into the parking lot of a drugstore, hurrying inside while I remained mystified in

the car, seeking to understand the apparition sitting behind me.

I turned around and stared at the boy. He stared back,
his eyes suddenly as placid and benign as a pond on a hot
afternoon. He had no quarrel with me. He had no need for
me. It was as if he was looking right through me.

The man was back within a few minutes, carrying a
paper bag filled with his purchases. I wondered what was
inside.

Within another few minutes, I knew where we were
heading. He turned into a familiar neighborhood, sped
past Robert Michael Martin's house with no sign of recognition, and kept going, past the intersection that divided the blocks around the playground from the area I
had just visited: he planned to confront the colonel. He
began to drive faster, consumed by a need to fight back
against the man who had manipulated him into taking
Tyler Matthews, and sought to orchestrate their dual ruin
for his gratification.

He parked his car a quarter mile away from the colonel's house, walking quickly past the handful of homes
on the block. Each one looked deserted under the night
sky. This was not a neighborhood where you moved to be
neighborly. This was where you lived when you wanted
to be left alone.

The colonel's van was parked in the driveway near the
ramp that led to the entrance door. Lights were on at the
back of the house. The colonel was in his computer room,
removing evidence before detectives arrived to search the
KinderWatch files.

The man glanced toward the lit windows, confirmed
the colonel was inside, and got to work. He took a coil of
wire from the bag that held his drugstore purchases and
wrapped wire tightly around the doorknob to the house,
twisting and doubling back repeatedly. He then wound it

around the railings of the ramp, over and over, snaking it up support beams and the handrail until a spiderweb of wire stretched from the edge of the ramp to the front door handle, cinching it firmly in place.

The colonel was trapped inside with no way to open his front door. If he pulled on it from the inside, he'd only tighten the wire that now bound it shut.

The man pulled keys from a pocket of his jeans and walked to the side door of the garage. He let himself in with an ease that told me he lived at this house with the colonel. In what kind of relationship, I did not know, but he knew his way around. I waited outside, one eye on the strange little boy with the vacant eyes; he had appeared at the house behind me. He was barely visible in the dark, yet I knew he was there. He was not done with the man who had taken Tyler Matthews. His need for vengeance hummed inside like a motor. He wanted to see it done.

The man emerged from the garage holding a can of gasoline. He ducked behind the house, and I followed. Quietly, without so much as a scrape, he rolled the gas grill on the back stoop closer to the back door and wedged it firmly against the frame. He poured gasoline beneath the propane tanks, soaking the wood until saturated, and then pouring even more until it formed a puddle. Done with that task, he began to splash gasoline against the wooden frame of the house, avoiding the brick foundation so he would not waste a drop. He worked with a fierce efficiency. His mind was blank, but his body burned with intensity, as if his need to avenge all he had suffered and all he had lost at the colonel's hands had transmuted itself into a physical need.

When he ran out of gasoline, he siphoned more from the tank of the colonel's van, kneeling in the dark and using tubing from the garage. His moves were so confident that I knew he had performed the same task many times before. I picked up on a sudden memory of his. He was kneeling beside a car on a blazing afternoon, surrounded by the desert sands and flat mountains of the Southwest, pouring stolen gas into the tank of a sedan while the colonel waited impatiently behind the steering wheel. It was a glimpse of what his life had been like as the colonel's companion, probably moving from town to town, evading the police, sometimes hungry and living on the edge of poverty, sometimes prosperous with a profitable scam like KinderWatch to support them. But always completely under the colonel's control, every movement dictated by his desires, as years of abuse crawled by.

His gas can refilled, the man set to work again, methodically soaking the sides of the house, not even hesitating when he was beneath the windows of the room where the colonel was transferring files onto storage drives and deleting the originals from his system, completely unaware that his victim had turned predator and was creating a hell here on earth, one designed to trap him.

There was nothing I could do. I had no power to stop the man from carrying out his plan. Nor did I know which side represented good in this battle. What do you do when evil is avenged? How do you justify stopping a force when it has rightly turned and is heading straight for those who created it in the first place? Besides, I could feel a new emotion stirring beneath the fury that drove the man to torch the colonel alive. It was a pain as deep and eternal as the oceans, with a power that ripped at his soul, leaving gashes that I knew could never be repaired. The terrible memories of his existence with the colonel tumbled over me now, flooding my mind with images so vile and emotions so painful that I thought I might combust and start the inferno myself.

How can I judge this man, so filled with pain, and say he is not entitled to revenge?

He pulled a pack of cigarettes from the drugstore bag and began to methodically light them one by one, placing each lit cigarette on the rim of the brick foundation where it met the clapboard frame. He started at the end of the house near the entrance door, as far from the colonel as he could get. Each time he laid a cigarette in place, he dragged a finger across the gasoline-soaked walls and then lightly tapped the barrel of the cigarette, as if he were anointing it. By the time he had finished with two walls, the house had begun to burn, the fingerprint of gasoline flaring and flickering up to join with the fuel-soaked wall above it. Once the first spark flared, the fire took on a life of its own, racing upward toward the roof and rimming the house itself in a ring of fire as precise as if Lucifer himself had dragged a finger around the house, leaving a trail to hell itself in his wake.

The little boy who had urged on this destruction stood at the edge of the fire, his flat eyes reflecting the dancing flames. His face was solemn and his thirst for revenge satisfied. He had done what he had come to do.

His job finished, the man who had taken Tyler Matthews stood by the colonel's van, took out his cell phone, and calmly dialed a number. I could hear it ringing nearby. A curtain at the back of the house flickered and the colonel's worried face peered out into the darkness as he held his cell phone to his ear. He saw the flames licking at the edges of his window and shrank back in fear. "What have you done?" he cried into the phone as he placed a palm against the window glass and snatched it away, feeling the heat.

The man's answer was serene: "You said tonight was the night I would become a man," he told the colonel. "That I would know what to do once I started." He paused, struggling to maintain his control. "You were right. I know now what I have to do. *I hope you burn in hell.*"

The man held his phone down by his side but did not disconnect it. The colonel punched wildly at the keypad on his phone, trying to sever the connection so he could call for help. With no signs of worry about being detected, the man stood only a few feet away from the house, watching the fire grow with a detached satisfaction. Suddenly, flames swept up the near side of the house in a swoop, as if someone had pulled a blanket of fire over it. Thick smoke rose from the other side, where the flames had sought and found more gasoline. It was astonishing how quickly the fire consumed the house and how little time the colonel had for escape.

I walked into the fire.

I knew the flames could not hurt me. More than that, I knew I needed to witness the colonel's suffering. I had long sought redemption, and I had never pursued vengeance against others, knowing it would threaten that redemption. But if I hoped to understand the mysteries of my lonely existence, I knew it was imperative I acknowledge the vast power of evil every bit as much as I acknowledged the power of good.

The colonel had thrown his phone on the floor and was wheeling toward the front door, his elbows pumping in his frenzy. He skidded to a halt, turned the dead bolt key, and tugged. The door did not give an inch as the wires binding it from the outside held firm. The colonel screamed in rage but did not waste any more time trying to force the door. The air was heavy with a thick, black smoke that reeked of burning wood and melting plastic. As the colonel began to choke on the noxious fumes, he wheeled to the kitchen sink, soaked a dishtowel, and placed it over his mouth. The air was so black with smoke that I could barely see him as he wheeled frantically back down the hall toward the narrower back door. Hands trembling, he fumbled with the lock and pulled it open, only to find the

way blocked by the massive gas grill. It did not stop the
colonel. He launched himself out of his wheelchair and
through the door, hitting the grill with a thud. It toppled
over and the propane tanks landed squarely in the puddle
of gasoline. He tried to drag himself forward, but the ring
of fire had snaked around the corner of the house and was
headed for the back stoop. The colonel smelled his hands
and looked down at his now-soaked clothing, realizing
what was happening. He crawled away from the grill, but
the flames were upon him. It was too late. With a massive
boom, the tanks exploded, the percussive wave bouncing
off the brick foundation and lifting the colonel into the
air. He was covered in flames now, his clothing soaked
with the fuel that had been splashed around the deck. His
body catapulted upward like a fireball, cleared the back
stairs, and hit the concrete of the pool deck. Screaming
with agony, the colonel writhed back and forth, trying to
roll toward the pool, his body consumed by flames.

I saw them then—black shapes that might have been
shadows from the flames dancing over the rippling, blue
surface of the pool, or maybe shadows inspired by the
wind that had sprung up inexplicably and was feeding
the fire, causing the tree limbs to dance as if they were
celebrating the death of evil. Except that the dark shapes
snaking toward him were not shadows. They had a power
of their own. Grasping, almost liquid black wisps were
surrounding the colonel, undulating beside his burning
body, inching closer and closer, as if hungry to drink from
his suffering. He was screaming in fury now, his pain
secondary to the rage he felt that his control had been
overcome. The colonel cursed and threatened the young
man who had taken Tyler Matthews with punishment,
as if he could sense that the man now stood, only a few
yards away, watching his torment with aloof curiosity.

Someone *was* standing only a few yards away, watching with aloof curiosity—the little boy apparition. His head was cocked and he had his hands on his hips, legs planted wide, as he watched the colonel writhing in agony. Satisfied with what he saw, he turned and disappeared into the shadows. I was not sorry to see him go.

Sirens howled in the distance, drawing closer. The colonel heard them despite his screams, and it gave him strength. He twisted and rolled, leaving a trail of flames behind him as he cleared the concrete lip of the pool and fell in with a splash. The dark shadows that had surrounded him now flowed over the surface of the pool like black water snakes, seeking a hold until, thwarted, they fizzled and disappeared. The colonel sank to the bottom of the pool, a black cocoon of burnt flesh and tattered cloth, then struggled toward the surface again, unrecognizable as anything human, his mouth little more than a bloodred hole in a mass of blackened flesh, gasping for air.

The man who had set the fire still did not move. He stood holding the can of gasoline, watching the colonel struggle. He did not care whether the colonel lived or died. It was his suffering that had been the point. Finally, job done, he placed the empty gas can inside the door of the garage and started down the driveway.

He had made his escape too late. Fire engines were pulling up in front of the colonel's house, followed by a squadron of department cars. Notified by an alert dispatcher, the abduction team was flocking to the scene. They knew that the fire roaring out of control in front of them had to be connected to the disappearance of Tyler Matthews. They'd recognized the colonel's address, and there were no coincidences in their world.

Maggie and Calvano were among the first to arrive. Whatever they had discovered on the computer files that Robert Michael Martin had brought them, they now knew the colonel was part of the abduction plan.

"Oh, god," Maggie cried as she raced across the front lawn. "Do you think he had the boy in the basement?"

"I should have run his background," Calvano said, his face stricken. He looked like he was getting ready to dive into the flames and search for Tyler Matthews himself.

A detective I did not recognize pulled Calvano back. "Get back," he said. "Let the firemen do their job." Even as he spoke, more fire trucks roared around a corner and in a squeal of brakes and grinding metal more men jumped from the trucks and uncoiled hoses, forming teams and shouting their strategy for stopping the inferno.

Maggie was staring at the fire, cheeks wet with tears, certain Tyler Matthews was inside. In the red light of the fire, she looked as holy as a Madonna in a medieval painting. Calvano was beside himself, pacing back and forth a few yards away, muttering that his carelessness in not questioning the colonel's credentials had almost certainly caused the young boy's death. "Stupid, stupid, stupid," he kept repeating until Maggie, at last, noticed.

"Stop it, Adrian," she ordered him. "You weren't calling the shots. It's not your fault. And we don't know anything yet. The boy may not be inside."

"I had to let some loser like that Martin guy do my job for me," Calvano said in disbelief. "I should have checked the hard drives myself. I should have picked up that something was off about the guy. I don't even know if he was really paralyzed. Oh my god, I've been so stupid."

"You aren't the only one who dropped the ball," Maggie said. "Pull yourself together before Gonzales gets here."

Calvano could not let it go. He paced restlessly toward the house and then darted up the driveway.

He came face to face with the man who had taken Tyler Matthews.

The man darted to the side, trying to outrun Calvano. Calvano grabbed at him, missed, and took after him a few steps too late. The man was far faster and was down the driveway in seconds, heading toward the neighbor's yard.

"Stop or I'll shoot!" Calvano cried, pulling his gun.

Maggie whirled around at the sound of Calvano's voice. "Wait!" she called to him, but it was too late. As the man disappeared into the darkness of the yard next door, Calvano fired, once, twice, and then one more time, as if his hand was no longer under his control and his adrenaline had made him reckless.

"Adrian!" Maggie screamed as she ran to him. She carefully lowered his hands and pried the gun from his grasp.

"It's him," Calvano croaked. "It's the guy who took Tyler Matthews. I looked him square in the face. He looks exactly like the sketch. It's him."

Maggie sprinted toward the side yard where the man had disappeared. He lay across the concrete of the neighbor's driveway, sprawled facedown, his T-shirt soaked with blood. Two bullets had entered his body through his back.

"Oh, no," Maggie said. She barked into her radio. "I need a bus now. Hurry. Critical witness down." She gave the address and knelt beside the injured man, placing her fingers to his neck. "Stay with me," she told him. She probed his injuries gently with her fingers and then rolled him so that he was staring up at the stars. His face was blank, his eyes closed, his life force fading to black as steadily as a twilight sky.

"Oh my god," Maggie said. "He's just a kid. He can't be more than twenty."

Calvano stood behind her, looking down, dumbfounded, as if not quite believing that he had caused such damage. "Is it him?" he asked. "The guy who took the kid?"

"If it is," Maggie said angrily, "you better hope to God he lives. If Tyler Matthews wasn't inside that house—and let's pray he wasn't—then this man is the only one on this earth who knows where the kid is. He's got to stay alive so he can tell us."

Chapter 25

I stood in the center of a maelstrom of emotions as rescue teams swarmed the scene, seeking to squelch the anarchy that had erupted. The firemen crackled with energy and exuded a recklessness outranked only by their courage. The abduction squad was frantic with worry that Tyler Matthews was inside, their confidence shaken that they had not discovered the colonel's involvement sooner. The feds were grim, as if this latest development was a personal affront to them. Noise, smoke, fear, anger: it all whirled around the house, seeming to whip the flames even higher.

An ambulance arrived, followed by another, disgorging EMTs. They moved through the chaos like beacons of light, their steady focus calming the others, causing them to pause and recover their professionalism.

"There's another one back here," a fireman shouted from the top of the driveway. An ambulance crew started toward him on the run, Maggie following behind them.

"Is it a child?" she screamed above the sounds of the fire.

"No," the fireman shouted back, his face covered in soot. "Adult. Unrecognizable." With these ominous words, he stepped aside as the EMTs raced past him. The fireman turned away from what he had seen. Having witnessed the agony of the colonel, he could not bear to look at it anymore. Even the EMTs slowed at what they saw: a blackened shape huddled over the steps in the shallow end of the pool, unrecognizable as human, a collage of black char, burnt fabric, and ruined pink flesh.

"Oh, god," one of the EMTs muttered under his breath. His companion glanced at him and tugged at his elbow, urging him to shake it off. Another human being was in pain, and it was their job to stop it.

They did what they could.

Maggie had returned to the injured young man's side as soon as she'd heard the second victim was not Tyler Matthews. She knelt beside him, holding his hand and murmuring to hang in there as the EMTs worked over him, assessing his wounds, slowing the bleeding, and containing infection for the moment. His eyes had opened and he stared at Maggie as if she were an angel, but he did not make a sound.

"Can I ride with him?" she asked as they loaded him onto a stretcher and began to race toward the ambulance.

"No room," the female EMT told her. "You'll have to follow."

Maggie was crestfallen. I marveled at the sympathy she was able to show for the man who had, irrefutably, taken Tyler Matthews.

"Come on, Adrian," Maggie told her partner. "Let's get out of here before Internal Affairs arrives. Someone's got to be by the kid in case he says something."

"You got my gun, right?" Calvano asked.

"Yes." Her answer was abrupt. "It's probably going to be a while before you get it back. Nothing I can do about that."

"Gonzales already knows, doesn't he?" Calvano asked miserably.

"Probably." Maggie took notice of Calvano for the first time since the shooting. She, like me, saw that something in him had changed, as if his ego had been popped by the jab of a pin and now hung deflated around him, leaving him with nothing but the saggy vestige to drag along with him. His cockiness, his confidence—it had all disappeared.

None of that had been real, I realized, his self-assurance, his self-centeredness. I had hated him for being someone who did not really exist. It was all a façade. And it all seemed like such a waste of energy now.

"Come on, Adrian," Maggie said more kindly. "Man up. I need your help."

Maggie could not ride with the young man to the hospital, but no one was going to stop me. I was inside the ambulance before the crew was, perched on a bench right behind the driver's seat, where I could watch the EMTs at work. They loaded the young man without any judgment about whether he was worthy of saving. I marveled at their objectivity. They sat on either side of him, checking his vital signs, hooking up intravenous drips, swabbing out what wounds they could. They did not care if he was a criminal or a victim. I could feel in each of the technicians an intense core of determination—as if they had anointed themselves knights sworn to defend all life against death, to the death, regardless of whether someone deserved it. They were not saving lives; they were fighting death.

"Why didn't you let her ride along?" the male EMT asked his colleague.

"She wants something from him," the other EMT explained. "She'd pounce on every groan or movement he made, wanting to talk to him. I can't deal with that. We're dealing with enough here as it is." A monitor began to beep and she quickly adjusted one of the clear bags of fluid dripping into one of the man's arms.

There was little they could do, really, given the devastating wounds, but their vigilance was relentless—and their stubborn refusal to give up on him was keeping him alive. As the young man lay in the dusk between life and death, his life force vibrated like a piano wire, swinging from faint to louder again, then fading away, only to be brought back once more. They were not going to let him die.

I could feel nothing else from him, just that faint thread of life and the remnants of whatever had kept him alive through all the years of the colonel's abuse: his will to survive. Whatever pain he had felt, whatever memories he held, they were of no importance now. His fight was simple: his body would either live, or it would die. Nothing else mattered.

We raced through the town, sirens screaming and red lights flashing, leaving a wake of chaos as cars pulled frantically to the side and then sought to recover from our passing. I saw the looks of terror on the faces of the drivers as the ambulance raced past. *Ask not for whom the bell tolls. It tolls for thee.*

We reached the hospital at virtually the exact same moment as the ambulance carrying the colonel, though he was little more than a ruined body. That he was still alive was no testament to his strength, I thought, but rather the judgment of a universe that had decreed he had not yet suffered enough to pay for the suffering he had caused.

A team of doctors and nurses rushed to meet us as we pulled up to the emergency room entrance. As my luck would have it, the great Christian Fletcher was back on duty, newly refreshed, and the first to take control. He took one look at the colonel and ordered him taken upstairs to the burn unit for "pain control." There was nothing else that could be done for him.

The young man was another story. Within seconds, the EMTs had summarized his condition to Fletcher and handed over the paperwork. As the young man was wheeled inside the hospital, a squadron of nurses fulfilled every order that Fletcher barked on the run. His authority was absolute; his concentration even more so. When Maggie and Calvano arrived a moment later, Fletcher was too engrossed in saving the young man's life to even notice that Maggie was watching.

Have I been wrong about him? Could a man so devoted to saving lives take a life, as someone had taken Fiona Harker's? As she watched him in action, it did not seem possible. And were he and I really all that different from each other? He fought to win the battle of the flesh. I fought to win the battle of the soul.

They were moving the young man into a trauma room. The nurses had changed from the warm, nurturing women I had observed days before into steel-strong instruments of efficiency, ruthless in their competence. They worked together as one, removing the boy's clothing and sterilizing the wounds. Fletcher did not even have to ask for an instrument or suggest an adjustment in the equipment now surrounding the man's body like a crowd of robotic onlookers. The nurses always seemed a step ahead of him, anticipating his needs.

Fiona Harker had once been one of them, I remembered. How ironic it would be, I thought, if the young man before me died because Fiona Harker was not here to help save him. She had been the best, the medical staff insisted, but if she had been better than the nurses I saw before me . . . oh, how very many lives she must have saved before hers was taken.

Maggie pulled aside one of the attendants and was outlining the situation in an urgent whisper, explaining the need to talk to the injured man as soon as they could, that he might be the only one who knew where the missing boy was. The attendant nodded, understanding, but jumped and then froze—as did everyone in the entire area—when the emergency room doors banged open and the federal agents stepped inside, looking like a posse of gunslingers about to take over the town.

"Get them out of here," Christian Fletcher ordered immediately. He glanced at Maggie and Calvano and I realized he had, indeed, registered her presence all along. "Those two can stay."

It was one of the few places in town where the feds were outranked and their outrage could not save them. They were swept from the treatment area by a pair of intractable nurses, but quickly abandoned the fight once one of the nurses told them the colonel was still alive and in a burn unit upstairs. They raced for the elevator instead.

Yeah, good luck with that one, boys, I thought. *The colonel's not going to be able to help any of you. He's busy fulfilling his fate.*

A nurse showed Maggie and Calvano to the staff break room and told them to wait there. She did not seem to agree with Fletcher's assessment that they could stay, and made a conspicuous point of removing a pile of patient records from a counter before she left the room. Neither Maggie nor Calvano noticed. They were too preoccupied with their troubles. They paced the room, both lost in their own fears. Maggie's worries were for the young man and for Tyler Matthews, who might have died in the fire. Calvano's worries were for himself. He knew his career was over if the man who had taken Tyler died with bullets from Calvano's gun in his back.

But Maggie's fears, at least, were lessened when Gonzales was shown into the room by an attendant. In my town, there was no force that could keep Gonzales from going where he pleased. He outranked God. I thought Calvano might crap in his pants when the commander walked through the door, but Maggie ran to him like a sinner seeking salvation. "What did they say?" she asked.

"No other bodies," Gonzales told her, grabbing her arm and holding her gently in place. I felt Maggie grow calm as relief and his steadying presence swept over her.

"Are they sure?" she asked.

He nodded. "The fire was contained pretty quickly. It's mostly smoke damage in the interior, except for a couple back rooms. They checked those carefully and searched the basement. There is no attic. And there are no other bodies. Which means Tyler Matthews may still be alive. Has the arsonist said anything?"

"No," Maggie said, sitting down abruptly and trapping her hands between her knees to steady them. "I'm not sure he's going to."

For the first time, Gonzales seemed to notice Calvano, although I knew he had been aware all along that he was waiting, stricken, in a corner of the room for his judgment. Ignoring him had only been the prelude to what awaited Adrian Calvano.

"You," Gonzales said, pointing straight at Calvano. Oh, this was bad. He was not even going to call him by his name. Calvano knew it, too; his face drained of all color. "Get out of here. Go back to the department and wait. A car's outside to take you. I don't want you getting near any case files or within two floors of the squad room. Sit in the lobby waiting area and wait. Talk to no one. IAD will be there when they can."

"The public waiting area?" Calvano asked, mortified. "The media can't be far behind. I'll be crucified."

Yeah, dude. I kind of think that's the point. I was suddenly very glad I'd been so low on Gonzales's radar while I was alive that he'd not ever even bothered to judge me.

"Then call your union rep and work it out," he told Calvano, unconcerned. "I'm busy. Just get out of here." Gonzales turned his back on Calvano. He was done with him. It was a devastating dismissal for someone who needed his approval as badly as Calvano did.

Humiliated, Calvano slunk from the room. I felt no satisfaction. I remembered all too well what it felt like to screw up that badly and, at least in my case, I'd had alcohol to blunt my mortification. Calvano would be facing his disgrace stone-cold sober.

Maggie's mind was already miles beyond Calvano and his well-deserved fate. "If Tyler wasn't at the house, where the hell is he?" she asked out loud.

"That's what I need you to find out," Gonzales said, pulling up a chair so he faced Maggie directly. I could feel his peculiar, supple energy reaching out to Maggie and wrapping around her. Gonzales was a chameleon. He could become whatever you wanted him to be, and he often did to further his own aims. He was going to be Maggie's father, a seasoned, older detective, treating her like a colleague who was just a little bit smarter than she was. And it was going to work.

"The feds will be raining down an army of people to find the boy," he explained. "But they aren't going to find him because they aren't from here, Maggie. You are. We can't count on that young man in there pulling through and telling us where the boy is. And Vitek is barely alive. He'll tell us nothing. He's in a medically induced coma, and we're not going to be able to countermand that order. He could die at any moment. The feds don't know that, so he's distracting them for at least a few hours. I need you to think, to think hard, on how we can find the boy."

Some people become detectives for the challenge: they thrive on puzzles and outsmarting criminals. Others love the ego trip. But some, like Maggie, do it for the victims. She was in it for Tyler Matthews, and her mind was uncluttered by anything but how best to find him. Gonzales was smart enough to know that, and so he had come to her. She would make him look good.

"The first thing we have to do is find out who that man is lying in the other room and why he set the fire," she said quietly as her mind began neatly cataloging her options. She was an amazing force at times like this, the human equivalent of a Porsche built for speed, beauty, and absolutely flawless performance. "He had no ID on him, so we need to find out how he got to Vitek's house, and then search his vehicle. The license plate is probably on the lists Martin took down near the park the morning before Tyler was taken. We can run the plates and see who it's registered to."

"Good," Gonzales urged her. "Go on."

"He's probably using a fake name—and so is Vitek, for that matter—so we need to find out who both of them are. Vitek's beyond fingerprints, but the boy isn't. And we can run DNA for both. And let's find out who owns the house where Vitek was living and how he ended up there." She was just getting started. Like Gonzales, she wanted a victory, and she wanted that victory to belong to the department, not to some faceless men in suits who looked down on the hometown squad.

"What else?" Gonzales urged her. "All that is going to take time."

"The disks," she said, looking up. "We have the files Robert Michael Martin brought into the station. The ones he copied off of Vitek's hard drives. If the boy is in some of them, maybe there's something in the background that will help us pinpoint the location?"

"They found footage of the boy a few minutes ago,"

Gonzales confirmed. "But there was a lot of material and they're still looking through it."

"Then we need to bring in Tyler's mother, sir," Maggie told him. "Have her look at the footage we have of her son. See if she recognizes anything in the house where he's being held. Stranger abductions are rare. Chances are good she knows whoever took him or that they at least had contact before. We need to bring her in again."

Gonzales nodded, but reluctantly. Callie Matthews was not in good shape. Seeing her son alive on Vitek's video files might reassure her, but it might also put her over the bend. I thought Gonzales might protest, but he didn't. Like me, he had noticed Maggie's expression, and it puzzled him. She looked almost shamefaced. I wondered what on earth she had to feel so guilty about.

So did Gonzales. "What is it, Gunn?" he asked.

"I apologize," she said quietly. "About Fiona Harker. Every time I think I'm getting somewhere, I get pulled onto the Matthews case. I haven't forgotten about her, sir. I will find out who killed her."

Gonzales looked bemused. "Gunn," he said, shaking his head. "The dead can wait. Let's just find the boy. But in the meantime, I'm giving you a direct order. I want you to go home and get some rest. I'll set the wheels in motion on everything else. I'll need you fresh in the morning. So go home, shower, and rest." His voice was surprisingly kind for someone whose entire existence revolved around self-interest.

His cell phone rang and he glanced at the caller ID. "Gonzales," he said into the phone, with the tone of voice he reserves for people more important than he is. He held his hand over the receiver and mouthed four words at Maggie: "Do what I say."

Yeah. As if that would stop Maggie from doing what she thought she needed to do.

Chapter 26

As soon as she left Gonzales, Maggie phoned her father. Colin had been waiting. He had his police scanner on and had followed the dispatches sent over the radio. He'd heard about the fire called in and had heard Maggie's call for an ambulance when she had tagged the man Calvano shot as a "critical witness" priority.

"What's going on?" he asked. "Is the fire related? Did they find the boy?"

Maggie told him about Vitek's sham background and his house burning. She also explained that Tyler Matthews was still missing, his whereabouts known only by the man whose life hung in balance.

"So you can't find the boy?" Colin said. "Not without this man's help?" He shook his head. "I don't think Calvano's uncle can save him from being sacked over this one. Barring a miracle, he's done. And that's too bad. Many a man has made a great detective once he's been humiliated. You just need to break him, like a stallion."

If that was the case, I'd have made a stellar detective. God knows, I'd humiliated myself often enough.

Maggie didn't want to think about Calvano. She had enough to worry about. "We're going to try finding the boy some other way," Maggie said. "We're not waiting on this guy to pull through. He may not make it." She outlined what she had suggested to Gonzales. "Can you think of anything else we could do?"

"Bring in the KinderWatch volunteers one by one," her father said promptly. "Find out every scrap of information they know about Vitek and the other man. You'll at least figure out what name he was going under. That may tell you something."

"*Yes,*" Maggie said, angry at herself. "I should have thought of that."

"The FBI would have suggested it soon enough. But it won't hurt to propose it first. That way, they'll overcompensate by taking over the questioning completely—and you can get out there and look for the boy. If you had to stay inside talking to people, knowing that boy was still missing? You'd go crazy, Maggie May. Trust me on this one. You're like poetry in motion. You need to keep moving."

Ah, but Colin Gunn loved his little girl.

"I love you, Dad," she told him. "I'll fill you in later."

"Wait," he added. "Don't go feeling guilty about Fiona Harker. Her turn will come. Things have a way of working out."

Maggie hung up and was pacing the halls of the emergency room wing when Peggy Calhoun arrived. Peggy looked distressed.

"You okay?" Maggie asked.

"No, I'm not okay," Peggy admitted. "I can smell that burned man in the emergency room. I can *smell* him, Maggie. I can only imagine what kind of agony he's in."

"I know," Maggie said. "But I'm betting we'll find he's left hundreds of victims in his wake, all of them kids. His whole identity was fake. Does that make it any better?"

"Maybe a little. How about the other guy? Is he going to make it?" She knew finding Tyler Matthews probably depended on it.

"We have no idea. We're hoping you can help us find out who he is. That way, even if he doesn't make it, maybe we can at least pick up his trail. Follow me." Maggie led her into the treatment room where Christian Fletcher was still working on the man. But fewer nurses surrounded him now, and the urgency in the room had abated.

Fletcher noticed Maggie the moment she approached. "He's stabilized," he told her. "I'm sending him up for surgery. And I apologize, but I just have to ask—were those your—"

"No," Maggie said, cutting him off. "My partner's."

Fletcher shook his head, disapproving. "At least he missed the spine. The kid may lose a kidney, but he's got a good shot at making it."

"How soon can I talk to him?"

"Anyone's guess. He's still under right now. Surgery is going to take at least three hours."

Maggie's frustration was intense but she fought to keep it under control. "We need to know who he is," she said. "For so many reasons."

"I can't help you there." Fletcher pulled off his gloves and handed them to a nurse. "I can only save them. I can't tell you who they are."

"I know. That's why my colleague needs to fingerprint him and take a DNA sample before you send him up."

At her words, the three nurses hovering over the man looked up. They stared first at Maggie and then at Fletcher.

"I can't let you do that," Fletcher said, trying to keep his voice neutral.

"Can I talk to you alone?" Maggie asked, her voice catching slightly, as if Fletcher had touched her most vulnerable spot.

Maggie, you didn't do that on purpose, did you?

There was no way Fletcher would say no, not to Maggie, not when she was acting like she needed him and only him. He gestured her over to a corner, where they huddled together, Maggie whispering furiously. Fletcher used the excuse to stand closer than was necessary, his head bent until it nearly touched hers. His professionalism had crumbled with his proximity to Maggie, and his face was a kaleidoscope of emotion as she explained why she needed this favor.

The nurses made no bones about shamelessly trying to eavesdrop. Neither did Peggy, for that matter. She didn't need a microscope to confirm that what she suspected was true: there was something between the two of them, whether they liked it or not. I fought my jealousy and thought of Tyler Matthews alone in the house near the old reservoir, waiting for the man to come take him to his mother. If this helped Maggie find him, so be it.

Fletcher put up a fight, citing protocol, but Maggie won in the end. Peggy could take her samples, no subpoena necessary. The well-being of Tyler Matthews overruled Fletcher's professional qualms about allowing his patient to be DNA-typed.

The nurses stepped back wordlessly as Peggy did her job, their eyes still on Fletcher and Maggie. I knew it would be less than an hour before word was out through the entire hospital that they had something going on, whether it was true yet or not. God help Maggie's reputation if he'd killed Fiona Harker. Her attempts at keeping distance between them wouldn't stop the gossip.

Peggy worked quickly as she took the unconscious man's fingerprints and a swab from the corner of his cheek. The nurses did not offer to help her, not even when she had to hold the air tube out of her way to scrape his cheek. They did not approve of Fletcher's decision, nor did they give a crap about how attractive Maggie was. They believed in protecting the patient's best interests, no matter what. And they did not have the benefit of knowing a little boy's fate was at stake.

Peggy stepped back when she was done. Fletcher nodded and two of the nurses began to wheel the man's gurney toward a back elevator.

Fletcher and Maggie shook hands, and she thanked him—rather unnecessarily, I felt. Also unnecessary was the fact that he was walking her to the exit door. This was not a cotillion. I turned away from them, determined not to torture myself, and saw a flurry of movement inside the wide steel elevator where nurses had loaded the man on the gurney while escorting him up to surgery. They were bending over him, but they didn't look alarmed. They looked surprised. The man's arm moved—I saw it distinctly. He reached out and touched one of the nurses. His lips moved and she bent closer, her ear nearly to his face. His hand fluttered again before he grew still. He'd said something to the nurses, I guessed, and then fallen back under, but what he'd said I did not know.

I do know that the two nurses looked up and stared straight at Maggie, their faces filled with synchronized indecision. Then they looked at each other and back again at Maggie, trying to decide what to do. But before either of them could react, the elevator doors slid shut, hiding them from view. They were on their way to the operating floor.

Whatever it was, if the man had said anything meaningful at all, it could be hours before Maggie would know. And that's if anyone bothered to tell her at all.

Chapter 27

As a wanderer through other people's lives, I have come to understand that human fate is shaped by random events colliding with events that are inevitable. But whether random or inevitable, each moment in a life carries the potential to become the point on which a destiny turns. Even the smallest of events can change the path of a life, if we choose to view it as important; even the largest of catastrophes can matter not a whit, if we choose to decree it inconsequential. But there is always a wild card in the deck of destiny—and that is the ripple effect of other people's lives on our own. We can never know when another person's choices will change our own fate profoundly.

So it was with Maggie that night. Unable to talk to the injured man until he was out of surgery, she headed back to the parking lot, knowing she'd never be able to sleep, and determined to use the long hours ahead to help find the missing boy. But Christian Fletcher followed her out to her car, his doctor's coat still soaked with blood.

"I'm sorry," he said from the edge of the shadows next to Maggie's car. He had moved as quietly through the night as me.

She whirled around, surprised to find someone behind her. I felt fear rise in her and just as quickly subside once she recognized Fletcher. A connection between them had taken root, and it was not based on fear. "Sorry for what?" she asked him.

"Everything. Meeting you when I did. Coming to you the other night like a crazy person. Not being able to help more when I know it means so much to you to find the boy."

She stared at him, not knowing what to say.

"Please just come have a cup of coffee with me. I need to sit across from you for fifteen minutes and act like a normal person. I need to hear you talk about your life, something that has nothing to do with people dying or hurting each other."

As he spoke, I felt the loneliness in him rise and seek out her own. I thought she would turn away, but the fire had unnerved her, and she needed the contact as much as he did. "All right," she said. "Just a cup. And we'll have to pretend I'm asking you about Fiona Harker. I can't be seen with you under any other circumstances."

"Fair enough," Fletcher said. Something inside him stirred to life, something light-filled and breathtaking. It was a hope he had not felt in a long time.

"I was going to go home and shower," Maggie confessed as they walked back into the hospital. "But I don't think I want to be alone right now. I can't stop thinking about that little boy."

"I know," Fletcher said, taking her arm for the moment it took them to reach the bright lights of the emergency room entrance. This time, it was something inside of Maggie that stirred at his touch, something she had not felt in a long time.

"I spend most of my life alone," he explained. "Even when I'm surrounded by others. And I don't mind it. In fact, I prefer it. I'm not sure I could do what I do if my head was cluttered with other people's lives. But there are times when I feel like I can't stand myself another moment, when I become so sick of my own obsessed need to keep doing the impossible, day after day, that I can't bear myself any longer. That's when I can't be alone."

"Exactly." Maggie stopped in the waiting room and stared at him. They smiled at each other. He was the first to drop his gaze.

"Come on," he said, guiding her by the elbow. "We'll go upstairs to the cafeteria. If we hide it, people will just talk more."

They sat at the back of the nearly deserted hospital cafeteria, surrounded by the smell of boiling cabbage and lemon floor disinfectant. The food looked bleached out and overcooked under the fluorescent lights. It made me glad I no longer had to eat.

They didn't seem to notice the atmosphere. They sat next to each other at a small table for two, chatting away as if they were sipping espresso at a Paris bistro.

A third wheel by fate, I could not bear also to be a third wheel by choice. I considered sitting at their table and turning their tête-à-tête into a threesome known only by me, but that seemed pathetic, even by my low standards. Instead, I sat a few tables over, across from an overweight Chinese man who was eating his third bowl of tapioca pudding. It quivered in his bowl like a lab specimen and made me even gladder I no longer had to eat.

I could smell their coffee from where I sat. It reeked like the boiled-down sludge I used to drink at the station house. I let the aroma fill me. How I missed the bitter taste of my morning ritual.

That wasn't what I envied most, of course.

Maggie and Fletcher sat only inches apart, but drawn in on themselves, as if they wanted to make the boundaries clear to anyone who might see them. That didn't fool me. Their energies were as intertwined as lovers curled up in bed. They talked about all the mundane details of their lives, the kinds of things you do not tell strangers, or even acquaintances, the kinds of things you only tell your lovers, because only a lover would find them fascinating. She told him all the things I already knew about her, the quirks and habits and daily rituals I had learned by watching her week after week. She was giving away what it had taken me so long to hoard, but I was helpless to stop it. There was something happening between them, fed by their shared proximity to death and their mutual concern for others.

I will kill him if he hurts my Maggie. I will find a way to make him pay.

They had just finished their coffee when Fletcher's cell phone rang. He started to ignore it, then saw the number and answered reluctantly. "What is it?" he asked. His face grew still. "What?" His voice rose. "Tell me exactly what he said." He was silent, listening. "Are you sure?" He glanced up at Maggie, his face grave. "No, you did the right thing," he assured his caller. He hung up and stared across the table at Maggie, as if not knowing how to begin.

"Who was that?" Maggie asked. "Why are you looking at me that way?"

"Your gunshot victim recovered consciousness briefly on the way to surgery. He said something I think might be important."

"Then tell me," Maggie said quickly. "What did he say?"

"It makes no sense." Fletcher's voice betrayed both his fear and his confusion. *An interesting combination,* I thought.

"What did he say, Christian?" Maggie asked again. She touched his arm and left it there.

"He said, 'I know who killed the nurse. I was at the playground that day.'"

Maggie froze, as if not comprehending.

"Did you hear me?" Fletcher asked.

"Yes." Her thoughts were already elsewhere. "Did he say anything else at all?"

Fletcher shook his head. "Not really. Nothing that made much sense. That was one of the nurses who actually heard him. She said he kept repeating: 'By the lake, by the lake, by the lake.'"

"What lake?"

Fletcher shrugged. "That was all he said."

"Why did the nurse call *you*?" Maggie asked, unable to ignore the flicker of suspicion her experience caused.

"She said it was because the other nurse told a few people, and she knew it would start going through the hospital like wildfire. Since he was my patient, she wanted me to know."

"Why did she really call?" Maggie asked more quietly.

Fletcher looked embarrassed. "Everyone assumes Fiona and I were having an affair. I think she was trying to be kind and thought I'd want to know."

I knew what Maggie was thinking: *Well someone was having an affair with her, and whoever he is, he probably has heard about it by now, too.*

"I have to put a guard on him," Maggie said. She sat up straight. "His life might be in danger."

"It *is* in danger," Fletcher said. "But not from whoever killed Fiona. He's in surgery by now and there's no guarantee he'll pull through. But at least no one can get to him, not for several hours."

"What if it was one of the surgeons?" Maggie sounded out of breath, even a little bit panicked, which was not like her at all. She never showed her vulnerability. Did it have something to do with Fletcher being here, with knowing he could comfort and sustain her?

For the first time, it occurred to me that maybe Maggie was stubborn and strong and stalwart—not because she wanted to be, but because she had to be.

Fletcher smiled sadly at her. "One of the surgeons? I'm starting to be glad I'm a doctor instead of a detective. All I have to do is fix people. You have to decide whether they're good or bad."

"Christian," she said, unwilling to give up her fears. "If that man dies, we may never know where the boy is or who killed Fiona Harker. He must be protected."

"He's not in danger from the surgeon," Fletcher assured her. "The guy just started his residency last week. He lived seven hundred miles away before then. With his boyfriend, I might add. And the nurses will be watching your man every moment. He will be okay. Don't forget that you won't be able to talk to him at all unless you let the surgical team do its job. You're just going to have to wait and accept that his fate is in other people's hands right now. There is nothing you can do but breathe."

"I can't just sit here and wait," Maggie said.

"You don't have a choice," Fletcher told her. "People come into this hospital all the time, thinking they have choices when they don't. Sometimes life doesn't give you any choices. You either live or you die and there's only one thing you can do to determine which it is. After that, it's up to God, or fate, or whatever you want to call it."

Oh, that wasn't going to work with Maggie. She wasn't one to give up control of anything, especially not to a force as nebulous as fate. It wasn't that she lacked faith. She just didn't trust it. She had seen the dark side of fate once too often.

The Chinese man sitting across from me eating tapi-

oca pudding grunted. I looked at him and realized that
he had a staff badge clipped to his shirt. I wondered how
much he had overheard of their conversation and why he
suddenly looked so alarmed.

For a moment, I thought he sensed my presence. He
was staring right at me with a look on his face that clearly
meant *trouble*. But then I realized he was staring past me.
And no wonder. Serena Holman was standing at the end of
the cafeteria line, cup of coffee in hand, dressed in an em-
erald green satin dress that clung to her as if it were painted
on. She was staring straight at Maggie and her soon-to-be-
ex-husband. Her heels were at least three inches tall and, I
had to admit it, the woman was smoking hot. If she'd been
at a fundraiser in that getup, which was my guess, I was
willing to bet she had raised a lot more than money.

The look she was sending Christian Fletcher radiated
hostility. Whether it was aimed at him or at Maggie or
both, I could not tell. But I was about to find out. She
started walking their way in that smooth, controlled gait
women who wear high heels learn, like they intend to eat
you when they get to you.

Fletcher saw his wife coming. "I apologize," he said
quickly.

"For what?" Maggie asked.

"For what's about to happen."

"Christian?" Serena Holman towered over them in her
heels. Her voice was carefully nonchalant, but I could feel
the anger simmering in her. It was a little over the top, I
thought. After all, *she* had left him.

"Serena." Fletcher's voice was as neutral as hers. It
was the vocal equivalent of two dogs circling each other.
"Been out rubbing elbows with board members again, or
are you planning to start a riot on the geriatric ward?"

"For your information, I was having dinner with our
largest benefactor."

But not his wife. That would have been counterproductive.

"My condolences," Fletcher said. "I've met him."

"Somebody's got to suck up to him if you want your salary paid," she snapped back.

Oh, no neutrality there. Miss Tall Blonde Doctor had slid right into nasty. She stared at Maggie and extended a hand. "Dr. Serena Holman. I don't believe we've met."

Liar. She knew who Maggie was. She didn't fool me. She didn't fool Maggie, either.

"Yes, I know who you are," Maggie said pleasantly. "We've met. Yesterday."

"Did we?" She peered down at Maggie. "The last few days have been a whirlwind. We've had a foundation grant up for review, tours of the wing, the dinner tonight, and, to top it all off, I've got a patient who's taken a turn for the worse who has to take precedence over everything else. I apologize for not remembering who you are."

Maggie smiled but said nothing. She was not going to engage. She was going to let Serena Holman's aggression wash over her like a wave until it receded back to sea. Not because Maggie was a student of Zen, but because she knew it would piss the lady doctor off royally.

"Oh, yes, I remember you now," Serena Holman said into the awkward silence. "You were asking around about that nurse's murder."

"Fiona Harker," Fletcher interrupted. "Her name was Fiona Harker."

His wife waved a hand gracefully, dismissing the information. Nurse's names, apparently, were one of the minor details she just didn't have time for on busy days.

"Have you made any progress?" she asked Maggie.

"Working on it," Maggie said, then looked at Christian Fletcher as if to say, *Let it be. She'll be gone soon enough.*

"Interestingly enough, I heard a rumor on the way in," Serena Holman said brightly, taking a sip of her coffee with a practiced gesture that had been perfected at endless cocktail parties. There would be no stains on her designer dresses.

"Did you?" Maggie said. She pretended to stifle a yawn. Serena Holman noticed, and the anger in her flared. She took herself very seriously.

"Apparently, some man was brought into the emergency room muttering about knowing who killed that nurse," Serena said, looking first at Maggie and then focusing on her estranged husband. "I imagine you saved his life, Christian. Surely you got the dirty details?"

"I wouldn't know about that," Fletcher said promptly, not needing Maggie's warning glance to profess ignorance. "I just fix their bodies."

"That's right," Serena Holman said coolly. "You're above all that gossip, aren't you? Saint Christian. Ironic, isn't it?" When no one asked her *what* was ironic, she flicked her spite on them anyway: "Ironic that a man who lets all the gossip go right over his head should be the single most popular subject of gossip in this entire hospital."

She smiled at them as if they had protested the truth of this statement, though both Maggie and Fletcher were staring resolutely at their coffee cups. "Oh, yes, it's true," she assured Maggie. "My husband here has ascended to the rank of most eligible bachelor in town. There seems to be a virtual sweepstakes to see who will land him next. In fact, I'm thinking of auctioning him off to raise money for the hospital. Would you like to put in a bid? Surely you can outbid a bunch of nurses? Even on a cop's salary."

"That's enough, Serena," Fletcher said sharply. "Don't you have a dying patient to attend to?"

"Of course. There's nothing I can do for her, though. Poor thing. But one must keep up appearances."

Why do I think that's her life philosophy?

Serena Holman turned on her three-inch heels and floated off, as if she had spotted someone across the room at a party and was just dying to confide in them.

"Like I said, I apologize," Fletcher told Maggie when they were alone again.

"It's okay," Maggie said. "My ex-husband was drop-dead gorgeous, and he taught me that incredibly beautiful people are often incredibly self-absorbed people. The world lets them be that way."

"She's not beautiful," Fletcher said. "Not on the inside and not the outside, either. She's plastic. Everything about her is an act. She doesn't care about anyone but herself. I was a fool to marry her."

No, my friend, I thought, moved by his humility. *You were human. What man under eighty would have been able to say no when a woman that perfect came after him? Sure, I know better now. Death can do that to you. It can open your eyes about what beauty really is. But you, my friend, you still live in the land of pheromones and self-delusion. I do not blame you for taking the bait.*

"It's easy to be blinded by the light," Maggie agreed. "Believe me, I've been there."

"She doesn't even care about her patients," Fletcher continued, either needing to confess his stupidity or wanting Maggie to know he was after something deeper with her. "It took me a long time to figure that out. Sure, she'll put on a show if the parents are around or, even better, donors. But when she's alone with them? She doesn't even like kids. Wouldn't have any of her own. Can you imagine? A pediatric surgeon who doesn't like children? She went into the field for the show. Because she knew she could go the fastest and the furthest with that specialty, that it would be her ace in the hole when it came to raising money. All she has to do is trot out some poor dying kid and people empty their pockets. But believe me when I say, she doesn't really even see them. They're invisible to her."

I knew how that felt, for sure.

Maggie was staring at Fletcher. He misread her look. "I sound bitter and petty, don't I?" he said.

"No," she assured him. "It's not that. It's just that I saw her in action yesterday, with some of her patients. I was waiting to talk to her in a playroom near the nurse's station. A little girl was there, drawing with crayons. She was precious, but very ill, I think. She made me a picture. It was lovely. She drew me a house by a lake with flowers and shrubs everywhere. And a little boy who lived in the house. She was telling me about it when your wife came in. She sent the little girl off with a nurse without so much as a smile because the girl had missed her radiation appointment. She seemed so angry at the child. I thought it was cold."

"And that story shows the difference between the two of you," Fletcher said. "You were in that ward for how long? Ten minutes? And you got presented with a picture some child lovingly drew for you? Serena has been there twelve years and she's never even brought home one memento. She probably throws them in the trash when she does get them. While I bet you put yours up on the refrigerator when you got home, didn't you?" He smiled. "That says a lot about you."

Maggie laughed. "Actually, I put the picture in Fiona Harker's case file. *That* says a lot about me."

Fletcher smiled. "Good luck explaining that in court."

"Yes, I will have to come up with a good reason why a map of a house by a lake is relevant to . . ." Maggie's voice trailed off and I could feel words connecting to ideas and then forming thoughts, tumbling through her brain in a millisecond. She made the connection. Then she discarded it. Then she made the connection again.

Come on, Maggie, I willed her. *Have a little faith. Have a little faith in me. Have a little faith in those things you cannot see.*

She stood abruptly. Fletcher looked alarmed. "I have to go," she said.

"You have to go?"

"Now." She glanced at him. "I can't tell you anything more, but I have to go. I'll send in someone to guard the gunshot victim's room when he's out of surgery. Can you clear that?"

"Sure," Fletcher said. "But where are you going?"

"I can't tell you. It would sound crazy anyway. I just have to go."

By the time she hit the parking lot, Maggie was running. I was right behind her.

Chapter 28

When Maggie is on a case, her determination manifests itself in velocity. Normally I enjoy it when she's driving like a NASCAR star on methamphetamines. But that night, she was so preoccupied with the thoughts tumbling through her head that she forgot to turn on her running lights. We were passing people at double the speed limit and burning through red lights with no warning whatsoever. I had no fear for myself—I was already dead—but I wasn't anxious for Maggie to join me. Not yet.

A particularly close call with a truck about five blocks from the hospital woke her from her reverie. She flipped on her lights, and I sat up tall and enjoyed the rush. My old partner and I had loved running with the lights on, damn the torpedoes, full speed ahead. We had pretty much peeled out for a run whenever the mood struck us, even if we were just going out for burgers and beer. I enjoyed it just as much with Maggie. We were on the move and, quite literally, it made me feel alive.

I wasn't sure what she was rushing toward, but I knew it had something to do with the drawing I'd had the little girl in the cancer ward make for her. I was exultant. Elements of it had been tumbling through Maggie's mind ever since she left the hospital: the blue-scribbled lake, the house, the little boy in blue shorts, the carefully outlined streets, even the little girl's reference to a boy drinking water. Maggie knew it was crazy to be pinning her hopes on something so out-there; I could feel her hesitation. I also knew she had nothing to lose and nothing else to go on for at least four more hours. There was a chance she'd go for it.

The station house lobby was quiet. It was after midnight on a Saturday night, and the reception desk was dark. The sergeant on duty was probably in a back room eating a late-night lunch or taking advantage of the distraction on the floors above, where the Tyler Matthews task force toiled, to watch television. Then I noticed a lone figure draped over a chair in the lobby, his long arms and legs sprawled out to each side as he snored, head back.

It was Adrian Calvano.

Maggie spotted her partner and woke him. He struggled to an upright position, recognized Maggie, and looked vaguely ashamed.

"What the hell are you doing still here?" Maggie asked him. "Where's IAD?"

"Don't know," Calvano mumbled, his New Jersey accent even more pronounced when he was caught in an unguarded state. "I've been here for three or four hours." He looked confused. "What the hell time is it?"

"It's almost two. Listen, Adrian, if IAD hasn't shown up by now, they're not coming until morning. Gonzales is just screwing with your head. He wants you to sweat it out all night. That's your punishment."

"I know," Calvano said. He hunched over, looking miserable. "But he told me to stay here and I am." He glanced up at Maggie. "I know you think I'm a joke. I know most of the guys on the force think I'm a joke, too, and that I just got my shield because my uncle pulled strings. But I like my job, Gunn. I know I'm a lousy detective. I'm not like you. You always seem to be one step ahead. I'm always running to catch up. But if I hang around with you long enough, maybe I'll catch up a little. I want to be a detective. I want to be a good detective. I'm sick of being a joke. So if Gonzales says to stay here until IAD arrives, I'm going to do it."

"Oh, Adrian." Maggie sat in the chair next to his. "Gonzales would probably respect you a lot more if you didn't act like his lapdog."

"What would you do?"

"First tell me what's going on upstairs," she asked.

"For starters, I've been bounced." He looked down at his empty holster. "Probably afraid I'd accidentally shoot Tyler Matthews if I did manage to find him. But some of the guys have been stopping by and updating me on their way out. You know what Colonel Vitek's real name is? Howard McGrew. He's some lifelong pervert who went off the radar in 1993, right after he got released from serving a stretch for abducting a little boy in Kansas. His DNA lit up CODIS like a Christmas tree, though. He molested enough victims to fill an elementary school."

"But no one knows where he's been living since 1993?" Maggie asked.

Calvano nodded. "Only if you follow his string of victims. He's been moving around constantly. His whole being-in-the-Marines story was bullshit. Should have seen that one coming. But he really was in a car wreck. He didn't have a wife and son, though, so they weren't killed like he told everyone." He shrugged. "About three years

ago, him and another male named Cody Wells were part
of a ten-car pile-up on a highway down in Florida. The
Wells guy was driving and Vitek—or McGrew, or whatever his name is—got thrown from his vehicle because
he wasn't wearing his seatbelt and got hit by another car.
That's how he ended up in the wheelchair."

"And Cody Wells?" Maggie asked. "The man driving?"

"That's the same name as one of the KinderWatch volunteers. Martin put him at the top of his list of volunteers
to look into. He's also the one a lot of the other volunteers
say was Vitek's right-hand man. We've showed them some
photos and they confirm it's the guy I shot in the back."

"Except Cody Wells probably isn't his real name,"
Maggie said glumly. "So knowing it isn't going to do us
any good."

"Probably not, but they're checking property under
that name and running it through the system anyway.
What else have we got to go on?"

"Anything come up after looking at the video files
again?"

"Only that the mother flipped out when they brought
her in to see the footage. She didn't recognize anything
about where her kid was being held, and she didn't recognize the Wells dude when he was in the shot, but she did
flip out when she saw her son and now she won't leave the
room. And I mean *she won't leave*. They couldn't pull her
up from the table. She's just sitting there, watching the
video of her son over and over and no one can get her to
budge. Everyone's just working around her."

"She needs to believe he's alive," Maggie explained.
"She needs to see him."

"Yeah, but the most recent video is from yesterday.
She acts like it's a live feed or something."

"She has to," Maggie said gently. "It must be terrible to

see your child and not be able to go to him." It was something Calvano would never have thought of, which was
the reason he'd never be as good a detective as Maggie.

"She's lucky he's alive," Calvano said. "You and I both
know that's a miracle. And lucky that he looks like he's
unharmed. You don't want to know what the colonel did
to the other little boys he took, at least until he landed in
that wheelchair."

"No, I don't want to know," Maggie agreed quickly.
"Has Gonzales said anything to you? Asked you to
help?"

"I'm dead to him," Calvano explained. "He's walked
right past me twice without even looking my way."

"He knows you're sitting here. That's the point."

"Like I said, what other choice do I have?"

I could feel Maggie hesitating, wondering whether she
should tell Calvano why she was there.

Come on, Mags, I willed her. *Have a little faith in
what you can't see.*

"Gonzales ordered me to go home and get some sleep,
but I've got a lead," she finally said. I wanted to jig with
joy. "More of an idea, really. Or a hunch. I need your help
with it."

She told Calvano about going to the hospital to question staff about Fiona Harker's murder and about the little
girl from the cancer ward who had come up to her and
handed her a drawing. "She said she drew it just for me,"
Maggie explained. "Then she said something like, 'A little boy who is lost lives there and drinks from the lake.'"

"So?" Calvano asked. "She's probably whacked out on
drugs."

"How did she know we were looking for a little boy?"
Maggie asked. "She even included him as part of the
drawing. He had curly brown hair like Tyler Matthews
and was wearing blue shorts."

Calvano shrugged. "Maybe she saw him on TV?"

"No way," Maggie said. "They keep a close eye on them. I saw Disney DVDs, but they're not letting them watch the nightly news."

"Maybe her parents told her?" Calvano suggested.

"Because when your kid is dying from cancer, it's so reassuring to talk about other little kids who've been kidnapped a few miles away?" Maggie asked incredulously.

"I don't know, Gunn. Have it your way. Somehow she knew you were looking for the boy. What are you getting at?"

"I think the drawing is a clue."

"Like what, a clue beamed from outer space?"

"Adrian," Maggie said. "Have a little faith."

Bingo.

"What do you mean?" Calvano asked. "You're telling me that you, Miss Show Me the Money, is actually going to believe in spooky shit like that?"

"Yes," Maggie said. "I am. I'm going to go upstairs and get the drawing and show you. I'm telling you—it's a map."

"A map?" he asked skeptically.

"If I remember it right, it might be a map of the old reservoir. The one they built that neighborhood around about fifteen or twenty years ago. There are a lot of up-scale rental homes in that area. It would be the perfect place to hide Tyler Matthews."

"How could a little girl who's been living in a cancer ward on the other side of town know where Tyler Matthews was being held?"

"I don't know," Maggie admitted. "But on the Kinder-Watch webcam footage that Martin brought in, Peggy told me that Tyler Matthews was talking to someone no one else could see, offering him toys and calling him Pawpaw."

"Which I heard the mother said was the kid's name for

his father, who's dead as a doorknob, thanks to a roadside ambush in Iraq."

Oh, that Calvano. Sensitive to the bone.

"Maybe Tyler *was* talking to his father," Maggie said. "Maybe the father is the one who told the little girl. She's dying. Maybe she sees things we don't."

Great. Even when Maggie figures out it was a ghost helping, I don't get the credit—she gives it to *another* ghost. It was the story of my afterlife.

Calvano and Maggie were staring at each other, letting her words sink in. Then they both burst out laughing. "We sound like idiots," Calvano said.

"Yeah, I know," Maggie conceded. "But come on, Adrian—what have we got to lose? Neither one of us is supposed to be on the job right now. No one else is going to listen to us if we tell them this crazy story and, I'm telling you, the drawing looks exactly like a map. Wait here and I'll show you."

Calvano, who was too afraid to do anything but wait like Gonzales had told him, shrugged as Maggie raced to the elevator, as if trying to beat herself to the squad room before she changed her mind.

The doors opened onto the bustling second floor, where, postmidnight or not, task force headquarters was teeming. Maggie poked her head in, with me right behind her, and it was just as Calvano had said. The mother of Tyler Matthews was sitting at the table, a laptop in front of her, unable to stop watching the footage of her little boy. A distressed friend sat next to her, trying to get her to drink coffee, but the mother was oblivious to all but the images of her son.

All around them, detectives and administrative support staff were sorting through files, searching public records, pulling up more people to interview, and making plans to bring in the few known associates of Howard

McGrew for questioning. They knew that all they needed to break the case was the tiniest detail—a name, deed, address, even just a neighborhood—anything that might narrow the search and lead them to Tyler Matthews.

Maggie had her own ideas about that. She ducked back into the elevator just as Gonzales looked up from a file and started toward the door, though clearly he had not seen her. She pressed into a corner and pressed the buttons frantically, not wanting him to catch her disobeying his order. I leaned against the elevator wall next to her, thoroughly enjoying watching her act this way. It was a new side of Maggie. She had gone off the reservation but good.

The elevator doors closed seconds before Gonzales reached them, and I enjoyed the hell out of the startled look on his face. He had not seen Maggie, but he knew someone had not bothered to wait for him, and he was not used to that kind of treatment.

As soon as we reached the fourth floor, she headed for the squad room and retrieved the Fiona Harker file. Its slender width reminded her of how the case had been put on the back burner for Tyler Matthews and would be again—at least for the next few hours, while the man who called himself Cody Wells was in surgery.

She unclipped the child's drawing and held it up to the light, turning it first one way and then the other, seeking to put it in context. Maggie had grown up in town like me, albeit years later. She'd probably played along the banks of the reservoir like I had as a kid, catching tadpoles and picking cattails she could wave around like swords until the cotton burst from their tips like snow. She'd have been a water rat like me, I knew. The rough-and-tumble kids of the local cops always were. And it was a certainty she'd been a tomboy. She knew the old reservoir; she just had to make the connection.

She turned the drawing several ways before zeroing in on the broad lines drawn along the bottom of it to represent the boulevard that ran across that side of town.

Come on, Mags, I willed her. *That's a road. That's a big, wide honkin' road. It* is *a map, Mags. It is.*

Her eyes widened. She saw it. I could feel the excitement in her. She recognized the reservoir. Folding the drawing so no one else could see it, she practically ran back to the lobby, forgoing the elevators for the stairs.

"I figured it out," she said breathlessly.

"Easy," Calvano warned her. He looked toward the exit doors. "Gonzales just breezed past. He didn't even look at me. Again."

"Then come with me," Maggie said slowly. "Adrian, look at this drawing. This is Fort Mott Boulevard. It has to be. See? Three lanes each way. Which means this is the old reservoir. Look at the dogleg on the eastern side of it. I used to play on its banks constantly as a kid, before they built the subdivision."

I knew it. Cop kid. Water rat. Tomboy.

"Okay," Calvano conceded. "Maybe you're right."

"No maybe about it. See the road that hugs the lake? That's exactly how it is. There's a two-lane road that circles the old reservoir, and every home in the subdivision is accessible from off that road."

"And we're going here?" Calvano asked. "To the residence of Mr. Willy Wonka, or maybe Harry Potter, or, I don't know, Alice in frigging Wonderland?" He pointed to the brown-crayon squares that represented the cedar-shingled house. Giant, colorful flowers and huge bushes had been carefully drawn to fill the yard. They were as tall as the upstairs windows. The stick figure of the little boy tilted crazily to one side, and the blobs on his shirt made him look like he had the measles.

Okay, so I hadn't had Leonardo da Vinci to work with.

What the little girl had lacked in skill, she more than made up for with enthusiasm.

"To the house of 'a little boy who is lost,'" she reminded him. "That's what the little girl who drew this said. And do you have any better ideas?"

"I definitely do not," Calvano admitted.

"If this map is right, then if we're heading west, we need to take a left turn off the road around the lake, and then we just have to take the first right onto a cul-de-sac to find the house. It's at the top of the cul-de-sac."

"There must be twenty or thirty roads like that around the lake. It's like a wagon wheel of roads."

"Fine. That's better than searching an entire town. Come on, let's go."

Calvano went. I didn't think he had it in him. "This is nuts," he mumbled as he followed her out to her car—but he went.

He was still amazingly self-absorbed, of course. I sat in the backseat and listened to his dire predictions about the future of his career, the only topic in his world at the moment, it seemed, even if there was a four-year-old boy still missing, stuck by himself in the house, in the middle of a massive subdivision, in the middle of a town where it would take weeks for the feds to check every home, which they wouldn't do anyway because there was no guarantee he'd even been kept in town and people had a pesky habit of not liking it when the government knocked on their doors and wanted to poke around.

But no, Calvano was obsessed with whether he'd get his gun back, what would happen if the guy he'd shot died, what if he got demoted, or—most important of all, apparently— would that hot chick in the property clerk's office find out about it and cancel their date Saturday night?

If ghosts had to worry about high blood pressure, Calvano would have put me in the hospital long ago. He'd shown flashes of potential, but clearly he still had a long way to go.

Then I realized that Calvano's self-absorbed whining served the useful purpose of keeping Maggie's mind off the desperate act they were attempting. "I am never telling Gonzales about this," she muttered to herself at one point. I realized she had tuned out Calvano before they'd even left the parking lot. She was skeptical, but at least she was still moving ahead with her plan. When Maggie got started, nothing stopped her.

"Okay," she decided as they drew near Fort Mott Boulevard. "Here's the plan." She killed the running lights and slowed to a sane pace, knowing that zooming into a neighborhood with red lights flashing was not the best way to maintain an unobtrusive presence while you conducted a clandestine search. "I'm going to turn into the subdivision right up here, by the CVS. Mark it down on the map."

"Huh?" Calvano looked at her blankly.

"Oh, for God's sake, Adrian," she complained. "We have to keep track of where we've checked and where we haven't. Everything looks the same in this neighborhood. Draw a little square and mark it *CVS*, okay? And every time we drive down a street and check it, I want you to add it to the map and put the name down."

"I can do that," Calvano agreed. "I got a badge for mapmaking in Boy Scouts."

Yeah, probably because your uncle was the scoutmaster.

Calvano carefully drew a small square, then sketched a miniature sign next to it and printed *CVS* neatly on it. Well, what do you know? I bet he'd gotten an A in drawing in third grade.

I wanted to be Maggie's partner. I was not taking this well.

"What's the name of the street we're starting with?" he asked Maggie, pen ready.

"Hope Valley," Maggie told him.

Hope Valley indeed.

Chapter 29

For almost two hours, Maggie and Calvano faithfully followed every road that led away from the lake, and then just as faithfully made each right turn, cul-de-sac or not. They checked each house for signs of occupancy, seeking out any that looked deserted. Just to be sure, they even checked the second right turn off each side road. They had to work slowly, to avoid detection and panicking the neighbors. They kept at it.

In the course of those first two hours, they did not find Tyler Matthews—but they did become real partners. Calvano marked down each road on their homemade map, they muttered back and forth to each other with their hopes of each road being the right one, and they reassured each other that the boy was safe and probably sleeping soundly, oblivious to all, and that no one else had been involved in the abduction scheme or they would have known by now. Maggie called the shots, Calvano obeyed without argument, and both seemed content with the arrangement.

This growing cohesiveness kept them going despite one discouraging turn after another. Whatever jealousy I felt at Calvano being Maggie's partner was overshadowed by my gratitude that they had become a team. I wasn't worried about Maggie quitting. Maggie would not quit until they had checked every single road that led off the lake. But I was worried Calvano would throw in the towel and distract Maggie from her task.

Calvano surprised me. He hung in there for every turn and every block they searched. Four times he got out of the car and crept around homes that looked like candidates for the hiding spot they were seeking. Each time he announced them as either shut down, without power or heat, or clearly not capable of housing the type of layout they had both seen on the colonel's video of the boy. Calvano was confident of his architectural prowess, as he had scored in the ninety-ninth percentile on the spatial sense section of his standard achievement tests as a sixth grader, a fact he only mentioned about three hundred times to Maggie over the course of two hours.

If he was so good at spatial relationships, why the hell had he shot a man running away in the back twice, missed with a third shot, and done this all in a yard clearly illuminated by a raging fire?

Still, he stayed. He did not abandon Maggie. He stayed, and he watched her back, like a partner's supposed to do. Not every guy on the force would have done that. I had to give him credit.

They finally reached the road that led to the house where Tyler Matthews was being kept. That was when a horrible new fear overcame me. What if Calvano hopped out of the car, confident he could assess the dark house accurately, and missed the fact that a little boy lay sleeping in a back bedroom—sleeping with the unbreakable pull of childhood slumber. I'd had two boys of my own.

I knew that sleep. It was almost narcotic. A child could dream through anything. If they pounded on the doors, it would do no good. If they shouted his name, he wouldn't hear it.

I beat them to the house, determined to do what I could to make sure Calvano did not simply peer in a window and walk away.

The living room was deserted, its interior illuminated by an odd glow. My heart soared as I entered the kitchen and saw the refrigerator door hanging open, drops of chocolate milk leading across the linoleum floor. Tyler Matthews had helped himself to a snack and, with the single-mindedness of a four-year-old, walked away and left chaos behind him. I followed the drops of chocolate milk out to the hall. An empty plastic quart bottle had been dropped on the carpet, a half-eaten doughnut next to it.

Tyler was in the back bedroom, fast asleep on the rug. His cheek was pressed against the carpet and his body was curled up tightly in a ball. He clutched a plastic soldier in one hand. The rest of his toys had been carefully divided into two equal piles, evidence of his willingness to share.

The oddest feeling came over me then: *There's someone else in the room.*

I looked under the bed, remembering when my own boys had asked me to check for monsters. Nothing. I searched in the closet and in every corner, trying to pinpoint the origin of what I felt—it was a pulsing of energy, a thickness of the air. It was an undeniable feeling more than anything else. Or maybe the faint smell of sweat and . . . was it gunpowder? A memory came to me, one from long ago—I was hunched over in a hallway outside my elementary school cafeteria, wrapping dozens of wooden matchstick tips in layers of aluminum foil. I was making a ball I would light and toss inside, filling the massive room with smoke and successfully clearing out the school for an hour, allowing me to avoid a math test I was unprepared for.

How had I ever become a cop?

Perhaps because of the firing range. The same smell reminded me of the firing range where I had once practiced for hours, early in my career, wanting to qualify with the highest possible marksmanship score.

But those were just memories. I saw no one in the room, no one but Tyler Matthews.

Leaving the boy behind temporarily, I checked the other rooms and assured myself that no one else was hiding nearby. Confident we were alone, I returned to the hallway and got down on my hands and knees, not to pray, but to exert all my otherworldly will toward something as inconsequential and yet as monumentally important as blowing a plastic bottle into the view of someone peering through the kitchen window.

It was all I had to offer. I had a little power over wind, and so could affect fire and water, at least a little, but that was all—that, and my ability to roam people's minds, sometimes shaping their thoughts or, more likely, their memories. It was a pitiful set of powers, one that made me no superhero. I wasn't even an ordinary man.

A familiar sense of futility flooded through me; the feeling was a remnant of my old life. I'd had few strengths as a detective. In fact, remaining upright was about the peak of my powers when I had been sleepwalking through work each day. I had celebrated my ineffectualness and exercised my sense of futility daily, wallowing in my failures and daring anyone to point out that I was impotent in every way. And it had gotten me nowhere but where I was now, trapped between the living and the dead. Yet, the familiarity of the feeling was hard to resist. Like Robert Michael Martin, I had been born to lose.

I would not let that feeling win. I was all Tyler Matthews had. I would have to be enough. Besides, that little boy had had even less to get him through the past few terrible days, and he had done it at the age of four. He had survived with absolute faith in the world and a handful of plastic toys.

I needed to make the most of what I had, instead of dwelling on what I did not have. However humble and ridiculous it seemed, I would kneel and do what I could to move that plastic bottle into the light. The world has been changed with less.

The irony of pushing a simple plastic bottle toward the light, instead of my own yearning soul, was not lost on me. But who among us has ever chosen our path to glory? Heroes are made from the smallest of gestures every day. It was my time to try, and I would not squander it.

I blew, and the bottle trembled. I concentrated on the atmosphere around it, focusing every scrap of energy I could gather on a single point in front of the bottle.

The damn thing skittered over the rug, jumped the metal strip divider, and spun crazily right smack dab in the middle of the kitchen floor.

What the hell? Or perhaps more accurately: *What the heaven?*

Someone—or some*thing*—had helped me with the task. I could feel it.

Would that empty bottle be enough? Would an idiot like Calvano put two and two together, notice the refrigerator door hanging open and chocolate milk on the floor, and have the sense to think *small child*?

I couldn't be sure. I needed Maggie at that window.

I saw their headlights turn into the cul-de-sac. The

car crept along the road, slowing as Maggie counted off the houses. She finally stopped at the end of the cul-de-sac and cut her lights. In the glow of the dome light, I could see her examining the child's picture, comparing the crude brown squares that represented cedar shingles on the drawing to the structure in front of her.

Come on, Maggie—see the glow from the refrigerator in the kitchen window? Weird, huh? Not a light, exactly, just some sort of reflected glow. And why in a kitchen window at this time of night? Get out of the car to see.

It wasn't going to be enough. Maybe the blinds or curtains were blocking all the light. I raced to the window and concentrated again, willing the air to move the curtains. They fluttered. I concentrated again, falling into a rhythm, making the curtains sway back and forth, hoping it would send a signal to Maggie and Calvano.

Two car doors gently clicked shut, followed by the crunch of feet on mulch.

"See what I mean?" Maggie said right outside the window.

Yes.

"It's odd," Maggie added. "It's like a signal or something."

"This whole thing is weird," Calvano muttered.

"Can you see inside?" Maggie asked in a low whisper. "There are no cars in the garage. There should be no one home."

"Hold on," Calvano said. I heard a rustling and a thump. "I found a concrete block. Help me with it." I heard dragging sounds and more thumps beneath the window.

I stopped my efforts. They would either get it or they would not.

Calvano's eyes appeared between two slats of the blinds. He searched the room, not seeing me, of course. His eyes lingered on the open refrigerator door and the empty bottle of milk on the floor. "It's kind of weird," he whispered to Maggie behind him.

"You're really going to have to be more specific than that," she said tersely.

"The refrigerator door is hanging open, and there's an empty bottle of milk in the middle of the kitchen floor."

"Break the door down, Adrian," Maggie ordered him in a firm voice. All hesitation and doubt was done. In a heartbeat, Maggie knew.

"This could backfire," he warned her. "If we're wrong, what the hell are we going to say? We saw a vision in a kid's drawing?"

"Break the door down, Adrian," she repeated—and Calvano could tell as well as I could that, until he actually did what she said, he would hear nothing but that phrase over and over again from her.

"Side doors are more vulnerable," he muttered. "That front door is going to have multiple dead bolts."

"Just break a door down," Maggie said. "Or pry open a window. I don't care. I want us inside that house *now*."

Calvano knocked over a trash can, and a dog started barking a block or so away. It didn't matter. They were on their way in. Without so much as a scratch of warning, he came crashing through the side door that opened into the kitchen. The door splintered in its frame and banged against a wall. The noise was as loud as a bomb going off.

Thank God. The noise was enough to wake Tyler.

He began to cry, his wails drifting in from the back bedroom. He had risen from sweet, childhood dreams, sleepy and confused, into an unfamiliar room without his mother nearby.

"Do you hear that?" Maggie asked Calvano.

"Holy shit," Calvano said, and crossed himself. "This can't be happening."

"Stay behind me," Maggie told him. "I'm not taking any chances."

She drew her gun and crept down the hallway, following the sounds of Tyler's sobs. Calvano cowered behind her comically. She flipped on the hall light and stopped outside the back bedroom. Tyler's sobs subsided when he heard someone at the door. His voice floated out into the hall, sweet and high. "Mommy? Daddy Two?" he asked.

Maggie opened the door to the bedroom, and Tyler Matthews sat up, blinking at her. He saw her gun and looked down at the plastic toy still clutched in his fist, then held it up to her and touched the gun painted on its hip as if to say, *See? I have one, too.*

Maggie lowered the gun and stared at the boy.

"Is it him?" Calvano asked, his voice full of disbelief.

"Yes," Maggie said. "It's definitely him."

"Holy shit," Calvano said, then reconsidered his choice of words. "I mean, holy something. No one is going to believe this."

"You're not going to tell them," Maggie told him. "We'll think of something else."

She scooped up Tyler Matthews in her arms. He was perfectly willing to let her hold him—which told me that, despite what had happened to him, Tyler Matthews's innocence was still intact. He still saw the world as full of one friend after another, all of them there to love and adore him. Talk about miracles.

I was so profoundly overcome with gratitude that this part of Tyler had been saved that I thought I might collapse. I did not understand why it had so much power over me, but the fact that I had helped save such purity, that he was still a little boy, even if only for a few more years, well . . . it overwhelmed me. It made me glad that I was what I was.

"I better call this in," Calvano said, forgetting he was on suspension.

"No," Maggie disagreed softly, holding Tyler against her. Inside her heart, a warmth had bloomed, a desire to protect and nurture and hold. Odd. I had never felt it in Maggie before, ever. This small boy had brought it out in her. "We're going to take him right to his mother."

"Mommy?" Tyler raised his head. He was still very sleepy, and his eyes had a dreamy faraway look in them. "I want my mommy and my daddy and my mommy."

"Shhh," Maggie said, patting his back. He obediently laid his head back down on Maggie's shoulder and drifted off to sleep again, perfectly confident that he was safe.

"We can't leave the scene," Calvano whispered, trying not to wake the boy.

"We are," Maggie said. "I've never been more sure of anything in my life. You drive. And you better drive carefully. Just get us there as fast as you can."

She carried Tyler Matthews out the front door of the house, and the little boy fell deeper asleep with each step she took. Life can be kind sometimes. He'd wake in his mother's arms.

Maggie sat in the backseat and cradled the boy during the ride to the station, her thoughts a jumble of so many memories from her life: the votive candles from the church she had attended with her father and mother each Sunday of her childhood; the moment in the hospital room when the little girl had handed her the drawing and said, "I made this for you"; the top of a stained-glass window flooded with light on the day of her mother's funeral; the instant she had spotted Tyler Matthews asleep on the rug, safe, and the faith it had restored in her.

"I don't believe this," Calvano said, just once, from the driver's seat. But he did believe it, I could tell. He was

like the family dog. He didn't sit around and do a lot of
questioning about life. He just lived. Things were. That's
the way it was.

In an odd way, I envied him.

"I know it's hard to believe," Maggie said. "Let's keep
it between us. We'll say the man in the hospital told us
enough that we could guess where to find the kid. It'll go
down better for you, too. The guy won't remember what
he said or didn't say."

"If he lives," Calvano said grimly, his own fate once
again on his mind.

"We should know that by now." Maggie turned on her
cell phone and it immediately began to vibrate. "I've got
two messages from the hospital already. Are you ready
to find out?"

Calvano let out a deep breath. "May as well. We're
almost to the station."

Maggie held Tyler gently with one hand, his head
slumped against her shoulder, and pressed redial on her
phone. It rang through, and I recognized the voice that
answered: the hallowed Christian Fletcher himself. Waiting for Maggie to call back.

"He made it," Fletcher told Maggie. I could feel the
relief in her. "You'll be able to talk to him within an hour
or so."

"Thank you," Maggie said as Tyler stirred in her arms.
"I've got to go. I'll explain later." She snapped her phone
shut and tossed it into the front seat, where it landed next
to Calvano. "You're off the hook," she said. "He made
it."

Calvano's whole body relaxed. He spread his hands
wide over the steering wheel and breathed deeply. "I'm
going to church when this is all over," he declared, and it
was as if he were channeling a different Calvano, one that
had lived long before the bravado and shiny shoes and

good suits and ridiculously styled hair took over. "I'm going to ask for a second chance at the job."

"We all deserve a second chance," Maggie agreed quietly.

I wasn't sure who she was referring to, exactly, but I seconded the emotion wholeheartedly.

Chapter 30

I will never forget the next five minutes, no matter how long I roam this earthly plane. As Maggie entered the station house, Tyler Matthews nestled in her arms, she was spotted by a handful of detectives and staff heading home for a few hours sleep. They recognized Tyler and immediately reversed direction without uttering a word, following her back upstairs. Calvano took the lead, gallantly opening doors and clearing the way for what quickly became a parade of people needing to be part of a happy ending for once, wanting to witness the miracle after so many days of nonstop effort and increasingly dark hours of despair.

It never ended like this. They wanted to be there when it did.

By the time they reached the task force room, Tyler still asleep in Maggie's arms, they looked like a mini-platoon on a rescue mission pushing through the doors. At first no one noticed. But as Maggie strode wordlessly across the room, pockets of people fell silent one by one, their conversations falling away in waves until the room was as quiet as a library. Callie Matthews was the only one who did not notice. She was still watching the footage of her son, unable to stop.

Maggie walked straight to where Tyler's mother sat, leaned over, and placed her son in her arms. It took a good five seconds for Callie Matthews to realize she was holding Tyler—her living, breathing son. During that time, no one in the room moved, not even the feds, who had turned as one at Maggie's approach and been stunned into open-mouthed silence. And then Callie Matthews, who had lived so long with sorrow and loss that her mind could barely comprehend the world around her, realized that Tyler was as safe and content as the day he'd been born—that he had, it seemed at first glance, slept through the whole ordeal—and an extraordinary transformation took place in her heart, even if, from the outside, she looked no different. It was as if Callie Matthews was reborn. Where once there had been grief, there was joy. Where once there had been a conviction that life was cruel—taking first her husband and then her son—there was an almost electrifying knowledge that, sometimes, miracles did happen. Most of all, her conviction that life was nothing more than a life sentence was instantly replaced with a sense of purpose and a determination to protect her son that was so fierce I could feel the evolutionary connection between human beings and other living creatures, a link long since forgotten in our quest to be what we call civilized. She had a reason to live.

Callie Matthews could not speak. It was too much, and words would never be able to express what she was feeling as she stared down at her child, safe in her arms. Tears poured from her eyes, not in teardrops, but in tiny rivers that flowed down her cheeks. She looked up at Maggie, opened her mouth to speak, and still could not find the words. Maggie didn't need words. She understood. She knelt before mother and child and gently touched Callie's arm. "He's fine," Maggie whispered. "He's going to be fine and you're going to be fine. It's all over now."

And with that, Maggie stood and left the room without a word to anyone.

It was unbelievable.

She didn't stay for her chance to be a hero. She didn't gloat to the feds. She didn't even look at the coworkers who had started to line the halls to see her pass by, the news being passed on through the building phone call by phone call. She just walked by them all with a quick glance at a terrified-looking Calvano, a glance that meant, *You handle it. I'm out of here. Don't screw it up, Calvano. It's your turn to deal.*

People need heroes. They need to be able to touch glory. They want to believe in beings larger than themselves. But there was no one left to worship other than the unlikely figure of Adrian Calvano, who had only a few hours before been hunched miserably in a chair in the waiting room, an abject failure who had managed to shoot a critical witness and prime suspect in the back. And now he was a hero. It was the fastest career resurrection in the history of the department and would likely be passed down as legend for generations to come. But for now, the others all clustered around him, asking questions at the same time, childlike and giddy with the unfamiliar feeing that something extraordinary had happened to them for once. They had been part of a miracle.

Maggie never even looked back. With each step that took us down the stairs and out the front doors, I could feel the determination in Maggie growing: "Fiona Harker has waited long enough. Now it is Fiona's turn."

Her cell phone rang incessantly during the drive to the

hospital. She ignored it. It was Gonzales. He'd clearly been wakened by a lackey and given the good news. But she had no time for whatever triumphant gloating he had in mind now that one of his own had trumped an entire task force and brought home the most famous missing child since the Lindbergh baby, or so the papers were likely to say by the time their next editions hit the streets.

Oh, Gonzales would milk this to the max. And Maggie wanted no part of it.

She muted her phone and slipped it into her jacket pocket as she neared the hospital parking lot. There was no room for thoughts of Christian Fletcher, not anymore, not when she had pledged her fealty to Fiona Harker and could, at last, carry the banner of her cause. Maggie pulled into a spot that had opened up near the main entrance, her adrenaline so pumped she nearly jogged into the building.

The first streaks of morning light were spreading across the sky as she flashed her badge at the bored night attendant. She was quickly directed to a room on the second floor and took the stairs at a run, too impatient to wait for the elevator.

I followed—and the moment I stepped out into the hall that led to the critical care unit, I knew that something was wrong. A dark vein of impending death snaked through the halls. I could feel it as clearly as ice water flowing over me.

A soul was in torment, struggling for life.

This is what murder feels like.

A cop was sitting in a chair at the far end of the hall and I was there in a millisecond. He was reading a magazine about boats, oblivious to the malicious cloud that swelled around the entrance to the room he was guarding.

The man who called himself Cody Wells lay writhing in bed, his mouth open wordlessly like a gaffed fish as he

gasped for air from a tube that was no longer there. It had
been ripped from his mouth and dangled over the edge of
the bed, bouncing each time his body flailed. His arms
would not obey him, but he was still instinctively trying
to grope for the tube, even as he tried to fight off the ef-
fects of the anesthesia.

And then I saw him, inches from the dangling
mouthpiece—the apparition of the little boy who had
followed me on and off over the past four days. He was
staring with his strangely blank eyes at the man gasping
for breath in the bed, and I could not read the emotions
welling up inside him. Had he done this? How had he
done this? What had the man done to him?

Cody Wells had started to turn blue and his movements were growing weaker. I had to try to save him.

I rattled the medical chart clipped to the end of his
bed, but the sound was pitiful. It would bring no one.

The little boy turned to me then, staring at me with his
blank eyes, but he seemed frozen, unable to react, so tied
to the man lying in the bed that he could not even move.

Outside, I heard Maggie questioning the guard on duty
about the last few hours and asking for details of the latest medical update.

Come on, Maggie. Your witness is dying. And there is
nothing that I can do about it.

For the first time, I realized the room smelled of a fragrance, something flowery and dusty and slightly exotic.
Perfume, I thought. Perfume that I had smelled before.

Perfume that smelled like funeral flowers. Perfume
that smelled like death.

Cody Wells was suffocating. Unable to breathe on his
own yet, his air tube had been ripped from his mouth. His
death would be as cruelly silent as my own existence.

I had to do something. I concentrated on the tubes that
led from the oxygen tank, the limitations of my powers

all too prevalent in my thoughts. A spark, I thought. I just needed a spark. I had done it several times before. What had I learned so long ago in science class? Fire is a combination of oxygen and what? What was it? Hydrogen? Carbon dioxide. Heat, that was it. Heat and fuel. Would the contents of the oxygen tank serve as the fuel? God, this was hopeless.

Just make the spark. The thought came to me from somewhere—the little boy?

Just make the spark.

I managed three flickers, a bright flare, and then more. A steady flame at the mouth of the breathing tube. The oxygen grabbed at the spark and pulled it inside the pressurized tank. Within an instant, the tank exploded and fire broke out in the room. Pandemonium followed. Smoke filled the air, the ceiling sprinklers activated, an alarm went off, and half a dozen people burst through the doors, Maggie wisely running to a corner, out of the way, as the medical staff responded in choreographed efficiency. One grabbed a fire extinguisher from the wall and attacked the flames; another bent over Cody Wells, administering mouth-to-mouth resuscitation as two more nurses secured him in the bed and began wheeling him from the room. The little boy followed, unable to leave the man's bedside. He was standing vigil—but over the man's life or his death, I could not tell. He looked at no one but the man who called himself Cody Wells.

They wheeled Wells into a room four doors down the hall and quickly reconnected him to a new respirator. When they were done, some of the staff left to check on their other patients, while others stood clustered around his bed, stunned at what had just happened.

Maggie was furious.

"That was deliberate," she announced. They all recognized her anger and knew enough not to argue.

"The explosion may have saved his life," the oldest of the nurses finally had the nerve to say. She was in her early fifties, plump with graying hair. Maggie did not frighten her. "His breathing tube had been ripped out of his throat. He would have died in another minute or so."

Now Maggie looked stunned. She had been through a lot in this long, long night. "Are you sure?" she asked.

"We moved the patient out of the recovery room and into a private room earlier than usual because of security considerations," the nurse explained to Maggie. "He was having some trouble coming out of anesthesia—that happens—and we had no way of knowing what he may have eaten or had to drink prior to surgery, so we had inserted a breathing tube to protect against aspiration." The nurse did not talk down to Maggie, and Maggie liked that. I felt a bond form between them. "We were monitoring his vital signs very carefully. His readouts indicated he was still at a stage of recovery that would mean he did not have the motor coordination nor the strength to take the breathing tube from his own mouth." She paused. "Or ring for help, especially if he was disoriented."

"You're sure?" Maggie asked.

"I'm sure."

The other staff members were looking back and forth between the two of them. I got the feeling the gray-haired nurse was the Maggie of the ward. No one questioned her judgment.

"It looks as if the breathing tube was removed with some proficiency, based on the condition of his throat," the nurse added. "It's also possible he was administered something to hinder breathing on his own." She was thinking the same thing Maggie was thinking: someone had tried to murder the man before he could talk to Maggie.

"Can you test for that?" Maggie asked her.

"Yes. It would be one of three or four drugs."

"Do it," Maggie said. The nurse set to work, unfazed. She trusted Maggie and she knew as well as anyone, at least anyone without blinders on, that Fiona Harker's killer was someone who worked at the hospital.

"You," Maggie said, pointing to a younger nurse. "I want you to stand beside him and not move until she can replace you." She touched the gray-haired nurse's arm. "Can you leave your other patients?"

"Yes," the older nurse said at once. "My staff is well trained."

"Good, I need you." Maggie spoke to the younger nurse again. "No one comes near him but me and doctors I say can get near him, understand?" She nodded. "You." She pointed to a tall man with dark skin who was a nurse's aide. "You stand outside the door and see that no one comes in. No one but me and medical staff members I personally approve. If anyone else tries to get in, ask the guard to hold them, and I want their names."

He nodded solemnly.

"And you—" She pointed to the panic-stricken patrolman who had been guarding the hospital room when the breathing tube was removed. "I want a word with you. The rest of you—out."

They scurried away like mice with a cat on their heels. The young nurse guarding the bed stared discreetly at the floor as Maggie lit into the shamefaced patrolman. Behind her, the strange little boy stood watch over the man in the bed, without any recognition of what was happening around him.

"You want to explain?" Maggie asked.

"No one went in and out but medical staff," the patrolman protested. "I swear to God."

"He was under danger from medical staff," Maggie hissed at him. "Did no one explain that to you?"

"He had to be treated," the patrolman shot back. "He just got out of surgery. How was I supposed to know who was legitimate? They were all legitimate. I let in a tall doctor with dark hair, a couple of nurses, two more doctors, a nurse's aide, and the same two nurses a couple more times. It wasn't like I let a parade of people come through."

"Describe them," Maggie ordered.

He did a credible job, considering he'd not known how important it might turn out to be. His descriptions matched the nurses on duty and the nurse's aide now guarding the door. The pair of doctors had included one taller man, possibly Indian or Pakistani, and a female doctor. They had walked in together, chatting as if they were a team, and then the male doctor had left a few minutes before the other one. The guard did not know much more about the remaining doctor. Her hair had been pinned up under a surgical cap and a surgical mask had partially concealed her face. In fact, both had been dressed in surgical wear. "It was clear they were part of his recovery team," the patrolman said. "I think the man said he was the anesthesiologist or something."

"And you are positive no one else entered that room?" Maggie asked, staring blatantly at the boating magazine that now lay in the middle of the hallway floor.

The guy was miserable. "Yes," he said in a low voice, but it sounded more like a question than anything else.

Maggie was so frustrated that I could feel the irritation growing in her. She was exhausted and she was hungry and she was really tired of putting her case behind other priorities. She wanted justice for Fiona Harker, and she wanted it now. It was time for all this bullshit to stop.

"Guard the door," she told the patrolman. "With your life. No one goes in and out unless they're with me."

"Yes, ma'am," he said meekly, and left the room.

"Who was his surgeon?" she asked the gray-haired nurse. She had returned after dropping off the blood sample and relieved the younger nurse standing by the bed.

"Dr. Verrett. He's new."

"Page him," Maggie ordered.

"Not Dr. Fletcher?" the nurse asked, and for the first time her voice sounded tentative.

"Definitely not Dr. Fletcher," Maggie answered promptly.

"But Dr. Verrett was his surgeon, not his attending," she said. "He's not really trained to—"

"He's new to the hospital," Maggie explained, handing her own cell phone to the nurse. "Page him."

"Got it." The gray-haired nurse took the phone and peered at the readout on it. "You have seven messages," she said. "All marked urgent."

"Page him," Maggie repeated.

She dutifully made the call but held on to the phone. She looked at Maggie as if she could not quite decide whether to speak up.

"What is it?" Maggie asked.

"If you really want the patient to be safe, let me make one more phone call."

"One phone call?" Maggie sounded skeptical.

"I'll call my friend Claudette in obstetrics and tell her the patient died. It'll be all over the hospital in five minutes. If they think he's already dead, who's going to try and kill him?"

"You should be a detective," Maggie told her. "Make the call."

The nurse obeyed and handed Maggie back her phone. "Maybe I should be an actress?" she joked, and the two women smiled at each other. I loved this sisterhood of competent women. It made me feel like the whole world was safer.

"Verrett doesn't sound Indian to me," Maggie told the nurse. "The guard said an Indian doctor was in here? Said he was the anesthesiologist?"

"He might have been. Or the woman doctor was and he was an attending looking over her shoulder," the nurse explained. "The hospital's a little paranoid about lawsuits, especially with Fiona being murdered. The big dogs are sniffing around a lot, second-guessing everyone. He was probably an attending who was checking up on staff and being very careful."

"What's his name?"

She looked apologetic. She wanted to help Maggie, but she was also part of a bigger team and she wasn't about to unleash a witch hunt based on skin color. "I'm not sure who it was. I didn't see them. I had a patient code on me around that time, and this man technically isn't my responsibility."

"He is now," Maggie told her. The woman nodded. She was willing to help Maggie any way she could.

"Did you recognize the female doctor the guard described?" Maggie asked.

The nurse's tone was apologetic. "About a third of the doctors on staff now are women. The numbers grow every year."

Maggie's sigh was eloquent. I almost pitied her. When she was focused, no one could best her. No one. But she had been going hard for days now, running on empty. Bulling through alone wasn't going to cut it.

"What's going on?" a voice asked. "He was fine an hour ago. What happened?"

"This is Dr. Verrett," the nurse explained. "The surgeon."

Maggie introduced herself and explained why she was there. The doctor was tall and thin with short-cropped dark hair and intense eyes that he likely used to intimidate other people. His energy was even more intense. He was as coiled as a cobra. Maggie had no effect on him whatsoever. But then again, he had no effect on Maggie in return. She was not intimidated by him at all. I don't think he was used to that, and it confused him.

"Christian Fletcher explained why you were here to me earlier," he said when Maggie was done. "Are you sure someone tried to kill this man?"

The nurse nodded and said, "We're sure." Dr. Verrett seemed to take her word a lot more seriously than Maggie's.

"Is he stable now?" he asked.

"Yes," the nurse said. "If he was given something to impair his breathing, it seems to be wearing off."

"Then there's nothing I can do." He turned to go.

"Wait," Maggie said. "Every doctor in this hospital is under suspicion except for you."

"Every doctor?" he asked incredulously. "Did Christian Fletcher not save this man's life just a few hours ago? Why would he do that if he wanted him dead?"

The nurse stared at Maggie, waiting for her answer. She had definitely heard the rumors about them.

"*Every* doctor," Maggie said firmly.

"There's nothing I can do for him," the doctor explained impatiently. He looked at his watch. "I have another procedure in an hour, and I'm hungry."

"Can't you bring him out of this faster?" Maggie asked. "Give him a shot?"

"I could," the doctor admitted. "But I won't. It's medically contraindicated, we have no idea what else may be in his system, and he's been through enough as it is." He stared at Maggie's gun pointedly. She got the meaning.

"I'm not the one who shot him," she said in an uncharacteristically defensive voice, perhaps realizing for the first time that, because she had helped redeem Calvano,

he was now going to be her responsibility for a long time
to come.

"Look," the doctor said, less impatiently. "He wasn't
deprived of oxygen long enough to cause brain damage,
and he's going to come out from under soon enough." He
checked the LED readouts on the medical equipment surrounding the bed and read through the thin strips of paper
containing the man's vital signs history. "You'll be able to
talk to him in about thirty to forty-five minutes."

"I can't wait that long," Maggie insisted.

"You're not used to waiting, are you?" the doctor
asked.

"You're not used to people arguing with you, are you?"
she countered.

The doctor sighed and gave the nurse some orders to
adjust the solution going into the IV inserted in the man's
arm. "I'm not doing anything but hydrating him more
quickly," the doctor told Maggie. "I can't agree to anything more than that."

"How long?" Maggie asked.

"Thirty minutes. Take it or leave it."

Maggie said nothing, and he turned to go.

"Wait," she told him. "You can't go."

"I can't go?" the doctor repeated slowly.

"If something else happens to him, I want you here."

"All this for a witness?" he asked impatiently.

"The only witness to whoever killed Fiona Harker,"
Maggie said angrily. "If we lose him, we'll never know."

"And Fiona Harker was a nurse in this hospital?" he
asked.

"Yes," Maggie said.

"The best nurse we had," the gray-haired nurse interrupted. Her voice was fierce, and she had tears in her
eyes. "Fiona Harker was the best nurse this hospital ever
had, and she deserves justice."

The doctor looked at her in surprise, but when he spoke, his voice was kinder. "Okay, then," he agreed. "I'll stay until you're done questioning him."

Maggie's smile was transformative. Even Dr. Verrett had to smile back.

Chapter 31

For thirty-three long minutes, no one spoke. The doctor sat in a chair and closed his eyes, taking the opportunity to enjoy a catnap. The nurse fussed over Cody Wells, constantly adjusting his pillows and checking the monitoring devices. Maggie leaned against a wall and lost herself in her thoughts. She was thinking of Christian Fletcher, I knew, thinking of him a floor below, knowing that he was probably feeling betrayed now that she had chosen Dr. Verrett to stand guard instead of him. She was wondering if he would ever get over what he was sure to see as a betrayal.

Ah, the job. I remembered it all too well. It always forced you to choose between the people in your life and life on the job. For a woman like Maggie it would be even worse. She'd dealt with it before by having no life outside the job. I'd dealt with it by having neither.

Somewhere during those thirty-three minutes, the little boy who had been standing watch over Cody Wells faded from view. One moment he was there; the next he was gone. *Does that mean the man's life is out of danger?*

"He's coming out of it," the nurse finally announced.

Maggie moved to his bedside.

"Not so fast, hotshot," the doctor told her. He bent over Cody Wells and checked his pulse and pupils, then made adjustments in the IV solution. "It's going to take him a while to regain full consciousness."

"Will he remember who took his breathing tube out?" Maggie asked.

"No." The doctor shook his head. "You'll be lucky if he remembers anything about the last forty-eight hours before he was admitted. Trauma can do that to you."

"But he'll remember four or five days ago?" Maggie asked, alarmed.

The doctor stared at her. "This is medicine. I don't give guarantees."

But the man remembered. Slowly he gained consciousness, his eyes clearing, his face regaining animation, his breathing strong enough for the doctor to remove the breathing tube. It was as if he were emerging from the bottom of a deep, deep sea. Maggie had to be patient, and she didn't do patient well. She fidgeted and kept darting toward the bed before being sent back to her corner by a look from the doctor or nurse. If so much hadn't been riding on the outcome, I'd almost have enjoyed her discomfort.

At last, Cody Wells was lying slightly elevated in bed, breathing under his own power, sipping at a cup of water the nurse held to his lips.

His first words were simple: "The boy?"

Maggie was at his side in an instant. "He's okay," she said. "We found him. He's with his mother now."

Something in the man let go. He seemed to melt into the pillows, as if he could drift back to a twilight world again.

"Wait," Maggie said. "I need to ask you some questions."

"I would never have hurt him," the man whispered to her. "I couldn't. I just couldn't."

"We saw the video," Maggie said. "I saw you taking good care of him. It's okay. I understand."

"I should never have taken him from the playground in the first place," the man whispered. "I was afraid if I didn't, I'd lose everything." Suddenly his eyes widened. He looked alarmed. "Where's the colonel? Does he know he's lost the boy?"

"The colonel is upstairs in the burn unit," the nurse interrupted. Her voice was tight. "He'll probably never regain consciousness. If fate is kind to him."

Maggie looked up at her, startled. The look the nurse gave her right back was very clear: *I'm sorry,* it said, *but I am a nurse, and this man hurt someone. No one should have to go through the agony that man is going through upstairs in the burn unit. No one. I don't care what he did.*

Well, I wasn't sure I agreed with her. The colonel had caused greater and more lasting agony in how many young souls? But that difference between us was why I had been a detective and why the gray-haired woman was a nurse. I wasn't going to fault her for it.

"Do you remember anything about the fire?" Maggie asked the man gently.

He shook his head.

"It doesn't matter," Maggie assured him. "I'm not here about that."

The man relaxed again, but I knew what Maggie was thinking: as soon as Howard McGrew's charred body gave up the fight, it was very likely this man lying in bed before her, so concerned about the boy, would be charged with his murder. And go to prison for a very long time because of it.

"Did you know the colonel's real name?" Maggie asked him.

The man stared at her with vacant eyes strangely reminiscent of those of the little boy apparition. "I called him Daddy," he explained. "I don't know his real name."

"What's your real name?" Maggie asked. "We know it's not Cody Wells."

Tears filled the man's eyes. His pulse raced and Dr. Verrett glared a warning at Maggie. She ignored him. "What's your real name?" she asked again.

He shook his head weakly. "No," he said. "I don't know. I don't remember. I don't want to know. I don't want to remember. I don't want people to know."

"You're going to lose him," the doctor warned her. "If you push him too hard, he'll just drop back down under. People's bodies take care of their minds."

Maggie did not want that to happen. Not until she knew what he'd seen from his vantage point in the park, when he'd sat on the bench right across from Fiona Harker's house, keeping track of everyone and everything around him.

"Right before you went into surgery, you told two people 'I know who killed the nurse,'" she explained to the man. "Do you remember?"

"No," he whispered back. "I don't remember saying any of that."

Maggie looked panicked "But do you know who killed Fiona Harker?"

"Yes. It was the doctor. I saw the doctor leaving her house the morning the newspapers say she died," he explained weakly.

"What did he look like?" Maggie asked.

The man looked confused.

"What did he look like?" she asked again.

"It was a woman," the man said. "It was a tall woman

with long, blonde hair wearing a doctor's coat and high heels."

"Why do you assume she was a doctor?"

"She drove a red Lamborghini, that's why. And she acted like she thought she was hot shit, like doctors always do. Like they're too good for the rest of us."

Dr. Verrett looked amused at this. I had to give him credit for having a sense of humor.

But Maggie looked stunned. I knew what she was thinking: Serena Holman had killed Fiona Harker for having an affair with her husband. Simply divorcing Christian Fletcher had not been good enough. No one crossed Serena Holman like that. Not without paying. No one.

Which made Christian Fletcher a big, fat liar. It meant he had, indeed, been having an affair with Fiona Harker.

"Are you sure?" Maggie asked. "Did you get a good look?"

"I'm sure," he said. "It was the third or fourth time I'd seen her. I recognized her from a few days before, and the week before that, too, when I was sitting in my car, watching the park, trying to decide if I . . ." He did not want to continue in that direction and returned to what he had seen. "One day, she walked right past me and didn't even give me a glance. Each time I saw her, it was always midmorning. She'd come on Mondays and Wednesdays, stay for a few hours, and then leave. It was always the same lady doctor. I just figured someone who was sick lived there."

That changed everything.

Fiona Harker had been in love with Serena Holman, not Christian Fletcher.

It explained why Fiona never talked about her private life, why she told no one else about the affair, why she lived so far away from her family. She was Catholic. She would have felt the need to hide it, and she must have felt so conflicted over her feelings for Serena. It also explained motive. Serena Holman had killed Fiona Harker to protect her reputation as a successful doctor and society queen, the tall blonde every man in the room wanted, the one they all opened up their checkbooks for.

I have seen people kill for many reasons, and I have seen many kinds of people killed. But I wasn't sure I had ever seen anyone as good as Fiona Harker killed by someone as worthless as Serena Holman, for the pettiest of reasons: social status.

The truth was going to devastate Christian Fletcher. Unless he had known about it.

"If I showed you a photo of the doctor, could you pick her out?" Maggie asked.

"Sure," the man replied. His voice was growing stronger.

The nurse did not wait for Maggie to ask. "I have something we can use," she said, and left the room, returning in a minute with a copy of the hospital's annual report. "We have about ten of these in every waiting room," she explained. She started to thumb through the brochure for a photo of Serena Holman, but Maggie stopped her.

"He has to be the one to pick her out. We can't just show him a photo."

The nurse handed Maggie the glossy booklet, and Maggie flipped through it, choosing several pages of photos taken at gala balls and other donor events. There wasn't a dearth of thin blondes to choose from. In fact, it was a three-hundred-person lineup of tall blondes. It would be an irrefutable identification if the man in the bed picked out Serena Holman from among them.

He went straight to her. He scanned two pages of photos, shaking his head, but the moment Maggie turned to the next page, his eyes stopped on a photo of Serena dressed in a black designer gown, smiling next to a trio of well-fed men in tuxedos, two of whom were staring at her in admiration.

"That's her," he said, pointing to Serena Holman. "I'm sure."

"You're sure?" Maggie asked.

"I'm sure."

"Is his mind medically clear?" Maggie asked the doctor.

The doctor looked at his watch. "I'll testify to it in court, if need be."

That was all Maggie needed to hear. "Get some rest," she told Cody Wells. "I know you've been through a lot. Tyler Matthews is back home safe. That's what counts. What you did today was a good thing. I'll make sure people know it."

The man closed his eyes and turned away. I was startled to realize he was crying at being called "good." *What had he been turned into?*

"Don't move for at least another twenty minutes," Maggie told the nurse, who nodded her agreement. "And thank you both very much," she added as she left the room. I was right behind her.

A pair of patrolmen had arrived to relieve the guard outside the room. One was going to take the end of the hall, the other the door. Instead, Maggie told both to come with her.

"Where are we going?" one of the patrolmen asked as they hurried after Maggie. She was walking with such a determined gait, I half expected her to go crashing through the elevator doors. Instead, miraculously, they opened at her approach, as if the universe wanted to escort her upstairs.

"We're going to arrest a murderer," Maggie said. "And if she won't come with us, we're taking her by force. Got your guns, boys?"

"Huh?" one of them asked, exchanging a glance with his buddy.

Maggie pulled out her cell phone.

"You're not supposed to use that in the hospital," a patrolman pointed out.

One glance from Maggie shut him up.

I thought she might call Gonzales. That was the sane thing to do when you had seven messages from him and were about to make a high-profile arrest. Besides, Maggie was by the book. She only made arrests after she had cleared them with Gonzales, who was big on having judges issue warrants first when the people being arrested had money. But Maggie knew enough about his priorities to guess that Gonzales might want to stall so he could milk both cases for maximum publicity, and Maggie was unwilling to wait. She was bringing Serena Holman in on her own. She had probable cause. So instead of calling Gonzales, she called Calvano for an update on Tyler Matthews and the reaction of Gonzales and the feds. But what she heard from him clearly surprised her. "So soon?" she asked. "When does it start?"

Whatever Calvano told her, after she hung up, it caused her thoughts to turn to Serena Holman once again. Maggie was angry, but she was more than just angry. She was determined to make the doctor pay for what she had done. I was pretty sure arresting her was not the only thing Maggie had in mind. She exited the elevator with such speed that the uniforms had to scurry after her to keep up. She greeted the nurse at the pediatric oncology ward station with a terse "Where's Dr. Holman?"

The nurse mutely pointed to the patient playroom, her eyes lingering on the two patrolmen accompanying Maggie.

The room was empty of patients. Serena Holman was sitting on the couch, an expensive coffee from the stand in the lobby at her elbow, flipping through a patient chart, clearly irritated at having spent Saturday night and into Sunday morning at the hospital. She glanced up, saw Maggie, and dismissed her. "I'm busy," she said, turning a page.

"Stand up," Maggie told her. She grabbed one of Serena's elbows and jerked her upright. The doctor teetered on her heels and tried to pull her arm away.

"How dare you?" she spat at Maggie. "I'm calling my lawyer."

"Good. You're going to need one." Maggie took the patient file from her and tossed it on the table, then twisted both of the doctor's hands behind her back. She clipped her handcuffs tightly around Serena's slender wrists. "You're under arrest for the murder of Fiona Harker," Maggie said. "You have the right to remain silent."

As Maggie recited the familiar warning, a white-hot fury started to grow inside Serena Holman. It was a typhoon of outrage—one of titanic proportions. "How dare you?" she hissed at Maggie. "I'll have your badge for this."

"Shut up," Maggie said calmly, shoving the doctor toward one of the uniformed patrolmen. "Just because I'm bringing you in doesn't mean I have to listen to your bullshit on the way." Even the patrolmen looked alarmed at the tone of Maggie's voice.

I don't think she had ever hated anyone more than she hated Serena Holman. I wasn't sure why exactly. It wasn't just what her arrest would do to Christian Fletcher; it ran deeper than that.

"You can't prove a thing," Serena snapped. "You're just doing this for Christian."

"We have a witness who puts you at Fiona Harker's house the morning she was killed," Maggie said. "And many mornings before that. A witness you failed to kill. Did I mention that? He's still alive. Can't wait for the lab tests to come back to see what drug you gave him. Or to have a chat with the attending who escorted you into his room. Or to get back the ownership search on the gun that killed her. Or to finish searching every inch of Fiona's house and locker for the tiniest scrap of your DNA. One single hair, and you're done. And I don't just mean because it will prove you're a bottle blonde."

I felt a crack in the doctor's arrogance. She was silent. Maggie shoved her toward the hallway door. "We're taking the long way out," she told her escorts, "Follow me."

By the time she reached the elevator, nurses had started to line the hallway and were madly dialing their cell phones. They stared at Serena Holman, their eyes bright and their anger obvious as she walked past, her heels clicking on the hospital floor and her doctor's coat hanging open to reveal the expensive dress underneath.

"Move faster," Maggie said, shoving the doctor into the elevator. Serena stumbled against a railing.

"What's your problem?" she asked Maggie. Her refined accent had been replaced by the raw vowels of a blue-collar Boston background. Was anything about the doctor real?

"All she did was *love you*," Maggie said, her contempt so great, her anger so immense, that the patrolmen averted their eyes. "All Fiona Harker wanted was for you to love her back. And she thought that you did. She told her friend that it was the real thing, that she'd finally found someone she could love."

"And you find that disgusting?" the doctor challenged her.

"What I find disgusting," Maggie said, anger rising in her voice, "is that someone gave you the gift of love, someone who was private and guarded and not prone to giving her heart away. You had to work for it. And you did. You worked until you had her heart and then you took it. And once you had it, you turned around and you killed her for loving you, all to protect your reputation. What's the matter with you? Do you even have a soul?"

I wondered that myself. Serena Holman had grown still as Maggie spoke, and her indignation had been replaced by a cold strength. I felt cunning inside her, cunning and selfishness and something darker—*Had she liked taking another person's life? Had she actually enjoyed making someone love her and then destroying her for it?*

Yes, I think she had.

I had sympathy then for Christian Fletcher. He still had his career, but she had pretty much devoured him, too.

"You don't know anything about me," Serena Holman spat at Maggie.

"I know you're going away for a long, long time," Maggie said. "To a place where you will not be able to wear your little ass-high dresses. To a place where no one is going to give a shit about how much you raised for this hospital. To a place you can't even imagine in your worst nightmares."

In that, at least, I thought Maggie was wrong. Serena Holman would use her beauty in prison just as she had in her life—to blind others so she could get exactly what she wanted. I was pretty sure she'd end up running the joint. And I was also pretty sure she'd killed Fiona Harker for a lot more than to protect her reputation, even if she didn't understand those reasons herself. I thought she'd loved Fiona back, maybe for the first time in her life. There was no other explanation for why she took the chance of becoming involved with her in the first place. And she had been driven to kill Fiona because of it, because her own ego would not tolerate the importance of anyone else.

Yes, Serena Holman would love prison. It was the one place where she could be herself.

"Let's go," Maggie said, pushing Serena out of the elevator toward the main lobby. For the first time, the doctor lost her poise and balked. No wonder. Word had gone out as swiftly as a call to battle. She had been arrested in the middle of a shift change, and hospital staff members were flooding into the lobby, wanting to see Serena Holman pay the price for killing one of their own. Nurses, aides, janitors, even doctors—all who had worked with Fiona Harker and loved her—were there, Christian Fletcher among them. There were surely a few left behind on the wards to make sure no patients died, but it seemed like every single person on duty in the hospital that morning was there, forming a phalanx of hostile onlookers that Maggie forced Serena Holman to walk through.

No one said a word. They just stood and stared at Serena. The air was thick with hate and sadness and contempt. But no one said a word.

And truth be told, no one seemed all that surprised. I guess beauty can't hide everything.

Serena Holman sailed through the crowd, head held high, as if she were a queen passing by. All she had left was her self-anointed superiority and she had no intention of giving that up.

No one even noticed Maggie. At least, no one but Christian Fletcher. He was standing toward the back of the crowd, a sympathetic nurse on each side as he absorbed the shock of seeing his ex-wife hauled through the lobby in handcuffs. His face was as easy to read as a billboard. His surprise was genuine. I was certain of that. And, grudgingly, I admitted that his sorrow was not for himself. He grieved for Fiona Harker, whom he had respected and relied on. He grieved for the person who had been his wife but was, apparently, someone he had never really known. And he grieved for Maggie. He knew he would lose her now.

At first, Maggie did not see Fletcher. She was grim but confident. She took no pleasure in what she was doing, but she felt it was her duty to do it. She owed Fiona Harker at least that much. Then Serena Holman stumbled and Maggie tightened her grip on the doctor's arm, steadying her. She looked over Serena's head and straight at Christian Fletcher. A look passed between them. It was an acknowledgment of what they had lost, of what they might have had. It had been real, and they had both felt it. Now they felt its loss.

Too late, I wished that I had helped them. I wished that I had brought them together somehow, instead of trying to drive them apart. Apart, they were just two more lonely people who lost themselves in work so they wouldn't have to think about the rest of their lives. Together, they could have been so much more.

Chapter 32

I couldn't understand why Maggie was driving so slowly. Even the patrolman with her looked puzzled. Reality was not matching rumor. He'd come along to keep an eye on Serena Holman, who was sitting in the backseat reciting the ways she intended to make Maggie pay for this scurrilous attack on her reputation. *Scurrilous?* That was a new one. My suspects had mostly shouted one-syllable expletives while inadvertently spraying booze-flavored spit on me.

I sat beside the outraged doctor, my arm draped over the seat behind her. I was like a child playing too close to the fire. I wanted to probe the self-assured darkness that filled her graceful frame. Evil took many forms, I knew, but seldom one as beautiful as this. It made her even scarier.

When we reached department headquarters, I realized why Maggie had taken her time getting there. Gonzales had called a full-blown press conference, hoping to catch the first cable news cycle after church let out. He was also taking advantage of the growing media crowd that had started to gather once word went out that Tyler Matthews had been found.

I loved the irony of it. Until that moment, the abduction of Tyler Matthews had done nothing but overshadow Fiona Harker's murder. Now Maggie intended to use the attention the media paid to the Matthews case as a way to punish Fiona's killer. Should I have disapproved? Perhaps. But then I thought of the dead nurse's body, as frail as a bird's, and of all the lives that might be lost because she was no longer there to greet the ambulances filled with broken beings in need of care. In the end, the truth is that I thought to myself, *Bring it on. Serena Holman deserves no mercy.*

News vans, cars, and pedestrians clogged the block leading to the station house. Maggie drove past them all, lights flashing, until every eye was on her. She parked at the far end of the lot and turned around to check on a seething Serena Holman.

"You bitch," Serena said to Maggie. She thought the press conference had been called for her. *Wow.* What a world she lived in.

"Uncuff her," Maggie told the patrolman.

"You sure?" the man asked.

"Uncuff her," Maggie repeated. "Please."

Serena looked vindicated, as if Maggie had finally realized that she was important and should be treated as nothing less than royalty in public. Me? I knew Maggie way better than that.

Serena rubbed her wrists and glared at Maggie with hate. "I'll have your badge by the end of the week."

"Now take your coat off," Maggie told her. "You're not wearing it when I walk you into the station. I'm not letting you taint the profession any more than you already have."

Serena Holman stared at her defiantly. That coat represented her power.

"Take it off," Maggie ordered.

When Serena didn't move, the patrolmen pulled it off her shoulders and down her arms, and then folded it awkwardly.

"I'll take that," Maggie said with a smile. "Evidence. Now put the cuffs back on her, please."

Serena threw a fit. She kicked the patrolman with the tips of her pointy shoes and began screaming expletives that my drunken losers had never even dreamed of.

Then Maggie said one word, and it stopped Serena cold: "Cameras."

Sure enough, a couple of news crews, bored with waiting for the press conference to start, had drifted toward Maggie's car, hoping for something exciting, perhaps even an arrest connected to the Tyler Matthews case.

Serena Holman quit struggling, sat up straight, and plastered a distant "I'm not really here" look on her face.

"Let's go," Maggie told the patrolman. She opened the car door ceremoniously for Serena Holman, almost as if she were a chauffeur. The news cameras recorded every inch of the doctor's emergence from the backseat. She swung her feet around first, unfolding from the car as if she were a movie star at a premiere. Reporters began shouting questions, asking who she was, until a few recognized her from prior fluff pieces about hospital fundraising events. The questions grew louder, the lights brighter, the crowd pressed in closer and closer. Maggie said not a word. She just grabbed Serena Holman's arm and pushed her through the crowd.

The patrolman with her grew drunk on all the attention and lingered behind to talk to the cameras. "She killed that nurse," he announced to a local station. "She's a hotshot doctor at the hospital, and she killed that nurse."

And thus did Fiona Harker's murder finally get the attention it deserved.

By the time Maggie reached the front entrance, Gonzales was on his way out to start the press conference. He looked like the president of a major European country dressed in his best suit. He sailed off the elevators, trailed by a parade of lackeys, a nervous-looking Robert Michael Martin, a beaming Noni Bates, and a cluster of women protectively surrounding a reborn Callie Matthews, who still held Tyler firmly in her arms. She had changed clothes; so had her son. They wore red, white, and blue matching outfits. He still clutched his toy soldier in one hand. The mood was festive and tinged with an air of disbelief—had the good guys really won?

The feds were nowhere in sight. They had packed and left as silently as they had arrived. Calvano was nowhere to be seen, either. He was no longer the goat, but Gonzales was not about to make him a hero, not yet, not even if Calvano had managed to find an entire Boy Scout troop.

Gonzales slowed when he saw Maggie coming in the door. His head swiveled to follow her as she walked right past, acting as if she did not notice him at all. His eyes narrowed, and I thought for a moment he'd call after her, but then his lackeys pulled both exit doors open wide and the shouts and cheers began. He gave Maggie a barely perceptible nod instead and kept going, into the cameras and lights.

I had a choice: watch Maggie haul Serena Holman up to booking or stay and watch the circus. I stayed. I'd had enough of Serena Holman.

Gonzales was slick. He managed—while thanking the feds for the immense number of resources they had provided—to make it clear that "one of our own" had found Tyler Matthews through "old-fashioned police work and astute questioning of a witness." He depicted

the man who had called himself Colonel Vitek, Howard
McGrew, as the lifelong pedophile he was, making it
plain that it was a miracle Tyler Matthews had escaped
his clutches. He reassured the public that McGrew was
no longer a threat to anyone, though he spared them the
details of the price he had paid—charred bodies, especially ones that are still breathing, can be a downer on the
nightly news. He then brought forth Callie and Tyler Matthews to cheers and tears. And he managed to find a hero
for the public in all of this after all, even without Maggie
or Calvano to pimp. With much ceremony, he bestowed
a Civilian Medal of Honor on Robert Michael Martin for
his help providing evidence that was crucial to identify-
ing Howard McGrew as a predator. Martin accepted his
medal with shy humility and a shaky voice, Noni Bates
by his side, beaming as proudly as a mother.

*Good for you, my friend, good for you. You are the
real hero in this.*

Not once did Gonzales mention Cody Wells, the man
who had actually abducted Tyler Matthews. I should have
known then that something was up, but at the time I just
figured he was playing his cards close to his chest, waiting to see if Wells turned out to be the good guy he had
seemed to be at the end.

The whole spectacle took less than twenty minutes,
but a good six of those were likely to make the news—
an extraordinary coup for Gonzales. Thanks to Maggie,
it had all broken his way, the dominoes tumbling in one
long, lucky path straight to his doorstep. He was a man
born under a lucky star. Or a man smart enough to hire
one.

When I'd finally had my fill of self-congratulatory
pomp and had listened to enough slick answers to stupid
questions asked by reporters who secretly half wished
the boy had died, because then the story could have been

dragged on for months, I left the press conference behind and found Maggie on the fourth floor, splashing water on her face and, I knew, planning how best to avoid
Gonzales.

I do not make it a habit to follow her into the ladies'
room, mind you, but it had been a long night and Maggie had seemed on edge. I was worried about her. It had
all come down to the personal with her. I knew Maggie
was all about the job. She needed the structure and the
distance it gave her from the world. It was a distraction
for her mind and heart. But the death of Fiona Harker,
the way Maggie had found Tyler Matthews? Both cases
had cut too close to the bone, brushing against her private fears and challenging a lifetime of beliefs. She was
shaken and exhausted.

She stared at herself in the mirror for a long time.
Where she may have seen the inevitable wrinkles starting at the corners of her eyes or noticed a few gray hairs
at the tips of her temple, I saw a woman of extraordinary strength and talent, one who made the world a better
place, which made her a rare person indeed. Sometimes
I thought the answer to good triumphing over evil was as
simple as understanding that it didn't matter if you made
the world a better place or not, you just had to try, and the
good in people would win.

Maggie dried her face and hands on a handful of rough
paper towels, tossed them in the trash, and left the sanctuary of the women's room behind to face Gonzales. She
had ignored his phone calls since midnight and turned
her back on his press conference; she had brought in a
suspect in a major case without obtaining an arrest warrant first; she had gone off the reservation, and everyone
knew it. Gonzales would make her pay, even with all she
had done to win his department glory.

When she walked into the squad room to await the

phone call that would inevitably come down from on high, the room was packed with detectives who knew Gonzales as well as Maggie and had also skipped the press conference below. They were busy bullshitting one another, gathering together personal belongings in anticipation of comp time off after all the extra shifts and calling their loved ones to give them the inside news on Tyler Matthews and Fiona Harker. But when they saw Maggie come through the door, each and every one of them stopped what they were doing. To a man, they stood and applauded. Maggie looked stunned. They applauded harder. And then the jokes began. They surrounded her, patting her back, calling her a hot dog, accusing her of taking all the glory so they would look like schlubs. They called her Top Gunn, congratulated her on outfoxing the feds and on finding something useful for that dumbass Calvano to do. They gave it to her good. They said she looked like she'd been sleeping with every doctor down at the hospital until she'd found the right one and could arrest her. They asked if she'd recognized Serena Holman from all that hanging out at girl bars that she did. They took a vote and decided it was really her father who had solved the cases. They weren't very sensitive, of course, and they insulted everyone up to and including Maggie's dead mother. But they said it all because they were proud of her. They were finally ready to accept her wholeheartedly into their ranks.

Maggie knew it, too. She gave it back as good as she got, and I felt the weariness fall away from her. She had worked for this moment her entire career. I think it was the best reward anyone could have given her, and certainly it meant far more to her than any public honor Gonzales might have bestowed.

At last they ran out of bad jokes and macho-crotcho comments. They returned to the unfinished business of their other cases just as a stocky black man in dress blues stuck his head in the door and called out, "Gunn— Gonzales wants to see you now."

Gonzales had given up on the telephone and sent his chief of staff to find her. There was no way she could avoid him now.

Amidst hoots and jeers, she left the comfort of the squad room and began the long, lonely walk to the commander's office, her mind lighting first on the injustice of the reprimand she was probably going to get for skipping the press conference, and then dwelling on what she might say to explain her need to go full speed ahead until she had brought Fiona Harker's killer to justice.

She'd need none of her explanation. As she entered his office, the administrative assistant at the front desk greeted her with a grave, sorrowful expression that sent a stab of worry through my gut. Something was wrong. The woman escorted Maggie into Gonzales's private office without a word. Gonzales sat behind his desk, staring down at its uncluttered surface, seemingly oblivious to his guests. Peggy sat in a chair to one side of his desk. Her eyes were red— she had been crying. Morty, the old beat cop Gonzales kept around because he'd been there forever, sat next to Peggy. He, too, seemed overcome with sorrow.

"What is it?" Maggie asked, her voice rising. "Is my father okay?" Peggy and Morty were old friends of her father's, and losing him was the worst fear she had.

"He's fine," Peggy said quickly.

"Sit down, Gunn," Gonzales told her.

"What is it?" Maggie asked again, looking from each grave face to the next.

"We have an ID on Cody Wells," Gonzales said. "Peggy made a DNA match."

Maggie looked at Peggy, who had started to cry even harder.

"Just tell me," Maggie said, her voice filled with fear.

It was Morty, the old beat cop, who spoke. "Cody Wells is Bobby D'Amato, Maggie. The little boy who was taken from the rest stop north of town sixteen years ago."

"Are you sure?" she asked him.

"We're sure," Gonzales said.

Maggie looked at him, tears in her eyes. "This changes everything."

Chapter 33

"We haven't told Rosemary D'Amato yet," Morty explained. "But I've already called the father, and he's on his way in from Scranton."

"We think it's best to wait until he gets here to tell her," Peggy explained. "It's going to overwhelm her."

Maggie and I were thinking the exact same thing at the exact same time, both of us remembering the apologetic woman who had sat in the lobby of police headquarters, sipping tea, grateful for every small gesture of kindness shown her.

Her life had become such a single-minded quest for her missing son that she had no friends beyond the people in this room.

Her whole world had consisted of working and waiting and the occasional interaction with Morty or Peggy, her sole allies in her lonely vigil.

And now, both of them, knowing how much Rosemary D'Amato needed them, were willing to be there beside her, guiding her through the heart-wrenching journey that awaited her. They knew what she did not—that as much as she would think she had her son back, the man lying in that hospital bed would not be the little boy she had once loved. He would be a stranger, and a bitter and cruel one at that.

There was no way to escape it. With the life he had led over the past sixteen years, it was impossible to believe he'd remember her or still carry with him even a scrap of the love she had once shown him. When she realized this, it would be a blow as massive as when he'd first been taken from her. They would be there to help her get through it.

The basic decency of what they had done for Rosemary D'Amato over the years, and what they were prepared to do for her now, shamed me. Between them, they had put in over seventy years of service to the department, yet neither had ever been noticed much by others or given the respect they had been due. Peggy had been ridiculed for her awkward spinsterhood; Morty for choosing to walk a beat, even when his gait had slowed with age.

And yet, I realized, they had been the conscience of the department for all of those years. They had accepted the insignificance their position of conscience bestowed on them, and they had continued to do the right thing regardless.

"I want to prepare Bobby for this," Maggie told Gonzales. "Please, sir. I've already talked to him. He didn't want anyone to know his real name. He wouldn't tell me."

"So he knows it?" Gonzales asked her, skeptical.

"I'm not sure. But he knows he used to be someone else, and he's ashamed of what's been done to him over the years, and he's terrified people will find out."

"Or what he may have done to others," Gonzales reminded her.

"Maybe." Maggie was reluctant to admit it. "I can't go that far, sir. I just know that we can't simply send two people strolling into his room who say they're his parents. Not without preparing him. Let me go to him and let me bring in the woman who hypnotized Robert Michael Martin. She's a trained therapist. She was very kind. She has experience with abuse victims."

Gonzales was not going to be the bad guy in this scenario. He had just emerged as the hero of the year, thanks to Tyler Matthews and Maggie, and he wasn't about to come off as the heavy now. "Do what you think you need to do," he decided. "Peggy and Morty are going to take care of preparing the family. Call the shrink and take care of the boy. But there's a news blackout on this until further notice, understand?"

"Thank you, sir." Maggie said.

Gonzales looked done with her. I think Maggie and I both thought she was going to get away with her renegade act, especially since both cases had ended so well. After all, the testimony of Bobby D'Amato, victim, would be more compelling to a jury weighing Serena Holman's fate than the testimony of Cody Wells, arsonist and murderer.

But we were wrong about Gonzales. He glanced up at Peggy and Morty. "If I could have a moment with Gunn?" he asked pointedly.

The old veterans rose as one and left the room, Morty giving Maggie a fatherly pat on the shoulder as he went.

Maggie started to explain, but Gonzales cut her off at the start. "Stop, Maggie," he said. "Neither one of us has the time. You get a pass on this one. You're the only one in the history of the department who has ignored seven of my phone calls and lived to tell about it." He smiled at her and she relaxed. A little.

"And I talked to legal," he continued. "We're in the

clear on the arrest of the doctor. We'll get her on the murder charges." He waved his hand, making it plain that Serena Holman was not going to pull rank on him. He loved bringing high society killers down; he loved hearing them rant about it even more. He had survived the poorest, toughest neighborhood in the state growing up. This was his revenge.

"She's going to be a pain in the ass, of course," he warned Maggie. "But there was probable cause and the arrest was a good one. I would have preferred it if you had been up there with me on the podium for the Tyler Matthews press conference, however. I can't let that happen again. That was your win, Maggie. You deserved to be up there."

"I can't do that stuff, sir. You know that. The guys would hate me if I became the department's pet detective, trotted out for sound bites. Can you imagine what the press would start calling me? I have to work with these guys."

Gonzales's smile was genuine. "Point well taken. But you may end up not getting the credit you deserve if you continue to take that approach."

"I don't care about the credit," Maggie explained—and she meant it. But Gonzales could not even grasp that concept. In the end, he let it go.

"Once again I find myself granting you a favor," he said to her instead. "I feel like a fairy godmother. But you've earned one. Name your price."

She was ready. But I was flabbergasted at what she wanted. "Sir," she said. "I want you to give Calvano another chance."

"Are you shitting me, Gunn?" he said, and I think it was the first time I had ever heard Gonzales use profanity. "That guy almost screwed up the case not once, not twice, but three times. He's a disaster."

"He'll learn," she promised. "I'll teach him."

"Please don't tell me that the two of you . . ." Gonzales began.

"God, no," Maggie interrupted. "It's not that. It's just that . . ." Her voice trailed off as she sought the words. "Sir, he wants it so badly. He really wants to be a detective, a good one. How many people in this building can you say that about? Let's just give him one more chance. He's learned his lesson. I'll keep a close eye on him. Please, talk to Internal Affairs. See what you can do. I know it won't be easy."

"I can get them to do whatever I want," he said, with no small satisfaction. "I just don't know if it's best for the department—or best for you."

"He helped us," she pointed out. "Do you want Bobby D'Amato to go to prison after all that's happened to him? Getting shot in the back like that will make him more sympathetic to a jury. So, really, Adrian sort of did us a favor."

Gonzales laughed. "Fine. I'll make it happen. But, Gunn, really—do you realize what you just said? With logic like that, maybe you should have been a lawyer instead of a detective."

Chapter 34

Maggie had not slept for a day and a half, but her fatigue was gone by the time she showered and changed and returned to the hospital. She knew that the rest of Bobby D'Amato's life depended on what happened now. Would he spend it harming himself and harming others, or would he find a way to reconcile what had happened to him and somehow keep living? She had seen the cycle too often in her career—hate and pain begetting more hate and pain. She wanted it to end here.

The therapist was waiting for Maggie outside Bobby D'Amato's room. I remembered her from the hypnosis session, when she had sensed sorrows in Robert Michael Martin that the rest of us had overlooked. Miranda carried with her an air that was as safe and welcoming as a sanctuary. I stood close to her, letting her aura of tranquility wash over me. I hoped Bobby D'Amato would be able to feel it, too. I did not know how this woman found the ability to radiate such serenity when she spent so much of her time around other people's pain, but she had a gift, and I was glad for it. Bobby D'Amato would need it.

"Ready?" Maggie asked her. They had already spoken by phone. Miranda was prepared. They entered the room together.

Bobby D'Amato was lying in bed, staring up at the ceiling, trying hard to keep his mind blank, with no inkling that he had not been alone in the room—the now-familiar little boy apparition stood solemnly by his bed. He looked at no one but Bobby.

"Bobby?" Maggie asked softly as she approached him. "How are you feeling?"

"Is that my name? Bobby?"

"Yes," Maggie told him. "Bobby D'Amato. Do you not remember?"

I could feel a slash of pain as deep as a knife wound surface in him. He'd known who he was; that was why he had visited his own grave the day I spotted him at the cemetery, hiding in the trees. He just couldn't face who he had become. "I don't like remembering," he said.

But he was remembering. Like a touchstone that would keep him safe, his mind was returning again and again to the moment in that small bathroom in the cedar-shingled house by the lake when Tyler Matthews had reached out and placed his chubby little hand on Bobby's head, trying to steady himself. It had been such a small gesture, and yet it had a power I did not fully understand. Perhaps it was his proof, I thought, the one scrap of proof he had that he was not the soul-destroying monster that the man who had called himself Colonel Vitek had raised him to be.

I'll admit it: I had no compassion for anyone when I was alive. I was too busy feeling sorry for myself. But compassion fascinates me now. It transforms ordinary people into avatars for what human beings can be at their best. When people are filled with compassion, it opens their senses to so much more than they might feel otherwise. It's almost as if a conduit opens between two hearts and souls, giving a glimpse of what we would be if we could be bigger than ourselves. I saw the power of compassion before me now: although neither Maggie nor Miranda could possibly know what Bobby D'Amato was thinking, both seemed to know exactly what he needed to hear.

"Do you remember what I told you earlier this morning?" Maggie asked him gently. "That the boy was home safe with his mother? He's safe."

Bobby nodded, eyes tightly shut. A tidal wave of emotions was overwhelming his ability to hear or see or think. But beneath this flood of regret and pain and fear, far beneath the surface, I felt a tiny spark of hope.

How can someone still have hope after all he's gone through?

I felt him thinking yet again of the little hand placed on his head, and his breathing grew more even. That was when I finally understood. That moment when he had made a choice, when he had decided to break away from the colonel at long last? It *was* his spark of hope. Reliving it was his mantra, his assurance that it had been real.

"I don't want you to worry about anything but getting well right now," Maggie said. "We'll work it out. Can you put those worries aside?"

No. Of course he could not. But it helped him to hear it.

"Bobby?" the therapist said quietly. "My name is Miranda. Maggie has asked me to be here as your advocate. To make sure you feel safe and feel comfortable, because a lot is going to happen to you now. Your life is going to change."

"Good." It was only one word, but he meant it.

Miranda took Bobby's hand, and he did not pull away.

I could feel her empathy washing over him like a gentle wave, easing his pain. "Did you know that for the last sixteen years, your parents have never stopped looking for you?" she asked. "They've never given up hope."

His body thrashed back and forth as if he was in unbearable pain.

Miranda's voice was soothing, almost hypnotic. "They're on their way here. They want to see you." Something in Bobby twanged: it was shame as dark and deep as an ocean. "They know what's happened to you. They love you so much. They need to see you and know that you are safe. They're so glad that you are safe."

As Miranda continued to talk, repeating the words *you are safe* over and over, the little boy specter standing by the bed inched closer, as if drawn in by her voice. His blank eyes remained fixed on Bobby's face as the therapist continued to talk, telling Bobby of how proud his parents were that he had had the courage to stand up to the colonel, that he had not harmed Tyler Matthews. A strange connection grew between the little boy and Bobby D'Amato in those few seconds. I could actually see it, though I am certain the others could not. It was like a tarnished gold ribbon that wound through the air, connecting a point on Bobby's breastbone with a similar point on the boy's. It was barely a shimmer, but it grew thicker and stronger with each word Miranda spoke. As the connection grew, I felt the fear in Bobby start to dissolve. The shame he carried started to crumble and dissolve. I felt the stranglehold of self-hate loosen and peace settle over him. Bobby's eyes were closed, but his heart opened, even if just a little.

The little boy disappeared.

He turned as translucent as smoke, and then he was a ripple of light pulsing through the air, and then he was gone.

I knew he would not be coming back. I understood at last what he was. I knew why he did not seem like me, why he had not been able to leave Bobby D'Amato alone.

He wasn't some victim Bobby had tortured. He wasn't some child the colonel had killed. He *was* Bobby D'Amato. He was the little boy who had died that morning sixteen years ago when a man had held out his hand to a trusting four-year-old trying to find his parents' car and said, "I know where they are. Come with me."

That silent apparition, devoid of all interest in others, capable of existing but just barely, was the child Bobby D'Amato had never been. The specter had been a deformed, lost soul, and perhaps there are some that would have called it an abomination.

I thought of it as an angel interrupted.

I was glad it had found its way home.

The knock on the hospital door was barely audible, but Maggie was waiting for it. "They're here," she told the therapist.

"Would you like me to stay with you?" Miranda asked Bobby. He held her slender hand, squeezing it tightly. She nodded and sat in a chair by his side, the only anchor he had in the entire world as he faced the life he had lost.

Morty was the first to poke his head in the door. "Come in," Maggie said to him brightly, then bit her lip as if she felt her mood was unseemly.

Morty was in full dress uniform, and he moved as carefully as if he were escorting the president. He opened the door and held out his arm. Rosemary D'Amato stepped through, stumbled, and was quickly steadied by a stocky man behind her. Bobby's father. He looked as fearful as his wife. They had lived on hope for so long that hope was all they had, and the possibility that it might be taken from them, that a mistake might have been made somehow, was too much to bear.

But then Rosemary D'Amato saw the man lying in the hospital bed, and she gasped. "You look just like my brother," she whispered. She appealed to her husband for the confirmation they both desperately needed. "He looks just like Dave, doesn't he?"

Her husband nodded mechanically, his eyes never leaving his son's face. Sixteen years of silence, of bearing the pain inside, broke in him. He rushed to Bobby and knelt, laying his head on the bed beside his son, hiding his face from the view of others. His body trembled with the sobs he could not hold back.

Bobby shifted awkwardly—and then he reached out and placed his hand on top of his father's head to comfort him. It changed everything.

His hope had been passed on.

Bobby's mother joined her husband and patted his back gently as she gazed at her son. "I knew you were alive," she told him. "I knew you were out there somewhere. I looked for you everywhere."

Bobby said nothing. He did not know what to say.

The therapist looked up at Maggie and Morty, then nodded. Silently, they left the room. I stayed. I needed to know Bobby D'Amato would make it.

His mother was crying now, too. She clutched her son's hand, and her tears fell on the thin, white sheet that covered him. She was trying to say something, but the words would not come. Her husband sobbed quietly in the silence.

Bobby was staring at his mother, searching her face. "I saw you at the graveyard," he finally said, his voice trembling with the certainty that she would be furious at him. "I was trying to find my grave, and I saw you there, visiting it, and I didn't come up and say anything. But I knew who you must be."

"It's okay," she told him without hesitation. "It doesn't

matter. Nothing matters except that you're alive and we're together. It's going to be okay. I promise you that. It's going to be okay."

It's going to be okay. Mothers' words, the kind they murmur when nothing else can be said. But I could feel she was right. It was going to be okay. They had come to their son without hesitation and without fear, even without forgiveness, because, in their minds, there was nothing in the world he could have done that would call for their forgiveness. They had come prepared to love him no matter what. And Bobby D'Amato could feel it. Something deep inside him shifted. Dark memories of terrible times faded. Years of pain fell away. The images in his mind that tormented him receded to a faraway land where, god willing, they would stay. The memory of a family speeding along the highway took their place. I could hear voices united in one single, glorious note as a father, mother, and son sang along to a song on the radio, each one knowing the words and knowing their part. Together, they made a whole new sound, rich with a harmony that delighted the little boy in the backseat. He banged his heels against the cushions and sang about a silver hammer, his heart full of happiness that they were all together, that they belonged, and that he was part of them.

They would get there again. I felt it. It would take time. but, with love, they would get there again.

Chapter 35

Colin Gunn was waiting for Maggie on the front porch of his house, a bottle of Maker's Mark at his side. He knew she'd be coming, and sooner rather than later. She always visited him after she closed a case.

"Did you hear?" Maggie asked as she mounted the front steps. Her smile was wide. Her father's house was the one place in the world where she allowed herself to show joy and pride in what she could do.

Colin raised a glass in a toast to her, even though it was not yet noon. This qualified as one of his many special occasions. "Eight phone calls from the boys already and the phone is still ringing. You've become a legend, Maggie May."

"Gonzales is pissed. I skipped out on his press conference."

"Gonzales is down at St. Ignatius throwing quarters into the votive box and starting a month-long novena of thanks that God sent you to him. You made that walking, talking, ladder-climbing, ass-kissing mannequin look good."

Maggie laughed and took her customary seat on the porch, in the rocking chair next to his wheelchair. "You heard who the perp was, right? Bobby D'Amato."

"I heard." Her father's voice was sad. He knew what the odds were and what lay ahead. "I thought the boy was dead. Not so sure it's better this way."

"I think his parents are prepared," Maggie said. "They seem willing to stand by him no matter what."

"The boy deserves no less after all he's been through. And the man who took him?"

"Still alive," Maggie answered. "If you call that living." She hesitated, not sure if she should even tell her father what she had to say next. "They're going to keep him alive," she finally said. "At least for as long as it takes to try Bobby D'Amato for the fire and for taking Tyler Matthews. The hospital is grateful to Bobby for his help solving the Harker murder, even if the killer was one of their own. This is their way of saying thanks. So long as they can keep Howard McGrew alive, Bobby D'Amato won't face murder charges, at least. And if he dies after the trial is over, the DA has already said he won't file new charges."

"That's a generous gesture on the hospital's part, considering how much it will cost them. They wanted four thousand dollars from poor Mrs. Nevins down the street just for setting her broken arm. And Maggie?" Colin looked at his daughter, shaking his head. "You will forgive me if I say that every minute that man lies in his bed in the burn unit consumed with agony is a minute of agony he deserves. He was going to burn sooner or later, whether in hell or here on earth. He brought that fate on himself."

"It's okay, Dad," she said. "You're not the only one who thinks that. Can I have a glass of that?"

He poured her a tumbler of whiskey. She took a deep sip, and then laid her head back against the rocker and sighed. "I asked Gonzales to give Calvano another chance."

"Did you?" her father asked, surprised. "Oh, boy. You've got more than a drop of your mother in you. The bums she used to feed. The old friends she never gave up on."

"Do you ever talk to her?" Maggie asked suddenly.

"Your mother? Of course I do." He was silent, thinking about it. "I talk to her more now than I did when she was alive."

"Does she answer?"

"Are you daft?" Colin took another sip of whiskey. "The day she starts answering me is the day I want you to wheel me down to the VA and put me in the drooler ward."

"I just wondered." Maggie hesitated. She wanted to say more but did not know how to begin.

"What is it?" her father asked. "What's got your mind buzzing?"

"If I told you, you'll think I was crazy."

"A hunch?" he guessed. "My little girl had a hunch that was heaven-sent?"

"What's that?"

"It's when you do something crazy because your gut tells you to do it, and it turns out you were right, and you can't tell anyone else because then they'll think you're either crazy or, well, they'll think you're crazy."

"You had those?"

"Sure I did. Solved a good eighth of my cases with them. You don't talk about it, though. It's like changing your underwear when you're on a winning streak. If you're smart, you just don't do it."

"I do," Maggie said emphatically. "Change my underwear, that is."

"Tell me about this hunch," he asked curiously. "I want to know what happened."

Another gulp of Maker's Mark convinced her, and Maggie ended up telling her father all about the drawing the little girl had given her in the hospital and how it had led her to Tyler Matthews.

"You see?" her father said when she was done. "That's why your mother and I made you go to Sunday school and church every week."

"I don't see what getting beaten with a ruler by a bad-tempered nun who smells like onions has to do with it," Maggie said grudgingly. I had to smile. I'd caught a glimpse of a reluctant young Maggie, being scrubbed for church, protesting the entire time.

"Oh, ye of little faith," her father retorted. He filled his glass again, happily, and I started to wonder just how long he'd been sitting out there on his front porch waiting for his daughter.

"Maggie?"

As soon as I heard the voice, I knew who it was.

He had come for her.

Christian Fletcher stood at the end of the walkway, dressed in a golf shirt and pants. The bastard even looked good out of his doctor clothes. He looked like the king of the country club.

Maggie stood so abruptly, I thought the rocking chair might tip over.

Oddly, her father seemed neither surprised nor perturbed.

"How did you find me?" Maggie asked him.

"Your friend Peggy told me." He glanced at Colin quickly. *Aha.* Colin had told Peggy that Maggie would be stopping by. Those two old lovebirds were up to something.

"Peggy?" Maggie asked. She was walking slowly toward Fletcher, as if she could not quite control her body. I don't think she was even aware of what she was doing. He was near—and she wanted to be nearer to him.

"Yes," Fletcher explained. "I stopped by the station house to offer my help with the case. To tell you what I know about Serena's movements over the past few months. Not that I know much, apparently, about my own wife." He looked Maggie straight in the eye. "I didn't know about it, Maggie. I swear to you, I didn't. I had no idea what Serena was doing or what she had done. It makes sense now, of course. I understand why Fiona was acting the way she was around me, the time she suggested we get coffee, and then asked me about my marriage." He ran out of words to say and just shrugged, hoping she would trust him.

"I know," Maggie said. "I believe you."

"Then why did you act like you didn't even see me in the lobby? Why did you avoid me in the hospital?"

"Christian, this is probably going to be the longest and most difficult court case of my career. Your wife is going to take us to the mat. I can only imagine the lawyers she can afford, the fight she'll put up. She's going to drag me through the mud, and you, too. I have to be able to sit up there on the stand and tell the truth when I'm asked if I have a personal relationship with you."

"I understand," he said quickly. "I get that part. I'm not here to ask you to do anything except promise me that you'll wait. That you'll wait until . . ." He searched for the right words. "Until we have the chance to give it a shot."

She didn't say anything at first, and I could tell Christian Fletcher's heart was undergoing a torturous moment of regret and indecision as he began to think that he had been a fool, that he should never have put his heart on the line. Oh, how people are like that. They offer their hearts, but a heart can never be offered without the fear of rejection attached—and that fear can be as paralyzing as tangled marionette strings. "I'm sorry," he said into the silence. "I never should have come—"

"Of course I'll wait," Maggie interrupted. "Christian, waiting is nothing for me. I haven't dated a man in . . . I don't know, two years?"

"Three and a half," her father called down from the porch.

Maggie turned and glared at him. *"Dad,"* she said firmly.

"I'm going to go freshen my ice," Colin Gunn declared, then wheeled his chair through the front door with a whole lot of unnecessarily conspicuous effort.

"Sorry about that," Maggie told Fletcher. He didn't care. Her father could have raced down his access ramp naked and done wheelies down the sidewalk for all Fletcher cared. All he saw and heard was Maggie.

I understood how he felt.

"You'll wait?" he asked, still not sure of his good fortune.

"Of course," she said, stepping closer. She looked up into his eyes, and I felt the thought pass between them again: *This is real.*

I knew it was real as well, and I knew something else that they did not know. I knew it because I had squandered moments like this in my life—laughed through them, slurred through them, run from them as fast as I could. Because of that, I had thrown away my chances of feeling what they were experiencing now. But at least I had learned from it. What I knew, that they did not, was this: It was real because they both had the courage to acknowledge it was real. It was real because they both had been through enough loneliness and unhappiness to realize how rare that feeling of two hearts merging is, and how much of a waste it would be to throw that feel-

ing away because you were afraid you might get hurt by it
one day. Letting yourself feel like that is like leaping off
a cliff into the darkness and letting the momentum take
you. Sure, you step out into the abyss, but oh, when you
do, what a rush it is.

"It might be a long time," Maggie told him. She had
put her hands on his arms, and he pulled her closer. It was
physics, I knew, physics of the heart. For every emotion,
there was a corresponding motion.

Oh, to be alive again.

"I don't care how long it takes," Fletcher said. He bent
down and kissed her, and when I felt what that kiss meant
to each of them, how it changed each of them forever, I
knew it was time for me to walk away. This was not my
world. It was not my turn. It was time to surrender the
battle.

And yet, I needed to be a part of their joy, even if only
by proximity. I returned to the front porch just as Colin
Gunn was wheeling himself back outside, extra glasses of
ice balanced precariously on his lap.

He did not give the walkway a glance. He wheeled
over to his favorite corner of the porch, where shrubs
hid Maggie and Fletcher from his view, and lined up the
glasses neatly on the ledge of the stone porch, filling each
one with two fingers of whiskey.

I counted the glasses: there were three of them. Was
he going to invite Fletcher to join them?

"The third one's for you, Fahey," I heard him say.

The shock electrified me to my core. *Colin Gunn was
talking to me.*

"Relax, Fahey," he said cheerfully, raising a toast in
my general direction. "I can't see you, but I know you're
there. You always smelled like tomato sauce and stale
beer. You still do. Here's to you, son—*salute.*"

He raised his glass to me, gulped at his whiskey, and

smacked his lips in satisfaction. He dropped his voice to a whisper.

"I won't say anything to Maggie," he promised me. "But I know you're here to watch over her. So long as you keep my little girl safe, you and I are going to get along just fine."

Epilogue

A man lies on an inflatable bed in a dimly lit hospital room. The air is hot and moist, though he can only feel it on his face, where the smallest of areas around his eyes remains uncovered. His body has been wound in bandages that peel off his charred skin when the nurses come in to change them. They reapply the salve that smells like metal and do not know he sees them. They think he is unconscious.

He knows he must stay awake.

The room is filled with soft hums. Respirators and humidifiers pump out the oxygen that keeps him alive. His lungs feel as if they are filled with liquid fire. Each breath sears his body from the inside out. The agony is unendurable, but he must endure it.

He knows he must stay awake.

Few are allowed inside his room. The risk of infection is too great. He sees only the shadows of people walking past in the hallway, voices hushed.

He sees the darker shadows, too.

They cling to the ceiling above him. They creep along the walls. They are gathering, watching his every twitch. When he closes his eyes, they inch forward, probing, tasting, feeding on his pain.

He knows he must stay awake.

It will get worse, the pain. He has heard the nurses whispering outside his room. When the blackened flesh is scraped away and the nerves regenerate, his present pain will seem like a respite. They want to put him under, to keep him deep in twilight where he will have no control. Where he will not even be able to open his eyes.

When the time comes, he will fight them.

He sees the shadows now, slinking closer. They hide in the corners of the room, biding their time. They live under his bed, and their dark power radiates upward with a magnetic pull.

Pain floods his body, but he fights to stay awake. He knows what will happen if he closes his eyes.

He knows they have come to take him.